A ROAD THROUGH THE MOUNTAINS

A ROAD
THROUGH
the
MOUNTAINS

Elizabeth McGregor

BANTAM BOOKS

A ROAD THROUGH THE MOUNTAINS
A Bantam Book / May 2004

Published by
Bantam Dell
a division of
Random House, Inc.
New York, New York

Book design by Glen Edelstein

Library of Congress Cataloging-in-Publication Data
McGregor, Elizabeth.
A road through the mountains / Elizabeth McGregor.
p. cm.
ISBN 0-553-80358-1
I. Title

PR6063.C+ R+ 2004   2003062831

Manufactured in the United States of America
Published simultaneously in Canada

10 9 8 7 6 5 4 3 2 1
BVG

for my father

My deepest thanks go to Carol David and her staff at the Arnold Arboretum, Boston, for their help in sharing their records of Ernest Wilson; Liv Blumer for introducing me to Grace's idyllic family home; Janet Bolam and James Purkiss for advising me on Oxford; and Sara Fisher for her unfailing support.

Readers should note that all Chinese place names are quoted from Wilson's original journals, and may not coincide with the modern-day names.

A ROAD THROUGH THE MOUNTAINS

One

MOST OF THE HOUSES at Ogunquit were shuttered against the
blinding day, silent in their gardens above the beach. They stood
back from the road, pale blue clapboard battalions on their green
lawns. By the Bay Cove Hotel on the corner, a smoke tree hung
over the gate to the pool, its spring bronze leaves now green, the
threadlike stalks of the flowers fluttering faintly in the July heat.

Anna came up the hill, looking back over her shoulder. Her
ten-year-old daughter was trailing her wet towel on the path, and
her feet were bare against the grass and stone.

"Honey, put on your shoes," Anna said. She walked back to her,
but in a second, Rachel was running past her, uphill, and into
Grace's yard, where she flung herself down in the shade.

Anna paused, then picked up the dropped towel, and followed.
As she turned in the gate, the suddenness of a memory surprised her.

Rachel, perhaps only two or three years old, in that same deep
shade, in this same garden, chasing Grace's cat, and wrapping it
in her arms. The cat, resigned to the show of ardor, submit-
ting grudgingly, with a single twitch of its tail. The shade of the
tree was dappled, the light a changing kaleidoscope on Rachel's
arms, on the fur of the cat, on the sparse grass. In spring, the sweet

chestnut shed its pollen in this same place of racing shadows and light.

And here was another summer. Another memory flooding in upon the first.

Rachel was eight; they were on the road to Provincetown in the early morning; sand was blowing across the end of the highway. Anna's broken-down old Chrysler was hiked on the verge, with the hood raised. As if they were there again in this moment, Anna clearly saw the repairman cocking his head toward her child, grinning; and Rachel, staring, rapt, into the smudged gray distance. Seven A.M., sand underfoot, sea grass, the sound of Provincetown boats setting out for the whales on Stellwagen Bank.

Anna had a sudden strange feeling, a sense of disorientation.

It was as if she had stepped out of the day, and, for the few short seconds that she had been gone, time had folded in upon itself, stretched like soft candy.

She heard the opening of the screen door, saw her mother emerge onto the porch. Anna walked down the path.

Grace was even taller than her daughter, and her hair that even up to last year had been a great iron gray color, was now almost white. She was sixty, but looked more. They regarded each other solemnly for a moment. Then Anna opened the door to the house.

The rooms inside were blissfully cool, blinds pulled down on the side of the sun, and windows open on the shade. Sea air was blowing through the house, caught from the edge of the bluff above the stony shoreline. From the back, they could see Perkins Cove, the arc of houses facing the Atlantic; beyond that, Grace's view, in winter, when the trees had shed their leaves, was almost completely ocean. Anna walked over to the lawn side, to the shade, to the ripple of air. She looked out the window at Rachel, who was still lying on her back spread-eagled, eyes closed.

"Did she say anything about going back?" Grace asked, as soon as the door closed.

"No," Anna replied softly.

Grace put an arm around her shoulder. Briefly, Anna rested her head against her mother's, before they both turned back toward the room.

It bore all the hallmarks of Grace's life. Anna couldn't recall a day when Grace's house had not looked like this: a deep couch with hand-sewn cushions, newspapers on the table, empty coffee cup. A pack of cigarettes. A big box of household matches balancing on the ashtray. The English Roberts radio on the fireplace, the old Norman Rockwell print, the basket of cones and wood. Anna's own paintings, and her mother's, everywhere.

The pictures traced the years. There in the corner were Anna's teenage collages, lovingly framed. On the facing wall, Grace's bold blue seascapes, and Anna's response—her miniatures when she had been pregnant with Rachel, when her world had seemingly diminished to tiny five-by-five watercolors. By contrast, over the fireplace, was an abstract riot, four feet by six, of Anna's first year in the Boston apartment: a blast of pleased independence. And, of course, the cartoons.

In her twenties, Grace had drawn comic strips. She had syndication in the Midwest, and down into Florida, for the *Daisy and Mike* series, and the raggedy Mike now hung at the foot of her stairs, framed in mid-fall over a muddy waterhole, fishing pole spinning out of his grip, while the freshly starched and aproned and plaited-hair Daisy held her hands to her face in the background. *You cain't catch 'em all,* read the caption.

Grace would repeat that when things got rough. It was her mantra; part too, now, of both Anna's and Rachel's childhoods.

Anna's gaze rested on Mike again now, faded by the sunlight of years, but still sailing into midair. She bit her lip unconsciously.

"You could go and meet James at Logan, and talk to him by yourself," Grace said, interrupting Anna's thoughts. "Come back for Rachel. Do it that way."

Anna looked at her mother, smiling at Grace's enforced reasonableness, the determined lightness of her tone.

"Why try to get her in the car?" Grace persisted. "She's tired. Leave her here, and come back. It's no bother. Come back in a couple of days."

Anna shook her head. "No, it's fine," she murmured. "She'll be fine once we get going."

"OK," Grace said, raising her hands, palms outward, to show that she was giving up the argument. "I said my piece."

"You said it over and over," Anna told her.

They set off at three.

James's flight got in from Dallas at five.

Anna took Route 1 first, instead of the turnpike, because they had always done it that way, from the time that Grace, eleven years ago, had lived briefly between York Harbor and Kittery.

Twenty minutes out, it began to rain.

Not a sweet soft rain, like the kind that sometimes drifted in from the sea with a slow-driving breeze, but a hard downpour, the sky blackening quickly. In her driving mirror, Anna now saw the billowing clouds, and the flash of lightning.

"Storm," Rachel murmured, from the backseat.

Anna glanced over her shoulder. She looked at her daughter's face, so fair and light, like a small round moon in the backseat. Her green eyes—eyes the same color as her mother's and grandmother's—were overly bright, as always.

"Soon pass," Anna reassured her.

The road surface was slick, oily: weeks had passed of hot weather, and, when the drops poured down now, there was an illusion of road dancing over road—one dark surface slipping over the other, like the mirage of water glimpsed in a desert.

Anna felt the wheel jump a little as she steered to overtake a station wagon, its roof crammed with children's bikes. She glanced at her speed. Not too fast. Forty. But the car was sliding, for brief moments. She braked a little. She caught sight of the trees to the side, leaves flipped to show a fainter seam of green. Spray fanned up; she turned the wipers to full, and flicked on the headlights.

There were trucks ahead, one loaded with logs. Her lights picked them out in sudden Technicolor. She saw a white pickup, and a dog in the back of it. She was distracted a moment by the dog, wondering why it was there, crouched up against the cab, a German shepherd, with a chain around its neck. It looked miserable in the rain, leaning against the body of the cab, ears flattened.

Then Anna looked behind her.

The Mack was accelerating to take the outer lane; huge, bright red and chrome, a blurred splash of color through the rear window. She had a second to think that it was coming too fast, not accounting for the jumble of cars and trucks ahead of her, all of them jostling for position on the greasy, rain-smeared road.

She thought she heard Rachel say, *Look at him, look,* and she did look, first back at the Mack roaring toward them, and then, very slowly it seemed, at the bikes on the station wagon. Their wheels were turning, and the taillights of the station wagon were suddenly showing. The crowded family car had braked hard. She heard the squeal of tires.

And then she saw the dog—*poor dog, poor dog,* she immediately thought, before anything else had time to register—the dog scrambling for purchase on the edge of the pickup, and the lazy circular motion of his tail as he lost his footing . . .

And the motion of the cat's tail in Grace's garden came back to her, and the flashing of sunlight through leaves, light on shade, and Rachel's hand slipping from hers as she pulled away from her in the street, and raced to the house.

It was over in an instant.

Anna's hands flew from the wheel on impact, as the station wagon slid sideways into the trucks, and the whole interior of their car filled with a strange watery light, the light from the Mack as it wailed into them, smashing the car like a mighty fist, lifting them momentarily from the road and slamming them back down hard to the grinding and keening of metal.

And—as the sound escalated to something hellish, demoniac— Anna was still thinking, still absurdly thinking, *poor dog, poor dog*— catching just a glimpse of its body thrown into the car on the near side. She saw the thick chains on the log truck, that smaller truck ahead of the station wagon, now slewed sideways, glisten as the load danced in slow motion against its restraints.

"Mommy!" Rachel screamed. A faint and receding echo of her own mind. "The dog, oh, the dog . . ."

And then, she was here.

She was here, inexplicably, at the side of the road, under the branches of the trees, watching herself.

For a while Anna concentrated on the people, on the purposeless way that they ran between the wrecks. There was a terrible noise, a grinding sound, something to do with the truck. The driver was still in the cab, still with his hands fastened to the wheel. Smoke poured from the Mack's engine.

There were the shouts of children in the station wagon, and a woman's voice raised in an agonized cry. Other voices joined them: people who had stopped on the other side of the road. Calls for help. Yelled instructions. Figures moved, it seemed, like silhouettes on a screen.

A magic lantern show, Anna thought vaguely, knowing full well that the thought was absurd. *A magic lantern show, just for me.*

For a while—and she had no idea how long—she waited for someone to come to their car, for someone to open the door and find Rachel. It took forever. If the accident had been over in a moment, the aftermath was long. Her body began to feel numb. She saw that she was standing at the fence, right on the edge of the trees, alongside them, almost enveloped by them; and she was part of that living scene, rooted to the ground, away from the crash. She was a dumb onlooker, part of the landscape.

She began to feel cold.

She watched the ambulances from Boston, and the warning barriers, and the trickle of other cars on the other side of the highway, slowing to rubberneck the drama. She waited until she saw Rachel on some man's arm, stumbling, her mouth a perfect little circle of dumb shock.

Anna sighed. And with nothing to carry but a handful of jumbled images, she turned away, and took a few steps back, into the woodland. She glanced up, and saw the tall alders swaying, the sky between them now striped with a brightening blue.

And then she drifted away, between the trees, into the dark.

Two

As soon as DAVID Mortimer put his foot on the stile and began to climb over, the dog began to dance.

It leapt about in front of him in the knee-high grass of the meadow, a black scribble of body outlined against the green landscape. David shaded his eyes against the morning sun. The dog looked like a cross between an Irish wolfhound and some other, smaller, darker breed. Gray wiry hair stood out in a shock all over its body, as if it were alive with static electricity.

He got down the other side of the stile, and the dog careered around him, its tail looping like a propeller. He watched the performance, waiting for the inevitable moment when it would stop in its crazy circling and stare expectantly at him.

He had no idea to whom the animal belonged; only that it came from the direction of the farm below, whose outbuildings—gray roofs, scattered sheds—could be glimpsed above the trees. He never saw it anywhere else but here; never in the village street, or in the back of some farm pickup, or skulking about, even, at the farm entrance. On cue, it skidded to a halt now, and stared at him, tongue lolling from its open mouth, eyes fixed on him in dumb entreaty.

It had a collar, even a tag hanging from it, but David had never learned its name. The dog would never allow him to come close

enough to read it. He had found, on the first day he saw it, coming over this same stile, that the moment you raised your hand to
this animal, even in friendship, the tail dipped down between its
legs and it skittered backward.

"OK," he said now. "Get going."

It scooted immediately for the next field gate, making straight
for Lewesdon Hill.

Lewesdon was a nine-hundred-foot-high outcrop at the very
head of the Simene River; a small, meandering water that eventually joined its larger sister, the Brit, and rolled out into the English
Channel at West Bay. Rising almost vertically on its south side
above the fields, covered by its huge beechwood, the hill stood inland by seven miles from the Dorset coast.

David had probably walked this hill a hundred times. He had
never tired of it. Nor of the country around it. Lewesdon was directly north of the great scoop of bay that sweeps from Portland to
Exmouth, with Lyme Regis at its halfway point. The landscape of
farms and fields and woodland, with its characteristically narrow
lanes and hidden valleys, had once, a hundred million years ago,
been a tropical sea, and the trees that grew here had their roots in
sandstone and chalk. At Lyme Regis, in the first few years of the
nineteenth century, Mary Anning had discovered the first skeletons of the ichthyosaur, plesiosaur, and pterodactyl in the ashy gray
cliffs of Lower Jurassic rock; further up the coast, where the Brit
merged, the great tower of East Cliff was sandstone, topped with a
narrow band of limestone, and the cliff glowed gold even in the
faintest sunlight.

But there was neither gold nor gray ahead of David. As he
walked up the long incline from Broadwindsor to Lewesdon, everything was green, a complete undulating fertile green world, from
the bright, almost acid green of the new beech leaves ahead of
him, through the lighter turf, to the tangled shades of the hedges:
a profusion of blackberry, nettle, hawthorn, and ivy.

He walked quickly, soon reaching the old embankment, a line in the grass where once a fence had divided the fields. He stopped, slightly out of breath from the climb, and looked back. The village, in its valley four hundred feet below, seemed asleep.

The dog was standing at the last field gate now, on the dried mud where the cows had trampled to get close to the water tub. David smiled at it. He opened the gate, and stepped into the wood, and then, as always, he stood for a few seconds, listening.

The very first time he had come here and seen the hill, he had thought it was like a cathedral, with the same hushed atmosphere. It was a vast room: a room that whispered and moved. One huge, heart-stopping church of trees.

It was different today—different in color, in sound. But then, it was always different. If you saw it in winter, it looked truly architectural, the gray trunks like bold watercolor strokes against the red woodland floor. In late spring, as today, the hill and the wood seemed intimately turned in one upon the other. Green pushed up from the leaf mold, and green reached down from the branches, and there seemed to be some private and ancient conversation being carried on. There was a friction, a rhythm.

He smiled to himself, and wiped the mossy smear from the palm of his hand, the legacy of the gate. He knew a lot about trees, but with all his academic theory and experience, he actually had a creeping conviction that he knew nothing at all. Not about what these mute creations really were. Nothing about what was actually going on.

Beeches were a case in point. They were beautiful monsters. Next to yews, they were mere adolescents, of course. They towered in their colonies, and looked designed or drawn, because they were so lovely in their shape, and so extraordinary in their colors. But there was a disquieting sense of their greediness and strength. As he passed the first few now, David touched the nearest trunk.

Beeches could grow up to a hundred and thirty feet high, with a hundred-and-thirty-foot canopy. They were also sensitive, probably among the most sensitive of all broadleaf species; sensitive to light, their leaves twisting on their stalks to face the sun; sensitive to injury, for the cambium layer, carrying all the functions of the tree's circulatory systems, was very near the surface of the bark. Despite its potentially huge size, a beech always looked delicate in woodland, with its smooth, tactile skin and lack of lower branches.

Woodland beech rose out of a naked woodland floor, because the beech sucked everything clean with its shallow, labyrinthine roots. Beautiful, beautiful monsters; sensuous, all-absorbing giants.

David began to walk up the rise. Sun was streaming through the new leaves, and there was an undulating light. For a second, he had the feeling of walking on the bottom of an ocean, with light shimmering down through fathoms of greenish water. The names of the common beech ran through his mind in their rhythmic, musical phrases, and he matched them to each footstep: *sylvatica, aspleniifolia, rotundifolia, rohanii, cristata. Fagus sylvatica*—smooth, silky-haired in spring when the leaf was unfolding, and as waxy as a playing card in summer; *aspleniifolia,* the slender cousin, thin and spiky, each lobe erratically cut and the vein showing up through the center of the leaf like a white thread; *rotundifolia*—the plain and homely sister; *rohanii* so purple it was almost black; and *cristata,* an irrational explosion of misshapen clusters, with leaves as pale and thin as rocket.

The dog was still ahead of him; it paused occasionally to look back, to check that he was still following. After five minutes, David reached a point where the track curved slightly to the right, and, now level with the tops of the lower trees, there was a break in the canopy.

He could see the landscape clearly. Out there, about a mile or so east, was Waddon Hill, a Roman fort with medieval strip lynchets on its eastern slope—a ridged reminder of a feudal history, showing like green steps under the pasture. The Wessex Ridgeway ran at its base, from Stoke Knapp, through Chart Knolle and down into Beaminster. Somewhere out there was Netherbury, where the apple orchards in full blossom stunned the senses in spring. Further east still was Eggardon, a huge treeless escarpment, jutting out above the farms and fields like some vast ship. It was always windy up there, even in summer, as if the great hill were just tethered to the land by the faintest of lines, and might break away, in full sail, at any moment.

The dog came careering down to David, and stopped at his feet. He looked down, and smiled. He picked up a stick, and threw it.

Then, turning away from the view, he followed where the dog had disappeared, over the crest of the rise.

It was mid-afternoon by the time he got back to Morton Abbas.

Despite its name, and its closeness to Morton House, an Elizabethan pile of some grandeur, the village was not pretty. True, it had some old sandstone cottages, and the church was twelfth century, and it had a bell tower that made the guidebooks, with a great cast bell called Arthur's Ruin inside it. No one knew why the bell was called that; the name was inscribed along the rim, along with the foundry mark and the date, 1766.

But, while the puzzling bell and the churchyard—bedded with snowdrops in February, like miniature blankets on many of the older graves—were certainly a talking point, nothing else about the village caught much attention. It was a working farming community. In the winter, the back lanes were ruts of mud. In the summer, it seemed to sag in a pall of dust. There was a garage at the north end of the main street; it had a single diesel pump and sold charcoal and fertilizer. There was Michaels Hill Farm, with its 1960's farmhouse and a few scrubby paddocks, and the whole of its badger hill turned over to a quad-bike track. And, at the south end of the road, was the shop, with a green Spar banner over the door, and firewood packs stacked out front.

David came down the hill, still swinging the stick that the dog had dropped four miles behind him on Lewesdon. He reached the stream, and stopped on the bridge, and looked for some time at the weed-thick water. Then, he walked on, and around the bend in the road to the shop.

He could see Sara as soon as he rounded the bend, her blond

hair scraped into a ponytail, her back bent over wooden pallets of groceries that had been delivered to the yard in front of the shop entrance.

David increased his step now, and called his sister's name. She didn't hear him: she was too busy trying to drag the potato sacks from the pallets, and into the store. As he watched, he saw Matt come out of the shop, Sara's husband. Matt noticed David at once and waved to him, then tapped Sara on the arm. She straightened up, and shielded her eyes.

"Well, hello," she said, as David got close, one hand on her hip. "I thought you must have emigrated."

"I haven't been gone that long."

"Five hours," she said.

Through the shop window, close to the till, he could see Hannah in her chair. The baby was staring out at him with round, china blue eyes.

"You've got a visitor," Matt said.

David looked at them both, one to the other, and back again. "Who?"

"John Crane."

David looked hard at Sara. "God," he said. "I don't believe you. You actually rang him."

"I rang him back, yes," she replied, meeting his glare. "He's left a lot of messages."

David glanced back at his brother-in-law. "Can you think of anyone in the world I would want to see less than bloody Crane?" he asked. "Anyone at all?"

She crossed her arms. "No dice this time," she told him resolutely. "This time you're talking to him. *And* you're going back."

David grinned at her. "You look like Mum when you're stressed," he said.

"Oh, yes?" she answered. "Well, here's another bit of Mum. Get a job and stick at it."

David sighed. He glanced at Matt, who was smiling to himself and trying not to show it, nudging the pallet with the edge of his shoe.

"How do you stand her?" David asked him. "What a gorgon." He looked back at Sara affectionately. "Look," he said, "I'm not arguing about it."

"That's right," she replied evenly. "Because for once in your life you're going to hold on to something. You're going back next term. You're going to do that, David."

David sighed, almost theatrically. "Right," he said. "Where is he?"

She caught his arm. "You go in there and tell him you'll come back," she said.

He didn't reply. He started for the shop. She held on to his arm, pulling on the sleeve of his shirt. "Listen, David," she said. "Don't do this all over again." By way of reply, her brother smiled, and blew her an elaborate kiss.

"I mean it," she warned him, as he went through the door.

John Crane was sitting in Sara's back room, wedged fastidiously in one corner of the overstuffed couch, trying to avoid the cat. The tabby was perched on the opposite arm, tail twitching, its glare fixed on Crane and the smoke spiraling from the cigarette. Crane was wearing a dark sports jacket, a pale blue shirt, and chinos. His hair had been cut, David noticed. Cut so short that you could see his scalp.

In Crane's hand was one of the children's toys, a hideous yellow pony with a purple mane. He was dangling it by its tail, and smiling to himself. He looked up as David came in. "Hello, David," he said easily. "Nice walk?"

David flopped down in the shabby armchair by the fire and started taking off his boots. "Hello, John," he replied. "Out of your usual stamping ground."

"I thought I'd look in on you."

The two men regarded each other. Crane continued smoothly.

"I hear you've been over to Morton House to advise them on their *Davidia*." He at last stubbed out the cigarette in a saucer. "Of course," he added, "there's no one more qualified to advise on *Davidia*. I should say that was in your blood."

David stretched out his legs. "Word travels fast," he observed, without trying to keep the sarcasm out of his voice. "Drink?"

"Too early in the day, thanks."

David smiled. "That's not like you, John," he said. "What's the matter? Blood pressure, or cirrhosis?"

"Neither."

"Angela getting on your back again?"

Crane flushed.

David looked at his watch. "I have to get my nephew from school in a minute," he remarked. "What did you come here for?"

Crane gave him a calculating look, and did not smile. "Child minder and gardener and shopkeeper," he said. "Still. As long as it keeps you busy." He laced his fingers over his stomach, looking David up and down. "Got any further with the Wilson book?"

David looked past Crane, out to the back garden, a bald patch of lawn edged by dilapidated flowerbeds. "I'm not writing a book."

"Oh?" Crane said. "You talked a lot about it a few months ago, when we interviewed you. I rather thought that's why you'd run out on us. To write your masterpiece."

David glanced back at him expressionlessly. If Crane wanted a rise out of him, he wasn't going to get it. "I haven't run out on you," he said. "I gave my notice."

"And left before the post was filled," Crane said.

David looked down at his hands.

"Your sister is very concerned for your welfare," Crane said.

"My sister worries a lot."

"And you don't worry at all."

David looked up again. "Actually, John, I don't," he replied.

Crane watched him. Only his foot, tapping slightly in midair from his crossed leg, betrayed his irritation. Crane did not like to be seen to lose his temper. He liked his reputation as an infinitely reasonable man.

"I've been having a long chat with Sara," he murmured.

"Oh, yes," David said.

"This is your fifth teaching post in eight years."

"And?"

"An observation."

"You knew all that when you took me on."

Crane nodded. "Yes," he mused. "A year at a private school, a year in voluntary work. Two years for the Woodland Trust ..."

"All on my C.V.," David said.

"And all very worthy," Crane admitted. "A year in Gambia, a year on VSO ..."

"Life is short."

"Is it?" Crane asked.

"I have a tiny attention span," David responded. He shrugged his shoulders. "So beat me with a stick."

"Your students are taking their A's."

"I do know that."

"Is it normal to leave a school while examinations are on?"

"I gave my notice," David repeated quietly.

"Your contract expires at the end of term, not three weeks prior to it."

"I worked a lot of overtime with my classes. I can't sit the exam for them."

"But their term of study doesn't finish with this year's exams," Crane said. "It finishes with next year's A-levels."

David closed his eyes temporarily, waited a beat. When he re-opened his eyes, he shook his head. "Pretend I'm pregnant suddenly," he said. "Who was it left at Christmas—Janine? She was pregnant."

Crane stared at him. "Is this a joke to you?" he demanded. "You never gave us any hint, David. We're a small school." He got to his feet. He smoothed out the creases in his trousers, took out another cigarette, and lit it. He walked over to the mantelpiece, where he picked up a photograph. He seemed to be trying to calm himself. "They are very pretty children," he remarked.

"They take after their mother," David murmured. "Matt is too ugly." He grinned at his joke.

Crane put down the picture. "How old are you, David?" he asked. There was an edge to his voice.

David put his head on one side speculatively, trying to guess where the question was leading. "I'm thirty, John. As you know. How old are you?"

"Thirty," Crane mused to himself. "Not married. Would you call yourself a dilettante, David?"

"I couldn't even spell it."

Crane looked at him with an expression of studied sadness. "A dilettante," he repeated slowly. "One who takes his subject light-heartedly."

"There's nothing wrong with being lighthearted."

"A person without depth."

David eyed him. "The two aren't the same," he answered.

"In this case they are," Crane said. "You're thirty years old and uncommitted to anything in life."

David at last uncrossed his arms, and stood up. "You don't know anything about me," he retorted.

"I certainly know what I've observed, and I know what Sara has told me," Crane replied.

"Look," David said. "What have you come here for, really? To lecture me on life? To get me to come back and stare at an empty classroom? What? Because it seems to me you're getting a hell of a lot of pleasure out of the lecturing."

"I at least recognize my responsibilities," Crane said.

David flushed. "Well, John," he answered. "I don't have any re-sponsibilities, so my condolences. I don't have Angela breathing down my neck, and I don't have a board of governors, and I don't have two monosyllabic sons to feed, thank God, and that's the way I like it."

They were standing face-to-face, almost toe-to-toe.

"You're a brilliant man, David," Crane said. "But even brilliant men need to live in the real world eventually."

David continued staring Crane down for a few more seconds; then, he shook his head, his body relaxed, and he suddenly grinned. He looked about him on the floor for his other pair of shoes, kicked them out from under the table, and put them on. "Thanks so much for the advice. And for coming all this way on a wasted journey to give it to me," he said. "Have a nice life."

In the shop, Sara was standing with Hannah in her arms. "Where are you going?" she asked, as David strode past.

"To get Tom."

"No, it's all right," she said. "I'll go." Her gaze anxiously went to Crane, who had followed David out of the sitting room.

David opened the door. He walked away, down the street, letting the shop door slam behind him.

Sara looked at Crane. "If you would just hold on for a while," she said. "We could talk him round. I know he did like the job." She glanced helplessly through the window in David's direction. "I don't know why he does this," she murmured.

Crane smiled at her. He reached out, and touched the baby's face momentarily. "Good-bye, Mrs. Reede," he said.

Three

THE OLD BLUE NISSAN slewed into the forecourt of Massachusetts General, and came to a halt in the road. Grace got out, and began to run up the ramp, past the orange-and-white ambulances.

After the storm, Boston was sweltering in ninety-degree heat and eighty-percent humidity. The journey had been hell. Boston's traffic, even to a native, was a nightmare; in the throes of major reconstruction, the city was a mass of temporary road junctions and crossings; turnpikes strung on box girders like a giant Erector set; great gaping holes in the ground shearing away from the side of every car on every snarled route. Grace, after spending almost two hours helplessly stuck in this mess, ran now with the clothes plastered to her back and sweat streaming from her face.

"Hey!" called the security guard. "You can't leave that car there!"

She stopped, stared at him, and dug the keys from her pocket. She was gasping for breath. She threw the keychain at him.

"You think this is a valet service?" he shouted back at her, as the keys fell at his feet. "You gonna get towed!"

"Do what you want with it," she yelled back, over her shoulder.

"Park it down the street!"

"Park it in the river, I don't give a shit," she muttered, pushing through the entrance doors.

The man behind the desk looked up at her.

"Accident," she told him, one hand to her chest. She winced at the stitch of pain there. "Accident out on ninety-three. Russell."

"Russell . . ." he said.

"You called me, for Chrissake. You called me!"

He was leafing through a directory. "I didn't call you, ma'am."

"Jesus Christ!" she said. "Someone did. An accident on ninety-three, two hours ago . . ."

He gave her the directions.

She hadn't run like this since high school. By the time she reached the ward, she could hardly breathe. She grabbed the first nurse she saw. "Anna Russell," she gasped. "Rachel Russell."

The nurse looked hard at her. "You OK?" she said.

"It's my daughter. My granddaughter." And then, without warning, an asphyxiating wave swept over her: a shoal of flickering lights.

"Sit down," the nurse said. "Sit down here."

"No. My daughter . . ."

"In a minute," the nurse coaxed. "Take a breath now."

Grace began to sob.

"You have an inhaler?"

She shook her head.

"You don't have an inhaler?"

The older woman's fingers fumbled at the catch of her bag.

"In here?"

"Glycerin."

The nurse squatted down at her side, took the bag, and looked in it. "You take nitro for your heart?"

The nurse found the bottle. She tipped the little white tablet into her hand. Gray in the face now, Grace took it and put it under her tongue. The corridor rolled and rebounded on her. She closed her eyes.

"Breathe," the nurse instructed. "Slow now. Slow."

"I am breathing," Grace muttered. "Oh, shit. Shit." Grace opened her eyes and grabbed the nurse's wrist. "Anna Russell," she said. "You tell me. You tell me now."

The woman looked into her eyes, and nodded. "Hold on," she said. "I'll check."

Sensation slowly came back to her. Grace sat with one hand pressed to her throat. She was in a corridor painted a soft gray, she realized. She was sitting opposite a picture of a snow-covered hill. Somewhere up the corridor, someone was laughing, softly. Softly.

She tried to focus on the picture. Snow. Snow.

Snow like the winter snow that surrounded the house near Shelburne Falls, her parents' home. It stood on a rise at the edge of woodland, with a view clear toward the Mohawk Trail. They had painted it white, with green shutters; it stood with its back to the long drop toward the valley, and its face to the trees. The years fell away. Her father was standing by the shed and the lumber room. The old house had once been a school, and, if you looked carefully among the piles of logs, through the pine-scented gloom, you could see children's drawings on the wall. Horses and cows. Cats. A bull. A giraffe with the longest legs. And Anna had brought the sled from out of this sweet-smelling darkness, and run it to the top of the hill, and bounced down what was, in summer, the track with a broad pasture on each side, full of knee-high self-seeded saplings and poison ivy. And Grace and her father had stood at the side of the track, their hearts in their mouths, calling, "Go careful, go careful," as Anna sped past the curve of the gate, into the woods, those dark woods, the last outlying spur of the Appalachians.

"Mrs. Russell," the nurse said.

She looked up. The hospital corridor washed back.

"Will you come with me?"

Grace got to her feet, and followed.

She walked with her head slightly bowed, staring at the white shoes of the woman ahead of her. She would give anything, she realized in that moment, anything at all, to find them both sitting in some waiting room. Waiting for her. With maybe a scratch.

Maybe some sort of slight, acceptable injury. Maybe with a card in their hands, an outpatient appointment. Anna with her car keys in her lap, and an apologetic look on her face, as if she had caused her mother trouble. Rachel curled in the next seat, thumb stuck in her mouth, looking acutely at her in that startling, unblinking way.

A door was opened.

They went through to the unit.

She saw Rachel almost at once, lying flat, with her arm in a splint, and tubes attached to her. Her granddaughter's eyes were open.

"Oh, honey," Grace said.

Rachel looked at her.

"How are you feeling, sweetie? How are you?"

To her surprise, Rachel held out her hand. As Grace bent down, Rachel's free arm locked around her neck. She pressed her lips to her grandmother's face, and to Grace's complete distress, the little girl began to whimper. It was like holding a small and frightened animal.

"It was a multiple fracture," the nurse murmured, in Grace's ear.

"It's OK," Grace murmured to her granddaughter. "You hurt your arm. They pinned your arm, I guess." She glanced up at the nurse, who nodded. "You feel sleepy? You went to sleep when they mended your arm...."

But Rachel didn't look as if she were just out from under anesthetic. Her face looked hollow, bruised and shadowed; but the eyes were coldly alive and so green, the color of the irises flat and startling, as if someone had dropped a watercolor onto them. Viridian, viridian. Grace pulled back a little, and tried to uncurl the arm. Rachel tightened her grip.

"Dog," Rachel said, suddenly.

Grace blinked. "A dog?" she repeated. There was only the stare by way of reply. "There was a dog?" Grace guessed. "On the road?"

Rachel's gaze flew upward, then back. "A car killed the dog."

"He ran out on the highway?"

"No," Rachel said. Her mouth turned down in an acute, clown-like bow of despair.

Grace kissed her face and ran her hand softly over her forehead. "You hurt anywhere else?" she whispered. "Anywhere?"

"The dog," Rachel said.

"OK, honey," Grace replied, soothing. "OK."

The nurse laid a hand on Grace's arm.

"Wait a minute," Grace told Rachel. "I'll be right back."

They went out into the corridor.

"Can we have something for our records?" the nurse asked. "A few details . . ."

"Sure."

They sat on two chairs by the nurses' station. Grace realized that she was trembling, faintly but steadily shaking, from head to foot.

"Rachel is how old?"

"Ten. Just ten."

"And she lives at . . ."

Grace gave the Boston address, and her own name and address as next of kin.

"And Anna Russell is Rachel's mother."

"Yes." Grace gripped the woman's arm. "Where is she? Anna?"

"I'll check again in just a second."

"But she's here?"

"In surgery."

"Oh, God," Grace gasped.

"I'll go back again in just a moment."

"But how long has she been in there?"

"About an hour and a half."

"An hour!" Grace plunged her head in her hands. "Jesus, oh, Jesus . . ."

The nurse paused, resting her hand on Grace's shoulder, until the older woman straightened up.

"I can see her?"

"Of course. If we could just finish Rachel's records ..."

"What's the matter with her? Why are they operating?"

"I'll find out." The nurse smiled gently. "OK? I promise. In just a second."

"All right. OK." Grace looked at the form, tried to concentrate on it.

"And Rachel's father ... ?"

"She doesn't have one."

"I see."

"They've never lived together."

"But he's alive?" the nurse asked.

"Yes."

"And his address would be?"

"I don't know. None of us knows."

"OK," the nurse said quietly.

"He's never seen her," Grace said, her voice little louder than a breath.

The pen scrawled across the page.

"Anna has a partner," Grace said. "James Garrett." She spelled the surname. She looked away, back toward the door of Rachel's room. "I guess he thinks of himself as her father," she murmured.

Down the corridor, she saw someone else come out from a patient's room: a couple, a man and his wife, holding on to each other. They walked very slowly toward the exit.

Grace looked back at the nurse. "There's something you should know about Rachel," she said. "She's an Asperger child."

"I see." The nurse nodded, writing. "Autistic."

Grace put her hand on the clipboard. "No," she said. "Not autistic."

"Asperger isn't a form of autism?"

Grace felt her heart skip. She waited, swallowing her irritation. Here it came again, all the things that she and Anna tried to avoid. The categories. The convenient boxes. "OK," she said finally, "you want to write autism, write it. But it isn't Rachel."

"I understand," the nurse said.

"I doubt it," Grace retorted. "But you write down autism, for your label."

The nurse held her glance for a second, but said nothing. She wrote *Autistic spectrum disorder* slowly on the page.

"I want to see my daughter now," Grace told her.

Four

JAMES GARRETT SAT BACK in the Logan Airport cab, staring at the traffic. The car he had hailed had no air-conditioning, but rolling down the windows—to the slow-moving congestion and the diesel-polluted air—was a much worse option than sweltering on the faux fur seat.

He looked at the driver: a kid in his twenties, black hair greased to the nape of his neck. He had his own window down, and was drumming his fingers on the outside panel of the car in a complicated rhythm.

"Plenty cars, huh," he shouted at James, looking at him in the mirror.

James said nothing. He glanced at his watch. Seven-ten. The arrangement had been to meet her outside Arrivals at five forty-five. The flight had been on time. He had waited in the claustrophobic heat for over an hour, while other travelers surged around him. He had watched an irritating number of courtesy buses arrive and depart, making for the rental-car compounds. He had let probably sixty cabs go past, until he finally hailed this one.

He watched as, distantly, the Hancock Tower came into view. He looked at his watch again, and then fished his cell phone from his jacket pocket. He had double-checked Anna's number and her house. He had even, with some misgiving, called Grace. All with no reply.

He looked, now, out of the window.

They had at last gotten to Tremont Street; the Common was just coming into view. He leaned forward and tapped on the back of the driver's seat. "Stop here," he said.

"We ain't at Irving yet."

"I know that."

He got out, paid the fare, and pulled his portfolio from the backseat. Crossing Tremont, he set off across the Common, past the souvenir stalls, the drunks on the bench near the fountain, the guy selling lemon ice, the chain of mothers pushing strollers. He walked briskly, linen jacket over one shoulder. More than one woman glanced at him.

Handsome and slim, and looking younger than his forty-two years, James Garrett gave off an air of understated but unmistakable wealth: the Italian suit, the open-necked cream shirt, the discreet jewelry. He looked European—Tuscan, perhaps. French. There was a distinguished scattering of early gray in the thick dark hair, and a slightly sallow, Mediterranean tone in his skin. He had dark eyes, with a sardonic glint in them. Only the mouth, thin-lipped and always slightly down-turned, betrayed a less than outgoing nature.

He crossed at Beacon Street, walking past the State House and turning up Joy Street. The brownstone mansions of Beacon Hill, rising above the Common, were in sharp contrast to the noisy city spread out before them. Here, the streets rapidly became quiet, even hushed. At the next intersection, Garrett stopped, and looked up at the ornate wrought-iron grilles and balconies.

When he had first come to Boston, twenty-four years ago, it had been his ambition to live here, among the Brahmins, looking out toward the Charles River and Cambridge beyond. He had coveted one particular house, at the corner of Joy and Myrtle, a beautiful French-looking frontage with shuttered windows. His hunger for a kind of life—the life he imagined was lived behind such shutters, behind such closed, expensive drapes—had struck him like a physical need.

He had been born just outside North Conway, in New Hampshire. It was at the edge of the White Mountains National Forest.

The forest was picturesque country. In the winter, it made money from skiing and sledding and sleigh rides; in summer, the tourists came for the walking and the wooded mountain scenery. Mount Washington was further up the valley, with the cog railway toiling up its scoured, windswept slopes.

His father had a job as caretaker in one of the resort hotels: an impressive, sprawling chalet-style building, set back on a private road high above the town. The hotel had four hundred rooms, and a swimming pool, and tennis courts, and a golf course. Every day, James's father towed the baggage carts, cleaned the filters of the pool, fixed the broken lights, mowed the grass, helped on deliveries. His mother was the housekeeper. Every day, James walked down the private road and got the school bus into town.

He had been a tall, thin kid, who had inherited his dark looks from an Italian grandmother. His father, by contrast, betrayed his Irish roots, with his pale blue eyes, and reddish face, and the urge to drink, and sing, and become sentimental. Father and son were an odd couple: a big, awkward man, clutching the hand of a ten-year-old silent boy. His father had always wanted to hold his hand. At ten. At fifteen. He saw nothing odd in it: he was a man in the grip of unfathomable passions that made him shake. Not with drink anymore, but with tearful concern.

If there was one thing that James had loathed as a teenager, it was to see his father weep, which he did often, and at slight and embarrassing events. Something on the TV. A guest giving him a tip. James's mother was a silent woman, and she kept both her son and husband at arm's length, her mouth habitually down-turned in cold stoicism. She had, she told James frequently, seen the worst of times with his father. Now they were here, holding down decent jobs, she would make sure that they kept them; and it was as if she believed that they kept their places by freezing out whatever feelings she might once have had.

He still had an image of her in his head, an image that he could never erase, and which would spring back at him sometimes at the darkest times, both figuratively and literally. It would come to him in the early hours, if he couldn't sleep. It would come if he were thwarted or at some temporary disadvantage: the image of his mother seated at the plastic-topped table in their basement apartment, her face stony with disapproval, and, behind her, the picture of the Madonna and child that she had carried from one house to another.

It wasn't a great picture. It wasn't by a famous artist. It was just a souvenir, a tacky and lurid portrait. The kind you saw in the worst roadside stalls in Cyprus or Greece, overdrawn and bleached by strong light, and side by side with playing cards and chewing gum and cheap leather purses. Nevertheless, her face had got into his head, his memory, and his claustrophobic, closed-off heart. The mother of Christ gazed out with piercing, questioning eyes, and a little bewildered smile; her skin was the color of skimmed milk, opaque, fragile. Her expression of both alarm and mystification clung to his soul. By contrast, her child was gazing at His outstretched fingers, His face averted.

James had tried not to think of his own mother for years. But instead, the Madonna would come streaming out of his subconscious and assault him with her pitiful five-and-dime purity.

If James's mother was cold beneath the weight of her frustrations, however, James's father was the exact opposite. All the emotions that had been drowned in the years of his drinking had come bubbling back up to the surface. For James as a child, it was like being stuck between a rock and a hard place. He didn't like his mother, but at least he could admire her rigid calm. His father was nothing but an embarrassment.

James had seen him standing in the hotel driveway one December, after a snowfall. He had been looking at the colored lights, reflected on the snow down the hill. He had turned to James, after meeting him from school, and held his son's shoulders, and shown him the colors on the snow, and his hands had been trembling with the pleasure of it. And all the while James had been thinking how unlike a man his father was, and how like a child. The kind of child you couldn't bear near you.

He made the kind of mistakes that James never forgot. Just after James had begun school, just after he got the job in the hotel and they moved to the area—James was perhaps six—his father had given him a schoolbag. It was a bag that a guest had given him.

As soon as you laid eyes on this bag, you knew that the man who had owned it had maybe been carrying it around for years. It had been good, once. So good that the owner hadn't been able to bring himself to throw it away. It was leather with a red trim, of which just a little scuffed red piping remained. It had a brass clasp. And whoever this guest was—James had never seen him—had finally handed the case to his father as a tip.

Inordinately proud, his father had given it to him, and insisted, with those watery blue eyes fixed on him, that he take it to school. He'd stood with him at the stop on the first day, and watched him board the bus, smiling hugely all the while, and nodding down at the case, as if James carried some fantastic prize.

Everyone on the bus had watched him board, too.

They watched this Hispanic-looking kid get on, and sit by himself.

They looked at the bag.

"What you got here?" some boy had demanded, when he was hardly through the gate of the school. Immediately, a pair of large, red-knuckled hands had fastened on the case. "What you got?" Shaking the handle. Ear against the leather, eyebrows raised in mock inquiry. A ripple of appreciative guffaws from the crowd. "Hey, kid. You FBI? Huh?"

The bag was grabbed, and kicked around the yard.

It was not the kind of thing he could tell his father. It was not the kind of thing his father could understand. The kicking, maybe. But not the loathing of the bag. He couldn't see what a hand-me-down it was. He thought it was valuable.

And his gratitude, and his tears, and his ridiculous trembling—all these things smothered James, and choked him.

When he told his mother about the bag, she had shrugged, and hissed a dismissive laugh. "Throw it away," she said. She had that familiar look on her face: tired cynicism.

"But what will I tell Dad?" he'd asked her.

"Tell him it was stolen."

He'd said nothing, merely looked at her.

She'd nodded at him. "A lie will get you where you want to go," she'd said. "That's a fact. You learn that."

Over the years, James had watched his father become narrower, smaller. He became a slow-moving, fastidious man, endlessly cleaning, repairing, polishing. Watching him one day in the summer, cleaning the restaurant windows with incredible care, James had felt the need to turn away. He had suddenly been suffocated by the movement of his hands, the way they described endless little tight circles. Because he was beginning to get arthritis, his father—sixty now to James's sixteen—took fifteen minutes to do a three-minute job, and a wave had swept through his son, something akin to revulsion, and it had added a secondary shame to the persistent feeling he carried around with him. That his father had finished with drinking and picked up his life again was, James supposed, good; that it had turned him prematurely old, slow-witted, and sentimental was not good. That he liked James to sit with him in the evenings, those he had free, was not good either. James wanted to be out, walking by himself. It was only then that he felt clean, as if his life stuck to him like a greasy skin. He wanted out. He wanted to shed that skin. He wanted to be someone else. Not the kid from White Mountain or North Conway. Not the kid with a reformed drunk for a father.

When he thought like this, he would get a great heavy beat in his chest, as if the person that he really was was fighting to get out of him, and throw this inconsequential identity aside. He didn't belong to his father, or the school, or any friend, or this place.

He had left high school without a diploma. He had simply walked out one day. He had walked the four miles back to the hotel, and gone to his room, and taken the hundred and twenty dollars that he had saved, and left. He had hitched all the way to Boston, without speaking to his parents, without even leaving a note.

★   ★   ★

James increased his pace as he turned into Myrtle Street.

His first job in the city had been at a bookstore on Brasely Street. It was no longer there now, but twenty-four years ago it had had a modest reputation, and the owner hired James for, above all else, his air of silent—even superior—calm. They had been short-handed that particular week. It had been his first stroke of luck.

And the second—perhaps the greatest piece of luck, indeed, of his life—had been Catherine Graham. She had come into the shop one morning, a glossy catalogue tucked under one arm. She was a tall woman in her early forties. She wore a charcoal-colored suit, low heels, and little jewelry. She walked slowly, with her head held up. Slowly, and smoothly, as if gliding, or sailing. She had come over, and asked him something. He had pointed her to a display. He remembered, even now, the amused expression in her blue eyes.

As she spoke, he had suddenly noticed what she was carrying under one arm: it was an auction catalogue. On the front cover was a painting.

"Jean Dubuffet," he said.

She had raised her eyebrows. "Yes," she murmured, looking at the catalogue, and then back at him.

"Art is nothing more than a product of exhilaration and joy," he told her. She frowned. He pointed at the picture. "That's what he said. Art is ..."

"Oh, I see," she murmured. And laughed, as if to herself, before turning away.

He saw her again two weeks later. She was on Congress Street, turning up toward Faneuil Hall. It was his day off, and he had been walking, as he always did, rather than stay in his one room on Braddock Parkway. It started to rain—it was February, and cold—and he saw her, through the crowds, begin to hurry, holding a newspaper over her head.

He had followed her. Right through Quincy Market, past the food stalls, past the tables where people were squeezed along the benches and around the walls, sheltering from the downpour—and he saw her run out and across to the shopping center opposite.

He caught up with her on the stairs, waiting for a family to come down the red-painted open walkway.

He had touched her arm.

"Hello," he said.

She had looked at him.

"The bookstore," he reminded her.

Her gaze had been blank.

"I work there," he told her. "You asked me . . ."

A hot flush of embarrassment had crept up his neck. She didn't remember him. The family passed them, a father and mother carrying a stroller between them, a little boy of four or five hanging on to his mother's spare hand.

"Dubuffet," he reminded her. He hoped to God that she wasn't meeting someone here. Some older man to whom she would turn, while casting a sardonic look back at James over her shoulder.

"I'm sorry," he said. He started back down the steps. She let him get around the curve of the landing before reaching down to touch his shoulder, where he stood on a lower step.

"Don't be sorry," she had said. "I don't meet many people who can quote Dubuffet."

Of course, he never told her. He didn't tell her when she bought him a cup of coffee that morning; and he didn't mention it when he arrived at a gallery that she owned, grasping the invitation to an opening that she had given him. And he didn't tell her when she took him home with her, and showed him the paintings that she owned in her house: the Rothko, the Ossorio.

He had never told her, even right up to the end, that the reason he knew about Dubuffet was that a previous tenant of his rented room had left a poster tacked to the wall. It was a print of Dubuffet's "Bustling Life," with Dubuffet's quotation running along underneath it. Up until that moment in the bookshop, he had never had the remotest interest in painting or painters. After she took him home, he never thought of anything else.

A lie will get you where you want to go.

Catherine Graham had taught him a lot, of course. Everything within her own strict, tight code. She had made the game plan very clear from the very first night he had come home with her.

"Don't suppose that I've brought you here for a sexual reason," she had said, in her loud, flat voice. She had slung her coat onto the nearest couch. "Everyone else will assume it," she said. "But you must not." She had eyed him from head to foot. "If that's what you're here for, you can leave."

"I'll stay," he said.

She had sat down, still staring at him. "I was married at twenty-one, and divorced at twenty-two," she said. "I tried it." She shrugged, smirking a little. "Like mealy grubs. I tried them once, too," she said. "And I didn't like that, either."

He smiled. She had started to laugh. "That's right, James," she had said. "Life is a sort of joke. If you can't look at it that way, you're lost." She had lit a cigarette, then stopped, and pointed a finger at him. "Except in business," she said. "That is serious."

He had merely nodded. He was overawed. He was in an amazing house. There was very little furniture, but what there was was rare, and expensive. There was a wonderful ormolu clock on the nearest cabinet, and two Art Deco figures.

"Where are you from, James?" she asked.

He had looked at her. A long beat passed. "Nowhere," he said.

"Nowhere," she repeated, slowly. "Not an interesting place."

"No," he replied.

She had leaned forward, elbows on her knees. "A blank page," she said. "Is that it?"

"Yes," he said.

"Was it so bad?" she asked.

"Yes," he repeated.

"You want something else."

Her fingers had described a slow, tapping rhythm on the arm of the chair. She had still not asked him to sit down. "Are you honest?" she asked him abruptly.

"Yes," he told her.

"Have you any money?"

"No."

"Are you in any kind of trouble?"

"No."

Her gaze flickered to the wall, where a tapestry hung. He could read her thoughts. Here was a young man with no money, who would say nothing about himself. And here was she, a wealthy woman, alone.

"I guess I could kill you right off," he told her, as she was still looking at the tapestry. "I guess I could make a lot of money out of what I could carry."

She glanced back, raised her eyebrows.

"You were thinking that," he said.

They had stared at each other for a few seconds. Seconds in which all the previous years fell into place for him, and he saw in her expression that she had always lived as he had lived, outside the world, looking in.

"And will you?" she said.

"Will I what?" he asked.

"Take what you can carry."

"No," he told her. "Never."

She leaned back against the chair. He saw something—a reflex of pain—cross her face. Although he was not to know it then, it was the illness that would eventually kill her, and the reason she needed help now. But, as suddenly as it had appeared, the expression was gone. "I used to run all over the place," she murmured. "Now I need a man to run for me."

"I can do it," he told her.

"We'll see," she replied.

Catherine Graham was a specialist, working as a consultant for major art and auction houses. She was asked to buy for corporations and for private individuals; she was called upon to authenticate recently discovered or long-lost works. She had once traveled in Europe, and had been based in London, but had come home to Boston that previous Christmas for a reason she wouldn't divulge. He grew used to Dubuffet, and Baziotes, and Motherwell. More used still to her personal favorites, particularly Leger and Braque. Schiele, Franz Marc, Theophile Steinlen.

She had a gallery on Newbury. It was a place that you couldn't enter without ringing a bell first. There was nothing on show outside, no plate-glass window. You stood on the stone step and waited until she answered, by intercom, from behind the black-painted door. If she recognized you, or you had an appointment, you were admitted. If not, you could wait outside until hell froze over.

Although the hallway was dark, the inner door led into a space flooded with light. Catherine had altered the entire ground floor, stripped it back to a beech floor and starkly plain white walls. In this long room hung maybe six, maybe eight paintings. Also perhaps three pieces of sculpture, or bronzes, or ceramics. She had been showing a new artist when James first came to the gallery, and he had hated the pictures of cafés and tables. To his eyes, the red tablecloths and blue bottles and yellow flowers not only clashed, but looked broken and misshapen. Dishes of food—a crab, a few pieces of fruit—would lie stranded in a sea of pink, with a pencil scribble indicating a bottle label, or a shadow, or a knife. Catherine explained to him why this artist was talented, and why he was worth so much. The whole collection, five in all, had been sold to a national bank for three million dollars only two days later, and, if James didn't see before, he saw then. Or, to be more accurate, he was damned sure that he would *learn* to see.

Catherine didn't give him any money in the first year. She fed him, she gave him the roof over his head, of course; she took him with her to auctions and parties and other collections and museums, and to some artists' homes. She paid for all his travel, and she paid for some of his clothes—the two business suits, one gray and one black. But she never offered him payment, and, after only a short while, he began to realize that this was some sort of test: whether he would earn anything on the side, or take tips from customers, or try the minor swindles of inflating the cost of the utilities he paid for or the tickets he booked. Whether, more outrageously, he would be tempted to steal from the purse she left lying around. But he never did. Neither did he go out in the evenings. Instead, with her permission, he read all the books she had, and he listened to all her music. And it was an education more important than all the years that had gone before.

Most important of all, he watched. He watched how she talked to customers, or how she didn't talk. He learned when it was best to keep silent. He learned not to flatter too much. He came to know the women, much like Catherine, of a certain age, involved with certain charities, invariably with very uncertain marriages, who invested their old money in new talent because they wanted to touch the artist in some way, or because spending their money gave them a little comfort, a few minutes of security. He watched the businessmen who were not interested in a painting, and how their gaze would skate over a picture; how they would stand with their hands locked behind their backs in front of a bronze, as if willing themselves not to connect with it at all. And he at last understood the peculiar conversation that went on between the piece of art and its viewer.

He reached his house now.

He took out his key, and opened the door.

When he had first bought this place three years ago, it had been split into three condominiums. One was for sale; one was usually empty, as the owner traveled. The third, on the ground floor, was owned by an elderly woman.

The top floor, which had been renovated, was for sale for three hundred and thirty thousand dollars. Over a period of eleven months he had bought out the other two. In the next year, he had stripped the house and refurbished it. The whole project had cost him a little in excess of two million. The ground floor was his office; the second, his sitting room, kitchen, and library. The third was his bedroom and bathroom. Let down through the center of the house, at enormous expense and through ever greater negotiation with the planning authorities, was a massive skylight that spilled light down the original wooden stairwell.

The house was minimalist in the extreme. Every floor was stripped, and every piece of furniture—of which there was little—was a neutral color. He had given space and air to his paintings, and, when he came home, as now, the first thing he did, before even putting down his bags, was to stand in the center of the second floor and look around him at the fortune that hung on the walls.

When Catherine Graham had died, she had given him the Rothko.

In addition, there were a Braque and a Lukaschewski.

Women had told him they were masculine paintings. Angular and uncompromising. They told him that the pictures said a lot about his own character.

And he was always surprised when they told him that. Because he thought of himself as the easiest and most compromising of men.

He walked over to the phone and listened to the messages, skipping through the business calls. He checked his watch again. Seven-thirty.

There would surely be something soon.

And, as if in answer to his thought, the doorbell rang downstairs.

He pressed the intercom.

"Yes?"

"James," said a familiar voice. "It's Grace."

He looked at the intercom grille in surprise. "Grace?"

"Let me in, James."

He paused a beat. "Of course."

He went out to the head of the stairs. She came in and slammed the door, and stood at the bottom of the steps, looking up.

"Are you all right?" he asked.

She didn't look all right. She looked gray.

"What is it?" he said.

She put a hand on the banister, and then shook her head. She bowed her head, and he realized that she was crying.

He began to walk down.

"What's happened?" he asked.

He drew level with her. He put his hand on her shoulder, but she moved away. She moved right back to the wall, and leaned against it, and her face was in shadow, and her hands, stained with paint and nicotine, were in the light, and she looked very old, much older than her years.

"It's Anna," she told him. "If you want to see her, you had better come now."

Five

THE DOVE TREE STOOD at the back of Morton House.

It was known by other names. The ghost tree. The handkerchief tree.

Standing underneath it, staring up through its airy branches, David watched the way that the white bracts moved in the wind. On a morning like this, a cool morning, with the sun just beginning to touch the uppermost leaves, the *Davidia involucrata* had first been discovered in the mountains of western China, in 1869.

The owner of Morton House had planted this particular tree forty years before, because he had heard the story of when the botanist Augustine Henry had first seen it flowering in Hupeh. Henry had told his wife that it was the strangest apparition of his journey, and that the bracts fluttered like a thousand small white birds on a mountain slope.

The dove could grow to sixty-five feet, and this one was already on its way. Light and vigorous, with beautiful heart-shaped leaves whose green tone was startlingly bright, each leaf ending in a pointed tip—a green flourish, a signature, like the tail on calligraphy letters—it seemed young, as if it were just a juvenile, racing upward.

David reached up and touched the leaves of the closest branch.

Davidia involucrata. It had come into flower in the spring, the small rounded heads with their bright purple anthers surrounded by protecting bracts, one always longer than the other. The flowers were partially hidden under the smaller bract, folded over it delicately, like a white fan hiding a face; the longer bract hanging down behind the flower, a palm of silky tissue paper, eight inches long. When the *Davidia* flowered, and the bracts covered the tree, it was like looking at a wedding dress, falling in loose silk tiers, fold over fold, to the ground.

David released the leaves. He looked down at the lawn underneath the tree, where the first dying bracts littered the grass. In a few weeks' time there would be nothing extraordinary to distinguish this tree from the others around it. Nevertheless, he envied the owner, Charles Augre, for his possession of it. No other tree had ever been so pursued and lusted after as this one.

Morton House had once been one of the flourishing estates that, a hundred years ago, had taken pride in propagating the first plants from trees like this. Lovely as the house and gardens still were—the Tudor chimneys rising like candy sugar twists above the knot garden, and the fountains, the laburnum galleries, the lawns and the lake—they were a shadow of their former glory. Here, the gardens had once held two great tropical glasshouses. Charles Augre's great-grandfather had spent his life breeding the finds that plant explorers, such as Ernest Wilson, had brought back from Asia, China, and India.

David stood with his back to the tree now, eyes shut.

Wilson again.

Anna again.

They came hand in hand walking through his mind, easily and softly, as if they had never left. He opened his eyes and looked up through the *Davidia*'s leaves, with that familiar ache in his heart.

Ernest Wilson was the man who had flooded the West with the prizes he had brought back from China. He had traveled for years— the first ten years of the twentieth century—to find flowers like the regal lily, the honeysuckle, and *Meconopsis integrifolia,* the astonishing broad-petaled poppy. It had taken him eight years to find the species that would eventually populate the western world with

China's children: the vanilla-scented *Clematis armandii* with its creamy white flowers; and the gorgeous *Clematis montana,* blanketed in ice pink blossom every spring. Twenty species of cotoneaster. The evergreen primrose jasmine. The beauty bush. Seven fantastic magnolia, fourteen different flowering cherries, eighteen varieties of climbing roses. The iris that was named after him, *Iris wilsonii;* the *Liriodendron chinense,* from the Lu Shan mountains, which the Chinese called the goose-foot. And three *Styrax,* known as snowbells in America because of their white, bell-shaped hanging flowers.

Wilson had traveled from Shanghai to Yichang, at the mouth of the Yangtze Gorges; across the Chengdu plain; as far as the China-Tibet borders to Tatsienlu, now Kangding, the Gate of Tibet; through the forests of Ta-P'ao and the wilderness of Laolin, and to the sacred mountain of Emei Shan.

It was in his second year at Oxford that David had found Wilson's book.

It was a chance discovery: he had been looking for something else, and stumbled upon the modest green cloth binding on the library shelves. He had taken the book down, and it had opened at a series of photographs: China in the first decade of the twentieth century. A picture of the Great Salt Road—a path only, passing through a fissure in a mountain wall. And someplace called Songpan, a cluster of poor tile roofs grouped around a stone fort. And, on the subsequent page, a scene of desolate beauty: *A view of the countryside above Songpan,* read the caption. Mountain ranges filled the horizon, the Kunlun Shan to the northwest, the Himalaya to the southwest. In their heart lay Lhasa; in their foothills, Kathmandu; at their feet, Lucknow and Dhaka, thousands of miles to the south.

David had weighed the book in his hand. He had looked along the library shelf. Nothing else by Wilson. He looked in the first few pages again, at the chapter headings: South and Southwest China, Indochina, Western China, Japan, Korea, and Taiwan, ran the list of journeys. He glanced at the facing page. *The Zhedou Pass at fourteen thousand feet,* began an introductory sentence.

He thought he recognized some of the discovery names from

his father's garden. *Viburnum,* for instance. *Rosa moyesii.* He turned to the index at the back, and saw page after page of discoveries. Photographs of maples, and sorbus, and primula. Seductive and unreal magnolia. A fantastic plant he had never heard of, with a light green spine running through each leaf, and the tips of the leaves turning copper. An orchid, with a great bell-shaped pouch like a fleshy mouth, almost with a tongue; candy-striped petals, green leaves like tulips. *Cypripedium tibeticum.* Brought from Tibet.

That lunchtime, David had showed the book to Anna. He still remembered her that day, coming out of Magdalen, carrying the thick drawing pad and her cotton roll of watercolors. They had sat down on the curb while he opened Wilson's book and folded out the maps, and she had drawn Wilson's *Lilium regale,* the fairy-tale white lily with its long yellow stamens and satinlike petals. She had held up the finished sketch at shoulder level.

"And this Wilson," she had said. "He found this where?"

"Near a place called Songpan."

"Where's that?"

"Western China."

"Romantic," she said.

He had leaned forward, pulled down the sketchpad, and smiled at her over the top of it. "Romantic?" he had repeated.

"Yes," she answered. "Why not?"

He opened the book. *". . . Barring absolute desert, no more barren and repelling country could be imagined,"* he read out. *"A fierce upriver wind blows regularly and it is difficult to make headway against it . . . the leaves on the maize plants are torn to shreds by the wind's violence . . ."*

She was listening to him. "Right up your alley," she commented. "I can see you doing that."

"What?" he had asked.

"Searching the world for a new daffodil," she teased. "Canoeing the Amazon for a chrysanthemum."

"That's Japan, chrysanthemums."

"Trekking Antarctica for a rare cabbage."

"Never have I looked upon a more savage and less inviting region . . ."

"I can see you now in a white hat, carrying a big net." She had laughed, throwing back her head. She had thick reddish hair that fell to just below her shoulders. He liked to listen to her, to hear the burr of her American accent. And she was forever in his head, now, like this . . . in faded jeans and T-shirt, and the turquoise-and-silver bangle on her wrist that she never took off, and her head rested on one hand, and turned toward him . . .

"Let's see what he looked like, this great explorer," she had said.

They found Wilson's photograph in the first chapter. A family man, at home in Boston, Wilson was the very epitome of Edwardian respectability, with a high starched collar and a dark cloth suit and a watch chain glimpsed at the waist. Below him sat his wife and daughter, in equally starched masses of white *broderie anglaise*. But, further on in the book, as they searched through it, they found another Wilson: sitting at the side of a mud track, with two dogs at his feet, a hat pushed back on his head, and a crowd of Chinese around him. Rain had splattered the camera lens. More mountains—endless, endless mountains—rose up in the background.

"Do you see where he comes from?" David had asked Anna.

"England," she said. "Gloucestershire. It said so, at the beginning."

"After that," he said. "Look—see? Hired in 1899 by the Arnold Arboretum in Boston."

She had smiled at him. "My mother lives just north of there."

"I know," he said, and he looked again at her quick, accomplished drawing of the lily.

He had first seen Anna three weeks before, in Roxburgh's on The High, sitting under the Matisse prints, making pocket money by drawing cartoons of customers in the style of famous artists. She was at a front table, pad propped on her lap, and a pastiche of Lautrec flowed from the pencil, and he had stopped. He had stopped and stared at her. And, miraculously, she had looked up, and smiled back.

"And this—this *savage region*—" she was saying, "that's where this lily comes from?" She, too, had looked again at her drawing, and then down again at the picture in Wilson's book.

"Lilium regale *luxuriates in rocky crevices . . .*" David continued. "*It grows three to five feet tall, ivory white suffused with canary yellow within, and is deliciously fragrant . . . the regal lily occurs here in abundance on the well-nigh stark slate and mudstone cliffs.*"

"How weird," she mused. "They look so fragile. Overblown, almost. As if they couldn't stand a breeze, let alone a desert." She frowned. "They look like a floral version of someone's mistress."

"A what?" he echoed.

"You know. All satin sheets and shaded rooms."

He grinned at her. "How did we get to satin sheets?" he asked. "And," he added, drawing her close to him, while the traffic rolled past just inches from their feet, and the crowds stepped around them, and the drawing of the lily fell between them, "what do you know about mistresses?"

"As much as you."

"I don't know a thing."

She'd smiled, kissing him. "You'd better not."

They had gotten up, eventually, and walked on down to Brasenose. "I could do my dissertation on someone like this," David had said, as they had stopped to cross the road.

"You could write a book," she'd replied. "A book would be better. You could do the text, and I could do the illustration. What would you call it?"

"*The Light of the World.*"

"No," she said, pulling a critical face. "That's already a painting. Don't you know that, you ignoramus?"

"*The World in Color,* then."

She'd started to laugh. "Oh, my God," she'd said. "That is so much worse. I can't tell you how much worse that is. That is awful."

They'd dashed across through a break in the traffic. "Well, I don't know," he'd said. "You choose."

She'd considered, mock serious. "*A Road Through the Mountains,*" she'd offered, finally. "Something to do with mountains, anyway."

He had kept the sketch of the *Lilium regale* for a long time.

Eleven years.

Long after she had gone.

★   ★   ★

"Mortimer!" called a voice.

He turned around. Charles Augre was walking across the grass. As he watched, the owner of Morton stopped, and beckoned him.

David started in his direction. "Yes?" he asked, when he was closer.

"Your sister's here for you," Augre replied. "Something urgent."

Sara was in the restaurant.

It was in the building where the horses had been kept, when Morton had had carriages. The Stables Bistro, said the sign over the door. The renovation had been one of the changes forced upon Augre to find income to run the house. Just one of the many changes that he hated. David often thought that Augre felt he had sold his soul to the devil, just to be enabled to keep Morton viable. If he had his own way, Augre would shut the gates and close the parking lot, and slam the shutters down on The Stables, just so he could have the luxury of being left alone in peace with his gardens.

"What are you doing here?" David asked his sister, as he came in.

Sara stood in the center of the room, watching the tables being set. It was still only half past nine; the grounds didn't open to the public until ten.

"They found you," she said.

Hannah was hitched up on Sara's hip, looking flushed and fretful.

"Is she all right?" David asked, nodding at the baby. "Is she ill?"

"She's got a temperature," Sara told him. "I'm on my way to the doctor's."

"Do you want me to come with you?" he asked.

"No, no," she said, shaking her head. "It's nothing serious. It's not Hannah. That's not why I'm here."

"Who's in the shop?" he asked.

"Matt," she replied. "Never mind that." She frowned at him, bit her lip. She stepped out of the way of one of the women, a stout lady in a checked apron, carrying a fistful of coasters and cutlery. The woman glanced from David to Sara, her gaze lingering a second on Sara's face. She could read the apprehension there. "When you'd gone," Sara continued to David, "just after you'd gone this morning . . . I got a phone call."

David was still distracted by Hannah, and the waitress, who was now making a hell of a noise filling the cutlery trays by the till. "Who from?" he asked, frowning.

Sara didn't reply. He looked back at her. "Who from?" he repeated.

"Grace Russell," she said.

The waitress came back. She smiled at Hannah. "Does she want anything?" she asked Sara. "A drink of juice?"

"No," Sara said. "Thank you . . . no."

"Oh, she's lovely," the woman said. "Isn't she a lovely one? Such a pretty little thing, in her pink outfit."

David watched her walk away. The doors to the kitchen rattled behind her.

"David," said Sara. "It's Anna's mother."

He lifted his eyes to hers.

"I know who Grace Russell is," he said.

"She's been trying to find you all night," she said. "Since yesterday." She took a step toward him. "It was just after nine when she got through. It's four in the morning out there."

He turned on his heel, went to the door, and pushed his way outside. Over the top of the restaurant, you could see the poplars that Augre had planted by the lake. The wind was plucking at them.

"David . . . David!"

He turned around. "The only time I heard from Grace Russell," he said, "she told me she didn't know where Anna was. And I rang her, then. Four times. The last time, she put the phone down on me."

"It doesn't matter now," Sara said. "It was years ago."

David's expression darkened. "That's right," he said. "It's years ago."

"You have to ring her," Sara said. She was taking a piece of paper out of her pocket. "I wrote down the numbers." She held it out to him.

He didn't take it from her.

"She had phoned all over looking for you," she said. "Your old college, London, Kew, VSO, Westonbirt, Bristol ... everywhere you've worked." She pushed the piece of paper at him. "If you think I'm standing here for my health," she warned. "Take it."

Grudgingly, he did so.

"Ring her," she told him. "It's about Anna."

He looked up. "What about her?"

"She's been in some sort of accident."

His hand dropped to his side, paper still in his grasp. "When?"

"I don't know," she said. "Yesterday, maybe. A road accident. She's in hospital." She nodded at the paper. "The first number is the mobile. The second is Massachusetts General."

In Sara's arms, Hannah began to cry.

"What happened to her?" David asked.

"David, I don't know." Sara looked closely at her daughter.

"Is she injured?"

Sara looked despairingly at him. "I don't know," she repeated. "I'm really sorry. I have to go. Ring Grace."

She turned, and walked to her car, glancing all the while at Hannah.

As she unlocked the door, David called to her.

"Why now?" he said. "After all this time?"

His sister put Hannah into the child seat. She straightened up, and leaned momentarily on the car's roof.

"Ring her," she told him. "Just ring."

Charles Augre showed him into the dining room.

It was the nearest phone. David didn't own a mobile.

He sat down on a chair, and looked at his watch. Ten-forty in the morning. It would be five-forty in Boston. Grace had rung Sara in the middle of the night.

He wondered if Grace still lived at Ogunquit. He wondered if Anna lived with her. He wondered if Anna had always lived with her, from the first days of going back there and deserting him without a word of explanation. Had Anna been standing close to Grace when he had phoned all those years ago? He wondered most of all what Anna had said to her mother, what reasons she had given her. The reasons denied to him.

He dialed Grace's number, and sat back and waited, staring ahead of him.

It was picked up after the second ring.

"Grace Russell."

"Hello," he said. "This is David."

There was a gasp on the other end of the line. "Oh! Thank you for calling. Thank you so much."

"You wanted to tell me something."

There was a beat of silence. "Yes . . . yes," she said. "I can't be-lieve it's you."

He gave a grudging half-smile. Grace's voice was full of the smoky breathlessness and warmth that he distantly remembered. "About Anna," he prompted.

"I . . ." Another silence. "Could you hold on?" she said. "The damned signal on this thing. Let me go into the hall."

He waited.

"David," she suddenly whispered. "I'm so grateful."

He said nothing.

"David, are you there?"

"Yes."

"Anna is very ill."

"I'm sorry to hear that."

Another silent second. "She just came out of surgery."

"Surgery?" he repeated. "What happened?"

"Her car crashed in a rainstorm. A truck went into her."

He balled his fist, knocked it against his leg, taking a moment to reply. "Is it bad?"

This time, the pause was long. "Yes," she said, and he heard her voice hitch.

"Is she unconscious?"

"Yes," she told him. "There's a head injury."

Immediately, irrationally, he thought of the reddish hair and the blond lily, side by side.

"I'm very sorry," he said.

"Yes, I ..." There was a jumble of voices, evidently of a group passing in the corridor where Grace was standing. "David," she whispered, "I need to ask you something."

He waited.

"I don't know what else to do."

He waited.

"David," she said, "will you come over here?"

He paused. Actually, he stopped breathing for a second, in surprise. "I'm sorry?" he said.

"Come over here. To Boston. To the hospital."

"What?" he said.

"Today. Tomorrow?"

He stared at the phone, then replaced it to his ear. "Is this a joke?"

"Do you think I would joke about this!" she exclaimed.

"You ring me up after eleven years ..."

"I know," she said. "I know how it must seem to you."

"It's out of the question," he told her. "No."

"Listen ..."

"I really am sorry," he said. "I'm sorry Anna's not well."

"You don't understand."

"I do understand," he replied. "But there's nothing I can do."

"Yes, there is!"

"No," he said. "No."

"Are you married?" she asked, suddenly.

"What?"

"Are you married?"

"What is that to do with anything?" he demanded.

"Your sister said you weren't."

"You've discussed me?"

"I'm sorry," she repeated. "It would complicate things. But it wouldn't change them."

"What the hell are you talking about?" he said.

"If you were married," she answered. Her words came in a rush, falling over each other. "If you had a wife ... if you had children ... but you would have to tell them. Nothing alters the fact ..."

"You aren't making any sense," he said. "I don't understand you. I'm not married. I don't have a family."

"Then will you come? Please!"

"Is Anna?" he asked.

"Sorry?" Grace said. "Is Anna what?"

"Is Anna married?"

"No," she replied. "She has a partner. An art dealer called James Garrett." He heard the coldness in her tone.

"Then it's certainly not appropriate for me to come there," he told her. "How would it seem to him?"

"You don't know him," she replied. There was a pause. "You don't want to know him."

He frowned hard. "I can't see what earthly good it would be," he said. "Anna wouldn't want me there."

"It's not for Anna," Grace said. "Not just Anna ..."

The line crackled heavily.

Someone—one of the stewards, the guides for the public in Morton House—opened the dining room door. She had a chair in her hand, and the rope barrier that kept the public away from the table and the furnishings. "Oh, sorry," she said, seeing David there. "But it's almost eleven. I have to open this room."

He put his hand over the receiver. "I'll be done in just a minute."

"David ... David ...!" Grace was saying.

"I'm still here," he told her. "But I have to go. I've borrowed this phone. People need to come in here." He stood up. "I'll ring another time," he said. "I'll ring in a few days and see how she is. If you want me to."

"Did you hear me?" Grace asked him, raising her voice.

"I can't just fly over there," he repeated. "It's absurd. I'm sorry. I'm not going to do that."

"Did you hear what I said?" she insisted. "Just now. Just a second ago?"

"No," he said. "The line . . ."

"It's Rachel," Grace continued. Now there were tears. He heard her sob, and then, almost in the same breath, curse herself. "Not for Anna, not for me . . ."

"Rachel?" he repeated, mystified.

He watched the double doors being opened now. There was someone—visitors to the house—already there, guidebooks in hand. They peered into the room curiously. "I have to go in a moment," he said, turning away, and cupping his hand over the receiver.

"She needs you," Grace was saying. "I'm afraid for her. I don't want her with him. It'll only get worse . . ."

"Who?" he said. "Don't want Rachel with who? Who is Rachel?"

Through the silence, across four thousand miles, he heard Anna's mother begin to weep helplessly.

"Your daughter," she told him. "Rachel is your daughter."

Six

ANNA SAT WITH HER hands resting on a piece of paper.

As she looked at it, it moved and flexed like water. Images bloomed and died, the colors merging and then just as rapidly draining away. Soon, as she watched with mounting confusion, even the paper itself disintegrated beneath her touch, and her hands sank through the watercolor cartridge sheet, through the table, through the air. Soon, her palms weighed down on her own body and passed through it.

She was made of nothing but filaments of dying color.

She looked around herself, and realized that she was in Oxford, in Roxburgh's. There was no one at the small marble-topped tables, and no one behind the bar. The whole room, which stretched far back from The High, was dim: the lights were all turned down.

She could hear voices behind the lacquered screen that led to the office. They were talking about her. Occasionally, she would hear her name, as if someone was calling her. Then, there would be a blur of conversation. There was a distant humming noise, like a generator.

A movement close to her caught her attention. There was a book on the neighboring table, and its pages were turning. Pictures of gardens. Pictures of trees. Here was Bonnard's "Almond Tree in

Bloom," with the blue pigment showing through the black-and-white branches. Paul Klee's "Night Flowers." Klimt's "Rosebushes Under Trees." She leaned forward, trying to remember exactly the way that the painting was composed, so that she could show Rachel. Three quarters of the canvas possessed by blue, gold, and greens. The bark of the trees, silver etched on gray. As she paused with her hand on the image, the page became fluid, and she could feel the coolness of the leaves brushing, whispering, against her skin. Plunging her hand deeper, she found it curling around the dense fluorescent mauve of Klee's sky, as though every particle of the twilight, all the breadth of the evening, had condensed itself into a few square inches of texture that could be flexed in her grasp.

"Can she hear us?" someone said.

She looked up, turned her head.

The High, that gold-shaded street, was gone.

Anna stood up, and walked to the window.

There was a river where the road had been.

It was not the Cherwell—although, for a second, she thought that she glimpsed the Meadow on the first of May, and felt the brush of first light, coming down past Magdalen to hear the choir sing in the tower at dawn, and David at her side, and the whole of the Meadow populated with the fritillary, their deep mauve flowers, almost the exotic opium poppy, almost Chinese lanterns in the eerie stillness . . .

But it wasn't the Cherwell.

This river was very wide and deep flowing. She could see whirlpools and eddies. It had no color at all. Everything was movement without tone or shade. She could see faces in the water; reflections of higher ground; wings and birds; rain slanting across the surface.

"She moved," said another voice.

But it was the river that moved. Now she could see more clearly. The faces were scattered grasses and reeds; the contours were rocks. There were men in the water, and the lines they were hauling were attached to flat-bottomed boats. They were crossing rapids, forty men or more on each line, and the pilot standing up in the boat.

The noise of the water swelled in her ears; as she watched, its sound filled the scene. Now there was only rising water, and the lines broke, and the flat-bottomed boat spun around, slowly, in the current.

It came alongside her. She stepped aboard.

It moved off, rotating gracefully in the flood.

Seven

IT HAD BEEN LATE October, and only three days after seeing her at Roxburgh's, that David had seen Anna again in Pembroke Street. Before the lily. Before Wilson. David had been cutting through toward St. Aldgate's when she came out of the Museum of Modern Art, and he saw her pause on the steps, a hair tie held in her teeth while she twisted her hair on top of her head.

"Hello again," she called. "You look busy."

His arms were full. "It's a project," he said.

"Remind me," she said. "I forgot what you're reading."

"Botany," he said.

She stood looking at him. She was not beautiful; perhaps she was not even pretty. But she had an unusual, appealing face: green eyes, and a broad smile, and the shoulder-length red hair. He noticed, for the first time, a little arc-shaped scar above one eye.

"You don't remember me," she said. "I talked to you in Roxburgh's. I was painting."

"Oh, I do remember," he told her.

She inclined her head toward the museum. "I work in the café," she said. "Just a couple of hours."

He looked up at the frontage, a white block that he had never really taken much notice of before. "I've never been in," he told her.

"You haven't?" she said. "Come and look."

He followed her. He didn't know how to interpret her easy manner. He didn't know if it meant she were being friendly especially toward him or that she was like this with everyone. He kept stealing sideways glances at her as she talked.

After a minute, he realized that she was telling him about the next exhibition. "It's going to start in January," she said. "It's called *Northlands*. Scandinavian artists."

He looked dutifully. He hadn't taken in a single word.

"This is called 'Book of Forms,' " she told him. "And this is 'A Sun.' " He looked at a photograph of Martii Aiha's mahogany sculpture, laid before a mirror-still lake.

"What do you think?" she asked him.

"Do you like it?" he asked her, doubtfully.

"Yes, it's exciting," she said. "It's wonderful."

"But why?"

She stopped, considering. "It makes me look."

"But so does anything. A traffic jam. A dog barking."

She laughed. "But to look three or four times; or even twenty times, and still be interested."

"Or confused."

She laughed. "But that's it exactly," she said. "While you're confused, you're still working things out."

He shook his head. They were now looking at a dark oil on canvas, by a different artist, for another exhibition. "It's dull," he said.

"But look at how the paint . . ."

"I don't want to look," he said. "If I look long enough at that, I'll run out in the street and throw myself under a bus." He grinned at her.

In return, she gave him a lingering, wry expression. Then, her face broke into a smile. "So what's this?" she asked, and she tapped the top book in the pile he still had balanced in the crook of one arm.

He looked down at what he was carrying. "It's a stone memorials project," he told her.

She prized the topmost book from his arm, and looked at the title. *"Characteristic Churchyard Species of Lichen,"* she read out. She raised an eyebrow at him, and this time it was her turn to grin: a broad, open smile that made his heart hitch.

"Churchyards are the most important sites for lichens growing on stone," he said. "There are over twenty thousand churchyards in England, and each one takes up roughly an acre of land. So that's twenty thousand—"

"Acres of lichen," she said, pretending to be breathless. "Really?"

He smiled back at her. "OK," he said. "But it's not dull, I promise you. Lichens are very old. And they're really resilient."

She had taken a fact sheet out of the book. " 'Guidelines for completing the mapping card,' " she intoned. She sighed heavily. "David," she said, "on a scale of dullness . . ."

"It's a pollution study," he explained. "For determining the levels of sulphur dioxide in the atmosphere."

"Ah," she said. "Determining levels. And what's this thing here?"

"A ten-times magnification lens." He pretended to be wildly proud of it, saying the words as if she were holding something of incredible rarity.

"My pulses quicken," she laughed. "Sulphur dioxide again?"

"Yes."

"Now I'm really excited. And this?" She was peering in his open rucksack now. He had to crane his neck to see what it was she was pointing at. He caught her scent: vanilla, rose. The scent of flowers. The skin of her neck was smooth, not downy: fine, sinuous. Smooth muscle under flesh. He watched the tilt of her head. Then, "Careful," he said.

"What is it?" she asked.

"Calcium hypochlorite and potassium hydroxide."

"For doing what?"

"Some lichens change color when they get zapped."

She was holding up something she had taken from the bag. "Ah—this is more like it," she said, triumphantly. "A razor blade."

"If the medulla reacts, a bit of the cortex has to be scraped away."

"You have to cut it?"

He made a mock-leering face. "You have to cut—cut—cut," he whispered.

She put the blade back, and let the top of the rucksack down, nodding and smiling. "Of course," she said, "with a kit like that, you could cease being fascinating, and just get to be a run-of-the-mill serial killer."

He raised his hands. "Goddamn!" he exclaimed. "Found out!"

They smiled at each other. As other people came in, they drifted over toward the catalogues on display. She flicked through the pages. Then, someone passed them—a boy—and called her name. She looked up and smiled. "Traggs. Eight o'clock tonight," he said. "Don't forget."

"Yeah, thanks," she replied. "Maybe."

The boy gave a thumbs-up signal, looked at David impassively, and then ran down the steps outside, and along the street.

David had the sudden conviction that Anna was not going to see this boy that night, or any other night.

"Would you come for a drink with me?" he asked.

She smiled at him. "Well, I dunno," she mused. "When were you thinking of?"

"Tonight," he said. "Eight o'clock."

"Ah," she responded, nodding. "I see." She scratched her neck, and looked him up and down. He wanted to take hold of her. A quick, urgent impulse. But she had already taken a step away from him. "Only if you promise to bring your calcium hypochlorite," she said.

"I never leave home without it," he replied. "And I could tell you all about cudweed if you like."

"Have you ever been slapped in a public place?" she asked.

That night, she mortified him by buying the first round in the Turf, and also by knowing the barman, with whom she kept up a casual banter. At David's insistence, they went over to the corner, to the smallest and most inaccessible table. He tried to take his eyes off the jacket she wore: a complicated quilted pattern, which looked hand sewn. It had all kinds of symbols woven into it—birds, clouds, trees.

"It's Indian," she said.

"American Indian?"

"No," she smiled. "Indian Indian."

"You've been there?"

"No," she said. "But I'd like to go. The colors, for one thing."

"Are you reading fine arts?" he asked.

"I'm studying history."

"I thought you were an artist," he said. "The drawings and caricatures . . ."

"I learned from my mother," she said. "But watching her trying to sell stuff, I decided from age six I was going to be a teacher."

"History teacher?"

"Maybe."

A silence fell. He looked at the upturned mouth. It was a slightly crooked expression, a repressed smile. He wondered what it would be like to kiss her. To taste that mouth.

"So," she said. "You're doing this project."

"Just in my spare time," he said.

"This lichen stuff is part of the course?"

"No."

"But you're doing it in a group?"

"No," he said. "I just go off at weekends."

She considered him. "You go off by yourself?"

"That's right."

"You go off by yourself counting lichens in churchyards?"

He saw the crookedness increase.

"It's better than beating up old ladies," he said.

"I guess."

She leaned on the table, arms folded. Now, she smiled. He liked that better. Out of the crookedness came that big, broad grin. She put her hand on his. Electricity swarmed through him.

"I could come with you," she said. "What do you do, take a tent?"

"Why would you want to do that?" he asked, amazed. He watched as she turned his hand over, and ran a lazy finger across his palm. "Long life," she murmured. "Loyal heart."

"What?" he asked, mesmerized.

"Here on your hand," she said. "You'll live to be an old, old man."

He grasped her own fingers, and raised them to his lips, and looked at her over their joined hands. She leaned forward, and touched his face. He had his wish then, the taste of that mouth. A roar of exultation in his head. A rushing sensation, as if the world were racing over him. The jolt of a journey's end, a journey's beginning. Opening his eyes, he saw her fair lashes, the lowered lids, and the pale skin.

"You know what I did after I saw you today?" she asked.

"No," he said. "What?"

"I went and looked up cudweed in *Flora Britannica*."

"You did?" He shook his head, started to laugh.

She smiled again. "Marsh cudweed," she intoned, "is a gray, woolly-leaved annual of damp or compacted soils on arable and new grassland, especially cart-tracks and footpaths."

"Latin name?" he asked.

She pretended to recall. *"Gnasher ugliflorum."*

He laughed again. "Well, close. *Gnaphalium uliginosum.*"

"Absolutely," she said. "Take two after meals until the symptoms clear up."

"It's part of the daisy family," he said. "Like thistles, and chamomile, and ragwort."

"Am I going to get a botany lecture?" she asked.

"Ragwort is all over the country now," he said. "It started from the Botanic Garden, here in Oxford. By 1830 . . ."

"OK. I *am* going to get a botany lecture."

"Listen, this is interesting."

"Yeah, I'm transfixed."

"By 1830, it had reached Oxford Railway Station, and it spread out from there, all along the tracks of the Great Western Railway, all over the country. Now it's, like, this really tough weed no one can get rid of."

She seemed to be studying his face. "What else?" she asked.

"It's called *squalidus.*"

"Try to concentrate on the real world," she said. "I meant, what else interests you?"

He shrugged.

"Music?" she suggested.

"Some."

"Play a sport?"

"No."

"But I thought all English guys liked soccer."

"Not me."

"Rugby, then. Rowing. Tennis."

"No, no." He spread his hands.

"Unicycle hockey player," she decided. "I met somebody in September, first week I was here. He plays unicycle hockey."

"He must be a laugh a minute," David replied. "But I haven't even got a bike. Sorry."

She sighed. Her fingertip described a circle in the spilt beer on the tabletop. "So," she said, "it's, like, lichens on gravestones, or nothing?"

"And trees," he told her. "I like trees."

He went to Salisbury that weekend, alone.

But two weeks after that, she came with him to the New Forest. It was the last weekend of the summer; the leaves were turning. They got a lift as far as Fordingbridge, and they walked through Godshill and up Godshill Ridge, and out across Ditchend Brook toward Island Thorns. It was warm, and there was a haze, as if the landscape had been merely sketched, and then erased with the edge of a thumb, so that shapes bled into one another across the heathland, and all the enclosures, the woodland—North Oakley, and Knightwood; Amberwood, Sloden, Holly Hatch and Beech

Bed—ran in mottled green shadow over the horizon. They reached the hilltop, and stood and looked out, south; and there, just at the foot of the rise, was a pool, looking like a piece of glass, reflecting the white sky.

They went down to it, and pushed off their rucksacks and stood looking at the water for a while. Anna sat down and took off her boots, and cooled her feet, stepping off the gravelly edge. The bottom of the pond, saturated peat, sank under her almost at once, and he caught her just as she lost her balance. They stood at the edge, arms around each other, and he saw the ripples spreading out over the surface, unhurried dark lines in the white.

They were headed for Fritham, and the campsite beyond it at Long Beech Hill, but they lost their way somehow. They never even found the narrow lane leading down to Fritham, and the evening light faded, and the night came on, and they pitched a tent on a slope above Latchmoor Brook. They hardly spoke; an absolute darkness came down. When he got into the tent, he asked her for the nightlight, because he couldn't see anything, not even a distinction between shadow and half-light, not even her face. She took his hand and guided it to her. She was naked. He kneeled down and took her in his arms, and couldn't have spoken then, not at all, not a word.

Sometime in the night, he woke, and heard her breathing, and the trees moving overhead. At once, he wondered what had brought this girl to him, and he thought about what she had told him about herself, the few and sketchy details. He sensed her deep privacy, and put it alongside the ease of her lying in his arms; and he felt a curious danger about her. Her unexpectedness, her sudden convictions.

In the end, he gave up trying to work it out.

He listened to the movement of the oaks for a long time, to their soft and beautiful conversation, lying on his back, holding her hand tightly over his heart.

Eight

"I WANT HER MOVED," Garrett said.

It was five-thirty. Dawn was coming up, and from the narrow band of black the night before, the corridor revealed itself filling with the light, the promising pink-gold of a summer's day. Grace had gone to the window, and realized suddenly that the room faced the Charles River. There was a yacht out there, early as it was: she saw it heading seaward.

When Garrett spoke, she turned back to him, and the room. Anna lay nearest the window. Machines hummed at her side. She lay immobile now, her eyes closed as if asleep, her hands at her sides; but restraints kept her in position. During the night she had been thrashing against the ventilator and the IV's. Her face was swollen and bruised, and her fingertips blue. Glass from the shattering windshield had peppered the left side of her head. Anna had turned on the point of impact, been thrown backward and then forward again, hitting the steering wheel. Glass from the side window had lacerated her arm. The ventilator hissed: a noise that Grace would never be able to forget.

Anna had come back from surgery at a quarter past midnight. The nurse had told them that a subdural hematoma had been operated on.

Grace and Garrett had stood in the corridor while Anna was

wheeled past them from surgery; speechless, Grace watched the transfer to the ICU. Grace had felt nothing at all at that moment; she was watching a TV screen—it was happening to someone else, someone else's family, someone else's daughter. She had looked away, and her gaze had fallen on another woman in the waiting room, whose door was open: a young woman, trapped in this same frozen stance, a friend on either side of her. Both were talking. The woman's eyes were dull, anesthetized with shock.

There was nowhere else to look, except to the floor. Grace didn't want to look past her own daughter and see this woman's sixteen-year-old son, the victim of a motorcycle accident, in the far bed.

The neurosurgeon came to speak to them.

By then, it was a little past two A.M.

Dr. Daniel Coram was a tall, elderly man, with a softly persuasive voice.

"We're interrupting a cycle here," he told them, quietly. "When a brain is injured, it swells. The compression that results decreases blood flow and oxygen. This, in turn, causes more swelling . . ."

He had held her hand. This kindly man.

She had started to cry again: unstoppable tears that poured out of her without warning.

"We've taken away the hematoma and repaired the blood vessels," he had continued.

It was almost a song, with its own gentle rhythm. She tried in vain to force herself to listen to him, and not the softly moving motion of the words. She heard their sibilance, the weight of them. But not their meaning.

"How are you?" Dr. Coram eventually asked.

She had trouble wrenching her gaze from their hands to his face.

"I'm fine," she said. Almost lightly.

"You'll get yourself a cool drink," he said. An instruction. "Something to eat."

"I couldn't eat," she told him.

Coram had looked at Garrett with a smile. "Anna will have a lot of tests," he said. "We'll monitor the pressure. It's a long process. It's a careful process. We may have to use a ventricular drain, or a shunt," he added. "But don't be afraid of what you see."

"She's moving," Grace interjected. She had suddenly noticed the flurry of activity behind his shoulder.

"We have to use a lot of tubes, and we have to use the ventilator," Dr. Coram said. "Sometimes the patient will react to that. It's reflexivity, nothing more just now." He had squeezed Grace's hand again. "I'll speak to you again in the morning."

Morning was here now.

Since four A.M., Anna had been still. Perfectly still and soundless.

Grace stared at James Garrett now.

"Moved?" she repeated. His murmured sentence, from the chair next to Anna's bed, where he sat, had only just filtered through to her. "Moved where?"

"A better facility."

She shook her head. "But there isn't a better facility," she said, in astonishment. "Look at this place. *Look* at it." She walked around the end of the bed to him. "Move her away from the surgeon, and the staff here?" she said. "You can't be serious."

"This is a public hospital," he told her.

She clenched her fists at her sides. She knew she was doing it, but she couldn't stop herself. "You don't know what you're talking about," she said.

"We'll talk about it later," he said.

"James," she said, "I'm not going to argue with you. Anna is lying here between us. There'll be no arguing."

"Good," he said.

She put her hand to her mouth, and laughed. A kind of deep, humorless exasperation. "Dear God," she told him, "you are astonishing. You want her moved simply because this is a public hospital? You are an astonishing fucking bigot."

He returned her look. He glanced, pointedly, at the fist pressed to her mouth.

"I don't mean right away," he said quietly. "When she comes around. For recuperation."

"Why don't you just leave her alone?" she demanded. "Why don't you leave them both alone?"

Garrett had remained perfectly still. "You're tired," he said. "We're all tired."

She turned away. She drew up a chair and sat as close to Anna as she could get.

"Go back to Myrtle Street," he told her, softly. "Here, take my key," he said, taking it from his pocket and offering it to her on the flat of his palm. "Have a shower. Sleep."

"No," she said, ignoring him.

"I'll stay with her."

"No."

There was silence.

He walked to the door.

"Then I'm going to sit with Rachel," he said.

Rachel Elizabeth Russell had been born at five in the morning four days before Christmas. It had been a bitterly cold winter. She was two weeks overdue. The labor lasted twelve hours, and the birth was breech.

Toward the end of the night the baby's heartbeat began to slow, and there was a flurry of activity, and talk of an emergency C-section. But Rachel appeared in a rush, finally: small for her term, at five pounds two ounces. As they handed her child to her, Anna had seen Rachel's wide-open eyes, and had a little frisson of disappointment as Rachel's attention immediately drifted away from her. Anna had read in a magazine that newborn babies held your gaze, apparently transfixed by the sight of their first human face.

"Hey," she had murmured, stroking her baby's cheek. "Say hello, Rachel. Here I am."

They lived with Grace; Rachel came home to the house on Christmas Eve. Anna had been touched to see how much effort

Grace had put into the decorations. All the trees in the garden were full of tiny white lights; the same lights were strung along the rails of the porch. Inside, a huge spruce was all colors—an extraordinary mixture of oranges and reds and blues, the Caribbean shades that both she and Grace loved. There was a big terra-cotta-and-blue angel on the top of the tree, papier-mâché, with outstretched wings of gold, all Grace's own work. In one hand, the angel carried a trumpet; in the other, a bottle of rum.

"Ma," Anna said, laughing. "You're incorrigible."

"Even the angels are celebrating," Grace said, winking at her.

They had gotten into a cozy routine over the months, one of these being that while Anna had her morning shower, she would leave Rachel with Grace, and then take the morning tea to her when she was finished.

One particular morning in September, there had been a gale blowing off the coast. There was a draft in the sitting room that Grace had complained about before; when the wind was in the right direction, like today, the blind on the window tapped against the frame.

Anna came out from her shower, hair still wet, dressing gown on, carrying the tea tray.

"I've noticed something odd," Grace told her.

She was sitting opposite Rachel, who was in a high chair.

Anna had put down the tray. "What?" she asked, pouring from the pot.

"Watch her," Grace said.

Anna paused. She looked at her daughter. Rachel was rocking slightly. "She always does that," Anna murmured.

"Watch," Grace said. "Listen." And she cocked her thumb at the blind, tap-tapping on the window frame.

After a few moments, Anna sat down. "She's rocking in time," she said. It was true. Rachel was pushing her back against the chair in beat with the tapping blind.

Mother and daughter looked at each other. "Well," Anna observed, handing her mother a mug of tea, "she's going to be a musician. A drummer, obviously." She leaned back on the couch. "She'll run off with a rock band when she's fourteen," she said. "A female drummer in a six-man band."

Grace didn't drink the tea. "Watch again," she said. "Look at her fingers."

Anna leaned forward. Rachel wasn't looking at them. Her gaze was focused on the tray of the high chair. There were eight or ten little squares of toast there, untouched.

"Do you see it?" Grace asked.

She did. Rachel's fingers on her right hand were also describing a beat.

"It's not the blind," Anna murmured. "It's the wires."

She glanced out of the window.

They had put a rotary drier in the garden. It was folded, but, in the high wind, that, too, was making a noise. The plastic-coated wires were moving against the metal pole.

"Two beats," Anna mused, looking back at her mother.

Grace nodded. "Did you ever see a child of that age even *hear* a rhythm, let alone hold two different beats at one time?"

"I don't know," Anna responded. "I don't know kids."

"Well, I do," Grace said. "And I haven't."

Anna shrugged. She got up, walked the couple of steps to Rachel, and held up a piece of toast for her. At once, the baby began to cry.

Anna lifted Rachel from the chair. Rachel's screams intensified. She arched her back, and tried to slide from Anna's grasp.

"So I've got an unusual baby," Anna told her mother, as she walked to their room to change Rachel out of her nightclothes. "That's fine by me," she added, over her shoulder. She turned back to Rachel, and pressed her lips to her face, ignoring the wails of protest. "Who wants to be ordinary?"

She shut the door behind her.

To tell the truth, she had been annoyed with her mother. She hated it whenever Grace suggested, even by a glance or an inclination of the head, that she knew better.

Well, she had thought to herself, hoisting Rachel off her shoulder and putting her on the bed, *she doesn't know better.*

She had looked at her daughter's creased red face, at the eyes screwed shut, at the fists raised and clenched at the shoulders.

"You're OK," she whispered. She tried to prize the tiny hands open, wriggling her index finger into the baby's grip. "You're OK, Rachel," she soothed. "You're OK. Hush now. Listen to me ... you're just fine."

A year and a half later, they were sitting in the children's ward of the hospital.

After a slow start—she hadn't actually walked until she was fifteen months old—Rachel was now extremely mobile. In situations like this, where it was necessary to sit for a while, and wait, Rachel could never be persuaded to stay still. She moved constantly, from the instant of waking to the instant of falling asleep. If she could be bribed into sitting for a few seconds, she would never sit in her mother's or her grandmother's lap. No one's lap, in fact. And not on seats with any kind of fabric covering. And not on plastic tub chairs, the kind they had at preschool. And she would not be directed: not even by a gentle fingertip on the arm.

When things got really bad—and Rachel was capable of working herself into breath-stopping storms of temper—Anna wrapped her arms around her and got her in a kind of wrestling hold, pinning her arms to her sides, while she waited for the piercing, high-pitched screams to subside. It meant squatting down on the ground and forcing the child into this human straitjacket. It could take anything up to twenty minutes to calm her—but the alternative was worse. If she wasn't held down at such a time, Rachel would run. Just run, full speed. She wouldn't look back. She wouldn't care what was in the way. Anna had seen her run at speed straight into a garden fence, cutting her face and upper arms. And God help any other children who happened to be in her line of sight.

In the arms-by-the-sides hold, Rachel's heels would drum

against her mother's knees or legs or ankles. Anna had long ago lost count of the bruises. And of the looks she had incurred in shopping malls or the street, or a park. Other mothers sometimes looked at her sympathetically, but, more often than not, she would get disapproval.

Older women were the worst.

They would lean down and try to touch Rachel. "What are you so cranky about?" they would say. "Oh, what a noise!" They would smile. "Is she holding you tight? Is it too tight?"

Of course, the running and the anger and the bruises were not the worst.

Not by a long way.

When Anna had been pregnant, she had had very little concrete idea of what her baby would be like. As an only child herself, her ideas about child care were at best hazy. She read what she could—she knew the bare facts—but she was totally unprepared for the mind-bending anxiety of bringing a child into the world. She often felt helpless: unprepared, naïve.

And yet, on one very specific subject, she had been totally, blissfully confident.

She knew that she and her child would have a deeper bond than most. She knew that they would be a support to each other. She would even allow her imagination to run forward through the years, to the days far in the future, when Rachel and she would talk together, or go on trips; even to the time when Rachel would have her own children.

When so much else in her life had been drifting and insubstantial, she would be able to depend on this, she knew. This deep and special understanding that she and Rachel would share.

There had been only one very small voice—one tiny, submerged whisper in the back of her mind—saying that Rachel would be her father's and not her mother's child. It was a voice she had preferred not to listen to, until that morning at the hospital. She hadn't even listened to it through Rachel's obsessions. Or the routines that became more pronounced with every passing week. Anna would watch her daughter play such odd games; and she

would watch the way Rachel held and carried herself—the spinning, the curled-up position against a wall, the hands repeatedly
hitting the floor, the long, long periods of complete dreamlike in-
activity.

Rachel had never made eye contact with her, never run to her,
never held up her arms or wanted to be kissed.

She lived in another world entirely.

"Mrs. Russell?" a woman said, breaking her reverie.

Grace touched Anna's arm.

"Yes," Anna responded, rising to her feet. "Actually, it's Miss
Russell."

Dr. Bauer smiled. "And Rachel?"

"Yes," Anna said. "She's here."

She walked a little way up the corridor, to where Rachel was
sitting on the floor.

"Rachel," Anna said. "Rachel . . ."

Grace had gotten up. "I could bring her in to you when she
gets up," she offered.

"She'll get up," Anna said. "Rachel . . ."

"You know," said Dr. Bauer, "that's not a bad idea. We'll talk.
Rachel can come in her own time."

Anna looked at Grace, who nodded encouragement.

Dr. Bauer's office was light and colorful. It looked out over a
garden, in which there was a child-sized chair and table. Mobiles
hung from the lower branches of the trees.

"We find it's a good idea," Dr. Bauer was saying, as she showed
Anna to a seat. "Except when it snows."

"Then they don't go out there?"

"Oh, they go out. But so do I," the woman responded. "That's
how my circulation stopped below the knees."

Anna smiled hesitantly.

"Make yourself comfortable."

They sat down alongside each other.

"You know how Rachel comes to be here," Dr. Bauer said.
"That this is a recommendation from preschool."

"It was a misunderstanding," Anna said.

Dr. Bauer held up her hand. "Can we go back a little?" she asked. She had a notebook in her hands. "Rachel is two years old ..."

"Yes. Just over."

"She was enrolled in the play group at fifteen months ..."

"I thought it was best for her to meet other children."

"So it is," Dr. Bauer agreed. "So it is."

"She just has her set ways of doing things. She doesn't mean anything by it."

"Set ways?"

Anna clasped her hands in her lap. "Well, if she comes into school, and finds something out of place ..."

"She notices placing?"

"Yes. The toys. The instruments."

"Does she relate to specific toys?"

"She's a little possessive over a few," Anna admitted, slowly. "She likes the ones that make sounds, you know ..."

"Does she sleep?"

"Excuse me?" Anna asked.

"Does she sleep well at night?"

"Well ... she does wake."

"How many times a night?" Bauer asked.

Anna shrugged. "I don't know."

"Approximately? On average?"

"Four. Five."

"And eating?"

"Yes, fine."

"No fads? Or preferences?"

"She ..." Anna stared out at the garden. "A few."

Dr. Bauer nodded. She regarded Anna closely for some moments. "Tell me what's great about Rachel," she said. "I get the feeling you're always having to explain what's problematic. But tell me what's good."

Anna turned, and met her gaze. The woman was in her forties, she guessed. Comfortable looking. Motherly. Anna wondered if she had any children of her own.

"She remembers," Anna said. "Patterns. Music. She loves music."

"Wonderful. Any kind in particular?"

Anna smiled. "Bach. Mozart."

"Good heavens! I wouldn't know the difference."

"Oh, she knows the difference," Anna said. She sat forward. "She gets the CD's. She knows the covers. She keeps time."

"Does she favor an instrument?"

"Yes," Anna said. "That's what this was about. That's where this started. It's the xylophone. You know, those toy ones, with the colored bands, the wooden ones?"

"I know."

"And we have a toy piano at home, very small, it plays its own tunes . . ."

Dr. Bauer was silent. She hadn't taken her eyes from Anna's face.

Anna stopped talking, feeling the intensity of the gaze. She dropped her eyes.

"Are you concerned?" the woman asked. "Are you worried?"

Anna started to protest, automatically, that she wasn't anxious. The words were in her mouth, the usual rushed explanation that Rachel was merely a little out of sync with other children; that her moods, the things she did, weren't malicious. She started to try to say that there was something—she was *sure* that there was something in Rachel, so far down, so deep, so hidden from them, and that she was exhausted with the effort of trying to reach it, but that, once found, this essential quality of her daughter would be amazing. Unique. As if there could be a key, and the key would be marked *Rachel*. One day, she was sure that she would find this answer, and use it, and release her child. And this daughter she so loved, and whom she so wanted to be near, would come running toward her, and Rachel would at last *look at her,* and she would . . . she would *say something to her* . . .

But the words didn't come.

Not the words she expected.

Anna looked at Dr. Bauer.

"Yes," she had admitted, at last. "I'm very worried."

Nine

DAVID WAS LATE GETTING home.

Sara had known that he would be; she would have guessed it even if Charles Augre had not rung her to say that David was still working, far up in the grounds, beyond the fringe of the woodland.

She and Matt closed the shop at seven and waited for him.

After she had come back from the doctor, Sara had hesitated only a fraction before ringing the number that she had copied from the message for David. She had listened intently as Grace described her conversation with her brother; she had said no more than a dozen words of quiet commiseration before putting the phone down.

"I can't believe it," Matt had commented, when she put the phone down and stared at him. "How old is this daughter of his?"

"Ten."

"And the mother is a girl David knew at Oxford?"

Sara had looked down thoughtfully at the cup of coffee he had brought her. Then looked up at him. "Anna was all he talked about that second year," she said. "She came to Mum's funeral, you know."

"What, came down from Oxford?"

"Yes," Sara said. "It was the first time I met her. As soon as they got off the bus, and I saw the way he looked at her ..." She shook her head.

"And she was American."

"Yes, she'd come over on one of those year-long exchanges."

"And she went back at the end of the year?"

"No," Sara said. "She left just after Easter. Just suddenly. Overnight."

"You mean she left her course," Matt asked, "and went home?"

"Yes."

They stared at each other. "She was pregnant," Matt said, voicing their thoughts. "And she never told him."

Sara put her hand to her head. "All this time," she murmured.

"Did he try to find her, go after her?"

"Yes," she said. "He wrote to her. He rang her mother ..."

They looked, at the same time, at Hannah, asleep in her Moses basket. "They never told him," Sara whispered. "Why would they never tell him?"

Matt blew out a long breath of air, and shook his head. "I can't see David wanting to know now," he said.

Sara glanced at him. "Why not?"

Matt raised his eyebrows at her. "David?" he said. "This is your brother we're talking about here. I've never seen David hold down a relationship for more than two weeks. He's a great guy and all that, good laugh, clever bloke, but he's not much on the commitment front, is he? How many women has he had in the last five years, since we got married? Eight? Nine?"

"Nobody serious," Sara admitted. "Nobody for more than a month or two."

"Exactly. And this is the man you think's going to take on a daughter?"

"He never used to be like that," she said. "Not so flippant. Not before Anna."

"You're saying this thing with Anna changed him?"

She looked at him, saw his disbelieving expression. "I don't know," she admitted. "He never said much. He'd get involved in his stuff, never take much notice of anyone ..."

"And that's how he was at home?"

"Pretty much. But that's how boys are," she countered. "Boys don't talk. Look at Tom. He'll thunder about on his bike for an hour, or build something. Girls don't do that, even when they're little. When Hannah is Tom's age, she'll be yattering away to her friends, and they'll be sorting out each other's hair, and even pretending their toys talk to each other. But boys? The closest a boy will come to getting his toys to communicate is pretending they're slaughtering each other."

Matt grinned. Then, just as suddenly, his face fell. "What are we going to do?" he asked.

Sara looked at him affectionately. Matt, who was an inch shorter than her, and always looked as if he'd dressed in the dark, was hardly film star material. In the past couple of years he'd put on weight, too. Probably the result of her cooking. But he was a good man. Solid and placid. And he adored his kids. He'd once told her that he never knew what life was really about until Tom arrived.

This thought suddenly galvanized her. "He's got to go and see her."

"Go over there?"

"Of course."

Matt laughed out loud. "He'll never do it."

"He will," Sara said. "After I've finished with him."

Matt gave her a long look, shook his head, then picked up the coffee cups and took them to the sink. "Bloody good luck," he said, over his shoulder.

After their supper, Sara went upstairs quickly, and took down the case from the top of the wardrobe. She slammed it down on the bed, went into David's room, and came back with an armful of shirts, jeans, and underwear. With determination, she began packing.

Half an hour later she heard the outside door open and close. A murmured conversation between David and Matt; the raised voice of Tom. Then, David's footstep on the stair.

She turned to face the door, hands on hips.

As soon as he reached the landing, he saw her. His eyes ranged from the opened suitcase to her face.

"I'm packing," she said.

"So I see."

"For you."

His mouth set. Then he ran a hand over his hair.

"Don't tell me you're not going, because you are," she told him.

He shook his head. "I'm hardly over the doorstep," he complained.

"I rang Virgin," she continued. "There's a cancellation on their afternoon flight tomorrow. You'll get to Boston just after five, their time."

He was silent. He stood staring at the floor.

She walked over to him, throwing down the folded towel that she had been holding. She had taken the first one that had come to hand from the airing cupboard and had been putting it in the case. He glanced at it, at the blue and white fishes on the pattern. It was Tom's swimming towel.

"You're hurrying," he remarked drily.

She looked into his face. "I'll drive you up there tomorrow."

"Sara," he said, "I'm not going."

She closed her eyes for a second.

"Look," he said. "Don't start shouting, and ordering me about. I've been thinking about it all afternoon."

"And you've come to this conclusion."

"Yes."

"Just like that."

"No," he said. "Not just like that."

"But you've decided that ..."

He gently pushed her to one side, went into his room, and looked down at the case. He picked out first the towel, then a pair of jeans: slowly, laboriously.

"They haven't wanted me for eleven years," he said.

"Oh," she responded tartly. "It's a sulk, then, is it?"

He glanced up. "Don't be stupid."

"Stupid?" she echoed. "*I'm* being stupid? Grace Russell rings up and begs you to come and see Anna and a daughter you didn't know you had," she said. "My niece, by the way. And Hannah and Tom's cousin."

"I'm not going."

She stepped toward him, after looking down the stairs. She closed the bedroom door behind her. "She rings you up, and begs you . . ."

"That's just it," he retorted, raising his voice. "Don't you understand? *Grace* rang me up. Not Anna. Anna hasn't changed her mind about anything. *Grace* rang me, because she doesn't get on with this partner of Anna's."

Sara stared at him.

"Don't you see?" he reiterated. "Grace doesn't like this Garrett character. Can't stand the sight of him. She said, *'You don't want to know him.'* You should have heard her tone of voice. She patently hates him. She just wants me to stand between him and Rachel."

"That's what's called a wild guess," Sara said. "An excuse you've seized upon these last couple of hours."

"She doesn't need me!" David objected. Color flooded his face. "Anna doesn't need me. Grace probably just wants me to go out there so it weakens Garrett's case. So if Anna dies she can say . . ."

He stopped abruptly. The color that had risen so quickly just as rapidly faded. "Listen," he continued finally, "don't you get it? If Anna died, there would be a court case, wouldn't there? I've been thinking about it all afternoon. This Garrett person would look for custody, residence, whatever it is. Of Rachel. And if Grace doesn't like Garrett . . ."

"But she's Rachel's grandmother," Sara said. "She'd get custody."

"Not necessarily," David answered. "But if the biological father were there, she might."

He sighed. He went to the bentwood chair by the window, and suddenly flopped down into it. The curtains were not yet drawn:

the view was dusky and insubstantial. A car was threading its way along Higher Lane. He watched the headlights appearing and reappearing between the hedges until it was lost to sight.

"An art dealer," he mused. "Ten to one, he's filthy bloody rich."

"What is that to do with anything?" Sara demanded.

"Because I won't be used like a bloody pawn!" David exclaimed.

"You haven't really thought at all," Sara said.

He covered his eyes with both hands. "Don't," he muttered, from behind his hands. "Just stop."

She strode to him, and pulled down his hands roughly. "We're not talking about James Garrett's partner's daughter," she snapped. "We're not even talking about Grace Russell's granddaughter. So what if they're into some weird fight? So what if they want to tear each other's hair out? What does it matter?"

"It matters," he retorted.

"It doesn't," she cried. "Because we're not talking about those things. Not at all! We're talking about *your daughter*, David. Your daughter! That's all that matters here!"

They stared at each other.

"Anna doesn't want me there," he said. He spoke very slowly. "Anna didn't ring me. Anna didn't ring me to say why she was leaving all those years ago, or where she was going. She didn't ring me when Rachel was born, or when Rachel was ill, or when Rachel first went to school, or passed an exam." He got to his feet. "And she was never going to ring me," he added, painfully. "Not when Rachel graduated, or got married, or when Rachel had children of her own . . ."

Seeing the expression on his face, Sara's eyes filled with tears.

He smiled faintly, then put his hand on her cheek. "I would only go if Anna wanted me to go," he said softly. "But she doesn't want that at all."

They remained where they were for a few more seconds. Then, Sara drew back from him. She wiped one eye with the heel of her hand.

"David," she said finally, "don't you want to see Anna?"

He gazed at her.

"I know you do," she said. "And . . . you ought to know, it's not just an accident. I mean," she added, frowning at herself, "it's more serious than you thought."

"What?" he said. "How do you know that?"

"I spoke to Grace this afternoon," she said. "Listen—listen, don't turn away," she said, grabbing his arm. "She said Anna's in a coma."

"A *coma*?" he repeated.

"The doctor spoke to them. It was just after she'd rung you," she told him.

"They can't know that," he said. "It's too soon."

"Are you going to risk it?" she asked.

"Sara, I can't go!"

"Yes, you can," she insisted. "What are you so afraid of?" She was almost shaking him now. He looked down at her hands on his shoulders. "Is it Garrett?" she said. "Is it Grace?"

"Of course not!"

"Then how can it be Anna?" she said. "How can Anna be angry with you? She's ill! She's unconscious! What, you think she's going to sit up in bed and tear you off a strip for flying thousands of miles to see her?"

"It's not what she wants!" he cried.

"It doesn't matter *what she wants*!" Sara screamed back. "Listen to me! It's not what Anna wants, because Anna probably won't live to say what she wants anymore! It's what *you* want!"

He took a breath, staring at her as if seeing her, horrified, for the first time.

"I'm sorry," she said, breathing heavily. "I'm very sorry." She pressed her fingers quickly to her mouth, as if she wished she could take the words back. "I understand what you're saying. But . . ." She touched his arm briefly, then let her hand drop. "Anna's wishes have been overtaken by her own mother," she reminded him. "You can't turn that back now, and make it what it was before. Grace took the decision to tell you and, whatever Anna wanted before, it's different now. Now it isn't Anna," she said. "It's you. You've got to do something about this."

He was looking at her intently.

But he wasn't seeing Sara.

He was seeing Anna, at nineteen, walking from Merton Field and through the Botanic Garden. He saw her, with her head down against a persistent March rain, coming to meet him, turning right at the gate as she always did, passing under the two-hundred-year-old black poplar with its massive branches and their vast and lazy curves.

And he thought of Anna that same weekend, that late March weekend when he first knew that something was wrong, going back to the Ashmolean after that conversation under the Magdalen Tower; and he had followed her there and watched her go through the door, and felt afraid, because he knew that something was wrong and he couldn't fathom it. She had a different look in her eye. She had that hunched-up walk that he had thought about so often since, and always decided that it had been the bitter weather of that spring.

And now he knew that it hadn't been the weather at all, but something else. A secret she was keeping.

He saw her often in his imagination. On the bridge or the water walks, or the Angel and Greyhound Meadows, or inside the Carfax Tower, on the steep stairwell where there was no room for another person to pass. They had kissed there, she on one step and he on the step below, and they had emerged at the top breathless and laughing. He had been suddenly struck by vertigo, and held on to the parapet, without knowing if it was the kiss or the height that had caused it. And, as they had come down, the quarter-jacks had struck. He had looked at his watch, and seen it was two-fifteen, and the hour stayed for months in his head, two-fifteen, two-fifteen, as if it were witching hour, white magic.

Anything could make him remember. It wasn't hard.

There was a piece of sculpture in the Ashmolean; not stone, but wood. "The Virgin of the Immaculate Conception." It was wood and polychrome. The label said that it came from a Jesuit mission in Pôrto Alegre, Brazil. Anna had loved that statue. It was a native carving of the Virgin, and Anna had loved how the hair, thick and dark and heavily stranded, like twists of fine rope, merged with the cloak. The sculpture was supposed to be an image of Christ's mother, but she was Native Indian, so much more powerful than the insipidly pale European version. Anna would look at her face, her eyes, at the folded hands. "Beautiful," she would murmur. "Beautiful."

She pointed things out to him like that. The monochrome studies of Peter Paul Rubens, drawn for a church in Antwerp and never used. "The Sacrifice of Noah" with its upward-flowing movement.

"What has he sacrificed?" he had asked her, peering at the little frame.

"I don't know," she told him. "It doesn't matter. Look at the rush in that drawing. Look at the horses in 'The Conversion of St. Paul' underneath it. Look at the way everything centers on him."

He had tried to see. He wanted to see through her eyes.

He had never felt that way about a girl before. Sometimes he had thought he had never even been alive before. And all the years growing up in the cool shadow of his father, trying to get out from under that blankness, that frigidity, that threat of being like him, that sense of being removed from the rest of the world—all of that had abruptly vanished under Anna's touch. When he was with her he was no longer worried that he would end up like his father. He was alive for the first time. The world was not behind some invisible sheet of glass, it was real and vibrant, and in his grasp. Anna was in his grasp, with her acute vision of color and movement, her connection with people, her quick intelligence. Anna was in his hands, literally. Anna's warm body, her urgency to be loved. Her kisses and whispers, the sensation of her fingers on his neck, his back, pressing over his heart so that he would have willingly, willingly done anything she wanted. . . .

She gave him the world; and it was a world he felt, at last, was his to take, his to inherit. He was sublimely alive and part of humanity at last.

It was just three months after they had met. It was just before Christmas. It was by another painting she liked, the picture of the chestnut tree. "Don't ever leave," he had told her.

She had looked at him with utter seriousness, in response to the words that he had tried to make lighthearted. "I have to go back to the U.S. in July," she told him.

"Yes, I know," he'd said. "Oh! Here's an idea. Maybe I'll come with you."

She had pushed back from him, and held him at arm's length. "Come *with* me?" she'd asked. "But, David, you have your Finals next year."

"I know that."

"You're surely not serious."

He had shrugged. "Who knows?" he'd said. "I could meet your mother. Who wants to sit Finals when they could be meeting your mother?"

"Don't joke about it," she'd responded.

He had wrapped his arms around her in front of Bevan's green-and-gray angular picture. Over her shoulder, he saw that there were animals in that painting. Pigs. There were pigs in the painting, grazing in the foreground.

The incongruity had struck him, how pigs couldn't be less romantic, and how an artist could put pigs in a picture and still get away with it, make it seem idyllic still, and he'd drawn back, laughing, just as she was now laughing outright at his own absurdity.

"You're crazy," she said. "You know that?"

"Maybe," he admitted. "But the world is that way. It's full of surprises. Maybe you could stay here. That's the other alternative."

"But I have a course to finish in the U.S.," she'd said.

There was, at last, a beat of complete seriousness between them. "So, what?" he'd asked. "You'll go back, and that's it?"

"No," she'd said. "I don't know. I haven't worked it out."

"Well, we should work it out."

She'd crossed her arms, hugging herself.

"Too soon to talk about?" he'd asked, trying to read the expression in her eyes.

"Yes," she'd said with a shrug. "Maybe. I don't know."

"Right," he'd replied, linking his arm in hers and casting one look backward toward the Bevan. "No M words."

"M words?" she'd asked.

They reached the door, and he glanced back at her. "Migration, master's degrees, marriage."

"Marriage?" she'd echoed.

He'd wagged an admonishing finger at her. To tell the truth, he had frightened himself in that moment. He took a small step backward, into his father's shade. "I said *not* to mention M words," he said.

She'd smiled. "Nothing beginning with M, right?"

"Right," he'd replied. *"Mertensia maritima. Menyanthaceae. Melilotus altissima. Myosotis scorpioides. Myosotis arvenisis.* No stuff like that."

"As if I would." She'd grinned.

He had lifted her hand, and kissed the warm flesh of her wrist, where the pulse beat under his lips. "Anyway, *Vergissmeinnicht* sounds much nicer than *Myosotis,*" he'd told her. "Even though it's the same plant."

"And what plant is that?" she'd asked.

"David," Sara murmured.

He came back to the present, to the bedroom under the eaves. To the sound of the children downstairs.

He looked down at the half-packed case.

"Forget-me-not," he said to himself. He picked up the towel, folded it slowly, and replaced it in the suitcase. "Forget-me-not," he repeated in a murmur. *"Vergissmeinnicht."*

Ten

IT WAS FOUR O'CLOCK in the afternoon; James Garrett and Grace sat on either side of Anna's bed.

An hour before, there had been a sudden rise in Anna's blood pressure, and her heart rate had increased. The nurses came to check on her; but, as suddenly as they had started, the pressure and rate dropped back down again.

"What caused it?" Grace had asked. "Is it a good sign?"

No one knew.

"Is it a bad sign?" To a closed door, afterward.

She looked across the bed now at Garrett. He sat with his hands on his knees, and his eyes closed, as if meditating. Rarely had he seemed so calm. Grace felt as if she could slap him. She *wanted* to slap him. She couldn't understand why he wasn't distraught, or how his anxiety couldn't be etched in his expression.

The last time that she had looked into the mirror in the ladies' room, she had seen some sort of wraith looking back at her. She had wet her hair under the cold tap, and combed it dry with her fingers, opening the tiny window and letting the sultry afternoon air rush in. Below her on the streets, people passed by; traffic moved. She had had a totally irrational desire to run out onto Longfellow Bridge, and scream and scream and scream. She wanted them to stop. She wanted the world to stop. It seemed so unfair that they should carry on with their normal day, when her daughter lay here.

She glanced up at Garrett.

"Did you know," she asked, "that she was in the hospital before?"

"Before?" he asked. "When?"

"When she was Rachel's age."

He shook his head.

"It wasn't even winter," she said. "You know? That's why I never connected."

He frowned at her. "I don't follow."

She looked away from him, out of the window. "It was August," she said. "The beaches get so crowded," she murmured.

Garrett regarded her levelly. She took out a handkerchief.

"It doesn't matter," he said. "Don't think of it now."

She ignored him. "We went down to the ocean," she continued softly. "And then ... always ... she never kept still. I kept saying to her, Look at the girls along the way. They're lying in the sun! Why don't you lie for a while in the sun?" She smiled to herself. "But not Anna. She was running in and out of the sea. In the afternoon, it got cool, and the crowds started leaving the beach, and she was still in the sea, and she had had a cold the week before, and ... it was just about five or six o'clock. I had been reading, and I heard ... I *heard* her come toward me, I heard her breathing ..."

The words fell into silence. Grace let go of Anna's hand, and got up, and walked to the window. "We got home," she said, "and we ate supper, and she went to bed. And I could still hear this breathing, this noise. I looked in on her, and she was asleep, and I went to my own room ..."

She felt in her pocket, and took out the pack of cigarettes, and shook one into her hand. "I woke up at two in the morning," she said. "Even now I don't know what woke me up. I went into her room, and she was making this ... *terrible,* this *terrible* noise as she slept. ... I just got her straight out of bed, and I put her in the car, and we drove to the hospital." At last, she turned around and looked at Anna, and then at Garrett. "She had pneumonia," she whispered.

"It won't be like that again," Garrett told her. "She won't come that close."

She stared at him. "And you know, do you?" she asked him. "You're certain. You're always so certain, aren't you, in this shit uneasy world."

He kept her gaze; there was a little tic of movement—a flex of disapproval—at one corner of his mouth. "Grace," he said, "I wish you wouldn't do that."

"Oh," she said. "Did I swear? I'm so sorry." She twisted the cigarette around and around between second finger and thumb, eyeing him wordlessly.

"I meant the cigarette," he murmured.

She looked at her hand, with the cigarette in it, then nodded slowly. "Come out in the corridor," she said, at last. "I want to talk to you."

They walked down to the water cooler. Each took a cup.

At the end of the corridor were four chairs.

"Sit down," Grace said.

Heedless of the signs, she lit the cigarette. Garrett took a sip of the water.

"Rachel's father is coming here," she told him.

He turned to face her.

"I found out where he was, and I called him," she said.

"Excuse me," he said. "You called who?"

"Her father."

"But you don't know who Rachel's father is," he said.

"Yes, we do."

He stared. For a few moments, she felt childishly pleased to see him, at last—finally, after the last five years of his curious complacency—so astounded.

"Anna has known who the father is," he repeated. "All along."

"Yes."

"I see," he said. "I see." He finished the water, crushed the cup carefully, and placed it in the bin.

She watched him.

Shout, she thought. *Shout and scream, why don't you.*

"Am I to be told his name?" he asked.

"It's David Mortimer."

He repeated it quietly to himself. "And he's coming here. Today."

"He's flying in from England."

He paused. He had clasped his hands in his lap, and was studying them intently. "British," he said.

"That's right."

"From Oxford."

"No," she told him.

He glanced up. "Oh, so this isn't a postgrad student," he said. "This is someone else."

"He was a student, at the same college with Anna."

"At Magdalen."

"Yes."

"And . . ." He stopped. To her surprise, he smiled at her. "I was going to say," he continued, "that I'm astonished that you should contact him without speaking to me. But of course I'm not astonished at that."

"He—"

Garrett held up his hand to stop her. "Did Anna ever tell this man about Rachel?"

Grace stopped. She didn't know exactly what had been said between Garrett and her daughter. She knew that Anna had always known the father's identity, but not if Anna had discussed this with Garrett. There was so much, so very much, in the last few years, which Anna would not discuss. Little by little, she had closed down; become—not secretive, not that—but wary. Guarded.

"I asked him," she said. "That's all. And he knows about Rachel. That's the story. And I don't care what you think," she added, standing up.

He looked up at her. "I'm well aware of that," he responded. "You have no need to bring a man halfway across the world to prove that to me. But you didn't answer my question." He considered her face closely. "He didn't know until now," he guessed.

"I did it for Rachel," she said, blushing.

"Rachel?" he echoed. Now he, too, stood up. "You did it for Rachel? How so? To disturb her further when she's already struggling to come to terms with a terribly disturbing experience?"

"Don't tell me how to care for my granddaughter," she warned.

"To unsettle her just a little more?" he said. "And to go against Anna's wishes. I take it, by your defensiveness, that that's what you've done."

"Don't pretend you're concerned for Rachel," Grace said. "Or Anna."

For the first time, he looked angry. "Anna's been my sole concern—Anna and Rachel have been my sole concern—ever since I met them."

"Oh, yes," she said. "You forget, I've seen you with them."

He gave a little laugh. "Grace, this is ridiculous," he said. "It's hysteria."

She turned away, and walked half a dozen steps up the corridor, muttering, "Jesus, *Jesus*," under her breath.

He walked after her. "And why should I not be concerned for Rachel?" he asked, without raising his voice. "When I've cared for her needs for the past five years?"

Grace wheeled back on him. "Oh, you've cared for her needs," she said. "And Anna's changed so much, I hardly recognize her."

He stared at her. "So," he murmured. "We're back to this."

"He'll be here in a couple of hours," she retorted. "There's nothing you can do about it."

"And you intend to take him to Rachel?"

"Of course."

"And Anna?"

"Yes."

Garrett nodded. She noticed that the little tightened reflex of annoyance was back at the corner of his mouth. "That's very unwise," he said. "Disturbing both mother and child with a visitor that neither of them wants to see."

"I'm willing to take the chance," she said. "He has a right. So does Rachel." She paused. "What's the matter, James?" she asked him. "Afraid Anna might remember what love is all about?"

He narrowed his eyes. "No," he said. "I'm not afraid of her seeing a man who abandoned her."

She gave a little laugh, crossing her arms.

Garrett paused. He seemed to assess her, and this unexpected reaction, for a few seconds. Then, "Where is David Mortimer staying?" he asked.

"I don't know," she said.

"I see," he repeated.

"I really don't know," she insisted. "And neither does he, I imagine."

"At the Holiday Inn, perhaps," he remarked. "As it's next door."

She looked at him. "He can stay with me. Rachel is being discharged tomorrow. They can both stay with me."

Garrett put his hand on her shoulder. The gesture was more shocking than a blow. His fingers exerted a gentle but insistent pressure. Instinctively, she pulled her shoulder back. But the touch remained.

"Grace," he said softly. "Wouldn't that be ridiculous, for the three of you to travel up and down the coast every day?"

"No," she said.

"In this heat?" he said. "So far?"

"It's no trouble."

"But for Rachel," he murmured. "What a trial for Rachel, when she hates the car—and along the road where the accident was . . . every day? Up and down, every day. Poor Rachel."

She started to speak, to respond.

But he suddenly dropped his hand.

And, still smiling to himself, he walked away.

★   ★   ★

He arrived at the Graham Gallery just twenty minutes later.

The people that passed by him in the streets looked worn down, wearied by the blast of salty humidity that was blowing in off the sea, and sweeping down Boylston and Columbus.

Summer was not his favorite season. In July and August, the crowds became almost unbearable here; fastidiously, he kept to the edge of the sidewalk, avoiding the strollers, tourists, and window shoppers. Stopping outside the Graham, he paused, and put his hand to the nape of his neck. He had a headache; a little crenellated chain of apparent reflection danced in the corner of his vision. He pressed a fingertip to the pressure point just behind each ear, in turn. Six beats hold. Six beats release.

He looked up at the gallery.

The Graham had no banners spread across its frontage; there were no boards advertising the exhibition. The doors were not open to the public, and the display was hidden. A piece of raw silk was drawn across the entire window, with a small and discreet handprinted sign.

Anna Russell.

Water and Light.

He stepped to the door, and opened it with his key.

Inside, there were two sets of glass doors. Beyond them, he could see Olivia, sitting at the desk in front of a computer. She glanced up as he entered, and smiled.

"How is business?" he asked.

"Good," she replied.

"Hawcross come by?"

"Yes," she said. "He took the ceramic."

He walked to the back of the building; here, down a shallow flight of six steps, was the inner gallery. On the farthest wall was Anna's largest painting to date. It hung in isolation on a white backdrop: a frameless fifteen-by-twenty-foot canvas. The predominant color was sienna.

James looked at the painting for a long time, without moving.

Then, he glanced to the side.

The paintings here were smaller. Six abstracts formed the center; at either end were two crosspieces of miniatures. Each miniature held a single panel of color, each with a different treatment—acrylic, pastel, inks.

Olivia walked to his side.

He looked down at his assistant. She was a very bright girl: a sophomore at MIT. But that was not why he had hired her this summer. He had simply liked her superior expression. She came from a family of old, old money. Her father had known Catherine. Olivia had a slightly Slavic look: black hair, catlike eyes; a residue, he thought, from some far-distant immigrant past.

"Everything is ready for the opening," she said. "Is it still going ahead?"

"Of course," he told her. He looked her slowly up and down, from head to foot.

"How is Anna?" she asked.

"Anna will be fine," he said.

He took her by the wrist.

She made no pretense of resisting.

They went forward into the smaller office, and, glancing back only briefly toward the street, he shut the door behind them.

Eleven

As the 757 made its final approach to Logan, David gripped the armrest and closed his eyes.

He had always hated flying. His mouth had been as dry as sand ever since they had left Gatwick.

The plane was packed to capacity, and, all journey, David had sat with his legs halfway into the aisle, and been kicked and tripped over regularly. It was holiday season: the schools in England had just finished their summer term. Opposite him, across the aisle, were a young family with four children: a teenage boy, who sat in front, welded to his Game Boy or his Walkman, and occasionally glanced at David with sulky defiance; and his three younger sisters, who sat behind him, arguing continually over each other's seat-back videos.

David had tried to ignore them. He had also tried to ignore that he was thirty thousand feet above the earth, and kept his eyes firmly away from the window. Most of all, he tried to forget what was to come. What he was going to say to this man Garrett. Or Grace. Or Anna. And what in God's name he could say to Rachel.

He tried to sleep; but the oblivion wouldn't come.

Instead, he could only think that this was the trip he had always planned to make with Anna. Almost the last time they had talked— they were on Deadman's Walk, alongside Merton, with the high stone wall on one side, and the iron railings of Merton Fields on their left—she wouldn't look at him. She had been almost completely silent.

"Coffee?" said a voice.

Startled, he opened his eyes. The steward was standing next to him with a tray. The man nodded at the empty cup in front of David.

"Oh ... no. No thanks," David said.

He pushed up the seat-back tray, and then sat, awkwardly, with the cup in his lap. When the man came past again, he gave it to him. It was taken without a word.

He turned in his seat and closed his eyes again.

In those last days with Anna he had had an idea. Looking back, he had probably only thought of it as a way to keep her. To hold back this shadow that was coming toward him.

"After Finals," he had said. "We'll go to China."

Maybe it was the fact that she had just kept on walking. She didn't glance up at him. She didn't unhook her arm from his either. But she just kept walking, looking at the frost-hardened ground.

"China," she had echoed.

"We'll go via Boston."

Still, she hadn't stopped. But she had looked. Glanced up at him, eyes screwed against the slanted, pale springtime sun. "Why the hell would you go to China via Boston?" she'd asked.

"We'll follow in Wilson's footsteps," he'd told her. "What d'you think? Isn't that a great idea? When we come back, I'll do my thesis on it. I'll write our book," he'd said. He had failed to notice that he was almost dragging her along with him, in an attempt to match his stride. "We could follow his route," he said. "Liverpool to Boston. Overland to San Francisco. Then Hong Kong. Veitch and Sons sent him to find Augustine Henry, the man who had first seen the dove tree. He had to travel into the Yunnan to find Henry, to get a map. To see exactly where it had been growing. Then he went back all the way to the Gorges, a thousand miles or more overland and by river, with this map ..."

He had gone on talking, he remembered.

He had just gone on talking, insanely and selfishly talking, while the shadow deepened between them.

It had taken twelve days, not a mere airborne six hours, for Ernest Wilson to reach Boston in 1899. On the sixth of May, Wilson had sailed from San Francisco for Hong Kong, and then straight on to the province of Yunnan, via Haiphong. After that, it was by river to Hanoi; by steamer on the Red River to Yen Bai; a transfer to a shallow-draft steamer to Lao Cai; then by native boat to Manhao, and by road, on mule and sedan chair, to Mengzi. From Mengzi, he took a caravan of sixteen mules to Simao, and he arrived where Augustine Henry was living on the twenty-fourth of September, five months after leaving England.

At last, Anna had stopped walking. By then, they had reached the junction of the lane by Corpus Christi. "You want to sail to Boston, and then to China," she had stated flatly.

"We'll fly to Boston," he had said. "We could get a train to the West Coast, like he did. Then take a tour. They do those tours. To the Gorges."

"And how do we pay for that?" she'd asked.

"We don't have to do it as a package," he had replied. "We could take our time. Work our way west. Work in Frisco for a few months. If it takes a year, or two years, what does it matter? And then the tours aren't too expensive." He'd grinned at her. *Fool. Grinned at her.* "What a journey to tell our kids," he'd said.

She'd suddenly pulled her arm away from him. "If there's one person I'm sick of hearing about, it's Wilson," she'd retorted. "Wilson, Wilson, Wilson! I hate this crap! Don't you ever think of anything else? Don't you *see* anything else?" She had put both hands to her eyes, then dropped them, and started to walk away, pushing him back with the flat of her hand.

He caught her arm, pulled her to him. For a moment, she relaxed into him, and he wrapped his arms around her, burying his face in her neck. "I love you," he whispered urgently. "I look forward, and I see us. I just see all these pictures of us doing things together."

He kissed her, and it seemed to him that she merely submitted.

It was not that usual urgent joining, the meeting of spirits. For months, he had loved her. Autumn days, winter days. Now he felt she was drifting from him. His head was full of her. Frost on the windows of her room; the two of them naked, with a blanket pulled over them, and her kisses as strong as his, her longing as deep. Nights where they didn't sleep, hungry for each other. Dawns on the long walks, meeting only early morning runners. He remembered being in the library, and feeling that he couldn't understand the words on the pages of books in front of him, because the shape of the paragraphs, the look of the letters, even the grain of the paper, seemed to be soaked in her presence. She reached up from the books, alive, lingering . . .

"I love you," he repeated.

She suddenly pulled away from him again, wiping her eyes. "And you think this is a reasonable thing to do," she demanded, "to travel all that way, with a fresh degree, and a mountain of fucking debt?"

It was the first time she'd ever sworn at him.

It was the last time.

He shifted in his seat now, feeling the plane altering course. Dropping in height. Pressure popped in his ears. He tried to pull himself away from the here and now. Backward, backward, to where he had last seen her.

He had bought a map of China to show her. Still bought the damned thing, even after such a conversation. Even after her objections. He had still bought the stupid bloody map. He had been brushing away that shadow. It was like whistling in the dark. Just plowing on, pretending that all the signs meant nothing.

Why didn't you just ask her.

*Why didn't you just **ask** her what was wrong.*

The plane lurched. David opened his eyes. The seat belt sign had come on, and a steward was standing above him, checking that the overhead bins were closed. He smiled at David.

"How long until we land?" David asked.

"Ten minutes or so," the steward said.

David shut his eyes again. He didn't want to be smiled at. He wanted to be on good, solid ground. And he wished that Augustine Henry—that soft-spoken Irishman who had lured Wilson to China—could have been there waiting to meet him. That was someone he felt he knew already.

In 1899, Augustine Henry had already been working as a medical officer for the Imperial Chinese Customs Service for eighteen years. He was eventually sent to Yichang, a Customs post at the entrance to the Yangtze Gorges, in 1882. And had been utterly smitten.

He had first seen the Gorges in winter, and it was an amazing sight. In total contrast to the country on the flood plain below, this place was savage and uncompromising, like some sort of prehistoric landscape. The Yangtze tore under two-thousand-foot cliffs, and hundred-strong teams of trackers hauled boats by hand over the rapids below. It was the land of Maeldune's ballad for Henry, perhaps: the Irish legend that Henry knew by heart—*... and the topmost spire of the mountains was lilies in lieu of snow ...*—for the first thing that Henry noticed, on a bare limestone ledge that extended for a quarter of a mile or more, was a huge winter flowering of Chinese primula, their colors merging from palest lilac to pink, like a drift of pastel snow hundreds of feet above his head.

But it was in the even more distant mountains of Hupeh that he had found the dove tree, the *Davidia involucrata*.

He never forgot it. He wrote to Kew and urged that botanists be sent to China in search of it. He was sure that it flourished on higher passes, and in ever more remote areas. He dreamed of finding its seeds, and shipping them back to Europe; and of the dove tree finally growing in Ireland, and America, and England. But the fruit that he finally sent back didn't germinate, and, ten years later, under Augustine's still persistent encouragement, the horticulturists Veitch and Sons sent Ernest Wilson to find the tree.

But first, Wilson had to find Henry, who was the only reliable

European who knew where the *Davidia* grew. And by then, Henry was no longer in Hupeh. He was in Yunnan; and Yunnan was far, far west of Hupeh.

Circular journeys, David thought.

The search for the beautiful, the unattainable, and the lost.

The pursuit of impossible dreams.

In his head, he saw the passes far above Yichang: the narrow valley north of Xiangtan where the foxglovelike flowers of *Rehmannia henryi* grew; the peak of Wan-tiao Shan, where the lilac flourished on the very highest summit; the remnants of the Great Salt Road as they reached Sichuan.

"Landing!" one of the girls cried, across the aisle of the plane. "We're there—we're landing!"

The wheels suddenly bounced onto the runway at Logan; the engines roared.

Immediately, every notion of Wilson and his journey vanished from David's mind. Mountains, gorges, lilies, rapids, rivers, and the ghostlike, supernatural *Davidia* disappeared from his head in a flash.

Forgetting them all entirely, he dug his fingernails into the armrest, and silently, feverishly, prayed.

It took him a long time to get through Customs, and even longer to find his suitcase. When he finally emerged into the main airport, David was dazed and disoriented. He could feel that it was hotter—much hotter—than England. The crowds swarmed past him. Even in the air-conditioning of the terminal, he was already sweating.

He stopped, and put his bag on the floor, and took the guidebook that he had bought in Gatwick out of his pocket. He thumbed through it, while other passengers pushed past him. It had a map on the inner leaf: Logan was marked, northeast of the city. He had to get to a place called Back Bay. That was where the hospital was. That was where Grace Russell would be.

He didn't know where he could find a bus, but he supposed that, if he just walked out of the airport, he would see something.

A bus, or a taxi. Maybe someone could tell him which one you had to get to reach Back Bay. Which number. Which route. He felt in his other pocket for the dollars he had put there. He pushed his bag to one side with his foot, and started doing what he should have done on the plane; transferring the dollars to his wallet, and putting the sterling in the pocket of his flight bag.

"David Mortimer?" said a voice.

As he looked up, surprised, he dropped the pound coins that had been in his hand.

"Yes?" he asked.

The man standing next to him, behind the rope of Arrivals, smiled. "Your money is escaping," he murmured.

David went after it, stamping on the rolling coins, fishing them off the floor, and turning back to see his bag being lifted over the rope.

The man held out his hand.

"James Garrett."

Oh, shit, was David's instinctive reaction. He wiped his own palm on the seam of his jeans, before extending it. "You knew who I was," he said.

"A lucky guess," Garrett replied.

David looked at him. Garrett, the older man, had that indefinable air of the rich: effortlessness and ease. He was wearing a gray lightweight suit, white shirt, gray silk tie. David was Garrett's height, but there any similarity ended. David didn't own a suit, let alone something as elegant as Garrett's outfit. He was broad-shouldered, not dark and slim. Garrett looked almost feminine in his suavity. It was almost as if, David suddenly thought, as if Garrett had been polished: steam-cleaned, polished, and manicured. Next to him, David felt suddenly too big, too untidy, too young.

"Why don't you come around the barrier," Garrett said.

David did so, after waiting his turn behind another family.

"Good flight?"

"Yes," David replied. "Thanks." He smoothed down his hair self-consciously.

"I thought I would come and meet you," Garrett said. "I hope you don't mind."

"No. Of course not."

Garrett walked ahead a little way, then stopped to make a call. "I'll just get the driver to come up to the ramp," he said. "I was stranded the other day, and had to make do with a taxi. I wouldn't recommend it."

By the time that they got to the exit doors, David saw what was waiting for them. It was a silver Mercedes, new registration. Garrett opened the rear passenger door for him.

"Is this yours?" David asked.

"No," Garrett said. "This company drives me."

They sat for some time in silence as the airport was left behind. It was only once they were on the turnpike that Garrett turned to him.

"Grace telephoned you, I understand," he said.

"Yesterday."

"And ..." Garrett paused. "This would be the first time that you've seen Rachel?"

"Yes."

"First time in Boston, also?"

"Yes."

Garrett nodded. He looked out of the window for a moment, then asked, "What is it that you do?"

David hesitated. For a second, he thought that Garrett was asking him what anyone did in the circumstances of meeting a daughter one had never known about. Then, he saw that it was simply a question about his work.

"I'm a scientist," he answered.

"Really?" Garrett replied. "In what field?"

"Biological sciences. Botany."

"You're a researcher?"

"I was once."

"That would be at Oxford?" Garrett asked.

"My Ph.D.," David told him.

"You have a Ph.D.?"

"No," David said. "I didn't finish."

The traffic was stop-starting. The air-conditioning hummed.

"Do you teach?"

"Sometimes," David said.

"In Oxford?"

"No."

"But you live there."

"No," said David. "I haven't lived in Oxford for nine years. I live in a place called Morton Abbas."

Garrett smiled again. "I'm giving you the third degree," he murmured. "I'm so sorry."

They descended into the city.

They drew up outside the house in Beacon Hill.

Garrett got out, and held the door for David. Inside the car, David looked up at him, questioning.

"This is my home," Garrett explained. "The hospital is just five minutes' walk away. I thought you would like to leave your bags."

David hesitated. He would much rather have gone straight to the hospital. He wanted to see Grace. But he felt awkward, churlish, to refuse Garrett's suggestion. He got out.

He followed Garrett up the stairs, and into the second-floor rooms.

Garrett went to the galley kitchen. "A beer?" he asked. "Coffee?"

David was still looking around him. He thought he recognized one of the paintings on the walls, but couldn't be sure.

"You like art?"

David glanced at him. "I'm sorry," he said. "This is quite a place."

Garrett smiled. He was holding up the coffeepot.

"Oh—something cold," David said. "Water is fine."

Garrett took a bottle of Perrier out of the fridge. "Sit down," he said. "Make yourself comfortable."

David sat on the edge of the couch, and took the glass offered to him.

Garrett leaned against the worktop, and crossed his arms. "Did you know that Anna was an artist?" he said.

"Yes, she painted."

"I mean now," Garrett said.

David glanced back at the walls. "She painted these?"

Garrett laughed softly. "No," he said. "But she's very talented. I represent her."

David said nothing. He sat wondering exactly what this meant.

"She has an exhibition at the moment," Garrett continued. "Perhaps you'd like to see it. See her work."

"Yes," David answered. He looked at his watch.

"How long were you two together?" Garrett asked.

David looked up. "I'm sorry?"

"You and Anna."

"A few months," David said.

Garrett regarded him speculatively. "Really?" he said, in a light conversational tone. "A short time?"

"Yes."

"And you're married to someone now?"

"No," David said. "I'm not married."

"You must forgive this rudeness," Garrett said. He took off his jacket, and placed it carefully on the back of the couch. "But I'm trying to catch up. You all know each other."

"I don't know Grace," David said. "And I certainly don't know Rachel. You've got quite a lead on me there."

Garrett nodded. "Of course, yes. But I'm actually asking you if Rachel has any other family."

"I don't have a wife and I don't have children," David said. "But she has cousins. My sister has a son and daughter."

In the silence that followed, David could hear the gentle, measured ticking of a clock. He stood up. "I ought to get to the hospital," he said. "I ought to ring Grace, at least."

"You must be hungry," Garrett said. "Let me get you something first. There's nothing at the hospital to speak of."

"I'm not hungry," David replied.

Garrett was pouring himself a drink. "Morton Abbas," he said, over his shoulder. "Where is that?"

"It's on the south coast."

"Portsmouth ... Brighton ...?"

"Lyme Regis."

"Ah," Garrett said. "Yes, I know that. I've been there."

David finished his water, stood, and handed Garrett back the glass. "Have you seen Anna today?" he asked.

"Yes."

"How is she?"

Garrett looked at the floor for a second before replying. "She's stable."

"And Rachel?"

"Rachel is fine," he replied. "She has an arm in a cast. She has a multiple fracture."

"I see," David said. This was news to him. He hadn't known. More specifically, he realized, he hadn't asked.

"Did you ever meet Grace?" Garrett inquired.

David put a hand to his forehead. Garrett's air-conditioning was chill. He felt clammy, almost cold. "No," he said. "But I ought to see her now. I promised I would go straight there."

Garrett nodded, but didn't move. "Perhaps we should talk about Grace before we go," he said. "Grace and Rachel." He indicated the sofa. Very reluctantly, David sat down again. Garrett took a chair opposite him.

"This must be very difficult for you," he observed quietly. "This whole situation. After so many years."

David said nothing. It occurred to him that this was simply stating the obvious.

"To come into a crisis like this ... cold, as it were," Garrett continued. "Without any information at all."

David looked steadily at him. "I feel as if I've had all the information I could handle in one day," he replied.

Garrett smiled sympathetically. "There's a little more you ought to know," he said. "About Rachel." David sat back. Garrett's expression was noncommittal, hard to read. "I don't suppose that Grace mentioned to you," Garrett said, "that Rachel is a very gifted child."

"Is she?" David said. "In what way?"

Garrett sat forward, elbows on knees, hands clasped. "Rachel has all sorts of gifts," he replied. "She's musical. She's very intelligent. Her IQ is high. She has mathematical ability."

"Musical," David repeated.

"She plays by ear," Garrett said. He nodded toward the back of the room; for the first time, David saw the piano there, set in a small alcove.

"Did Anna teach her?" David asked. "Does Anna play?"

"No," Garrett answered. "Rachel doesn't read music."

"But . . ." David paused.

"Rachel," Garrett told him, in a measured voice, "isn't a typical student. She isn't even typical of a gifted student."

"I don't understand," David said.

"She is completely self-motivated," Garrett told him. "She's an innovative child. She needs something more than an ordinary school. She needs individual care."

David leaned forward now, too. "I don't know what you're telling me," he said. "Are you saying that Rachel can't go to a normal school?"

"That's right."

"Because she . . . she's what?" he asked, puzzled. "She's too clever? Won't they have her?"

"It's not a case of the school system not having her," Garrett replied. "It's a case of us finding something more suited to Rachel. Suited to her abilities."

"She's not in school," David said. "Is that what you're saying?"

"Yes, she's in school," Garrett said. "But that will change. I'm arranging a private tutor."

David rubbed a hand over his forehead. "You're allowed to take her out of the school system," he said. "And you'll do that?"

"Yes."

"Here?"

"Here in Boston. At Anna's home."

David paused. He sat back, trying to assess what this meant. "Anna doesn't live here with you?" he asked.

"No. They live in Jamaica Plain."

"And Rachel lives with Anna, and she'll have a private tutor come to Anna's house?"

"That's right."

There was a pause. "That would be very expensive," David said.

Garrett smiled, and spread his hands in a gesture of modesty.

David tried to think, to work it out. "She'd miss other children," he murmured, finally. He looked up. Just for a second, he saw something in Garrett's face. A flash of something. A defense mechanism.

"Rachel doesn't really need other children," he said.

"Every child needs other children."

"You don't understand," Garrett countered.

"Yes, I do," David responded quickly. "My sister has children, and I see how much they need other kids. Play school, school . . ."

"You don't understand," Garrett repeated. "Rachel doesn't *want* other children."

"What do you mean?" David demanded.

"She's autistic," Garrett said.

David sat back. He felt winded, as if someone had punched him. He couldn't think of a single response.

"Grace didn't tell you," Garrett murmured. "I didn't think she would."

Still, David said nothing. He had no idea of what autism meant, only that it was one of those words that carried a threat of the unknown. He remembered Sara being worried about Thomas having the MMR vaccine, because of the rumor that it was somehow linked to autism. He tried to think. To remember what the hell he knew about this subject. Autistic children were talented. There had been a boy in England, famous for his architectural drawings. There had been an article on the TV news one night, and another little boy there was spinning; just spinning around in the background while his mother was speaking.

"Autism," he repeated, slowly. "I thought it was something that just boys had."

"More boys than girls," Garrett corrected.

"Autistic," David said. Then folded his arms across himself, and pressed his lips tightly together. He was afraid that something sublimely stupid would come out of his mouth. Something that showed his ignorance to this calm, polished man in front of him who knew only too well what autism was, and who had tended his daughter through it.

"David," Garrett said softly. "Forgive me. But is there anyone in your family with such a condition?"

David blinked. "My family?"

"It's . . ." Garrett paused, apparently choosing his words carefully. "As far as I know, this condition comes down through the male side," he said. "Would your father, your grandfather, your brother . . . ?"

"I don't have a brother," David said.

Garrett was looking steadily at him.

David got up. There was no way he was discussing his father with Garrett. "I think I should go now," he said.

Garrett got up also. "David," he said. "I've offended you."

"No," David replied. "I'm shocked. That's all."

"I wouldn't have offended you for the world."

"It's OK," David said. It was true that he was affronted by Garrett's implication. It was as if Garrett were telling him that Rachel had inherited a gene from him that he, Garrett, had been forced to tend. He looked around for his things. He wanted to take his bags and go. He had a sudden overwhelming feeling that he shouldn't be in this man's house. The sensation of being a trespasser in a world he couldn't understand washed over him.

"I felt you ought to know," Garrett was saying. "To be forearmed."

David said nothing. He was thinking of Anna. He was thinking of her hearing this diagnosis for the first time. He was thinking again, for the thousandth time, of why she had never rung him. He could have helped her. He could have done something.

What were you going to do, said a small voice inside his head, *on the other side of the Atlantic?*

"Thank you for the glass of water," he said. "I have to go."

Abruptly, Garrett gripped his arm. "David," he murmured. "There's Grace."

"What?" He was standing at the head of the stairs. Behind Garrett's head, the painting loomed, an exclamation of design in the white box of the room. It was lurid, dominant. Faces leered from the canvas. Colors fought for space. Yellows, blues, reds.

"You know ... you can see how Anna has had her problems," Garrett said. "And Grace ... well, frankly, to phone you like this, to bring you over here without any discussion, without any thought ..."

David raised a hand to his eyes. "Is there something about Grace?" he asked.

"You know her background?"

"No," David said.

"That she and Anna's father were never married?"

David looked up. "Does that matter?"

"That Anna's father was, in fact, a married man, and that Grace had been his mistress? And she lived in a house he had given her, but that Anna never once saw her father?"

David's eyes ranged over Garrett's face. "No," he said. "She never told me that."

Garrett shook his head sadly. "She never saw her father because he abandoned Grace, giving her an annuity as soon as he knew that Grace was pregnant," he murmured.

"That's very sad," David commented. Anna had never told him this. He mused on it for a while, thinking of Grace struggling to bring up Anna alone. How many echoes she must have seen in Anna's situation.

But, when he looked up, there wasn't an echo of sympathy in Garrett's face, rather disapproval. "This is Anna's mother," Garrett told him. "This is her background."

David frowned. "You don't like her."

Garrett laughed shortly. "David, as you will see," he said, "it's not a case of liking or not liking, it's a case of trying to make sense of this woman. She's an enormously difficult person to get along with. In fact . . . I worry about her."

"You worry?" David said. "Why?"

Garrett looked embarrassed. "Well," he said. "She's an odd lady. She . . . she can forget, she's a very heavy smoker . . . and her language . . ."

"You're saying she's senile."

"No," Garrett replied swiftly. "No, no, not at all . . ."

He left the denial hanging, unconvincingly, between them.

"Where does she live now?" David asked. "Does she live with Anna?"

"Oh, she has a house. In Ogunquit. It's north of here."

"And she and Anna . . ."

"David," Garrett interrupted. "I'm going to be perfectly honest with you here. Grace will do everything she can to divide you from both Anna and Rachel. I should know. I've seen this for the last five years. I've been at the receiving end of this treatment."

"But she rang me," David said.

"Because she resents Anna's relationship with me. She resents the things we have done for Rachel."

"Do you mean that she rang me because she wanted some sort of leverage with Rachel?" And his conversation with Sara came back to him. *I won't be used like a bloody pawn.*

Garrett hesitated. "David, I'm sorry," he said. "But Anna and I have agreed on Rachel's care, and Grace has not agreed. And I would have consulted you. Naturally, I would have consulted you. If I had known who you were, or where you were."

David bit his lip. He could feel the unspoken insinuation: that Anna hadn't wanted him to know. That Garrett would have spoken to him willingly, but Anna had prevented it.

"And you think that Grace sees this as an opportunity to stop that happening," he asked dully. "By recruiting me?"

"I wouldn't put it that way. I wouldn't think even Grace could be so crude."

"But that is what you think," David said. "That's what you're afraid of." He looked directly at the other man.

You're worried I'm going to break up your family, he thought.

"Look," he added, "I didn't come here for any other reason than someone rang me and told me I had a daughter. I couldn't ignore that. I just couldn't ignore it. I don't want to come between you and Anna."

Garrett smiled at him. "Oh, you won't come between Anna and me," he told him softly. He reached for his jacket from the back of the couch. "There isn't a chance of that."

Twelve

ANNA STOOD IN THE lane, and looked at the last house.

It was a double-fronted Victorian cottage at the end of a long terrace, bordered by a blackthorn hedge at the front. Beyond it, the lane rolled away in a long arc, disappearing into the dip where the stream ran under the road, and the woods rose up on the other side. Unsurfaced and narrow, the lane was a white line, and each leaf of the bordering hedgerows was outlined with the delicate perfection of a deep frost.

There had been snow recently: a scattering that turned the fields and the woods white, and lay in stripes on the plowed hillside. It was December. The fifteenth of December, the year that she was nineteen.

She saw herself walking down the lane. David and Sara were next to her. David's sister was sixteen years old, and she wore a yellow PVC coat and Wellington boots, and a hand-knitted scarf wound again and again around her neck.

Sara had met them on the road, at the bus stop, and, as they had gotten off the bus, she had launched herself at David, and hugged him almost wildly. Her embrace of Anna had been no less fierce. Standing back from them, she had wrung her hands together; they had betrayed her below the smile.

"We had better go to Martock's first," she'd said.

"Is Dad here?" David asked.

"No," Sara had replied. "He wouldn't come."

The bus had pulled away, toiling up the gradient of the Wells-Bristol road. They crossed the road, jumping the brown slush gutters. Martock's was only a few yards down, its memorials lined up outside the single-story building whose corrugated iron roof dipped almost to the pavement.

They went in, and a woman met them. "David," she said.

He shook her hand. "This is my friend Anna," he murmured.

Miss Martock held out her bony fingers, and gripped her. "I've known him since he was a boy," she told Anna. "And his poor mother. Poor Kathleen."

They went into the workroom. "We've had a family business here for a hundred and thirty years," Miss Martock said. "You go and look in the churchyard. You'll see our names on the stones. A hundred and thirty years."

The workroom, under the corrugated roof, was still. There were three large panes of glass in the roof, letting in a dusky, rain-smeared light. On the floor were puddles of water, where the snow and then the rain had come through.

"I've shown Sara the book," the woman said. "She chose a marble. Like this one."

And she showed them the texture of a half-finished headstone on the workbench. Anna looked at the lettering. It was not for David and Sara's mother, but some other death. Lines were marked out in readiness on the surface. *Beloved son,* Anna noticed. Involuntarily, she shuddered.

"Sara thought, as you would be going back to Oxford, you had better choose now."

Sara looked at her brother for approval, her face a mask of anxiety. "Is it right?" she asked.

"Yes," David said.

That was all.

As they came out of the workroom again, and stood by the door of the house, Anna saw David look up. There was a holly tree in the garden.

She put her hand up now to the memory, to the image of the three of them standing by the headstones by the door. Beyond the ilex at Martock's, she touched another, the tree that stood in the New College cloister, whose green crown could be seen above the roofs as you walked down New College Lane toward the bell tower. She pressed a little harder, and the ancient imprint folded. She grasped it in her fist, and pulled it away, and deeper still in her mind came others that David had shown her: the beeches at Addison's Walk. The great plane tree by the President's Lodgings. Deeper still, into her own childhood; the sugar maple by the summer cottage, with a gray-brown bark furrowed with age. The lovely acer in her grandfather's garden, splashed with yellow, the one called Drummond. Fruit wings of sycamore dropping into her lap in the fall. Green flower clusters like small, spare lanterns of the spring.

There was holly in the church at the funeral.

Holly and ivy, like the Christmas carol.

She had felt like a trespasser. She had known David for only two months. The church was cold, and full of the villagers that had been David's mother's friends. Since they had gotten the news just a week ago in college, David had been unnaturally—or perhaps, in the circumstances, naturally—silent. She had treated him with studied care, not knowing what was needed from her, and feeling isolated in his company. Yet, when she had suggested that she should not come to the funeral, he had been wounded.

"Of course you'll come," he had insisted.

"Maybe I shouldn't," she'd said.

"OK. If you don't want to . . ."

"I want to," she'd reassured him, puzzled by the touch of impatience, and his inability to understand her reluctance.

The church stood at the top of the village, near the main road. It was eleventh-century, Sara had told her. Anna looked up now, through the memory, through the air that showed their breath, to the timbered vault of the roof.

They sang "Dear Lord and Father of Mankind," because it had been David's mother's favorite. And as they began the fourth verse, "Our words and works that drown/the tender whisper of thy call,"

Anna looked along the row of the pew, and saw the family's faces in profile: Sara's grieving gaze; her father's silent face. David, mouthing the words but not singing them. Anna had looked again from father to son. David's father was fair; both his children were dark. She had been shown several photographs of Kathleen Mortimer, and saw how David and Sara took after her in coloring. Sara especially had her mother's open, smiling expression.

That morning, Anna had found Sara crying downstairs, and the two of them had sat, in the silent hour before breakfast, by the range in the kitchen, looking through the photograph albums, and the kept cards and pressed flowers, and the keepsakes of childhood. The first drawings and paintings. The Mother's Day messages. And Anna had felt drawn to this woman, who had died so suddenly at fifty-five, and whose imprint was all over this warm and homely house. Drawn, too, to Sara, who had wiped her eyes, and made the breakfast with a ghost of cheerfulness.

But the men. There was no way to get close to the men. As the hymn finished, they had closed their prayer books. The priest had come forward to them, as the coffin was lifted onto the shoulders of the pallbearers. Some question was asked about the order of service at the graveside. David's father answered in a firm voice, almost bright. Anna looked from him to David again, and saw nothing. No interchange of looks. No hand on an arm for comfort. No contact at all, in fact. They kept themselves away from each other almost fastidiously, elbows pressed to their sides.

David had gazed out at the grave. He had looked away from the lowering of the coffin. His eyes had been fixed on the valley beyond the chalk walls of the graveyard. Anna had linked arms with him, and gently pushed her hand into his pocket to clasp his fingers.

She held out her hand now; this fragile and translucent hand that didn't belong to her, attached to a body that had ceased to matter. She flexed her fingers this way and that, and thought of Sara's warmth as she passed the photograph books, and unwrapped the tissue-guarded memories.

And David's father, the following day. He had gone out early to work in the garden behind the house; an unfenced path of ground that had once been allotment gardens. They had walked up the path toward him to say good-bye. His attitude, she had thought, was almost jaunty. Good-humored.

"Will he cry?" Anna had asked David, as they waited for the bus to take them down to Bristol and the train. She was worried about him. Worried at the unnaturalness of it all.

"Cry?" David had said, and looked astonished. "I've never seen him cry."

His expression had suddenly altered in that moment. As the cold wind blew around them, and the traffic roared past up the long winter hill, David's eyes had filled with tears. She had put her arms around him, stroking his hair, gently kissing him, feeling him tremble.

"You can go back," she'd whispered. "We don't have to go to Oxford right now. Go back to the house, stay with them. Stay with your father."

He'd pulled back from her abruptly. "Stay with him?" he'd asked. He rubbed his eyes, shook his head. "I can't stand being around him," he murmured. "He's dead."

She'd blinked in shock at his tone, at the words. Felt his sense of utter rejection from a father he longed to know.

David had met her gaze. "He's dead and buried inside that face," he told her. "That's one thing you have to understand about my father. He's not in this world. He's not here. He never was."

She came back now, down that winter lane, across the flattened grass of the fields, the uncut hay lying in frosty swathes, the stream running over stones in the darkness under the little bridge; to David's father's garden, and its neatly symmetrical rows and beds, the plants white in the frost, white from the snow. She looked hard at the field in front of the house, and saw something infinitely strange there: contour lines and lettering. Blocks of color. A map was unrolling over the field, molding itself to every rut and furrow and blade of grass. It swept away from the lane toward the trees of the hill, wrinkled under fences and hedges, smoothed over the rise where the oak trees grew. She saw it unraveling for miles, away from the valley, over the landscape, through Somerset and Dorset and down to the sea.

A map. A map . . .

He had bought a map, those last weeks. Those last days in March.

"What is this?" she'd asked.

"The route," he'd told her.

"What route?"

"To China," he'd said.

They had been in his room. She'd turned around in sudden fury—rolling, unrolling contours, rolling road and trees—and flailed her hands against things: the table, the desk, the chair. The bed.

"What are you doing?" he'd asked, mystified. "What's the matter with you?"

"With *me*?" she'd cried. She'd pushed him in the chest. "It's you!" she'd shouted.

"What have I said?" he'd asked.

"It isn't what you've said," she'd replied. Her throat was hot. Her whole body was hot.

"But I don't understand," he'd told her.

"No," she'd said. "You don't understand." She'd lost control of herself completely, suddenly possessed by the panic at her situation. She'd hit him, a clenched fist, in the center of his chest.

Darkness stepped between them. She'd purposely ignored the confused, hurt look on his face. She was so wound up that all she could think of was to find something to hurt him with.

"You never cried about your mother," she said. "Your father never cried. You told me that yourself. It's not right! It's not *human*! What's the matter with you both?"

"I think about my mother," he'd said. "I do cry about her."

"Do you? You never say so. I've never seen you."

"I do. Of course I do."

"And your father?"

His face had darkened. "I'm not like him," he said.

"There's something missing with you," she'd whispered.

He had flinched. She was glad of it at the time, in that desperation she felt.

"He never spoke to me," David said. There was confusion and pain in his tone. "That's how it was. He never spoke to any of us."

"Not to your mother?"

"He worked very hard, and he read the newspaper, and he had his little projects—"

He suddenly realized what he'd said.

"And you're just like him," she whispered. "You remember how he was talking about his garden, that morning after the funeral? You're just like him, talking about Wilson all the time; about some person who's dead . . ."

"I'm not like him," he'd said. "I want to talk to you. Anna! I want to talk to you." And he'd snatched for her arm, while she simultaneously pulled away from him.

"And some dead place that doesn't exist anymore," she'd gasped. "That's what you want. You want to be far away, don't you? Up on some mountain. That's what you talk about all the time, isn't it?" she'd demanded. "How Wilson went where no one had ever been before. Up to the places where even the Chinese were afraid to go. Into places where the *dead* don't want to be, for Chrissake!"

"It's not true," he'd said. "I'm not my father!"

"If you tell me one more thing about trees or plants or flowers—"

"I'm not like him," he repeated. "That's not fair. It's not fair . . ."

She had floundered for the words. The right words. The right blade to sink in his flesh, to make him suffer. She had been so afraid that night: afraid the world was slipping away. All her plans, her vision for the future. All disintegrating. If she told him the truth, he would leave her. Just like her father had left her mother, for the same reason. That was what terrified her. David would vanish into Wilson's world.

"You're living in some place," she told him, "some far-off place and you don't care if that connects with anyone else." She'd sobbed, "You *are* him. You and your father are the same."

She saw she'd succeeded. Confusion was replaced with hurt in his expression. She had touched his innermost fear, that one day he would find himself in some remote, unreachable place.

She'd turned, and run out of the room, down the stairs. Hatred for herself welled up, for using that weapon against him. And the blind terror at her own predicament. She remembered stone steps, those little narrow stairwells. The black boards with gold lettering by the cloister. She'd run. Away from the noise of The High. Down Longwall and St. Cross. She had an insane thought in her head, that she would throw herself in the Cherwell. She'd stopped and run halfway back to the edge of the Deer Park, and halted there, gasping for breath.

It was getting dark. And she thought of the river, and suddenly, of her mother, and the ocean.

The physical, physical ache to go home. To see Grace. To hide.

And the map of China still rolled away now, out of David's hands, out of the streets, out of the quick brown water flowing under the bridges.

On the surface of the water were leaves, torn by the spring gales, beating their endless circles to the sea.

Thirteen

DAVID AND GARRETT REACHED the hospital at seven o'clock.

A haze of humidity hung over the city. The traffic at Cambridge Street was heavy, grindingly slow: still, they waited for some time to cross.

As they walked toward the front door, David noticed a woman sitting to the right hand side of it. There were dozens of wheelchairs here, and she was in one of them, her head down, her elbows on her knees. A cigarette hung from her fingers, burning down to untouched ash.

Garrett touched his arm, and turned to him with an apologetic look. Then, saying nothing further to David, he walked up to the woman.

"Grace," he said.

She looked up.

David stopped. Anna's mother had been crying. Her eyes were red, her face mottled, stained as if by bruises. She got to her feet, dropped the cigarette, ground it with her heel, and took a handkerchief from her pocket. Garrett was speaking to her in a low voice. Without looking into his face, turned solicitously to hers, she wiped her eyes. Then, quite suddenly, she looked up at David.

The first thing he thought was that he could see Anna in her. She had the same slightly broad face that would be quick to break into a smile. She was tall, like Anna. He saw the same long-fingered hands, the same way of carrying her head, almost too upright, with the chin tilted upward.

She walked forward. "David?" she asked.

"Yes," he said.

She shook his hand. "I'm so glad you've come," she said. Her skin was warm, dry. The touch was almost muscular. "Are you tired?" she asked. She seemed to be making a superhuman effort to speak. "How was your flight?" The same politeness that Garrett had used. All the while, her eyes searched his face.

"Fine," he replied. "Fine."

She was still staring at him. "Anna has a photograph of you," she said. "You look exactly the same."

"A photograph?" he repeated. It seemed inconceivable to him that Anna should have kept a memento of him. He had long ago imagined that she had cut him completely from her life; burned the letters, thrown the photos away.

"In the picture, you're standing in a street," she said. "There's a building behind it, a dome . . ."

"It's the Sheldonian," he said. He remembered the day it was taken.

"I have to take Rachel home," Grace murmured distractedly. She looked at Garrett, then back at David. "She's ready to be discharged. She's been ready since two o'clock." He saw her hands shaking.

Something slammed into him: a wave, a force of some kind. Everything around him took on a surreal detail: the thick gray plastic handles of the wheelchairs, the color of the brick. The glare of the pavement and the glass of the windows.

"I'm too late for Anna," he guessed, and at once felt nauseous. He had a sudden conviction that he was going to be violently ill. Then, it receded as quickly as it had come. He took a breath, like a swimmer surfacing.

"Anna?" Garrett said, coming alongside them. "Has something happened?"

"They took her back into surgery," Grace said. "There's another bleed somewhere. She'd been stable. Then, this afternoon . . ."

The light refracted, relaxed.

"And Rachel?" David asked.

"She's waiting."

"Does she know about this?"

"Yes," Grace said.

Garrett made a motion with his hand that David couldn't interpret. Then he glanced pointedly at Grace. "I wish you would go to the house, and rest," he said. "Take my key."

"I don't want to rest," she replied.

"You've been here two full days."

"I'm all right," she said. "I know how long I've been here."

David looked from Garrett to Grace. "Some sleep," David suggested. "You must be exhausted."

"I slept last night. I slept in the chair."

"I wish you would take my advice," Garrett said.

David looked from one to the other. "You can't sleep in a chair," he said.

"I have to see to Rachel."

"Rachel can come with me," Garrett said. "You can both come."

"No," she said.

"We're just five minutes' walk away," he continued, in a soft, persuasive tone. "You can take my bed. You and Rachel." He put an arm around her shoulder.

She stepped away. "I'm going to Anna's."

Garrett smiled. "But it's a long way, Grace."

"I'm going to Anna's," she repeated. She looked at David. "She has to go," she said. "She wants to go. I'll take the T."

"You're taking Rachel on the T all the way to Jamaica Plain," Garrett said. It was a flat statement. "It will take forty minutes. The crowds."

"She is perfectly OK on a train," Grace told him. "She likes the train." But her voice wavered and cracked.

"Look," Garrett suggested, "you can have the house tonight,

and, if you really don't like the thought of sharing it with me, David and I will stay at the gallery." He nodded at David, and smiled. "I have a small arrangement at the back of the building," he said. "Just two rooms. A sitting room with a sofa bed. A kitchenette. It's very small. But it's functional."

"I was going to get a hotel," David said.

"I won't hear of it," Garrett murmured.

David looked again at Grace. He was confused now. Grace had a desperate pleading expression on her face that he couldn't fathom. "Don't worry," he told her. "We'll go back inside and wait. We'll wait together."

"It's Rachel," she said. "I must look after her. I was trying to think while I waited for you. I was trying to think what to do...."

"Where is Anna's house?" David asked.

"It's close to the Arborway," Garrett said. "They'd have to go all the way to Forest Hills."

"I can get on a train," Grace insisted. "It won't take forty minutes."

"There won't be food in the house," Garrett pointed out. "Anna hasn't been there in four or five days, has she?"

"There is a store on the corner of the street," Grace snapped. "I can walk into a store."

"And you're doing this tonight," Garrett said. "What about Anna? Are you intending to stay until she comes out of surgery? What then? Go back then on the T, at midnight?"

Grace's mouth buckled. Helpless defeat.

"I can stay with Anna," David offered. "You can't go three nights without rest. You could stay at James's house with Rachel," he suggested. "And James could stay at the gallery ..."

"No," Grace whispered.

"You can't be in two places at once," Garrett pointed out. "You can't be here with Anna, and with Rachel at the house in Jamaica Plain."

"Rachel can stay with us in Anna's room in the hospital," Grace said, suddenly. "Until tomorrow. Until we see how Anna is. Just for one night."

At this, Garrett laughed. "Oh, no," he said. "No, no. With a woman in intensive care? No."

"Can we go inside," David said. Garrett's words drummed in his head. *A woman in intensive care. A woman . . .* "We're arguing out on the street here."

"David is right," Garrett said.

"I'm not leaving Rachel," Grace told him. "And I'm not leaving Anna."

"You can't do both, that's obvious," Garrett told Grace. "If you insist on staying here again tonight, I'll take Rachel home with me."

Grace gave David a glance of complete despair.

"Let's go inside," Garrett said.

As they came up to the ward, David had a moment of panic.

He was going to see his child. He was going to speak to his child.

Irrationally, after coming so far, he had a sudden impulse to turn and run. He took a breath. *Don't be stupid.*

They came out of the elevator, and immediately he saw two couches in a glass-fronted room; a girl was sitting inside, watching television. A nurse stood by the doorway; she turned to them as they walked up.

"We're watching *Fantasia*," the woman said. "It's for the kids, you know. Not grown-ups like Rachel." She smiled indulgently. "But I couldn't find anything else."

David could see only the child's profile. She was fair-haired. That was all he could see: her head, and her hands, as she sat in the chair. Her feet were tucked under her. Her head was leaning on one hand.

"Rachel," Grace prompted.

The girl glanced around. She looked at the three of them, then back at the screen.

Grace walked forward. "Rachel," she repeated.

"It's the thunderstorm," Rachel said. Her voice was clear and rather low. At Grace's back, David stood looking hard at her, trying to find Anna in her face, and failing. Nor could he see himself. Rachel had fair skin; her face was very pale, quite round. Her hands, too, holding the remote, were large. Her fingertips were slightly flattened, he noticed.

On the TV, the picture faded, and returned showing an orchestra in half-light, preparing to play.

"This next one is Ponchielli," Rachel said. "If you listen, he says it. He says, 'The Dance of the Hours.' "

The announcement duly came up on the film.

"Rachel had this tape," Grace said. "She watched it all the time when she was younger. Didn't you, honey?"

"Yes," Rachel responded. She looked at Grace, and put down the remote.

"Switch it off now," Grace told her.

"Ponchielli," Rachel repeated. "He was Italian."

"Rachel is studying composition," Garrett said. "And the composers, of course."

For the first time, Rachel looked at David.

His heart pounded hard.

Grace held out her hand to him. He took it, and she pulled him in front of the seated girl. "Rachel," she said, "this is David Mortimer. He's come to see you, and your mother."

"She had an accident," Rachel said.

"You had one, too," David observed. "How is your arm?"

"I have to come back. I was in the car."

"She has to have a checkup in a week or two," Grace murmured. "Rachel," she said. "David knew your mother in Oxford, a long time ago. Before you were born."

Rachel looked again at him, her gaze settling on him this time.

It was then that he saw the resemblance. He saw his father in her; the same hair color and texture. The same direct gaze. He sucked in a breath, shocked. His father had died two years ago; yet he was looking out at David through this girl's eyes.

"Oxford, England," she said.

"That's right," he replied. He felt terribly moved. He wanted to touch her. He wanted to take her hand. Put his arms around her.

"Rachel," said Garrett, behind him. "Your grandmother is stay-ing here with David. You and I are going home."

"I have to come back," Rachel said. "I was in the car."

"But not yet," Garrett told her. He had picked up a little bun-dle that the hospital had made for her, wrapped in a white plastic bag. "Are these all your things?" he asked.

"They didn't find Mofty," Rachel said.

Garrett looked at David. "It's her little mascot," he explained. "We're not allowed to call it a toy."

"Mofty," David repeated.

"It's a model," Grace said. "A bridge." She smiled wanly at him. She tucked the remote back next to the TV set, and held Rachel's hand. She smiled. "Just a little bridge, you know? Not a big one."

"You can see it," Rachel said to David. "It was in the pocket of the door. There's a pocket in the door. It was in that pocket. You can find it if you look."

"It was in Anna's car," Grace told him. She gave an infinitesimal frown, and shake of her head. Then, she stepped directly in front of Rachel, and bent at the knees a little, so that she was looking straight into her eyes. "I'm coming to see you," she said. "I'm coming over soon. Tonight, OK?"

"We're going to my room," Rachel said.

"You're going to James's house."

"My room."

"No, Rachel," Grace reiterated gently. "You're going to see your piano at James's house."

Rachel looked at the bag in Garrett's hand.

"Her clothes are in there," Grace told Garrett. "They've been laundered."

"We'll see," he remarked.

The two stared at each other.

David reached out to touch Rachel. Just her arm. He just wanted to touch her arm.

She stepped back, into the chair, sending it skidding back on the floor.

"It's all right," David said.

"Rachel," Garrett warned.

David didn't want to let her go.

"Which band do you like?" he asked.

She looked toward him mutely. But not at his face. She gazed at a point somewhere just past him, just a fraction over his shoulder. He resisted the urge to turn and look at whatever she was staring at. "Do you like any bands?" he repeated. He was thinking that he could buy her a CD. He hadn't come with a present for her. He ought to have done that. He ought to have thought of it, to have come with a gift. He could have bought something at the airport. He tried desperately to think. She liked music. "Rock music?" he guessed. He just didn't know. He didn't know what music girls liked.

"Rachel prefers classical music," Garrett said. He had put his hand behind Rachel's shoulder, and, without gripping her, was guiding her. She moved unwillingly, her eyes now glancing toward Grace.

"I will be there," Grace told her. "I will be there by nine o'clock. I promise. Look at the clock. Watch the time. Wait for me. I'll come by nine o'clock, OK?"

They went out of the door.

Neither Garrett nor Rachel looked back.

They watched them go to the elevators, and get in. David stayed where he was, looking at the indicator as it gradually lighted the floors below.

Grace stepped up to him, looked anxiously at the expression on his face, and then put her arms around him.

"She takes time," she whispered to him gently. "That's all. Don't worry. Just time."

Fourteen

IF YOU LOOKED CLOSELY, and for long enough, you could see the kestrel above the water meadow. Just about this time of the evening, he patrolled the valley, and the ridge between this village and the next, along a strip of woodland that ran along the top of the hills. Sara was watching him now, as she sat on a quadrangle of turf next to the stream near the shop. Tom was in the water of the stream up to his knees, standing stock-still, waiting for the stickle-backs. He had seen three, he had told her, and the next time, he was going to catch one. He stood poised, fishing net in one hand, jam jar in the other, with the water almost coming in over the top of his Wellington boots.

"Are your feet cold yet?" she asked.

"My socks is wet," Tom replied absentmindedly, without look-ing up. His tongue rested on his bottom lip: acute study in con-centration.

"What was Charlie's party like?" she asked. Next to her, Hannah's buggy—with Hannah slumped asleep in it, hand still gripping her feeder cup—had two balloons tied to it.

"Good," Tom said.

"What did you play?"

"Stuff," he replied.

She smiled to herself. It sounded like a conversation with her

father; although, thank God, Thomas wasn't like his maternal grandfather. Normally he could string more than two words together,
and make a conversation.

Dragonflies darted over the water. She took off her sandals, and
lowered her feet into the stream.

"Ouch," she said, at the temperature.

"Mind my fishes," Thomas warned her. "Don't scare them."

She had a photograph of herself at Thomas's age. Perhaps
younger. She was wearing a party frock in the photo, too; and her
mother must have done her hair, because it was all bunched up in
curls. She didn't remember the dress, but she remembered the
shoes: black patent. Her first party shoes. She hadn't been able to
take her eyes off these shiny things on her feet: even in the photo,
she was staring at them.

Her mother took a lot of photographs. And her father's reaction had been the same that day as it was any other day. As her
mother had tried to persuade him to come and sit with Sara, he
had grumbled to himself, complaining at the fuss. He had come
down the garden path to the gate, and, reluctantly obeying his
wife's instructions, taken Sara on his knee. His big hands, with the
soil-darkened fingernails, had enfolded her.

The memories of her father's touches were few.

Because he only really got close under orders, at special occa-
sions, most of these same touches were actually preserved on film.
But every now and then, he would be taken unaware, stuck in a
family group, looking oddly isolated. There were plenty of pictures, for instance, taken by beaches where they had gone, as a
family, for days out. Always the same kind of photograph, taken by
those professional photographers who pursued you, snapping away
as you walked, and then pressing a card into your hand, so that you
could collect the developed photo later from a kiosk near the
sands.

Her mother would always be smiling broadly, loaded down
with bags and the picnic basket; her father would look bemused, carrying the windbreak and the mallet and the deck chairs. David, looking serious and shy, a gangly nine-, ten-, or eleven-year-old, always

half grown out of his shorts and T-shirts; she, much smaller, wrapped up in one of David's sweaters, her hair stuffed behind a hairband, and sticking out in a mad triangle around her face.

Her father's role would be to position the deck chairs and the windbreak. It was a work of art, determining the exact wind direction and the height of any incoming tide, and it was a task taken with deadly and silent severity. Once the windbreak was up, and the tea was distributed from the thermos, her father's work was over. He never swam, and he never made sand castles. He read his paper, behind a pair of clip-on dark lenses that he put over his regular glasses.

Her mother was the one who did things with them. Walked the beach looking for shells and stones and pieces of wood; waded into the water, holding Sara's hand. Her mother was also the one who put them to bed, and fed them, and entertained them. She was the one who kept scrapbooks, and all their drawings, and who packed their lunches, and cooked their suppers, and cleaned their shoes, and sewed their clothes.

The day that her mother had her heart attack, Sara had come home from school and could feel the loss in that house before she even saw her father's face. Power had drained from the rooms. It seemed as if even the color had gone. She remembered looking at the furniture and the carpets and curtains and thinking that it was like the posed studio pictures of her grandparents and great-grandparents. Monochrome, dusty, with a kind of etched-in backdrop of false flowers and someone else's ornaments and vases and books. Unreal. Drained.

She had been left alone with him. And subject, quite suddenly, to the true nature of her father's character. He was not resentful, or aggressive, or needy, or any of the predictable things that a bereaved man might be to his daughter. But she had come to realize, with both her mother and David gone, that her father was a cold man. It wasn't that he didn't feel things; it wasn't that he didn't have opinions. It was that they were expressed so rarely and so formally. When he talked, it was always about the same thing and in the same fashion. He would almost lecture her on the merits of some piece of machinery. A car, or a television. He would read all the reviews and books, and pontificate—there was no other word for it—stand pontificating in a shop in front of the same television. After days of longing for him to speak, she would find herself wishing that he would keep his voice down.

You just couldn't hold a conversation with him.

You couldn't just talk—meandering, aimless talk. The kind of talks she had had with her mother. There always had to be a point with Dad. There always had to be some sort of reasoned progression, and a conclusion. It was like sitting through a science experiment: method, variables, result.

And so, in the end, she started not to talk to him about anything. At school, all her friendships flourished; but at home it was like drawing a curtain down. Her words, and especially her emotions, weren't wanted. They were superfluous. They got in the way. And she felt that her father was rather glad of her silence.

It was then, when the whole truth of this hit her, almost a year after her mother had died, that she really mourned. She would go upstairs, and close the door on the empty-feeling house, and cry and cry for her mother. Cry for them standing side by side in the kitchen, talking while they made a meal. Cry for her mother reading out the horoscopes.

Strange, to need a person for details like that. In the end, she couldn't even face the crosswords in the paper that they used to do together when she had come in from school. She never looked again down the horoscopes, because she would come to her mother's star sign before her own. It was the little things. The little inconsequential things.

When she had met Matt, she had worried that her father wouldn't like him. Because Matt did talk. He talked to anyone. He was always the one standing at bars talking to the barmen, or with a crowd of people around him. He talked for a living, in fact. Long before they had decided upon buying the village shop and working it together, Matt had been a salesman, and he sold printing and copying machines. It had suddenly occurred to Sara, with that same overriding sense of strangeness, that her father liked Matt because of the machines. Her father would look at the brochures, absorbed by them. And this impressed him more than anything else, it seemed. That Matt had some sort of understanding, some innate grasp, of a machine.

Her wedding day stuck out in her memory more than any other.

It had been a blustery day in June. It had rained at first light, and the garden was wet. Clouds scudded across the sky, and the rain was shaken from the trees. It seemed to her that the world had been washed and painted for her. All the colors stood out. There was a breath of salt in the wind.

When everyone else, including David, had left for the church, and it was only them remaining in the house for the last few minutes, her father had wandered back and forth between the downstairs rooms, fiddling with things: pulling chairs square, winding the already overwound clock. Frowning in the direction of the lane, where green leaves, torn from the hedges, skittled about in the road, keeping a private dance of celebration.

"Do I look nice?" she'd asked him. She had dressed alone, missing her mother.

He had turned to look at her.

"Very nice," he told her.

She waited. She waited for him to say something else. To offer her advice. Or to say that he loved her, perhaps. To wish her well, at least.

He pulled at the edges of his jacket, and shifted from foot to foot, glancing at his watch. She could see that this was some sort of agony for him, and pitied his nerves.

"I've got freesias in my bouquet," she said. "Look."

He did so.

"Do you remember?" she asked.

"Remember what?"

"Mum's favorite."

He had just nodded.

They heard the car draw up; they went to the door.

It was two years ago that he had died. Thomas was two, and she was pregnant with Hannah. One morning when she was trying to get Tom ready to go out, her father's neighbor had rung to say that her father had collapsed. She had driven to the hospital, alone and full of dread; when she walked into the ward, she saw him, sitting up, and awake, hooked up to oxygen. She had gone to his bed and sat alongside him, and taken his hand.

"I haven't had anything to eat," he told her.

Relief drenched her. He was all right. "OK," she had said. This kind of statement, without any greeting or preamble, was exactly like him. "Shall I ask the nurse?"

"They moved all the walls," he murmured.

She glanced back at him. "They did what?" she asked.

"The walls," he repeated. "They move the beds, and they move the walls."

She had looked around at the other patients: all elderly.

"There's a boy that comes," her father announced suddenly. "He stands by the door."

It was another hour and a half before she managed to see the doctor.

"It's not him," she explained. "My father doesn't talk like this. He's not a fanciful man. He's very practical. He doesn't imagine things."

"We think there's been a stroke," the doctor told her.

"But he's not paralyzed. He's talking."

"That can happen."

"You don't understand," she said. "My father doesn't speak like this. He's not making sense."

"It could just be disorientation," was the reply. "He has a chest infection."

"And the collapse?"

"We'll see what tomorrow brings."

But the next day was worse.

They had moved him to a side ward. She was rung at five o'clock in the morning, with the simple message that her father was asking for her.

When she arrived, alone, having left Matt to look after Thomas, she found her father lying in bed, his face turned toward the window, where the dawn was just beginning to show. The light was on to one side of him; it cast a yellow glow over the bed and his face.

"Daddy," she said. "How are you?"

"They're building the trees," he said.

She was so grateful to find him alive that she began to cry.

He put his hand on her head and stroked it; this man who had hated to touch and be touched, all his life.

"My wonderful daughter," he whispered.

And he had started to weep with her; not silent tears, but great wrenching sobs. It so shocked her—both the words and the tears—that she could only hold his hand and watch him.

The chaplain came.

He read verses that Sara heard, but instantly forgot. Nothing made any sense to her, least of all prayers. She stopped him as he spoke.

"This isn't my father," she repeated. She was feeling light-headed by now; the breakfast hour had come and gone. None of the nursing staff had brought a tray: some secret was being shared, Sara thought. But not with her. A pall hung over the room as if her father had already died.

"My father isn't like this," she said to the priest. "I've never seen him cry."

Later on—midday came and went, and other visitors, the regular visitors, coming at the regular time, passed along the corridor outside—she went to find the ward sister.

The woman sat her down in a dayroom, where magazines were scattered among the ashtrays.

"A stroke in some parts of the brain can release inhibitions," the sister said. "It can change personalities. It can completely alter all sorts of perceptions."

"Is he in pain?"

"No."

"Does he know me?" Sara asked. "Is it me he's seeing?"

For almost three hours that afternoon, her father talked.

David had arrived by then; he sat on the opposite side of the bed. He had been teaching in Bristol, and had left his classes. He looked much older, and had lost weight. He listened with his head bowed.

"I'm going to see that man," her father murmured. "There's a cut to be done. We'll ask Kate about it. They'll close the windows. There's the borders. The rosebay came up after the fires. Bringing them down from Hertfordshire. They set up the table, and they took it away . . ."

Sara had looked at David. "It's been like this all day," she told him. "What is it about? What does he mean?"

It got to six o'clock. It started to get dark.

Quite suddenly, in the dimness of the room, with the light still casting its yellowish pool, her father opened his eyes and looked at her, with a perfectly lucid expression.

"Kiss her when she comes," he said, "for all the love she gave me."

He died at six-fifteen; softly, gently. Breathing out with a sigh.

Sara looked at Tom now.

He had caught something: a little minnow. It was wriggling in his jar, and he let out a shout of triumph, holding the jar up for her to see.

"There's stuff under the stones," he shouted. "Come look at it. It's yuck."

She hobbled over, her feet icy in the stream's current. Over the flint and pebbles.

Tom had turned over one of the little rocks, and pushed it up the bank from the shallows. "Look at all that stuff," he commanded her.

There was some sort of colorless algae on the underside of the rock. Tom was busy prizing it loose with his fingers.

"It's a house," she told him. "If you pull it off, it'll have no-where to live."

She persuaded him to put the rock back.

They sat on the bank, and she took off Tom's Wellingtons, and his saturated socks.

She thought of her father, who had never shared a minute like this with her. And she thought of David, all those miles away, in another country, seeing the face of his daughter for the first time. She thought of all the times and opportunities that had been missed. Opportunities to love, and be loved, and to say the things that needed to be heard, and kept in the heart.

On an impulse, she reached over and grabbed her son, swinging him off his feet, wrapping her arms around him, squeezing the breath out of him, and kissing him hard.

"Stop it," he yelled, wriggling in disgust, trying to get down and out of her grasp. "Kiss Hannah."

"I love you," she told him. "Remember, remember. I love you."

Fifteen

"I BROUGHT THIS TO show you," Grace said.

They were sitting in Anna's room. It was almost eight o'clock in the evening. Anna was still in surgery. Grace took a piece of paper from her bag, crumpled and creased; she placed it on the bedcover, and tried to smooth it flat.

"Do you see what it is?"

David leaned forward. It was a map. Drawn on a piece of school graph paper, about two feet square. "It's a coastline," he murmured.

"It's where I live," Grace said. "You see the road, the house? The lighthouse?"

"Yes." He sat admiring it; it was rather beautiful, with Gothic lettering for the place-names, and pictures of the seabirds. He turned it around, seeing that there was a scale at the bottom.

"Rachel drew this when she was eight," Grace said. "The cottage here is mine—it looks exactly like that. All the details are right. She did another one, after this. Of the city center, with the State House and Hancock Tower, and the Freedom Trail marked in bronze, like the plaques on the sidewalk. And the parks all drawn in green, with beautiful trees, and a frog sitting in the middle of Frog Pond..." She looked up at him, with shining eyes. "It was maps for a long time," she told him. "All kinds of atlases. She could sit for hours, just looking. She drew a map of her own room first, and then the road, the town ... She's drawn maps of the state. And she loves place-names. She can tell you what place-names mean, and she knows every capital...."

"You're proud of her," he said.

"Of course I am." She sat back, and considered him. "Garrett told you about her."

"Yes, he spoke to me."

"That's why you were late."

"He insisted we stop at his house."

She smiled thinly. "He does a lot of insisting," she said. "Quiet, you know? Refined. Like sugar. Refined the hell out of himself. Took all the gritty bits away."

He smiled back at her. "Well," he said, "he's told me about Rachel."

She laughed softly. "Then you know all there is to know," she said.

He heard the sarcasm.

She looked at the empty bed, at the equipment lying still. "Do you know anything at all about Asperger?"

"About what?" he asked.

She glanced back at him. "Asperger syndrome."

"I don't understand," he said. "I thought Rachel was autistic."

She nodded, slowly, assessing him. "Would you prefer her to be?"

"*Prefer* her ...?"

"That's Garrett's theory. She's autistic."

"And she's not?"

"Look," Grace said, "she's Asperger. Officially, as of nine months ago." She spread her hands, indicating a fait accompli.

"I'm lost," David said. He was beginning to feel the long day: pain drummed faintly behind his eyes.

Grace paused, then she pointed down at her bag. "It's just like a map," she said. "Do you remember those old ones? You've seen them, surely. Where the countries beyond the known world just said, *Here be dragons*?"

"Yes," he replied.

"OK," Grace said. She leaned forward, elbows on the bed. "So say we put autism with the dragons. We're guessing at the country. We think it's a long way off, so far on the edge of our own world, that it's really *another* world. But it's not. Aspergers are closer to us than that." She nodded down again at her bag. "At least they can *tell* you where they are. Some Aspergers are incredibly vocal. They can talk about themselves. But autistic children might be so distant that they can't distinguish just how deeply different they are. Whereas an Asperger, like Rachel, knows she's different."

"Rachel knows this?" he repeated. "She knows she's different?"

Grace smiled at him sadly. "David," she said, "Rachel is only too well aware. Other kids tell her all the time."

"They do?" he asked. "They tell her?"

"Yes," Grace said. "They tease her."

He frowned. "You mean, they pick on her."

"Sure."

"They bully her?"

"Yes."

He flushed.

"Look," Grace said. "One of the things about Rachel—about any kid like Rachel—is that she'll just speak up. Sometimes that earns her enemies." She smiled, and then sighed. "It's not that she's trying to be aggressive," she explained. "It's just that she doesn't have a set of social rules in her head. She doesn't recognize subliminal stuff, messages that you or I pick up instinctively. You know—say, for instance, if someone rolls their eyes when we're around. We know what that means, don't we? We think, OK, so I've said something stupid. Or they don't like me. And we store that information away. We'll maybe be more circumspect around that person. We'll watch them and ourselves. Or we might choose to avoid them."

"And Rachel doesn't store the information."

"Oh, yes," Grace said. "She stores information like a computer hard disc."

"But not anything that helps her with relationships."

"That's right."

"And she doesn't want friends?"

"She wants friends," Grace answered. "But making them, keeping them—that's really hard for her. It's as if it's conducted in a foreign language to her. All the nuances are lost. All the little clues and lead-ins for a conversation. All the jokes. Plus," she said, "Rachel can't lie, and she won't break a rule, and she won't bend. Try having a friendship where you can't tell that little white lie, the one that stops you hurting someone's feelings."

David got up, and walked to the window. The lights of the city were spread out in front of him. He was struck hard by the poignancy of this lost child, who could not grasp the way others behaved, drawing maps for herself. "I'm not surprised that Anna wants to take her out of school," he murmured. He had his back to Anna's mother. He didn't see her face. "Garrett told me about the tutor."

Grace got up. She came alongside him. "Rachel doesn't need a tutor," she said.

He looked at her. "But James . . ."

"Oh, let me guess. Rachel will be having a tutor at home."

"You mean she won't?"

"No," Grace said. "She damn well won't." She put both hands on the windowsill, closed her eyes, drew in a breath. "He's been brainwashing Anna with this stuff for weeks. Weeks! It's just a way to control Anna, insisting on expensive schooling the child doesn't need. Making Anna feel she's mistaken. Fucking octopus."

David stared at her. She opened her eyes. He shook his head, spread his hands. She started to laugh. "Well, that's what he is," she said. "Greasy tentacles everywhere, you know? Pulling you in. All in that nice soft voice of his. That very reasonable voice. Rachel would be *so* much better off with a private tutor, she would get along *so* much better in a calm atmosphere . . . You can see Anna waver. Is she doing the right thing? Is James right? He undermines her all the time." She made a gesture, both hands to her head, as if she'd tear her hair out. "Oh, for two cents, I'd kill him," she muttered. "I really would. I'd go down there right now and shoot him." She glanced at David's perplexed face. "I threw you to the lions," she said, apologetically. "I called you here, to this mess."

David frowned. He had no idea what was going on here. "So Rachel's still in school?"

"Of course she's in school, of *course* she is," Grace retorted. "It's what keeps her in the world. You want her to be out there with the dragons? You want her lost?" She put both hands on his arms. "Look," she said. "Sometimes it hurts her to get face-to-face with people. She struggles to understand. She literally has to learn such-and-such an expression; she has to learn that that particular way a face looks means that the person is upset. And another expression means happy. She has to learn what silences mean in certain situations, and what they mean in others. It's like she's battling to stay afloat. But *she has to stay afloat,*" Grace insisted, her fingers pressing into his flesh. "She has to stay in touch with us. What's the alternative? The alternative is, she drifts away, she goes over that ocean, we lose her. And worse still, at some point in the future, she's alone, when Anna and I aren't here anymore, and she's left without any clues, any strategies. *That* is the world that Garrett wants for her," she said. "He wants to set her apart, and hothouse her, and turn her into a freak show. He wants her to have special math tutoring, and to take her college exams early."

She sighed, running a hand through her hair. "And all the time she'd be shrink-wrapped against the world, and she'd be helpless. Helpless."

David stared at her. An image sprang back at him: waiting for a bus in a winter landscape, with Anna at his side.

My father is dead and buried inside that face.

Grace dropped her hands. "Excuse me," she said. "But I get so angry about this. We've had her for ten years, and he's known her for five, and he knows everything. He knows best. He'll talk and he'll talk and he'll talk. He'll talk at you until you get so tired of listening to him. And it's all the same tone, the same sound. Eventually you get like you'd agree to anything, just to get him to stop. He's been like that with Anna. It's a slow drip. You know? Like a slow-dripping tap."

"But why would Anna let that happen?" he asked. "This is her daughter."

Grace shook her head. "You haven't seen," she said. "You can't imagine what he's like."

"You mean he just imposes what he wants?"

"He grinds her down."

"Oh, come on! The Anna I knew wouldn't let anyone grind her down," David objected.

Grace looked at him for some time before replying. "Put yourself in her shoes," she murmured, at last. "She's a single mother. And an artist. She really struggles financially. She's worn down with trying to work, and looking after Rachel, but she wants to be independent. She moves to Boston because she enrolls Rachel in a school here, one with a good record. It's mainstream, but it understands. Unlike the other two schools that Rachel's attended, this one is prepared to listen. And Rachel is five now."

Grace interrupted her own story with a sudden, wide smile. "Oh, David, if you could see this school," she said. "They have a parent support program; they're flexible. They let Rachel go in before she started full-time, and they asked her to write down a description of herself."

The smile became positively glowing now. "I've kept that description," she said. "I'll bring it. She wrote down what she liked best. The maps came into that, then. And playing an Autoharp. It's just a little instrument we found in a store; you press down a band, and you make all sorts of chords ... and she wrote about the tapping, and turning around."

David frowned.

"Bouncing, tapping, whirling around," she explained. "Of all the autistic traits, that's the one that makes people think *That child is crazy.* It's hard to look at sometimes. Or they bang their heads against the wall, or hit themselves."

"My God," David whispered.

"And you know why?" Grace said. "I read this only the other week. They believe that it's because autistic children hear and see so much better than anyone else. Their senses are all tuned up.

They're wildly sensitive. Living in a superheated world. Have you seen that TV ad, the one where the person with the sore throat is sitting there, and he has—it's a graphics effect—thorns wound around his throat?"

"I don't know ... maybe ..."

"That always makes me think of Rachel," Grace said. "Living in a world where a screech of car brakes sounds like a whirlwind, or the taste of orange marmalade on toast tastes just like eating an actual orange, pith and skin. And so many other things, so many others ... the noise of waves, or of feet brushing against a carpet, or a cat's fur under your fingers ..."

Grace's attention had drifted away from David and had settled on Anna's empty bed. "They turn around, or move, or hit themselves, to concentrate on that vibration or pain, to temporarily tune out the overload." She suddenly turned back to him. "Don't you think that's rather incredible?" she asked.

"Yes," he said. And the thought swept over him. The thought of himself walking in Lewesdon, repeating the names of trees. Hanging on to his private mantras and his solitude. The overriding feeling he had had since Anna's departure—that he was not quite part of the rest of the world. Without her, he had slowly, slowly drifted away.

He thought of the last woman he had known—she was a teacher, near Bristol—telling him that he was so hard to know. It was New Year's. They had been in a crowded pub. Someone else in their party was at the bar, shouting their order over the heads of other people. The music was deafening.

"What?" he'd said, cupping his hand to his ear, pretending to be both old and deaf. "What did you say, young lady?"

"Hard—to—know," she'd answered, mouthing the words at him exaggeratedly.

"I'm not hard to know," he had retorted, grinning. "Look at me. I'm Mr. Nice Guy."

"Yes," she'd said. "You are. You're the life and soul of the party."

"Yeah," he'd retorted. "Mr. Cool!"

She had furrowed her brows. "It's all the talking."

"All the *what*?" he'd repeated.

She almost had to shout. "You talk so much."

"And that's what?" he'd asked, tipping his head down low to her now, to grasp the real meaning of what she was saying. "That's a fault? All I ever hear from women is how they wish men would talk to them."

She'd smiled. The drinks came back from the bar, together with much pushing and shoving. In the background, the radio was turned even higher as the countdown to New Year started. He had gripped her arm.

"All about your work," she'd said.

And it was like it always was when his relationships finished. He would think of Anna. Not the woman he had lost. But Anna . . .

"David," Grace said.

He jolted back to the present. "Sorry."

"Do you want to hear about Rachel?"

"Yes," he said. "I'm sorry. Go on."

She paused just a fraction, then went on. "Well, Rachel starts this school, and it's good. There are bad days—she is suspended twice—but, on the whole, it's progress. We begin to relax a little. Just a little. But there is a downside. Living in Boston is expensive, and money is tight. Anna isn't selling too well in Boston. We shuttle back and forth, and we talk about maybe me moving, or the two of them traveling back and forth every day, and there seems to be no right way to do it. No easy way. Anna gets tired, and Rachel gets tired. . . ."

She took a deep breath. "Then, out of the blue, here comes along a very wealthy man. A very quiet man who understands what she does. Who's willing to look after this very challenging, different child she has. He doesn't run away. Most men do, you know. They take one look at Rachel—"

"So there's nothing wrong with him," David interrupted. "Nothing wrong with Garrett."

"No," Grace responded sharply. "What could be wrong? He's like manna from heaven. He gets Anna work. A showing, an exhibition. Money, a name. And everything suddenly starts to change. Everything's easier, because he's around. She doesn't have to live in a one-room apartment anymore. She can afford a house. Not a great house, but a house. She feels less alone. He's very understanding."

"I don't know why I'm here," David observed.

Grace ignored him. Her voice was full of intensity. "And everything's wonderful, and Anna paints, she paints like crazy, everything's fine. And then he starts criticizing, just a little, he asks her to repeat work that sold, tells her the new routes she wants to take don't work, he takes on commissions for her. And then the paintings change. Do you know what that means? Do you know the significance of that?" she asked. "They start looking dark, they lose their color, and she produces tone-on-tone. She produces single-color canvases; she produces modular stuff, that crappy mix-and-match stuff for banks and corporate dining rooms and airports; she sits in her studio and paints from photographs, predictable things, the same over and over."

David still wasn't looking up.

"He puts her on a production line," she insisted. "Do you know what that means, David? To an artist? To be on a production line?"

David put his elbows on his knees, and held his head in his hands.

"Garrett looks and he sounds like an understanding man," she said. "But he doesn't understand. He doesn't understand Anna. And he doesn't understand Rachel. And they're both crumbling away. And I have to watch."

There was a long silence.

Grace got up. She pulled her chair around the side of the bed, next to his.

He sat back. "I've got no business here," he said.

"What?" she gasped.

"I shouldn't have come here," he told her.

"David . . ."

He stood up. "How can I help Rachel?" he asked. "How can I help Anna? I can't help them."

"Of course you can!" she cried.

"How?" he demanded. "I don't live here. I don't have any money. And," he added, "I don't know them. Either of them."

She stared at him.

"Even if you don't like Garrett," he said, "he's a better bet than I am."

"How can you say that!" Grace objected. "You're Rachel's father."

"No," he replied. "Her father is the one who looks after her."

"You're wrong," she said. "Garrett will never be a father. He's a manipulator. Haven't you heard what I've been saying? For Christ's sake!"

"Well, he's all she's got," David replied. "Because Anna chose to leave the father she had."

They stared at each other.

Then, down the corridor, they heard the heavy swinging doors open, and the sound of voices.

Sixteen

EVERYTHING WAS STILL.

The noise of the torrent had gone. The water flowed noise-lessly now, soft as a breath in the darkness. Anna was standing on the bank, her naked feet on the grass. Something like snow was falling. The ground was covered with the grainlike seeds of the poplar. The names of the Salicaceae were like incantations: balm of Gilead, *lasiocarpa, szechuanica, babylonica, pekinensis, thibetica. Alba* and *aurora.* Aspen, the whispering tree, the messenger of the gods, the crucifixion tree that trembled at its memories; the white poplar, sacred to Persephone; and the black poplar, perpetually weeping on the banks of the Eridanus, mourning the death of Phaëthon.

Under the black Lombardy poplar that she could see close to the gate, the glasshouses rose like ghosts in the night, barely con-taining the giants that pressed against the roof, the palm fronds spread like hands. Here by the entrance crowded the magnolia, all ashy pink opalescence, a crowd of luxurious heads, like flushed faces gathered together, pressing forward; white faces and pink throats, and the *delavayi* behind them, with glossier and darker leaves, and their six yellow petals that opened only at night, and faded the next day.

It was so long since she had been here. She looked around her-self for something to catch hold of, to remember. She walked toward the magnolia, but her feet passed through the snow-wash of seeds on the midnight grass without leaving any kind of trace.

He had been going to take her from here—from the little Cherwell dividing into two as it raced toward Christ Church Meadow—to other gardens, eight thousand feet high, unseen and unpictured and unpainted before. Wild gardens dominated by the lily, and by the rose and musk rose; wind-torn valleys in the mountains where, on the gravel shores below, were the tamarisk and meadow rue, and barberries with masses of red fruit, and mile upon mile of the silver-gray artemisia.

She had refused him, and now she would never find the way alone.

She wanted to give him all the paintings she had made in her mind. And now, time was short. She had to seek him out, and give him the thoughts that tied them together. She had sketched them over and over again, on margins of other paintings, in the flyleaves of books. All the lily family, spread over her paper, trailing down through his text: the lily of the valley, the snowdrop, the meadow saffron. The May lily, with its heart-shaped face; and the summer snowflake, exquisite, delicate, with the flower almost impossibly suspended on a green stem as thin as a strand of cotton. The fritillaries, the Oriental lantern-flowers that grew in the Magdalen Meadow in the spring, the only place in England where they grew so freely . . .

All the honeysuckles: the elder, the dog tree, the borewood, whose heartwood and roots were as hard as ebony, whose flowers tasted of muscat; the guelder rose, twelve feet tall, scarlet-leaved in the autumn, with rings of china white blooms.

The *Meconopsis,* the yellow poppy, so very beautiful, with its six-inch petals, spreading in the wild all the way from Tibet to Burma; the plant that died when it gave up its flower. An ancient, ancient species, the poppy family Papaveraceae, whose seeds were found mixed with grains of barley in twelfth-dynasty tombs; named daughters of the field by the Assyrians, and a sacred plant of the goddess Ceres to the Romans. Gardens of sleep to those who cultivated the opium. Gardens of death on Flanders Field.

And she would draw him all the roses that Wilson had brought home. Eighteen of them, and among them *Rosa helenae,* named for his wife; *Rosa murieliae,* named for his daughter; and *Rosa sino-wilsonii* for himself.

Rosa moyesii was her own favorite. Wilson had found it in Tatsienlu, and called it one of the most beautiful of roses, and she had found it once, growing in Boston in a public garden, and she had stopped, her hand to her throat, looking at the open, five-petaled flowers with their immense yellow centers, struck by the colors that ranged from darkest red to a delicate and soft cerise, and she had thought then of David, and wanted him. Wanted him, suddenly and passionately, just because she had seen a flower; a Tatsienlu rose in an American street.

Everywhere she went, he touched her. She couldn't look into a room with flowers in a vase, or see the lilies that James habitually put in the gallery, or pass a flower shop, without David's hand restraining her and turning her to look back at him. The rose family, of course, spread far and wide: in meadowsweet, whose frothy white flowers, on roadsides and in fields, smelled of musk and honey, and whose leaves smelled sharper, almost of vinegar. In the cloudberry, and raspberry and blackberry, all the rose's cousins; in wild strawberries, and agrimony, and in all the wild roses, and wild cherries and wild plums. In rowan and hawthorn, in medlar, and Juneberry, and whitebeam. He was everywhere, everywhere; wherever she turned.

She held out her hands.

The poplar still rained its soft, cotton-wrapped seeds on her. She let herself go, dropping down through time, her fingers fleetingly touching echoes of colors and shapes, faint traces of her own compositions; passing the river, and the trees, and sinking further down still, into the water of the greater river that came now to engulf her.

And, as she fell, she looked down to see that her still-open palms were full of the *moyesii* rose: blood red, and growing rapidly darker.

Seventeen

GRACE WALKED OUT OF the hospital, and crossed to Beacon Hill.

As she got to the other side of Grove, she looked back, once, at the curved white frontage of the hospital tower, standing out against the darkening night sky. Then, she walked on up the slope, staring down at the cobbled road and pavement. At the corner, she stopped again, breathing heavily.

It was still warm. Hot, even. She waited for the dizziness and the stitch in her shoulder to subside. Over the other side of the hill, she could hear the ever-present rumble of traffic. But here it was quiet, thank God. Only the wheezing drone of air conditioners, and, from somewhere above her, music. She leaned on the wall of the corner house, and looked up Revere Street.

David had insisted upon seeing the neurosurgeon. She had been surprised at David's immovability: literal immovability. He had stood by the nurses' station and waited, his hands in his pockets and his face blank.

"He'll find us," Grace had urged him. "Come and stand near Anna. You can see her. They'll let us get closer to her in a minute."

"I hate the noise in there," he'd muttered.

"What noise?" she'd asked. She had long since ceased to hear the ICU.

Even when Dr. Coram came, David would not sit down.

"What's happening?" he asked, without any preamble.

"There's a secondary bleed," the surgeon said. "And a paren-chymal injury."

"A what?" Grace said.

"A contusion in the brain itself."

"How bad?" David said.

Dr. Coram looked at him, and at the rigid, unmoving way that he was standing. "It's early days."

"It's been fifty-two hours," Grace said. "She hasn't opened her eyes. She hasn't moved since the ventilator."

"We have a CT scan," the surgeon replied.

"And?" David demanded. "What else?"

"They do tests all the time," Grace murmured to him. She was holding his arm. It felt like stone.

"The GCS shows us the level of consciousness and the degree of dysfunction," Dr. Coram explained. "It's a test for coma. A high score would be fifteen—that would be a relatively mild injury . . ."

"What is Anna's score?" David asked.

The surgeon looked first at Grace, and then at David. "These are early tests," he repeated. "Only one of those at our disposal. They test verbal responses, motor responses . . ."

"What is Anna's score?" David insisted.

"Nine."

Grace took a huge intake of breath.

"Nine," David repeated. "That's . . . that's nothing. No re-sponse."

"Brain injury changes almost from minute to minute," Dr. Coram told him. "Hour to hour."

"But to take her in for a second operation," David said. "That's not so good. That's an emergency."

"Everything we do here just now is urgent."

"A second bleed into a bruised brain," David murmured. He seemed to be thinking out loud, his eyes fixed on the physician.

"It's a blunt head trauma," the man told them. "She hit the wheel, the dashboard."

"What are the chances?" David asked.

Grace gripped him harder. This was a question she didn't want answered. She didn't want to hear. "We'll go sit with her," she urged.

The surgeon put his hand on David's shoulder. "We'll see how she gets through the next couple of days."

"The chances," David repeated. "Please."

Dr. Coram's hand dropped. "I'm not a gambling man," he said. "I don't give odds, Mr. Mortimer."

When Grace got to Garrett's door, it opened before she had a chance to ring. She saw at once that Garrett was standing in the hallway, and Rachel was on the stairs, taking two steps up and two down again. When she saw her grandmother, she stepped up to the door, and then back to the stairs.

"You're late," Garrett said. "She's been anxious."

"OK," Grace said. She held out her hand. "Come on then, honey."

"It's time," Rachel said. "It's nine-sixteen."

"I know that," Grace admitted. "Let's go." The child's hand in hers was loose, the fingers uncurled. "You've got everything?"

"Where is David?" Garrett asked.

"He's with Anna."

"She's back from surgery?"

"Yes," Grace said.

"What did the doctor say?"

Rachel was repeating her two-step on the pavement, up and down the curb. Distracted, Grace glanced up at the man in the doorway. "I gave David my phone," she said. "Call him. Or go down."

"I can't do that," Garrett said. "The reception is tonight. I'm late already by an hour."

She stared at him. It was a second or two before she found she could speak. "You mean to say it's going ahead?" she asked.

"Of course it is," he told her.

"Tonight?"

"Anna has worked for this all year."

"You couldn't make it another day?"

"The invitations were all sent out."

"Oh, right," she said. She started to laugh, mirthlessly but steadily. The absurdity of it overtook the exasperation.

"What do you want me to do?" he asked. "Go down there and bolt the doors, and turn everyone away? There are two hundred people coming."

"Yes," she said. "Turn them away. Let's see, what could you say? 'The artist is indisposed.' Try that."

"Anna set this date," he said. "It's what she wanted."

Grace looked at him in astonishment for a few seconds longer. "I've got to go," she said at last.

"It's what she wanted," he repeated.

"Have a wonderful night," she said.

They started down the street.

All the way to Downtown Crossing, Grace's heart kept up the almost visible patter in her chest. She put her hand to her skin once or twice, pressing her fingertips to the depressions between her ribs just under the clavicle, and she kept it there as they stepped down to the T platform, and waited for the train.

When it came, it was, miraculously, half-empty. She subsided gratefully into a seat, with Rachel beside her. After a while, as the T accelerated, she glanced at her granddaughter's face, and saw her watching the wires, walls, and road signs beyond the window, head tipped very slightly to one side. Rachel would blink as walls ended and began again, and as streetlights flashed for a second and were gone. She took no notice at all of the man opposite them, who had fallen asleep with a newspaper in his hand, whose pages were ticking back and forth with the motion of the rail.

They got off at Forest Hills and walked along the street that was separated from the Arborway by a steel fence. Anna's house stood on Devonshire, facing the traffic across a phalanx of lime trees:

gray-painted board with tall, dusty windows. A few kids played in the street, or slumped on the porches. Through open windows came the blue glare of TV's.

As Grace walked up Anna's porch steps, her neighbor came out, a plastic bag of rubbish in one hand. The woman stopped as she saw the two of them on the step.

"Grace," she called. "Is it true?"

Grace looked across at her. Anna's neighbor, Jen, was young. She had two children, and a husband who worked abroad. They had talked many times on nights like these, watching the bikes in the road, the trees gently moving, the continual drone of cars beyond.

Jen leaned now on her rail, holding out her hand. "Grace ..."

"Inside," Rachel said. She was tapping the lock with her fingers. Rhythm. Traffic, doorstep, rattle of the key in Grace's hand. Step, rattle, tap.

Grace put the key in the lock, but couldn't make it turn. All the while Rachel kept up the rhythm. She shuffled from side to side, concentrating on the door, fingers tapping.

Before Grace knew it, Jen's hand was on her shoulder.

"I can't work the damn key here," Grace said.

"Give it to me," Jen told her. She opened the door, let Rachel go ahead, and put her arm around Grace's waist. In the darkness of the doorway, Grace leaned on her, and wept hard: a twisting, deep, physical exertion.

"I've been waiting all day," Jen said. "Someone in the store said they were in an accident."

Grace leaned against the hallway wall.

Rachel was at the foot of the stairs, waiting.

"Honey," Grace said to her granddaughter, "tonight, I have to help you wash."

"My shower," Rachel said.

"Not tonight," Grace told her. "Because of your arm." She felt for the light, but missed the switch. It didn't seem to matter. She stood with one foot across the doorway, one foot in the hall, breathing slowly, as if through some sort of mask, such was the effort.

"What happened?" Jen whispered.

"They were on ninety-three. A truck came into them from the back."

"And Anna . . . ?"

"She's still unconscious. She's got a head injury."

"My God," Jen breathed. "Oh, Lord."

"Grandma," Rachel said. "My shower."

"You can't put your arm in the shower," Grace repeated quietly. "We have to work something out, OK? For your cast. Let me think a minute."

"We can take it off."

"You can't take a cast off," Grace said. "There's a break in your arm. It has to heal, OK? Remember? We looked at the pictures."

It seemed weeks ago that they had stood together and gazed at the fracture showing on the X ray. Weeks, months. Another life. It had only been this morning.

"I'm going to come and help you," Grace said. She tried to work it out. "OK, let's see, you could stand in the shower and wash, but not let water get to the cast," she explained. "And you have to take your soap in one hand, Rachel. One hand, all right? I'll come and help you."

"No," Rachel said. She was halfway up the stairs, running full tilt.

Slowly, Grace went through to the kitchen. The whiteness of chairs and the table, luminous like ghosts. A jar in the center of the scrubbed oak tabletop. In the confined space, the cut climbing roses imprinted their scent on the room, soaking the shadows.

"I'll check on her," Jen murmured. "Sit down. I'll put on the light and make you some tea."

"No," Grace told her. "Leave the light, dear. I've been seeing white light in that hospital for so long. The dark is nice."

They stood for a second, listening to Rachel's footsteps above. Grace knew what her granddaughter was doing. Rachel was figuring spaces. It happened every time something new came into the house. She would measure the room in steps, almost as if she were checking how much space were left. She would do it tonight, because of the cast, and the way it threw her, and disturbed her pattern. To watch her engaged in the silent measuring would be to witness a private, meticulous dance.

"What can I do?" Jen asked.

Grace took out a tissue, and blew her nose. "Oh, Jen. I just need to sleep. That's all."

"You want me to take care of Rachel?"

The shadows were intimate: a meeting of faces and hands. The younger woman's warmth, the smell of other children. "We'll be fine," Grace said. "Really."

"You'll call over, phone me," Jen said. "If there's anything to-night . . ."

"Yes."

"I'll get some groceries for you tomorrow?"

"Thank you."

Just one hand left, pressing hers now in the silence.

"Go on," Grace urged.

"I'll come by in the morning . . ."

"OK," Grace said. "OK."

The house smelled stuffy, overcooked. Grace listened to the sound of Jen opening her own front door, and the slam of the screen. Then, she pushed open the windows, looked at the square of grass in the backyard, the red swing, and the jungle gym, their colors just glimmers in the half-light. She turned back and went through the ground floor of the house, opening each window, let-ting in the drizzle of night air and the smell of the street. In the long room at the back, she switched on the lamp and sank down to the blissful respite of the couch.

On the opposite wall was a painting that Anna had done when she first came to Boston. When her colors were still blazing. It was a painting of the famous red corrugated iron wall by the dock at Rockport, with dozens of fishing floats: blue and white, red, green, terra-cotta, yellow, set against the red, with a mid-blue sky hanging over the tile roof above. Grace looked at it hard. She reached into her bag and found the cigarettes, and lit one, and her heart sank back again to a sluggish murmur. She closed her eyes.

Her parents had first brought her to Rockport. They would come down in the fall, when the worst of the crowds were gone. It was where her father had been brought up as a boy, and they rented a cottage every year, right up until the fogs rolled in off the Atlantic. He liked those long gray twilights of the year; evenings on the beach watching the indigo color in the sea. It was here that she herself had begun to draw: cartoon men in cartoon boats; the faces in the stores; white spits of sand, and brown-laced rock; and her father's hands and face—his fist around a cup of coffee; the set of his mouth while he concentrated. And the lobsters at Pete's Café. Looking into the murky holding tank, watching the claws scuttling on the glass. She used to draw them, fascinated by their elongation, their primeval shape and Day-Glo bodies when they were served up on the plates.

When she herself had grown up, she had come to Boston to work, on no more than a whim. It was only to be a summer. A fall. A winter. Perhaps a spring. No more than a year. She had felt claustrophobic in her hometown, with its single store and fill-ing station, the two hand pumps on the single street, the Baptist church, the long ride up to Springfield past flat hilltop fields, green square and gold square, green square and gold square, in drowsy repetition; tired even of the blood-chill threat of bears on the slopes below, in the unmanaged tiers of Appalachian trees, and of the curiously still meadow at night above the house. Tired perhaps of the summer trek to the coast. She had wanted to be in the city through four seasons; that was the single scope of her ambition. She had never counted on meeting a married man when she was eighteen. Or falling deeply in love with him, a love that was un-returned for more than ten years. Last of all, she had not foreseen—

the reckless stupidity of passion—getting pregnant by him. Or losing her child's father back to his wife.

She had sold the Deerfield house when her parents died. It was, above everything else, the thing that she regretted. More so even than Anna's father's absence, or her own naïveté, or at being the recipient of the coldly charitable check through the door every month. She had missed that old house like hell. Its icy washroom with a tin jug and bowl and a wickerwork table that never stood straight, and the blue rug on the floor as you came in the door, that particular blue, a shade of blue almost gray. Her father had died when Anna was six, never having brought himself to terms with Grace's unmarried life, or the fact that she lived in the Ogunquit house, neither mistress nor wife, but something else. Driftwood, maybe. Cleanly polished and put on a mantel to look at. Not truly belonging there, or anywhere.

She told herself that she was too independent to go back home, and bear the sidelong looks. Sometimes, to herself, deep in the night when she gazed into darkness, her conscience would whisper to her that perhaps she was ashamed. But, in truth, it was neither independence nor shame. It was her father's sadness for her that she couldn't bear.

He was eighty-two when he died. After falling down in the meadow one late September afternoon, trying to cut a sapling by hand, he had complained of the pain in his back. He wrote her that it irritated him not to be able to get on the truck and haul out the stumps; that one of the youngsters from the village had had to come up and that he had been forced to watch him do his work. Six weeks later, he died in the county hospital of a cancer in the spine. She went to the house and took away the rug, and the tin jug and bowl, and some of his pictures and photos, and she had stood looking at the old school drawings in the outhouse, the giraffe and cow and drop-eared dog, and at his immovable white 1938 convertible with the torn black cloth roof.

She dreamed sometimes of the house now. She would be young—curiously young when her father was young. Like brother and sister, they would stand on the outhouse step next to the convertible. Sometimes it would be summer. Sometimes the snow would be falling, and Anna running through it, arms outstretched.

She and Anna had walked down to the Ogunquit beach a week after Anna came back from England.

It was early in the morning; too early for the crowds. They sat on the jetty and looked at the sea. Nothing had been said until that moment, and there was suddenly no introduction, no small talk. The question flew into Grace's head, and straight out of her mouth.

"How many weeks?" Grace had asked.

Anna was taking little stones from the wood platform, little pieces of grit and gravel, and throwing them into the sea. She had a palmful of them. She showed no reaction: no surprise, no denial.

"Sixteen," she said. The stones made lazy circles where they had fallen, and the circles, equally lazily, were pulled out of shape by the tide. Waves washed the jetty, little waves making a hushing sound.

"What is it that you want to do?" Grace asked.

"I don't know."

"Did you make a decision?"

"No."

They watched the first tourist boat of the day go out just beyond the shore, tacking up and down parallel to the beach.

"I wanted to be home more than anything else," Anna told her.

Grace was having trouble. She had fisted her free hand and tucked it under her leg, so that the knuckles actually hurt against the wood, just to stop her saying something she might regret. But it came out anyway.

"Of all the things I didn't want for you," she said, "it was to be like me."

Anna shifted away from her, slightly raising her head.

"What did David say?"

"I didn't tell him," Anna murmured.

"You ...?" Grace raised her eyes to heaven. "Oh, Lord God

almighty. You came all this way, and you never told him? You ran out on him? Are you crazy?"

The two women had stared at each other.

"Do you know what?" Anna had demanded. "Look at this family."

"What family? Ours?"

"Yes."

"But, Anna," she said, "who are you talking about? Your grand-parents?"

Anna had pouted like a child, and looked away.

"There couldn't be a more ordinary couple ..."

"I don't mean them."

"Who, then?"

Anna shook her head.

"Is it David?"

"No."

"Something about his family?" Grace asked. "What did they say to you?"

A long, breathy hiss escaped Anna; a kind of laugh.

"What did they say?" Grace insisted.

"Nothing," Anna replied.

"I thought you liked his sister."

"I do."

"Well, who?"

"Forget it," Anna had said.

Grace looked at her. "Something in David's family drove you away," she said.

"No," Anna told her. "Not exactly," she murmured.

"Something you saw in David?"

Silence. Grace took Anna's hand and stroked it. "Remoteness," Anna murmured. "I'm afraid he'll ... draw back. Disappear."

"So you did it first?" Grace said. She shook her head. "Sure, that makes a whole lot of sense."

"I don't know," Anna told her, "I can't think."

"Well, you can't go on not thinking."

Anna's mouth wavered. Rachel had just the same expression now, when frustrated or exasperated.

"You gave up your studies," Grace said. "We have to find a way around that. Your father wanted an education for you."

"What did he care?" Anna said.

Grace had to take a deep, deep breath. "He left you well provided for," she said. "He was proud of you."

"Yeah, right," Anna murmured. "So he told me on Christmas cards."

Grace had tried. She had tried so hard. When first pregnant, she had visited him in the offices where he worked. It was a bank. He was director of something. She saw the brass sign on his door in her mind's eye. He had been appalled at the news. In that first minute, she had lost the sweet-natured man who had shared her bed for months, and found him replaced by a cold-faced and dutiful stranger, who respected her decision to keep her child, but told her emphatically that he would never see his offspring. He had a reputation to keep up. He had a large family to maintain. A house in the Hamptons. A condominium in Florida. A house in Grenada. He had listed them for her, all these things he could lose, while she listened in dazed horror. He had promised her money for secrecy.

What do you do, faced with this?

Go back out into the street and walk right down to the church underneath the Hancock Tower, and stare at the crucifix outside the door. The church where he devoutly worshiped every day. Turn away, with the taste of dust in your throat, and a fierce pain burning.

She sighed to herself as she looked at Anna. The sun was getting higher. The first families were coming onto the beach below them.

"Anna," Grace said, at last. "You have to tell David about this. That's the first thing you have to do."

"Why?" Anna said. "So he can run a mile? So I take him to court for child support?"

Grace paused only a second. "Is he going to run a mile?"

"Maybe."

"He'd really do that? He'd really run a mile?"

Anna threw down the gravel, and wiped her hands on her dress. "I don't know."

"My God!" Grace had exclaimed. "How much longer are you going to stick your head in the sand? What's the matter with you?"

Anna had stood up. "I'm pregnant!" she'd cried. "And I don't know what to do!"

Still sitting, Grace had gazed up at her. Then, she scrambled to her feet. Anna had begun walking back; Grace ran after her, and grabbed her by the arm, and turned Anna around to face her.

"Why did you come home?" she asked.

Anna didn't reply.

"Did you come to hear me tell you it's OK?" Grace demanded. "Because I'm not going to tell you that. Do you understand? It's not OK."

"Fine," Anna said.

"Oh, for Christ's sake, don't give me all that shit," Grace exclaimed.

"I'll go somewhere," Anna said. "Then you won't have to watch me. And I won't have to listen to you, either."

"Anna, Anna, please ..."

"I'll just go somewhere ..."

"Stop it," Grace warned. "Anna! This isn't a game."

"Oh, I know that," Anna retorted. "I'm not like you, and this isn't a duplicate of your life. Because I'm not doing what you did. I'm not going to be abandoned. To see his face when I tell him. To see him slowly vanish from me." She almost spat the last sentence out.

Grace looked at her aghast.

Anna walked quickly away. Grace watched her, the set of her shoulders, the thin body in the blue dress.

She started to run. After a few moments, she caught up with Anna. She looked into her daughter's face—this beautiful, clever daughter she had raised—and saw the utter confusion there. "Don't be alone," she said. "I love you so."

Anna's face crumpled. Grace took out a tissue, and wiped

Anna's face. Just like she used to do when she was a toddler. And Anna meekly allowed it, tears pouring down, hands hanging by her sides.

Upstairs, now, Grace heard the water running.

She could hear Rachel's voice. Whether it was a song, or whether her granddaughter was calling her, she couldn't tell. For a moment, the nineteen-year-old Anna, so thin in the blue dress, swept back into the room and into her embrace, her head on her mother's shoulder. She could still feel Anna's hand in hers, and she saw the bitten quick of the fingers.

She had held that hand today, and yesterday.

She smoothed her fingers over her own face now, drawing the skin tight over her cheekbones. Then, she got up from the couch.

"Rachel?" she called. "Rachel . . . ?"

She took one more long look at the exuberant painting on the wall in front of her; then, she walked out into the hall, and started, slowly, up the stairs.

Eighteen

DAVID WAS ASLEEP WHEN the nurse touched his shoulder.

He woke, disoriented and dry-mouthed, in the corridor; and realized, as he looked up at her, that he must have been slumped at an awkward angle. His neck cramped; he put his hand to it with a little grunt of pain.

"How are you doing?" the woman asked.

"I'm cold," he said.

He wondered how it could be true; the hospital was almost too warm. He looked at his watch. It was two A.M. He still had his jacket wrapped around him.

"You want some coffee?"

He smiled at her. "Yes . . . thank you."

"You can go in to her," she said, softly. "You can sit with her." She was nodding at him encouragingly. They had all seen him, he supposed, after Grace had gone.

He had stood uncertainly for a long time near the nurses' station, pacing up and down. Then, he had suddenly walked away, gone down in the elevator, got out at the ground floor, and found himself in the reception area that looked out onto the ambulance circle where he and James had first seen Grace. It was deserted, the white lights blazing outside at regular intervals along the sloping drive. He wanted to go home. He wanted to run.

With an effort, he turned away from the doors, and walked down a corridor, and found himself at a junction of several others; in the corner was a vending machine. He put in the little change he had, and took out a can of soda and stood with the ice-cold surface pressed to his face. He saw that, in the wastebasket next to the machine, there was a sheaf of papers and leaflets. *The Heritage of New England,* read one. *Writers and Thinkers, The Concord Circle, The Berkshires, The Hartford Colony.* He stared at the brochures, trying to make sense of the names. Above the soda machine was a wall poster. *The Isabella Gardner Museum, Tapestry Room open September to May,* he read. He stared at the Venetian-style courtyard in the picture. He picked up one of the tourist pamphlets and turned it curiously. *Naumkeag . . . Mission House . . . Herbarium, daylilies, shrubs, and wildflowers, Berkshire Botanical Garden . . .*

He had dropped the leaflet, and then the can, unopened, into the wastebasket, and walked back to the elevator.

He stood up now. The nurse was still at his side. They walked to the door of the ICU. "You can talk to her, you know," she murmured.

He looked everywhere but at the bed. Opposite him were the three women who kept watch over the teenage boy, like a trio of ghosts. They caught his glance, but they were only reflections of themselves, fighting with the unreality, nurturing the hope that they were about to wake from the dream. He could see it in their stillness and suspension. As if they were all holding their breath interminably, waiting for the moment that would flex them back into their lives.

He gave them a nod. He knew that feeling. They looked back to the boy.

For the first time, he looked at Anna.

Arc-shaped scar above one eyebrow. And her eyes were half open, mere blanks, filled with mucuslike tears. The nurse stopped to wipe them, and checked the monitors.

Arc-shaped scar over one eyebrow.

Tears.

The nurse came around to his side of the bed. "Sit here," she urged gently. "It's all right."

"But she's awake."

"No," the woman murmured. "But talk. Hold her hand. It's OK," she repeated.

He did as he was told; sat down, breath coming in little shallow drafts.

"Why didn't you talk to her?" Sara had asked, eleven years ago.

"I did," he had replied. "I tried."

"Anna," he said now.

Now Sara is following him along New Building, under the carved hyena, panther, griffin, and Anger. The stone carved figure of Anger.

"Anna," he said. "Anna." He touched the back of her hand with his fingertip. "Anna, it's David."

He had met Sara at the Oxford station.

It was six months after their mother had died. She had come for a visit.

She got down out of the train and threw herself into his arms. "I'm so excited," she said. It was a bright afternoon. He had arranged with Anna that Sara could stay with her in her room. The blackthorn was in bloom in the parks; the cherries were just beginning to show. Somehow he had equated this, in his head, with a change in Anna's attitude. All the misunderstandings of the previous few weeks would blow over. The cold would be a memory. But all the time, as he had waited on the platform for Sara's train to arrive, the gnawing unease in the pit of his stomach had grown. Anna had promised that she would meet him at twelve-fifteen.

It got to be twelve-thirty. The train was late. So was Anna.

The train came.

Anna did not.

After dropping him from her bear hug, Sara had immediately started to rifle through her shoulder bag, all the while grinning up at him. "Here," she said, pushing a packet into his grasp. "Don't say anything, it wasn't my choice. He told me to bring them. All the way! I ask you! But you know what he's like."

David had peered down into the brown paper bag. It was full of apples; last year's apples, carefully preserved by his father over that winter; russets, wrinkled and sweet-smelling.

He'd smiled sadly. His father never wrote a letter. The gift of the apples was the best he could do; a greeting from the depths of his slow preoccupations.

"Where's Anna?" Sara asked.

"I don't know," he told her.

"Is she going to meet us?"

"I don't know," he said. "I think I got it wrong."

He'd walked her along Broad. "This is the Sheldonian," he told her. "Old Bodleian Library. Catte Street . . ."

"Stop running," she begged. "Stop the guided tour. I can't hear what you're on about."

"I'm not running, I'm walking fast."

"You can have my bag then, it's killing me."

As they stopped and she handed the bag over, she suddenly saw the expression on his face. "What's the matter?" she asked.

"Nothing. It's a misunderstanding."

It was a Saturday. Crowds filled the streets. Still, he felt totally removed from the people around them. He and Sara had strayed into some other reality. He was not here, and Sara was not here. As he took the bag, he thought of them in years past, getting off the same school bus at the bottom of the hill in the village, he taking Sara's bag then, a smaller Sara running ahead of him along the lane, or careering from side to side on her bike, or dancing in circles with the dog from the house on the corner, the spaniel. Years collapsed in on themselves. Holding Sara's hand as she leaned out over the stream; finding her alone in the orchard at the bottom of the wood, cross-legged under an apple tree, obliviously chewing on a piece of grass.

"Don't tell me nothing's wrong," Sara was saying. "Have you had an argument with Anna?"

He didn't want to walk on. He clung, for a few seconds, to the long-ago image of Sara in his head.

"David," Sara had urged, pulling on his sleeve.

"No," he told her. "No argument."

"A fight?"

"Of course we bloody haven't."

They'd got to the High, and Roxburgh's was facing them. As they crossed the street toward it, he had a sudden piercing conviction that Anna was gone. He almost tripped over the curb in a blind panic.

"Wait," Sara begged. "Wait."

They reached Anna's rooms. "Stay here," he told her, leaving her at the foot of the stairs. His heart was pounding by now. It seemed to be right in his throat, choking him.

Two steps at a time, he reached Anna's landing. A girl was walking along it, another American girl, and he caught her by the arm. It was someone that he had once or twice seen Anna talking to. "Is Anna here?" he asked.

She had shrugged, disengaging her arm with a frown.

"Anna Russell," he said.

"How would I know?"

He went to the door, and knocked. There was no answer. He tried it. Locked. "Anna," he shouted, face pressed to the door.

The next door along opened. This girl he thought he knew. She was from New York. An Irish name. Caitlin. Or Colleen . . .

"David?" she asked.

"Have you seen Anna?" he said.

"Are you David?" she asked, evidently not remembering him.

"Why?" he said.

The girl rolled her eyes. "Look, what's your name?"

"David Mortimer," he told her.

"Just a minute," she said.

She went into her room, and came out again, holding an envelope. It had his name written on the front.

"She left you this," the girl said.

He stared at the envelope, then back at her. "Where is she?" he demanded.

"Listen," she said, "I don't know anything, believe me."

He tore it open.

David,
I've got to go home. I'm sorry. I will write to you.
Anna

He stared at the girl in the doorway.

"When did she give you this?"

"This morning."

"When this morning?"

"Early. Before seven."

Sara was coming up the stairs, bumping her bag against her leg. He glanced at her once, then back at the girl.

"Did she say where she was going?" he asked.

"No."

"She must have done!"

"She said nothing to me. The first I know, she's giving me that." And she nodded at the paper in his hand.

"Was she going home?"

"I don't know," the girl answered. "What does the letter say?"

He took a step toward her, the letter in his fist, his hands shaking, the paper fluttering. "But she must have said something to you," he said. "She must have said she was getting a train, or going to a hotel, or visiting somewhere ..."

The girl stepped back defensively. "There's no use getting angry with me," she retorted.

Sara was at his shoulder. "What is it?" she asked.

"I'm not getting angry," David said, "I just want to know where she is."

Sara was trying to take the letter from his grasp.

"How am I supposed to know?" the girl snapped. "You're the one with the letter."

"But she must have said something to you!"

"Look," the girl replied, "I know nothing about it, OK? All I know is she knocks at the door at the crack of dawn, and she gives me this." And she indicated the letter with a flourish of her hand.

"David," Sara said. "Come downstairs."

"I'm just asking a simple question," he said. "She lives next door to her, she lives next door . . ."

"I know," Sara said. She was pulling on his shoulder, trying to turn him around.

"It's a simple question . . ."

"Come downstairs," Sara said. She pushed and pulled him along the corridor. They went down the stone steps, back to the ground floor. Sara took the letter. She read it, then folded it silently, and put it in her pocket.

"Sit down," she said.

"No."

"Walk, then," she cajoled. "Come on. Walk."

They went out, and along the street, and over the bridge.

"We'll get a cup of tea," Sara said. "Where is a good place? Show me."

They sat somewhere. Not Roxburgh's.

For a long time he stared down at the cup of tea, then, with a sudden thought, looked up at his sister.

"Which airport would a flight to Boston go from?" he asked her.

"It doesn't matter," she said. "Because you're not following her."

"Is it Gatwick?"

She held his hand. "David," she said, "it's half past one in the afternoon now. She left at seven."

"It won't have gone yet," he said.

"Even if that were true now," she pointed out to him, "it wouldn't be by the time you got to the airport. It would take you hours by train. Even by car it would take too long." She gripped his fingers tightly. "It can't be done," she whispered softly. "She's gone."

"It's a mistake," he said.

"Mistake?"

"She didn't understand."

Sara frowned. "Understand what?"

"It wouldn't have mattered," he said. "We could wait. She could have gone back at the end of the year. China doesn't matter. I could have come to Boston. You could work that out, couldn't you?"

She shifted her chair closer to him. "What's all this about?" she said.

"I wanted to be with her," he said. "After her course finished here."

Sara closed her eyes briefly. "Oh, David."

"What?" he said. "What's wrong with that?"

"You've only known each other a few weeks!"

"Five months," he said. "We've known each other five months."

"Even so."

He stared at her. "It wasn't a joke," he said.

"I know."

"Then what the hell are you smiling about?"

She shook her head. "It's you," she said. "Just obliviously plowing ahead with your pet scheme."

"What are you talking about?" he demanded.

"Look," she replied, "what did you ask Anna to do?"

"Just be together. Maybe go to China."

"China?" Sara repeated. "And what did she say?"

"She . . ." He stopped.

"You fenced her in," she told him.

"I didn't," he said.

"So she said yes?" Sara asked. "She agreed?"

"Not exactly," he told her. "She didn't say no."

"But . . ."

"She asked me not to keep talking about it, so I didn't. I stopped."

"OK," Sara said. "So then what?"

He shrugged. "We talked about what we would do at the end of this year," he said.

"And what's all this about China?"

He looked away from her, back to the nearly empty cup. "It's a book," he said. "I wanted to write a book."

"About what, exactly?"

"Someone who went there. A botanist. A plant collector." She was watching him intently. "It was just an idea," he muttered.

"And you suggested that Anna go with you?"

"Of course."

"After you finished at Oxford."

"Yes."

"And she finished at Harvard."

"Yes. Kind of."

"And *she* said . . . ?"

He looked away, at the people around them. Families. Other students. Tourists.

"David," Sara prompted. "What did she say to you about this trip?"

"She didn't want to go," he murmured.

Sara sat back in her seat. She looked at him with pity; glancing up from the table, he caught her expression.

"Everything was all right," he said. "I don't know what went wrong."

Sara said nothing for some time. She drank the last of her tea, and then gazed out of the window. Eventually, she looked back at him, and gave him a small smile. "You aren't Dad," she said, finally. "But you can get detached—off in your own little world. That's when you remind me of him."

He shook his head, mouth clamped shut in a defensive grimace.

Sara began to talk, almost as if to herself, in a musing voice. "Have you any idea what it's been like at home, since Mum died?" she said. "I can talk to Dad, and he doesn't listen. He's somewhere else in his head. He's thinking about some job he's got organized. Do you know what it was last week, do you know what the sole topic of conversation was?" She shook her head, half smiling, half grimacing. "Somebody's bloody lawn mower! He's repairing a lawn mower, and he was out in the garden shed every night last week. And I can't get two words out of him, except to talk about this bloody mower, and do you know what?" she demanded, leaning now on the table, and pointing at him. "Even if I could, even if I could make him see what I was talking about, even if he tried to be interested, it would all be for nothing."

"Why?" David asked.

"Because he doesn't understand," she replied. "If I get upset about *anything,* he stares at me as if I've grown another head. I feel like I'm living alone."

David looked down. "Anna wasn't alone," he muttered.

Sara sighed. "And I suppose you talked and talked at her about this book," she said, "when you already guessed she was feeling something else?" She put her hand over his. "Am I close?" she murmured.

David pushed his cup away, and stared at the tabletop.

Later that week, after Sara had gone, he went to Magdalen Chapel.

Near the door was a blue notice board, where visitors pinned little pieces of paper. They wrote down names and prayers. Hopes and memorials.

He had found himself staring at the messages, while in the screened-off chapel beyond, a single voice read and reread a passage from the New Testament, practicing for the service the next day.

He had to lean down to read the messages in the gloom, with only the faint ochre lights above the board, and the blue reflection from the Nativity Window.

After a while, he had written his own message, and pinned it to the board.

It was just Anna's name.

He had gone back week after week, to make sure that it was still there.

Nineteen

THE WOMAN IN THE red Donna Karan dress pressed James's hand tightly. He smiled at her. The last of the clients were leaving; the champagne bottles were empty. "I think it's what she would have wanted," he said.

"Of course it is," the woman told him.

He looked over her shoulder as she took her coat from her husband, at the display behind her. James had counted eight red dots. Eight pieces sold.

"How long, do you think," the woman asked him, her hand returning to press his forearm, "before Anna begins work again?"

"I can't say."

"But soon." She smiled. "As the injury isn't too severe."

"Absolutely," he lied.

"She'll be thrilled with tonight."

"She will indeed."

"And you have another planned?"

"In New York."

The woman was rearranging her hair in the reflection of the glass door. "Well, y'know, you have to get right back again," she said. "I had an accident myself. I broke a bone in my wrist." And she held the wrist up, obligingly, for him to see. "Here," she demonstrated. "Two little hairline fractures, but the fuss! You must get right over it. You must tell Anna to ignore it, you know."

"I will," he murmured.

They were almost at the door. It opened, and let a wash of hot air into the cooled gallery. The woman turned on the step, and held out her hand. He pressed it to his lips. She gave him an intimate glance, and walked off down the street, her husband two steps behind her.

On another hot evening like this, five years ago, he had knocked on Anna's door for the first time.

They had made the arrangement a few days before, but she had forgotten that he was coming.

She answered the intercom, but silence met his name.

"James Garrett," he had repeated.

"Oh!" she said. "Well . . . you'd better come up."

The first thing he noticed in the three-room apartment was the child. She was running everywhere, weaving about the room. Anna Russell was standing in the center, under the open skylights which formed half the ceiling; he could see the reflection of her as he glanced upward. She looked smaller than she had in Quincy Market, dwarfed by the scale of the loft space. She wore a blue T-shirt, stained with pastels; a pair of jeans; her feet were bare. Behind her, a large sugar cane paper sheet had been primed, and washed with diluted inks.

"I'm sorry," she said. "I forgot you were coming. What time is it?"

"Just after eight."

The little girl stopped; then she tilted her head to one side and back again, lifting her arms.

"This is my daughter Rachel," Anna said.

"Hello, Rachel," he said.

Anna wiped her hands on the seams of her jeans, and picked Rachel up. "Please sit down," she said. "I'll be back in a second."

"May I look around?" he asked.

"If you like," she said, over her shoulder.

He watched her go, then walked to the kitchen, and put his bottle of red wine down on the counter.

There were close to thirty paintings leaning haphazardly against the walls. He looked at each one, slowly, appreciatively. Most were acrylics, or mixed media. All were abstracts. He went to the easel, and considered the latest work; there was a photograph pinned to the top left-hand corner: Rachel running through a fountain. He recognized Frog Pond from the Common. Sketches were stapled together alongside the photo: angles of light on the water. On one, he saw the blotchy imprint of Rachel's palm in green paint.

He turned, and looked more closely at the room.

The half under the skylights was Anna's working space: there was a plan chest in the center, on which her paints were assembled; paints, and a jumble of magazines, and glass pots, and the discarded nubs of pastels, worn down to the last speck in their paper wrappers.

In the other half of the room was a large red couch, and a red rug over the stripped floorboards. Bookshelves lined one wall, and a TV sat in the far corner, with a small CD player. Dominating the whole of this area, however, was the painting on the wall; not an abstract this time, but a map of the world. Each country was delineated in a different color or shade; rivers snaked luridly across continents; jungles swarmed over Asia and South America. A childish hand had built the bridges of San Francisco, and London, and Paris, and New York in meticulous detail.

From the bathroom, he could hear Anna singing some repetitive refrain to her daughter.

He opened the bottom drawer of the plan chest, and saw pencil drawings, a contrast to the abstracts around him. They were minutely observed studies of leaves and blossom. He bent down and saw their names written in calligraphic script: lacebark, mountain ribbonwood, paper mulberry, Osage orange. He stared for a moment or two at the representation of the common fig, *Ficus carica*.

The fruit was shown cut in half, the outer green flesh concealing the heavily seeded interior, the seeds radiating from the center, pink against the outer rim of pale yellow, like a pursed mouth.

Anna came back into the room, Rachel hooked up onto one hip, now with a towel in her grasp.

"I hope you don't mind," he said.

"No," she replied. But she had flushed, and seemed embarrassed.

"Are they botanical drawings?" he asked.

"Not quite."

"Recent?"

"No," she said. She came and closed the drawer.

"I rather like that sort of thing," he said. "Do you know a book called *Women of Flowers*?"

"No," she murmured.

"The Victorian plant illustrators . . . and Walter Hood Fitch?"

"Yes," she said. "I know Fitch."

Rachel was observing him silently. He was taken aback, for a moment, by the flatness in her expression.

He changed the subject. "Did you sell much in Quincy?" he asked.

She smiled. "Two."

"And you're there every month?"

"Yes."

"Would two be an average day?"

"No," she said. "Two is a good day." She shrugged.

"How long have you been selling there?"

"Not long," she said. "I just moved six months ago, from Ogunquit."

He looked from her to the child. There was quite a contrast: the little girl looked heavy and was fair; her mother was slight, red-haired, and the hair cut in a close crop, where the little girl's was long.

"Did you read my prospectus?" he asked. When he had seen her with her paintings, on the pavement outside the market, he had given her a brochure of the gallery. He had been amused, that day, by her reaction. Most of the artists, even the amateurs, knew who he was, but if she had heard of him or the gallery, she had not shown it. Merely thanked him for the prospectus, politely explained the title of each painting, and sat down again on her folding stool, her hands crossed in her lap.

She had gone now to the kitchen, and taken the brochure from a drawer. "I can't say I've ever seen such a thing," she told him. "It's like a book."

He nodded, pleased. "My printing costs are high," he told her, "but presentation is everything."

She felt the warmth of the coffee on the stove. "Would you like a drink?" she asked. And she noticed the wine. "Your wine?"

"Thank you."

She let Rachel down while she opened the bottle. He caught her glancing at him several times, with an expression of bemusement. The child sat on the floor. He felt himself under inspection from two pairs of eyes.

When she handed him the glass, he said, "I would like to show several of your paintings."

"Not buy," she said.

"That's not the way it works."

"No," she commented. "Wishful thinking."

He sipped his wine, and regarded her. He saw that the child had a pencil in one hand; she began drawing circles on her forearm.

"Rachel," Anna chided.

"It's quite a map," he said, nodding at the far wall.

She followed his glance. "Oh, yes," she answered. "For Rachel."

There was a silence. He wondered at the extreme indulgence of allowing a child to paint an entire wall.

"This is lovely," Anna said. She was holding up the wineglass.

"You like it?"

"I do."

"It's one of my interests," he said.

"Drinking wine?"

"Investing in wine."

She nodded. She was half smiling.

"What else do you invest in?" she asked.

"People like you," he said.

"Ah." Gently, she took the pencil from Rachel's grasp. "I've never thought of myself as an investment."

"Perhaps you're not interested in an exhibition," he said. "I've known artists who aren't."

Anna looked from Rachel to him. "You would exhibit me?"

"Yes. In time."

"Truly?"

He smiled at her. "Some of the work here is quite salable."

She got to her feet. "Show me," she said.

They walked from painting to painting in the studio. He chose according to a theme: the semiabstracts of Boston and New England; the recognizable locations of Nantucket; the Center Methodist Church's white tower rising above the gray stacked roofs of Provincetown; Nobska Light at Falmouth.

"But these aren't the best," she kept saying.

"You would have to trust my judgment," he told her.

"What about my judgment?" she said.

He considered her. "Show me the best," he said.

She went away into what he assumed was a bedroom, and brought back three framed pieces. He looked at them carefully, but their color was very high, almost backlit, in shades of orange.

"What does this remind me of," he wondered.

"Vermont," she said.

He nodded. "Vermont in the fall. Very Technicolor."

"You don't like them," she said.

"They're not as commercial as the others."

"I don't want to be commercial."

He smiled. It was an old argument. He fingered the nearest painting, the molding around the frame. "They would need remounting," he said. "Who did this for you?"

"My mother," she said.

He managed to say nothing. It struck him as rather comically naïve.

He had finished his glass of wine, and placed it, precisely, on the kitchen counter. "You must trust my judgment," he repeated.

*   *   *

She was hard to impress, to win over.

He rather liked her for it.

She would not give him the New England pieces at all, because he would not take her favorites. They had parted company that warm July night with perfect politeness. He was not prepared to push her.

As he walked away, he had felt irritated at her obstinacy; then, grudgingly, he admired it. He went back to the market the following week, but she wasn't there. In fact, she wasn't there for a month. At the end of August, one lunchtime, he had called at her apartment again.

This time, she was alone. All the loft windows were open. A less humid breeze was blowing. That morning, there had been a squall of rain, and the drops still marked the open windows. She was not working at the easel, but on the floor, printing a pattern on a collage.

"A new departure," he observed.

"Not really," she said.

He looked around. "Is your daughter here?"

"No," she said, "she's with her grandmother for the week." She looked at the floor, and paced up and down, judging what she had done that morning. Then she turned away from it. She snatched at a denim jacket that was hanging over a chair. "I was just going out," she said.

"For lunch?"

"Some groceries. There's no food in the house."

"Let me buy you lunch," he said.

She indicated her clothes: another T-shirt, and a pair of fraying shorts.

"I'll wait if you want to change," he said.

She hesitated, the smile twitching at her mouth. "Are you taking me somewhere exotic?" she asked.

"Wherever you like."

"Is it gentle persuasion?"

"To what purpose?"

"To give you the New Englands."

"Not at all," he said. "I have too many paintings and not enough space to show them."

"I see," she murmured. "You wouldn't make an exception, then, to show mine?"

He smiled at her. "Since you won't give them to me, that is an academic question," he said.

He took her to Gyuhama.

As they sat down, she said, "I've never eaten sushi before."

"Do you not like seafood?" he asked.

She grinned at him. "Born in Boston, and I don't like seafood?"

He began to like her. She ate quickly, as if all life were a hurry.

"Tell me about yourself," he said.

She ate for a second, then tilted her chin. "Twenty-five, single mother."

"Were you married?" he asked.

"No."

"So you bring Rachel up alone."

She eyed him. "And?"

"Nothing at all. Just an inquiry."

"My mother helps me," Anna told him. "In fact, we lived with her until a while ago."

He watched her as she tasted the miso soup. "Rachel is a striking child," he said.

She looked up. "You think so?"

"Yes."

She simply nodded.

"Have you always lived in New England?" he asked.

"Most of the time," she said. "Have you?"

"Yes."

"But you must travel."

"Yes. I go to Europe a great deal. London, Paris."

"London, Paris, New York, and Rome," she said. "Like the perfume bottles."

"I'm sorry?"

She smiled. "My mother's perfume bottles always had those cities on the label. When I was little, I thought I'd travel to all those places."

"And have you?"

"No," she said. "But I will."

"You should," he told her. "Italy and France, for an artist."

"I couldn't afford it just now," she told him.

The soup was taken away; the treasure boat arrived. She peered down at it, intrigued.

"How do you eat this?" she asked. And, when shown, "What is this? And this?" He explained the dishes to her.

She was rather childlike herself, he decided. Or perhaps that was an illusion. Perhaps it was simply that she seemed to have no idea of herself, no egotism. She was totally unself-conscious.

"If you let me sell your paintings, you might be able to afford a trip," he pointed out.

She sat back and considered him. "Mr. Garrett," she said, "if you sold my paintings, I would pay off my credit cards."

"Are you in debt?" he asked.

She started to laugh. "You sound like an old man."

"I am an old man," he said.

The laugh was genuine. "Right," she murmured. "Right." Then, "But you're very formal," she told him.

"Is that wrong?" he asked.

She rocked her hand from side to side in a *maybe-maybe not* gesture. "You're telling me you're *not* in debt," she said.

"I'm not in debt."

"To anyone? A loan, a mortgage?"

"Nothing," he said.

"Jesus," she muttered.

He let this go. After a moment, he said, "Let me help you."

She shook her head. "More debts, Mr. Garrett."

"Not a debt," he said. "A gift."

Her mouth hung open for a second. "Why would you want to do that?" she asked.

He didn't answer directly. "Then let me sell your paintings," he said.

She sighed. "All of them?"

"No," he said. "I'll take two."

"But that's less than you offered to take a month ago!" she objected.

"And how much did you spend on your credit card this month?" he asked her.

"That's not fair."

"I'm not the one with debts," he said.

By December of that year, by Christmas, she no longer had to worry about her bills. The first exhibition had finished in November. He had sold fourteen pieces.

On the night before Christmas Eve, she walked into the gallery in a heavy wool coat, in which she twirled for him. "Do you like it?"

"Yes."

"A Christmas present from Ma."

He had met Grace by then. One afternoon in the summer, they had stopped by his house to pick up a check. He had sold the first two paintings straightaway; four more had followed. One was very large, the first really giant canvas that Anna had attempted. Grace had said very little that afternoon: she was extraordinarily polite toward him—an attitude that he later learned hid her immediate dislike.

That Christmas, the gallery was showing the more figurative paintings that traditionally did well in the festive season. On his urging, Anna had produced four small paintings in oils of winter landscapes. Grace had exclaimed when she had seen them hanging: they were of a house in woodland, with a long sloping drive.

Anna had stood in the gallery, dwarfed by the floor-length black coat. A blue velvet scarf was wound around her neck. He was struck by her heightened color from the cold outside, and the luminosity of her eyes.

Then, it struck him. It struck him like a thunderbolt, and he knew then why he had returned to see her in the loft apartment, and why he had persevered with her, and why he thought of her as so different from the other women who inhabited his life, darkening shadows with their sordid tastes, and their ability to be degraded.

Looking back at him across the gallery now, above the blue velvet of the scarf, were the eyes of his mother's stainless Madonna.

"I have something for you," he said suddenly.

He went into the office, and brought out the gift he had bought for some grasping Brahmin wife who kept him secret from her self-satisfied husband. She didn't matter anymore.

He handed the box to Anna. She opened it slowly, and stared at the gift. She said nothing at all.

"It's an antique," he told her.

It was a rather beautiful item. Victorian, in silver, and made in London, it was a neck chain of entwined petals.

"Flowers," she said.

"I believe they're lilies," he told her.

She stood with it in one hand, the other gently touching it. She didn't look up at him.

"Put it on," he said. He walked forward.

She was biting her lip, that familiar habit.

"Would you like to put it on?" he asked pointedly.

She closed the lid of the box. "Thank you," she said. "But I can't take this."

He frowned at her expression. "Is something the matter?"

"No, no."

"I thought you liked silver."

"Yes," she said. "I do. It's lovely. But I can't possibly take it from you. It's too expensive."

"You have a silver bangle ... I thought ..."

"It's lovely," she repeated. She nodded her head once or twice, almost too emphatically.

He had closed his hand over hers, over the proffered box, and pushed it gently back toward her. "You can take it, and you will," he said. "Or I shall be very offended."

In March, he arranged the first exhibition in New York. It was not easy to do; the venue was inappropriate at first, and then the replacement was horrendously expensive. But he had the first of the corporate orders for her: a fashion house wanted six of the very spare, almost colorless works.

Anna herself was distracted; Rachel had been recommended for a residential school at Easter. It was a new departure, for Rachel had never left home before, even for a single night, away from her mother or grandmother.

"I don't know what to do," Anna had said to him, when he arranged to meet her for lunch. She came into the restaurant looking fragmented and anxious. She went very pale at such times.

"Who suggested the residential course?" he asked. The waiter was hovering, waiting for the order; Anna had not even noticed him.

She fumbled with the menu. "The school," she said. "It's highly thought of, this—this—" she searched for the word. "Program."

"Then take the opportunity," he suggested.

She stared at him. "You heard what I said?" she asked.

"Yes."

"A *program*," she said. "That's what they call it. Like machines."

"I'm sure that's not the meaning," he told her.

"Oh," she remarked. Her hands, and the menu, dropped to the table. "You're always so sure about everything."

He asked the waiter to come back.

"You're annoyed," he said.

"Life is so simple for you," she told him.

"Excuse me?"

She waved her hand. "No children. No wife. No partner. No one to please."

"I only try to advise you . . ."

"Well, don't," she said. "Don't advise me."

And she got up, and walked away.

The evening before the exhibition, they were due to drive to New York. He was taking her; the car drew up at the curb and she was waiting already outside her apartment, wrapped in the long wool coat and the blue scarf, an overnight bag at her feet.

"You're prompt," he remarked, as the driver packed her bag into the trunk. He couldn't take his eyes off her. She seemed so fragile, so untouched.

"Rachel isn't here," she reminded him.

There was silence most of the way; even when they checked in, she barely said a word. They went straight to the gallery, and examined the way the paintings had been hung. For a while, she became coolly businesslike, insisting on two moves. She wanted a duo interchanged, but one was smaller than the other. It created a domino effect, other pieces having to be shifted to accommodate the change in sizes. But she was adamant, standing with her arms crossed, her face set. He couldn't decide if she were angry or not; she seemed so controlled. The changes took three hours, and it was after eleven o'clock at night when they emerged. All she wanted to do was go back to the hotel.

He walked her to her door, out of politeness. She got out her key, and only then did he see, to his complete surprise, that she was crying.

"What is it?" he asked.

She shook her head, opened the door, and went in without closing it.

He followed her, and saw her sitting on the edge of the bed, looking desolate. She was as thin as a rake, and hollow-eyed.

"Are you ill?" he asked.

He opened the minibar, and poured her a brandy. She took it meekly.

"Is it the show?"

"No."

"Then what?"

She was silent. She picked up the TV remote, and began to flick through channels at high speed. The colors from the screen chased over her face; then, as quickly as she had picked it up, she switched off the TV again, and threw the remote down. It clattered against the bedside table, and fell to the floor.

"Am I doing anything right?" she asked.

He sat down opposite her. "You paint reasonably well," he observed.

She glanced up, and gave him a crooked smile.

"You're dissatisfied," he said.

"Yes."

"With the exhibition?"

She shook her head. "No, no."

"Then it's Rachel," he decided.

She was staring at the carpet. "It's a very curious thing," she murmured, "intimacy." She looked up at him. "How can you survive without it?"

She must have gleaned something from his expression.

"I'm sorry," she said. "That was rude."

"No," he told her. "Actually, you're right. There's no one I'm close to."

"Your parents?" she asked.

"They both died in the last three years."

"I'm sorry," she repeated.

He leaned forward. "If you don't feel intimacy with a child like Rachel," he said, "that is hardly your fault."

She grimaced. "She shares things in her own way," she said. She put her face in her hands, and lay back on the bed, palms pressed hard to her eyes. "But I . . ."

"Is it money?" he asked. "Do you need any more?"

"No," she said. She began to sob.

"Is there something Rachel needs?" he asked.

"No," she said. She put down her hands, and immediately replaced them with an arm across her face. "Would you please go?" she said.

"But there's something else I can help with," he said. "There must be." He kneeled down at her side. Almost a supplicant. He lifted down the protecting arm; she stared at him.

"Don't you know how much I want to help you?" he asked.

"I can do it by myself," she whispered.

He turned her hand over, and kissed the palm softly.

"You've been alone for too long," he told her. "Too long."

Twenty

DAVID REACHED ANNA'S HOUSE at ten the next morning. A slight rain had fallen; the street was cool.

He pressed the bell. A woman came to the door that he didn't know.

"Is Grace here?" he asked.

Jen looked at him speculatively, wiping her hands on a cloth. "She's at the store," she said.

"I'm David Mortimer," he said; and, seeing her blank reaction, "I wanted to speak to Grace. I've come from the hospital."

She let him in, leading him through to the kitchen. There was a coffeepot on the table, a set of used dishes, a cut loaf of bread. "We just finished breakfast," she said. "Would you like some coffee?"

"No, thanks," he said. His head was buzzing from the coffee he had drunk during the night. He sat down heavily.

"How is Anna?" Jen asked.

He paused, not knowing who this woman was. Exhaustion was making the world blurred; taking the taxi just now had been almost surreal. It had suddenly seemed strange to him how the world was revolving in its persistent way. He couldn't fathom why there was so much traffic. From the ICU to the street was too far, stepping off one planet and onto another.

"I'm sorry," he said. And he rubbed his face with one hand. "Are you a friend of Anna's?"

She sat down opposite him, and held out her hand. "I'm Jen Ashton," she told him. "I live next door."

He shook the proffered hand. "You've known Anna long?" he asked.

"About three years."

He looked at her expectant face. "Something happened today," she said. He noticed she had folded the cloth, and put it down on the tabletop. She sat straight-backed, looking into his eyes. He realized that she was steeling herself for the worst. "Is it Anna?" she asked.

"Not Anna," David told her. "A boy. He was sixteen."

"This is a boy in the ICU?"

"Yes," he told her. "He died there an hour ago."

About five-thirty, as it was getting light, David had left the room for a few minutes. When he came back, the boy's mother was standing in the center of the corridor. She was alone for a second; she held out her hands from her sides, as if she were trying not to touch anything. Almost as soon as he noticed her, he saw the two other women come out after her; they took hold of her arms, and tried to pull her to one side, talking to her. He heard the broken tone in their voices.

As David got closer, the woman started to walk. She came right up to him, pulling away from the grasp of the others. He stared at her. Her eyes were wide. She said nothing to him, only looked at him with that flat glare. Just for a second, he thought she was going to hit him, such was the heat in that look.

When he got to the door of the ICU, he saw the movement around the boy's bed; he looked behind him, and saw the women trying to persuade her to come back inside. The nurses were slowly disengaging the lines. He stepped back in horror and embarrassment, realizing he had waded through grief at the door without recognizing it.

He took a chair in the corner, backed up from Anna's bedside. He saw the boy's hands and arms, grazed by the road where he had been dragged. The marks showed as gray lines, no longer livid. He saw the fingers of the nearest hand, loosely cupped. He looked at Anna's hands, in the same faintly curled position on the sheet.

Garrett had arrived at eight o'clock.

He looked fresh. Almost jaunty. He was wearing a dark suit and white shirt, and a tie with a silver-and-black pattern. As soon as David had seen him, he had thought, *You look like the fucking under-taker.*

By then, the boy's bed was empty.

Garrett had held out his hand. For a second, David recoiled. It was something to do with the flesh of the palm and fingers; he had to steel himself to respond. He had not touched Anna since the boy's death, the handling of the inert body.

"You look tired," Garrett had said.

They had spoken for a minute or so, Garrett offering him the apartment. He had taken the spare key that Garrett gave him, and walked out of the hospital, fully intending to go to the Beacon Hill address. But, just as he stood at the crossing, everything about Garrett's tone, and the way he dressed, and the cool ease of the conversation, overwhelmed him. He thought of the paintings in the apartment and the smell of the icy air-conditioning, and, suddenly, he had wanted to see Grace. He had hailed the first taxi that came along.

Jen Ashton, he realized, was still looking at him.

"David Mortimer," she said.

He frowned. "Sorry?"

"You're David Mortimer," she said, and she laughed a little suddenly, and blushed. "You must think I'm stupid," she said. "I heard your name, and I never connected." She got to her feet. "Look, I'll make some fresh," she said, lifting the coffeepot. She started to smile all over again. "Can you believe that?" she asked. "I never connected."

"I'm sorry," he repeated. "You've lost me."

"You've come from England?"

"Yes. But—"

"You came from England ..."

"Yesterday," he said. "Grace rang me."

Jen's eyes widened. She put the coffeepot on the stove, and pressed both hands to her face, laughing and sighing at once. "She did? My God," she murmured. She dropped her hands. "And you came. You came."

"Yes, I—"

She looked at him; looked him over from head to foot, looked at his clothes, his hands, his face. "I've seen your picture," she said. "Dozens of times. And here you are. You materialize."

"My photograph?"

"No," she said. "A drawing of you."

"A drawing?"

"You don't know," she said. "Of course, you wouldn't."

"This is a drawing of Anna's?"

"How long is it since you saw her?" Jen asked.

"Eleven years."

She smiled again, shook her head, looked at the floor. "Oh, my," she said to herself. "Imagine that." Then, she looked back at him. "Did you see Rachel?" she asked.

"Yes."

"She's upstairs. Would you like to go to her?"

"No . . ."

"She's drawing. Did you know she draws, like Anna?"

"Yes."

"And you wouldn't like to see her?" Jen persisted. "Go ahead. It's just on the right, the room on the right at the top of the stairs."

"Look, Gemma—"

"It's Jen. Jennifer."

He nodded an apology. "Jen. I can't stay."

"Oh," she said. "You're going back to the hospital."

"No," he said. "I'm going home."

She stared at him. "Home?" she echoed. "Not to England? Not now?"

"I don't expect you to understand," he said. "I can't help Anna, and I don't know Rachel, and there's no way I can get through to her, and that was the whole reason for coming here. To know her, and to have her know me. But that's never going to happen."

"Of course it will happen!" Jen protested.

He looked at her directly. "Let's face it," he said. "She won't make any distinction between me and any other man."

"Oh, you're wrong," Jen said. "If you just got to know her . . ."

"When all's said and done, there's nothing I can offer them."

"There's nothing you can offer?" she echoed.

He stared pointedly at her.

"I'm sorry," she said. "I'm sorry to argue with you."

"I shouldn't have come at all," he said.

"Maybe if you just stayed a few days, just for Rachel."

"And what good would that be?" he answered shortly. "What the hell difference will it make to her?"

She watched him as he turned away. "It would make a lot of difference," she murmured.

"I doubt it," he said.

There was a long pause, during which Jen Ashton continued to stare at him. "You don't know how much you're needed here," she said, eventually. She walked across the kitchen, opened the door, and stepped out into the hall. "Would you do something for me?" she asked.

"What is it?"

She held out her hand. "Just come with me," she told him.

She walked up the stairs, past Rachel's room, where he could hear the TV playing, and on up another flight to the third floor. Here, the landing was narrower, and the ceiling lower. Jen opened a door that faced them, and smiled at him as he ducked his head, went through the door, and into Anna's studio.

It was a large room, as wide and long as the house. Two enormous windows set into the roof lighted the loft. In the center was a stripped pine table. On either side, storage had been built: low shelves ran around the outside of the space, deep enough to take whole sheets of cartridge paper, rolls of tissue and sugar cane paper, and canvases, with other fancy units at intervals, all sizes and shapes, to house the inks and pastels, paints and brushes. There were two easels, one open and one stacked, and a massive wooden structure, a kind of giant easel in itself, racked into the ceiling with bolts.

Jen had come in after him.

"James built this for Anna," she said. She paused, raised her eyebrows. "She hated it."

He looked at her, and started to smile. "She did?" he said. "It looks perfect."

"That's why she hated it," she said.

He ran his finger down the nearest wall rack: it was wood, light oak; not melamine. "Expensive," he said. He walked around, looking.

"She said she'd been straightened out," Jen added.

He smiled. The Anna he had known was full of idiosyncratic economies. He remembered the rolled-up towel that she used to carry her paints in, with small pockets sewn into it for the tubes of color; and the piece of flannel and the sea sponge she used to get light-through and water-through effects; and what she called her cheating tape, a roll of masking tape that she could tear into strips or shapes, put on the paper, and use a watercolor wash over. Removing the tape would show a disc of sun through cloud, or white shadow on gray, like a photographic negative.

"Clever," he had once said to her.

She'd shrugged. "Kind of a trick," she'd said. "Cheating tape."

"You could get masking fluid," he'd suggested.

"Money, money," she'd told him.

He walked the length of the room. At the far end was an old red leather armchair, its surface rather cracked, the brass beading on the armrests and the seat polished light by wear. He ran a hand over it.

"It was her grandfather's," Jen said.

He could feel her on this. He could feel her in the grain of the leather. He ran his index finger over the rounded right arm, where another hand had worn a small shiny patch, a tawny circle little bigger than a fingertip.

"Sit down," Jen said.

But he couldn't sit in the chair. It seemed too intimate. He sat down on the floor alongside it, drawing up his legs, resting his elbows on his knees, and his head on one hand.

"You're tired," Jen said.

"Yes."

"Did you sleep at the hospital?"

"No," he said. "I dozed a little."

"Sometimes they give you a little room, or something ...?"

"I couldn't sleep in a room there," he murmured. He put the hand over his eyes.

"You sit by the bed?"

"They told me ..." He stopped, moving the hand from his eyes to his mouth.

Jen had moved closer to him. "Told you ...?" she prompted.

He shook his head. "To help her. They gave me ... these things ... like a plastic ball you can squeeze, and a piece of cloth, it's soft on one side, and it's a kind of rubber, corrugated rubber on the other ..."

"For sensation?" she asked.

"Yes," he said. "To give different sensations."

"To wake her."

He frowned, looked at the floor, the skylights.

"Maybe it's just sedation," she said. "After the operation."

He shook his head. "There's no response," he said. "They did a new test. Even her reflexes ..."

"Oh, God," Jen murmured. "Does Grace know?"

"Not yet."

The two of them fell silent, each with their private picture in their head: a parody of sleep.

"She really doesn't look that bad," he whispered. "This boy, you could see the side of his face, his head ... but Anna ..." He looked up at her. "I'm no good at this," he said. "Really no good." He dropped his hand, glanced at the chair. "When they gave me this piece of material, this two-sided thing . . ." He sighed, grimacing at himself. "I couldn't even pick it up," he confessed. "Someone else should be there. That's what she needs. Someone else."

Jen looked at him for some seconds.

Then, she went to a desk on the other side of the room. She reached behind it, at floor level, and eased a key from underneath it. Then, standing, she unlocked a drawer and carefully took out a wooden tray. "David," she said. "Come over here."

He got off the floor, and walked toward her. When he got level with her, she pushed the tray toward him across the table.

There was a parcel in one corner of the tray, wrapped in an odd kind of checked tissue paper.

"What is it?" he asked, his eyes traveling over the remainder—sheaves of paper gripped by a thick elastic band; several drawing pads; other, smaller cardboard boxes.

"Go ahead," Jen said. "Open the package."

He did so, glancing at her, puzzled.

It turned out to be a book. It was large; about ten inches by eight, and two inches thick. The cover, lovingly protected under plastic, was a gold design on black, resembling the bark of a tree. The edges of the pages were gold leaf. He opened the cover to a similarly etched inner page, this time of brilliant orange and gold. He turned the title page. *China*, it read, *Mother of Gardens*. And the author, in a flowing, upright pen had signed it: *E. H. Wilson, Keeper of the Arnold Arboretum of Harvard University.*

David looked up at Jen.

"This is a first edition," he said. "This is Wilson's own signature."

"Yes," she said. "Anna bought it two years ago."

"But it was out of print long ago," he said. "You can't get a modern version: these are all there are left. And I don't know how many there would be . . . half a dozen? A dozen? Anywhere."

"She knew," Jen told him.

He returned her look for a moment, then carefully turned the pages.

This was Wilson's preface, written on February 15, 1929. David had seen it only once before, quoted in the biography he had found in Oxford. The familiarity of the opening sentences struck him.

. . . from the bursting into blossom of the forsythias and Yulan
magnolias in the early spring, to the peonies and roses in summer,
China's contribution to the floral wealth of gardens is in evidence . . .
    It was in 1899 that I first set foot in China, to leave it finally in
1911 . . .

"Where did she get it?" he asked.

"At an auction."

"A book auction?" he repeated.

"Yes, antiquarian books."

"But how did she find out about it?" He stared down at the pages. "I suppose Garrett bought it."

"No, David," Jen said softly. "James never knew she had it. He didn't know about the auction. He didn't know how much she paid. He doesn't know now."

He frowned at her. "You mean she was looking in antiquarian auctions . . ."

"For a long time," Jen confirmed. "Ever since she started to break even, to make a little money."

"For this one book?"

"For this book."

He shook his head. Slowly, he turned the pale yellow pages with their uneven, hand-cut edges. Here were Wilson's own photographs: *Paulownia fargesii, 55 feet tall, in blossom . . . Sapindus musko-rossi, 80 feet tall, girth 12 feet.* This black-and-white plate showed the soapnut tree, curved in silhouette against a mountain slope; leaning at first to the left, a large branch, weighted by low-hanging leaves, spread forty feet parallel to the ground; then the crown soared upward, compensating for the lower growth by arching to the right another sixty feet. Underneath it, and standing in its shade, was a temple memorial with three pagoda roofs. To the left-hand side of the picture, a stone track undulated through fields.

Rice fields in the Red Basin . . . the market village of Tan-Chia-Tien.

Tan-Chia-Tien was crowded into the banks of a river, a collection of wide-eaved roofs hanging over a drop to the water. It looked like some kind of angular debris that had been washed into the shore by a flood. Above it, on either bank, vertical limestone walls rose out of view of the camera; only in the distance could a horizon be seen, a triangle of sky above another peak.

Chinese Tulip Tree . . . this on a tremendous incline. Below, clouds filled the valley; opposite it were line after line of mountains, each with serrated outlines, like well-used saws. Wind blurred the leaves of the tulip tree, a ninety-foot monster defying gravity. This was much larger than anything that grew in cultivation. The leaves that gave it its name, with their curious, indented tip exactly like the shape of a tulip flower, turned yellow in autumn and were almost blue underneath. He knew a cousin of this, the ordinary tulip tree, a hundred and fifty feet high, at a manor house in Wiltshire; and there was one at Kew Gardens, a hundred and ten feet at last measurement, brought to England for Charles the First from the rich deep soils of Virginia and Kentucky.

David glanced at the text opposite the photograph.

". . . A rugged, precipitous, sparsely populated country is this, and I never wish to see it again . . . magnificent from the scenic point of view, but arduous beyond words . . . the final stage was through jungle . . . one mass of purest white was conspicuous from afar . . . walnut trees . . . varnish trees . . ."

The poisonous varnish tree, whose sap made the black Chinese lacquer. The leaves could be two feet long, and looked a little like bay. David liked these trees. They were beautiful, sensuous things, with a slender, sinuous stem holding these great green flags; shiny, seductive, and dangerous. David didn't know if they grew on the eastern seaboard; but their sisters did, the dwarf sumacs, small dancers with a shape like a posy, tightly packed leaves on a short body, clustered with yellow flowers in summer.

He turned another page.

Here was Songpan, the town that Wilson loved so much, a highland fortress with a vast number of terraced fields outside the city walls, and the Min River curving through the city in a broad S bend. *"The people are very fond of flowers,"* Wilson had written, *"China asters, and small-flowered poppies and Tiger Lilies."* He had visited Songpan three times, and left it each time with regret. Songpan, in modern-day Jiuzhai Gou, a country of lakes and waterfalls. Sichuan, Emei Shan, Chengdu, Jiuzhai Gou, Leshan, Qingcheng Shan. Even the names were songs.

He ran his finger over the spine of the book, the red-and-gold binding just visible.

Other photographs.

Chinese dogwood, Mandarin Orange, China Fir . . .

Another.

Musk rose . . . Davidia involucrata . . .

He stopped, his hand flat on the page. Then, he raised his eyes to Jen.

She nodded toward the rest of the box. He glanced from the tray to her hand.

"She kept these under lock and key," he murmured.

"She didn't want James to find them," she said.

He picked up the first thing that came to hand: a thick folder, held with an elastic band. Taking off the band, he saw that it was a collection of essays, seminar papers that she had written eleven years ago. He looked carefully at their titles, and at her own scribbled notes in some of the margins. In the same folder was a guidebook, much thumbed and creased. It was the kind for sale in every bookshop in Oxford; inside it was a map from the Information Centre, the colleges illustrated in a lurid cerise pink, the streets in blue. The great meadows ringed the northeast: Music, Angel, Magdalen, Merton, and Christ Church. He stared at the Magdalen Bridge by the Botanic Garden, and the Cherwell running so close to the Thames at Folly Bridge.

Also, inside the same cover, were four postcards: an aerial view looking over Merton and Oriel; Deadman's Walk; the Cathedral Chancel of Christ Church, and, lastly, Magdalen itself—*perhaps the most beautiful college,* ran the description on the back. He put it down, his expression unreadable.

"Did she tell you about me?" he asked.

"Yes," Jen answered. "A little."

"Did she say why she left me?"

He met her eye; held her gaze.

"David," she said, "I don't know."

"I tried to find her," he said. "I went to the university; I gave them letters to forward to her. I even rang Grace."

"I know," Jen murmured. "She received the letters."

"She did?"

Jen glanced at the box.

"You mean they're in here?" He stared down at the cardboard boxes. "And she told you all this," he said, "but she never told you the reason for leaving?"

"I guess she was afraid?" Jen suggested softly. "Panicked?"

"She said that?"

"Not in so many words," she admitted. She watched him for a second longer, then lifted out the largest drawing pad. She held it out to him. "But she did say that this meant a lot," she told him.

He looked at it: a sixteen-by-twelve Langton watercolor pad.

He opened the pad, knowing already what he would find. There on the third page was a copy of the sketch she had made of the regal lily, drawn from the color plates in the Wilson biography. An exact copy of the one that she had given to him, and that he had kept.

"Garrett said he didn't know of my existence, didn't know who I was," David murmured. He looked again at Jen. "So he wouldn't know that all this is here. . . ."

"No," Jen said.

He looked up at her. "I would have come," he said. "If she had talked to me once. Written me just one letter."

Jen said nothing. She took out the smaller cardboard box. She pushed it across the tabletop. Inside was an envelope: opening it, he tipped out the contents.

Oak leaves, from Island Thorns.

He held them in his palm for a few seconds, remembering the night, and the following morning, when she had picked these up from the ground and put them in her pocket between the pages of the map. Oak leaves, once freshly opened, and the yellow-green catkins attached to the stem. But the flowers were gone now, and the color had faded.

He looked up again at Jen, at the friend to whom Anna had disclosed this secret. She was gazing at him with an almost apologetic smile.

"She never forgot," she murmured.

He went back to the chair.

He tried not to close his hand over the leaves.

"When you say that there must be someone else," Jen told him, "you're wrong. I don't think there's anyone else who could bring Anna back."

He sat down slowly in the red leather chair, in Anna's silent embrace.

Twenty-one

GARRETT TOOK ANNA TO Italy after the first New York exhibition.

Other than England, she had never been abroad before, and was loath to leave Rachel. But James wanted to introduce her to Italy; it was important to her, he said. "You can't live in one place all your life, and bring anything fresh to your work," he told her.

She had her doubts. "Other artists do it all the time," she'd said. "A place becomes their trademark."

"If you don't want to travel with me, that's fine," he'd replied.

They arrived in the spring, to a cold Milan. The city looked pale to her, the buildings faceless. They stayed in a hotel whose restaurant James favored and, on the first night, James insisted that they eat there.

"Are we going out?" she asked. It was still only nine when they had finished eating.

"Aren't you tired?" he asked.

"Not really."

"We have a meeting in the morning," he told her. "I would rather rest."

She went up to the room with him, and sat on the edge of the bed, watching him in the bathroom. He undressed and showered. On the TV above her head, fastened to the wall of the otherwise opulent bedroom, a satellite news station rotated endlessly, like *Groundhog Day,* in the corner of the room.

"How many times have you been here?" she asked, when he was combing his wet hair. "In Milan?"

"Eight, nine," he said.

She looked at his spare, tall body. His slim frame showed the first, faint signs of blurring slackness in the muscles of the arm above the elbow, and in the small of his back, and on the skin just below his shoulder blades. He was twelve years older than she was. Out of his clothes he looked, if anything, more contained, almost ascetic. His skin tone was unusual: blemish free, and uniformly the color of very pale coffee. He had long fingers, long joints, long calves, like a runner. He ought to be, she thought, a very attractive man. But he was, even with the first hints of age, still so curiously flawless.

He had caught her glance through the mirror, and stopped what he was doing.

She stood up. "I'm going out for a while," she said.

"Now?" he asked. "Alone?"

"Yes."

He frowned. "I'll get dressed," he told her.

"No," she said. "It's all right. I'll only be a few minutes."

"You can't go out on your own," he protested.

But she had already closed the door, softly, behind her.

She walked down the nearest street on a dark pavement thronged with crowds. It was January, and the air was icy sharp, almost taking her breath away. The orange trolleybuses and the ubiquitous, swarming motorcycles swept past. She followed the direction of the crowd and suddenly found herself in a widening space. Under the Palazzo Marino and the statue of da Vinci, tourists were standing, drifting, gazing. She turned to the right and saw La Scala and, as the lights changed, she was propelled forward with the stream of pedestrians, crossing in front of the opera house toward the center of the square. She let herself go with it. She liked the crowds, the noise, the seemingly self-assured, sociable Italians, and the men who looked directly at her with interest and approval, as they looked, she noticed, at every woman who passed.

She walked past the front of the town hall and into the Galleria Vittorio, over the mosaic floors, past the seductively lit windows, and under the great glass roof, lit blue against the night sky. In the arcade, diners were still sitting at café tables, their cups of espresso, cell phones, and packs of cigarettes laid out before them like icons. She walked down the central aisle, and suddenly saw before her the next square, the front face of the cathedral, looking like a spun sugar wedding cake. Far above the Duomo, the gilded figure of La Madonnina, with her halo of stars, looked up to heaven, away from the world.

When Anna got back to the hotel, James was still awake. With his dressing gown wrapped around him, he was sitting on the bed. He looked up from his book as she came in.

"I've seen the Duomo," she told him.

"Good," he remarked, noting his page and putting down the novel.

"Could we go back tomorrow?" she asked. "It must be wonderful inside."

He smiled at her. "It has three thousand five hundred statues, the Trivulzio Candelabrum, five aisles, and a door relief by Ludovico Pogliaghi," he said.

"But I would like to see inside," she told him. She had a picture in her head that they might walk down the Galleria, in front of the gleaming, gold-accented shop fronts with their high arches, and stop at one of the coffee shops, and be like the Italians, and watch the world go by.

He walked up to her, took off her coat, and kissed her.

"I want to be a tourist," she said. "I want to look."

"But I've already told you everything a tourist needs to know," he said.

They were up at eight the next morning, but not for the Duomo, or to sit at café tables. James had ordered a car that took them to the northwest of the city near the Castello Sforzesco. But they were not to see this fifteenth-century palace, either, and the gardens of Parco Sempione and the Arco della Pace passed them by through the car's windows, a haze of stone and statues and a lake glimpsed through the winter trees. They drew up outside a peeling façade, a five-story apartment building.

"Where are we?" she asked. "What have we come for?"

He handed her out of the car with his usual delicacy. "This is something you will never quite see again," he told her. "This is not for tourists."

They rang the bell, and were admitted to an inner courtyard. High windows were masked by drapes; verdigris coated the sad little fountain in the center. As they mounted the inner stairs, there was a funereal air to the black marble steps and gold handrail, inlaid with a black pattern.

A man was waiting for them at the top. Anna glanced at him with a smile. He nodded at James, and ignored her. He walked ahead of them, opening high brass doors to a dark hallway.

Anna blinked as she accustomed herself to the light. They were standing in a drawing room of classical proportions: high ceiling with ornate plasterwork, a vast marble fireplace, a stone floor with one large rectangular rug in shades of ochre and blue. In the center of the room, with her back to the light, sat an elderly woman, who must have been at least eighty. She was overweight, with a patrician face—the kind of face that Anna had seen about her many times in the last twenty-four hours: once beautiful, with full lips and hooded eyes. She wore an air of frigidity, as if the world, and her disapproval of it, were a burden.

She held out her hand, and James lowered his lips to it, only barely brushing her skin.

"James," the woman murmured.

He stepped back, and held out his hand to Anna. "I've brought someone to see you, Countess," he said. "This is Anna Russell."

"Hi," Anna said.

The countess paused, then nodded. "Your assistant?" she asked James.

"My friend," he said. "An artist."

She raised her eyebrows. Closer to the woman now, Anna could smell the unmistakable, heavy cloud of scent that she wore. Expensive and old-fashioned, it drenched the air.

"If you are an artist," the countess murmured, "you will appreciate what I have to show you."

She got up, and took James's arm. Anna followed behind them, feeling rather like the lowly assistant that the woman had taken her for.

They passed into a long, narrow corridor. It had no furniture in it, and only one window, as thin as an arrow slit. The only light that it afforded fell on the painting on the wall directly in front of it.

The woman dropped James's arm, and motioned him forward to inspect the painting. He did so, approaching it slowly. He stood before it, considering it for some time. Then he took out the kind of lens favored by jewelers, and looked very closely at the canvas from several different directions.

The countess turned to Anna. "You paint?" she asked.

"Yes," Anna said.

She felt herself under even closer scrutiny than James was giving the picture. The countess's gaze had lingered first on her shoes, then on her hands, and, finally, on her face, from which she did not now take her attention.

"What kind of paintings?" the woman asked.

"Abstract. Seascape. Watercolor. Acrylics."

The woman nodded. "So many things," she said. Anna couldn't tell if this were sarcasm or not. "And for long?"

"All my life," Anna said.

"You are a protégée of James," the countess observed. It was exactly that: an observation, a statement, and not a question. Anna was suddenly certain that she was not the first protégée that James had brought to Italy.

James came back to them. "Very fine," he said. "My compliments."

Anna caught his glance: his color was heightened. He stared at Anna with intensity, an almost sexual look.

"You recognize?" the countess asked Anna.

"I'm sorry?" Anna asked.

"You recognize the painting, naturally."

Anna looked along the corridor in confusion. That it was an eighteenth- or early-nineteenth-century picture was obvious. But the artist was beyond her.

"Do you like it?" the countess persisted.

She couldn't in all honesty say that she did. It was a religious subject, a Nativity scene in a very mannered style. What drew her eye were the infinitely badly drawn angels that festooned each corner of the canvas. "It's very striking," Anna at last said.

There was a moment of complete silence.

"It is a masterpiece," the countess told her.

They sat together in the salon for twenty minutes, and were served tiny cups of the bitter espresso that Anna had so craved the evening before. As Anna sat in her chair, however, it was James, and James alone, who was given the tour of the room. The countess's voice murmured in lilting tones over her treasures as she pointed them out. "In the style of Ramanino ... rumored to be from Grotte di Catullo ... Reni ... from Villa Sirmione ..." At each introduction, James, following a half-pace behind, bowed his head in appreciation. *You're like a courtier,* Anna thought.

Eventually, they rejoined her.

"Are you fond of antiquities?" the countess asked.

"I do like old things."

Somehow it came out as something of an insult. Not to the woman, but to the house. It sounded like condemnation by faint praise, which had not been Anna's intention. She blushed.

The countess rang a handbell, and the manservant who had first shown them into the room came again to the door.

Once they got to the street, Anna took a deep breath. "Oh, my," she said, fanning her face with her gloved hand. "The smell!"

James looked at her as they waited for the car. "What smell?" he asked.

"The perfume, the damp."

"It didn't seem damp to me."

"You could see it on the walls!" Anna said. "How on earth does she live there?"

"She lives there because her family has lived there for six generations," he told her.

Once in the car again, she glanced at him. "You're angry with me," she said.

"Not at all."

"You're angry, but I don't understand why."

"I'm disappointed at losing the purchase," he said. Then he picked up her hand and pressed it to his lips. He was looking at her with that same sensual, disturbing gaze he had given her in front of the painting.

"But I thought you were interested in the picture," Anna said, her eyes running from his face to their hands, and back again.

"I am. But she won't sell it to me now."

"Why not?"

He said nothing. He smiled, and dropped her hand, and sat watching the streets go by, the fingers of one hand tapping his knee.

"Something to do with me," Anna said.

"She's an eccentric woman," he murmured. "She can be difficult."

"You think you've lost the picture because of me?"

"Don't worry about it." He smiled again, almost secretly, to himself. "I won't."

She snorted. "I'm not worried," she said. "I'm outraged."

He looked at her. "Why?" he asked. "I'm the one who lost the painting. There was a considerable profit in it."

"Listen to you," she said. She shook her head. "I'm not outraged you've lost the sale. I'm outraged that you think it's my fault. Or worse still, you know that it's my fault, and accept it."

"I don't accept it," he said. "I already told you she is a difficult woman."

"Just because I didn't know the artist," Anna said.

"It wasn't that."

The car came to a halt in the traffic. She glimpsed a group of women going by—the wonderfully supercilious-looking, beautiful, sensual, Italian women.

"Well, I wish you'd told me I needed a degree in fine arts to come with you on this trip," Anna remarked.

"It wasn't that," he repeated.

"What then? What?"

He shrugged. "One does not simply say 'Hi' to a countess," he murmured.

For a second, she stared at him.

Then, she began to laugh.

He turned to her in the car, put his arms around her, and, to her discomfort, pressed his mouth to hers. It was the first time she had seen him even come close to losing control of himself. For a moment, he seemed possessed by passion. His breath was hot; his hands moved on her. Then, just as suddenly, he drew back. She stared at him, strangely threatened by his look. Threatened at an instinctive, visceral level.

"You are my own Madonna," he told her.

A week later, they went to Rome.

It was not a city he enjoyed as much, he told her. The Romans were too relaxed, he said; they wore their heritage badly. He said this as they were walking from their hotel one night. She looked in his face to see if he were joking, but he was not.

"I expect if you pointed it out to them," she said, "they would line all the monuments up in an orderly display for you."

She warmed to the Romans more than the Milanese. She liked the restaurant where they had lunch, on the edge of a street, under a yellow awning. The cars and motorcycles edged close to their table, and the wall bore a green tattoo of ancient advertisements; tables were crammed up against each other. She liked the pushing and shoving, the expressiveness of people, their gesturing hands. She drew a neighboring family on her paper napkin: the wriggling child in a blue-and-white-striped dress, the mother talking to the waiter, two faces almost intimate above the red paper menu.

"We'll buy you some clothes," James said.

She looked up from her drawing, distracted. "Sorry?"

He was peeling notes from his wallet to pay the bill. "Clothes."

She put down the pencil. "I've got clothes."

"Do you see anyone in jeans?" he asked.

She bridled. "Yes, I see plenty of people in jeans."

"Teenagers," he said.

"Jesus Christ, James," she said, affronted. "I live in jeans at home."

He smiled at her. He was getting up. She stared at him angrily. He took her arm and persuaded her to her feet. "I had no idea I was such an embarrassment to you," she said.

He started to laugh. "Don't you know how I worship you?" he asked, as he pulled up the collar of her coat.

He looked at her now, all this time later.

Sunlight had been streaming into the ICU until the blinds had been drawn. Now the faint thin lines of light ran down the length of Anna's body. She seemed much smaller now, much thinner than the woman who had come with him to Italy. More childlike even than the woman who had been in Paris, and cried so pitifully and so much.

His face fell in an unconscious grimace of failure. A failure to secure the whole Anna, heart and soul.

A movement distracted him; he concentrated on her fingers. As he watched, he saw them flex. Once, twice.

The seizure began slowly, as slowly and concentratedly as the first steps in a dance. She might have been turning her hand back on the wrist to test its slenderness; then the tremor passed up the arm, and, at the same time, her back arched. With their own peculiar staccato music, the machines at her side, wired to her system, began to accompany her.

He listened to their alarms for a moment, and then got to his feet, and walked to the door. Here, the two nurses who had run along the corridor and into the room glanced at his face as they rushed past.

"It's no good," he murmured to himself. "It's no good."

Twenty-two

As THE T ROLLED out of Forest Hills, David looked at Rachel.

She was sitting next to Grace, her hands clasped in her lap.
Occasionally he would see her index finger describe a shape, a rectangular pattern, on her wrist. She looked out of the window, past
his shoulder, at the districts of Franklin Park and Roxbury passing
by; when the main line tracks ran parallel to the T for a while, he
saw her gaze flicker. She glanced once or twice at him, and the
book he was carrying.

He had brought Wilson's biography.

As they had prepared to go out, after both he and Grace had
caught just a couple of hours' sleep, Jen had brought Rachel down
to the kitchen. The book was open on the tabletop, at a picture of
the An-lan Chiao suspension bridge, on the route to Tatsienlu.
What had prompted him to look at the chapter, he couldn't say.
But he had woken up in the red leather chair with Tatsienlu in his
head.

Rachel had stood at his shoulder in the kitchen, leaning slightly
forward.

"Have you seen this bridge before?" he asked her.

He watched her eyes stray across the page.

Grace smiled at them. "Rachel," she murmured. "This is
David, remember? Say hello."

"Hello," Rachel said.

David wanted to touch her. He wondered at this strange, impulsive instinct. He only wanted to put his arm on her shoulder, or his hand on hers. But, after the reaction the day before, he dared not. "Hello, Rachel," he said.

"Have your sandwich, Rachel," Grace instructed.

"I have bridges, too," Rachel said. She had sat down in front of the place set for her.

"This is in China," David told her. "This is your mother's book."

"Three hundred and forty-three, six hundred and seventy-six, three hundred and forty-three feet, like that," Rachel said, putting her palms flat on the table, side by side, three times. "Flatiron bed, fixed saddle, anchorages."

She was smiling with some kind of inner delight. It was the first smile he had seen, and his heart knocked unexpectedly in his chest. The smile transformed the face, but, more than that, it was terribly unusual. It was the kind of smile you saw sometimes on the faces of much younger children, completely without guile or hesitation.

Grace was cutting bread at the table. "Clifton," she guessed.

"No."

"Oh, my goodness," Grace complained, making up her own sandwich. "I'm out of practice with this one." She shrugged. "Windsor."

"No," Rachel repeated. She pressed her palms again to the tabletop.

Grace glanced at David. "It's a game," she explained.

"Three hundred and forty-three, six hundred and seventy-six, three hundred and forty-three."

"It's Wales somewhere," Jen suggested. "Or the Great Western."

"No."

"Got it," Grace said. "Hungerford."

Rachel began to eat, satisfied. She rocked from side to side a little.

Grace looked back at David. "That's your part of the world," she said. "Hungerford Bridge, London. Built by Isambard Kingdom Brunel in 1845."

"And Clifton is Bristol," David said, understanding now. Rachel kept the precise dimensions of bridges in her head. Strange. Amazing. He joined their smiles. "Even I know that. You can't exactly miss Clifton Gorge."

"Ten cables, twenty-one inches," Rachel said.

"Clifton has ten cables?" David asked, puzzled.

"Eat," Grace told her. "No talking, Rachel. Enough."

It wasn't until they got up to go, as David closed the book, that he saw, toward the bottom of the page opposite the photograph of the An-lan Chiao high in the Min River mountains, Wilson's diary notes: *". . . the floor of the bridge rests across ten bamboo cables each 21 inches in circumference, made of bamboo culms split and twisted together . . ."*

And the idea came to him then.

Right then, watching his daughter pick up her things, with the book in his hand.

They went on to the State station.

"Sometime today I have to find my car," Grace mused, as they stepped out into the street. "God alone knows where it is."

She turned as if to walk down the long haul of Cambridge Street to the hospital, but David held her arm.

"Did James ring you yet?" he asked.

She shook her head.

"Do you think we could spare a half hour?"

"What for?"

"Something I need to find," he told her.

She took her cell phone out of her bag and rang James's number. After a slight delay, he answered.

"How is Anna?" she asked. She paused for the reply. "Any change?" He must have replied in the negative. "We'll be there soon," she told him. She made to switch the phone off, then put it back to her ear. "Excuse me?" she said. David saw her face darken. "I see," she replied. "Then we'll make it sooner." She flicked it off, and put it back in her bag. Then, she stood with both hands on her hips, gazing sightlessly at the buildings across the street.

"What is it?" David asked.

"That bastard," she retorted. "He isn't there."

"Isn't at the hospital?"

"No."

"Well, where the hell is he?"

"At the gallery," she said.

David looked at the ground for a moment. "What did he say about Anna?"

"No change," Grace whispered.

David set his face. "Come on," he told her. "We'll hurry."

They found the huge bookstore on School Street.

"What are you looking for?" Grace asked.

"A map," David told her.

"A map?" Grace repeated. She gave him a curious look.

"Bear with me," he told her.

"You should have told me maps, and not books," Grace said. "There's a better place on State Street. It's a travel store."

"Is it far?"

"Not too far . . ."

They found themselves almost running.

Inside Rand McNally, Rachel began pulling Grace's arm. "We used to come here all the time," Grace explained. "Atlases."

They found the section for China. David took down one of the books that boasted a foldout map in the back pocket. He sat down on the floor, and spread it out. *Zhongguo*, said the back title, *Carte Chine, Mapa touystyczna Chiny* . . .

He flattened it out. It occupied fifty inches by thirty-five.

"China," Rachel said. "India, Kazakhstan, Taiwan."

He looked up at her, smiling. "That's right," he said. "That's right."

They stared down at the piece of the world revealed at their feet. In the bottom right-hand corner, Shanghai occupied the easternmost part of the continent, the Yellow Sea stretching out toward the fragmented coastlines of Japan and Korea. Rounding the coast came Kowloon, Hong Kong, and the Gulf of Tonkin. From their vantage point directly above it, the enormity of the mountains dwarfed even the vastness of China's interior: the Altun, Qilian, Kunlun, Gangdisê, Nyaingêntanglha, and Himalaya Shan all swept down in one extraordinary arc. Two colors alone dominated the map: the green of the huge river plains, and the stony gray of the interminable mountain ranges. Almost through the center, dividing mountain from tundra and China from Mongolia and Russia, ran the Great Wall.

David got up. "Stay here," he said.

Rachel got down on her knees, and ran her finger along the eastern coast, and then inland, following the blue line of the river from Shanghai.

David was back in a minute or so, with a highlighter pen in his hand.

He kneeled next to Rachel. He began to underline the place-names. They showed in vivid pink.

"Yichang," Rachel read out, "Chongqing . . ."

He found the others that he could remember. All traveling west, higher and higher: Chengdu, the last great city before Sichuan really began to climb; Chongqing, Emei Shan, Hanyuan, the Zhedou Pass, Danba, Batang.

"Do you see this?" he asked Rachel. He pointed to the site of the Zhedou-Shankou Pass, at eighteen thousand feet, far away from the green, far into the gray.

"Where are the bridges?" Rachel asked.

"This is Zhedou," he told her. "I think there's probably a bridge there by now. There certainly used to be a village. It's a thousand feet below the pass. A man called Ernest Wilson walked through here a hundred years ago. He was from England, and had come to live in Boston, right here in this city. Near where you live now, Rachel."

She said nothing. He persevered. She was looking off to the side now, along the tall racks.

"When he walked up to Zhedou, it was a horrible journey," he continued. "It was so cold that the rain froze on their clothes. They passed the skeletons of animals that had died on the road—horses and mules, animals that were supposed to be able to endure places like that. The Chinese men who walked with him said that they were afraid of the pass, because the wind made a noise, a howling and grinding, a wailing noise as if someone was crying. They thought that something was mourning the dead. They thought ghosts lived there."

"There's no such thing as ghosts," Rachel said. Her head was still turned in the opposite direction.

He smiled. "Maybe not," he said. "But the men who were with him thought so. In China, there were spirits who controlled the human world, and there were the *shen* that belonged to trees, and rivers, and rain. Then there were the *gui*. They were the ghosts. They were people who had done something terrible in life, and had been reborn as demons, always hungry, always crying."

"There's no such thing as ghosts," Rachel repeated.

David glanced at Grace. She had pursed her lips at Rachel's pragmatism, and now simply rolled her eyes at David in good humor.

"Well," David said, "then there was a snowstorm, and two men got lost. They found one the next morning. He'd been hiding under some rocks all night, and he was too frightened to go on."

"Where was the other man?" Grace asked.

"They didn't find him until two days later," he said. "He was alive, but frozen to the core. They had to leave him behind in the huts they'd used for shelter."

"Why?" Rachel said.

"Because he was too slow to walk with them."

"Why?"

"She means why were they walking in the snow," Grace murmured.

David sat back on his heels. "Because, in all this snow, where
nothing else was growing, where nobody lived, and where not
even animals could live, there were plants. Orchids. Poppies. Things
that no one in the West—in England, in America, in Europe—had
ever seen before."

"Orchids are flowers," Grace explained. "Your mom drew
them."

She looked at David over Rachel's head, and gave a little smile.

She knew, he realized; she knew that her daughter had remembered him.

"Where are the bridges?" Rachel repeated.

David turned back. Now, his daughter was looking straight at
him.

"You know what?" he said to her. "This is why I bought the
map. We need it. We need it for when we go and see your
mother." He stood up, picked up the map carefully, and began to
fold it.

Grace put her hand briefly on his arm.

"We're going to build a bridge," he said quietly. "She'll come
back. Just like the orchids. Just like the lilies."

"David," Grace warned, in little more than a breath.

"We'll build a bridge," he said. "We'll build a way through the
mountains."

Twenty-three

GRACE REMEMBERED THE DAY that Anna had come back from Paris.

It had been Rachel's birthday the week before, and the first regular birthday party that they had managed to arrange for her. For the first time they were able to make out invitations, because for the first time Rachel had made friends.

It was hard to watch the isolation of her world, and also wildly intriguing to watch her interpretation of the parallel life that went on alongside her. Grace sometimes thought that Rachel was a witness to humanity: it was just as if she had been dropped on Earth by some advanced species who, it turned out, had not been so advanced as to teach her the meaning of living.

She would sit in front of the TV incessantly, and play the same video over and over again. Aged six, she became attached to two things that totally ruled her waking hours, and the two became bizarrely entwined. She knew every song from *The Little Mermaid*, and would sing them to herself. Sometimes the whole song, and sometimes just one line. She had no interest in the mermaid herself, but she loved the conversation about the human—as opposed to the mermaid—names for things, and she would carry a fork around with her, an ordinary table fork that she had taken from the kitchen drawer. She could not be parted from it, and wrapped it in a little towel, and took it to school with her, and insisted on it being in a bag that fastened on a strap around her waist. It had been the subject of many phone calls from the principal. *Could Rachel not bring the bag,* Anna was asked. Then, *If she must bring the bag, could she be persuaded to leave it in the principal's office each day?* And finally, *If Rachel must bring the bag, and have it with her, could the metal fork be exchanged for plastic?*

The compromise was achieved only after three months. Rachel relinquished the fork and took a pink plastic version, but she cried bitterly about it, and mourned the other fork as if it had been a pet, something living that had left her.

The second attachment was even stranger.

At that time, Grace had owned a number of videotapes of old movies; she would play them especially on long winter weekend afternoons, if it was raining or cold. Rachel would sit motionless in front of them on the carpet, taking in every detail. One in particular appealed to her, a very old English Ealing comedy called *Kind Hearts and Coronets.* It wasn't, perhaps, an ideal subject for a child; although a comedy, it concerned the revenge of a disinherited man against a wealthy family. He decided to kill them off one by one, so that he could inherit the title. The actor Alec Guinness played each one of the titled family's roles.

A woman whom the hero eventually married, the widow of one of his victims, fascinated Rachel. She was called Lady D'Ascogne, and there was one particular conversation, in a horse-drawn carriage, that Rachel would incessantly repeat.

"Thank you for intervening when you did," Lady D'Ascogne murmurs, pressing a handkerchief to her lips.

"I could gladly have struck him," answers the hero.

At the end of the same scene, there was another exchange.

"I am sure that Henry would not profess one thing and practice another," opines the hero.

"I, too, am sure," replies his companion.

This became the conversation at their dinner table for over a year. Rachel repeated it word for word.

"I, too, am sure," she would profess, her fingers to her mouth, holding the imaginary handkerchief, and her face turning away to an imaginary window of an imaginary carriage. "I, too, am sure. I, too, am sure."

They would hear her at night saying the same thing to herself in bed, in the darkness.

"*I, too, am sure . . . I, too, am sure . . .*"

It would make Grace's heart ache, hearing that thin little voice telling herself over and over that she was sure. Because Rachel was not sure about anything. Her whole landscape was a constantly unraveling mystery, one that she tried to pin down with lists of names, and rules, and repetitions. The other kids thought her weird and stupid. And they said so every day. Sometimes Rachel would respond by running out into the grounds, and hiding in the thick beech hedges that bordered the play area. Sometimes she would respond by pummeling the teasing children, drumming her clenched fists on their backs and shoulders.

Twice she was expelled from school, and twice taken back.

Some of the less experienced teachers still had trouble grasping her difficulties, or understanding the condition.

"I'm sure that Rachel understands the boundaries," one very junior teacher had said, within her hearing, with all the confidence of the Asperger textbook she had skimmed the previous evening. "And so do I."

"I am sure that Henry would not profess one thing and practice another," Rachel had retorted loudly.

Grace remembered having to turn her face away, biting the inside of her cheek to stop laughing out loud.

And then along came Jessica Murphy, a bright little girl who did not have any kind of learning difficulty, and who, after six months in Rachel's class, suddenly decided one day that Rachel was both smart and funny.

They formed an exclusive group of two, both being mermaids, with and without forks, and quoting whole streams of dialogue to one another. Jessica also decided that Rachel could draw good stuff—accurate renditions of mermaids, for one thing, and curiously alluring pictures of horse-drawn carriages with ladies inside

who had lace handkerchiefs. For the first time, Rachel was invited
to a child's house for supper, and Rachel's rote-learned ability to
say please and thank you at every possible opportunity suitably impressed Jessica's mother.

By some miracle, Jessica accepted that Rachel did not hold hands.
She also seemed to accept that Rachel's ability to name every state,
and their populations and climates, was a reasonable alternative.

In return, Jessica initiated Rachel into the rules of girls' friendships that no adult could have translated for her.

Grace had overheard this conversation one afternoon, just before
the party:

"You and me," Jessica said, "that's best friends. Then there's
next-best friends." She was ticking them off on her short, stubby
fingers. "Then there's a friend. That's like Tania Wheeler. That's
an OK person."

"OK person," Rachel repeated.

"Then," said Jessica, "there's bitty friends, who hang around.
And hang-ons. They kind of are there with the bitty ones. Then
there's hi-yas. You say hi-ya but you don't say stuff to them. Then
there's everyone else."

Rachel took a long time to grasp this.

Up until then, she thought friends were people who spoke to
you, or gave you a crayon, or nudged you when standing in line. It
was work for her—really tough work—to learn the distinctions.

Soon after meeting Jessica, Rachel began to say things to Anna
and Grace. Peculiar little signposts along the hitherto empty road.

"You sound like the ocean when you walk," she told Anna.

"The floors move in the last room."

"People listen with half faces."

"I have spans."

This last, with both hands extended, had seemed easy to trans-
late. She had spans—she had hands. Only when Anna and Grace
connected it to the bridges did they realize how hands and
bridges—the flat surface that carried the bridge traffic—were somehow related. They were lines of communication, a lateral-thinking
revelation that astounded them.

People with half faces were those not paying attention, with their faces literally turned half-on to a speaker.

The floor in the last room of the school, before the cafeteria, had a pattern of square tiles of different colors. For Rachel, they moved. They began to understand the sensory overload of patterns, and how important it was for Rachel to discipline them into working order.

"You sound like the ocean when you walk." For this, Anna had kneeled down beside Rachel and held out her arms, and been rewarded with that rarest of things, a returned embrace. Anna had been wearing a floor-length taffeta skirt, a present from James Garrett. It was green, and it whispered like the soft, incoming tide of the sea.

"You sound like the ocean when you walk," Grace had murmured to Anna many times as she left her, on the steps of the apartment in the city, or at the front gate of her own garden. It always brought a beaming smile to Anna's face.

And so Grace thanked God daily for Jessica Murphy, the savior of the second grade. It was a moment for breathing out.

Rachel had missed her mother while she was on the Paris trip.

She began a map of Paris, and then a greater and more detailed map of an imaginary place that Grace had never seen before.

"Where is this?" Grace had asked.

"Another country," Rachel answered, and could not be persuaded to say anything else.

Anna got home at seven in the evening; they saw the car pull up outside the apartment. Anna got out, but James did not follow. She slammed the door and hauled her own case to the steps, and did not turn around as the car left the curb.

Grace ran down the stairs to meet her. She held out her arms and hugged her. "Good trip?" she asked.

"Fine," Anna answered.

"Here. Let me help you."

"Don't be ridiculous," Anna retorted.

Grace stepped back in surprise, and watched her daughter carry the case upstairs.

At the door, Rachel was pacing. She had the Paris drawing in her hand.

Anna kneeled down, and looked at it carefully. "The Eiffel Tower," she said. "The Sacré-Coeur. Montmartre. We went there." She sat down on the floor, opened her case, and gave Rachel the presents that she had brought her: Métro tickets; a menu with a floor plan of the Pompidou Center; a brochure of the Louvre and the Musée D'Orsay. Last of all was a little chess set.

"They play outdoors, in the Luxembourg Gardens," Anna told Rachel. "James said you would like to learn."

Rachel took the maps and the pictures of the Musée D'Orsay clock, and left the chess set sitting noticeably alone on the floor.

That night, Grace and Anna sat by the open window and watched the lights come on over the city. Anna, back in her worn-out sweatshirt and old cotton shorts, sat with her knees drawn up to her chest, and her glass of wine held on her feet. She made a play of balancing it there; when Grace smiled, she looked at the glass, and promptly drank half of the Rioja.

"You might as well tell me what it is," Grace said. "I go home tomorrow."

Anna shrugged infinitesimally.

"Are you tired?" Grace asked.

"Yes."

"Anything else?"

"No."

"OK," Grace said. "I'm going to bed."

Anna put down the glass, and put her hand on her mother's.

"Is it so terrible?" Grace asked. She couldn't read Anna's expression.

"Do you think I could go to England?" Anna said.

"England? Why England? You mean for a vacation? You just got back."

"Not for a vacation," Anna said. "To see David."

It was the first time that his name had been mentioned for two or three years. "David," Grace repeated. "David Mortimer."

"Do you think I could find him?" Anna asked.

Grace, who had been in the act of standing up, sank back down to her chair. "How long have you been thinking this?" she asked.

"Not long."

"Since you were in Paris?"

Anna glanced away, back to the window. "He might still be in Oxford," she said. "If not, I could go to his father's house."

"He might, and you could," Grace murmured. "But why would you?"

Anna put down her glass, and got up. She paced about the loft space, and eventually stood in front of the world map that she and Rachel had painted across the wall. "I wish we could take this with us," she said. In less than a month, she and Rachel were moving to the house in Jamaica Plain.

"Maybe James will pay for the block to be taken down and moved downtown," Grace joked. "Ask him."

Anna walked up and down in front of the map. She trailed her hand over the green mass of the Amazon. In its depths, Rachel had drawn complicated leaf patterns, and insects. Crocodiles moved in the rivers; whales in the sea.

"I went to the café you told me about," she murmured distractedly. "Where Hemingway drank. In St.-Germain-des-Prés."

"What did James think of it?" Grace asked.

"He wasn't with me," Anna said. Behind her, Grace frowned.

Anna walked the length of the map. Across the southern oceans. Across Antarctica and South Africa and New Zealand. "Fuji, Hawaii," she whispered. She turned her face to the wall, and pressed her forehead to it.

Grace got up in a hurry. Anna turned to her with a stricken face. Grace held out her arms; they stood in the blue-swirled vastness of the Pacific, among Rachel's white-topped waves.

"Tell me why," Grace said. "Why did you leave David?"

"We went to David's mother's funeral," Anna said slowly. "And

his father had this . . . vacancy. It's all I could see. It's all I could remember. Sometimes I thought I saw it in David. I thought I heard
it in him. It's a kind of . . . unconnectedness. I would think, *He's
talking at me, he's far away.* I didn't want to tell him that I was pregnant, and see him go further away still. I couldn't bear to take the
chance. I was afraid."

Grace guided her to the couch. They sat down together, Grace
holding Anna's hands.

"So you just ran away."

Anna made a little moue of despair, then shook her head. "I
can always trust you to hit me right in the mouth," she complained.

"You did a cruel thing, Anna."

Anna wiped her eyes. "OK, I ran away," she admitted. "And
when I got the letters, they made it worse."

Grace had seen David's letters. They were short. Very short.
Just naked pleas.

"I thought I would wait until she was born," Anna said. "And
then I wrote to him."

Grace did a double take. "You wrote to him?" she echoed. "To
David? When?"

"When Rachel was two months old," Anna replied. "I told him
he had a daughter."

"But you never told me this!" Grace exclaimed.

"I didn't want to raise your hopes."

"You mean you thought I'd put pressure on you?" Grace said.
"But, Anna . . . !"

Anna held up her hand. "Or *my* hopes." She took a breath, ex-
haled slowly. "And he didn't reply," she said. "So there it was. That
was my answer. I couldn't blame him."

"And you just sent the one letter?" Grace asked.

"Yes."

"But maybe he never got it? Did you think of that?"

"I sent exactly the same letter to his college and to his father's
address," Anna said. "Two copies."

"And . . ."

"Nothing. Nothing at all."

The two women sat side by side, hands entwined.

"And why do you think he would have changed?" Grace asked, eventually. "If you found him now?"

Anna was completely silent.

"Anna?"

Anna disengaged her hands. "He wouldn't have," she said. "You're right. He wouldn't." She got to her feet. She picked up Rachel's jacket from the nearest chair, and her own case. Grace followed her into the bedroom, where Rachel was sleeping. Anna's own bed stood at right angles to her daughter's.

"What happened in Paris?" Grace whispered.

Anna unlocked the suitcase, glancing at Rachel's averted face.

Grace took the clothes which she had just taken out of the case from Anna's hands. "Come out of here and talk to me," she said.

"Look," said Anna, "forget David, forget Paris. Everything's fine."

"If you don't stop lying to me, I'll crack that damned suitcase over your head," Grace hissed.

They began a conversation in urgent whispers.

"What did James say to you?"

"Nothing."

"You went to Les Deux-Magots on your own."

"He was busy. He had a meeting. I went a lot of places on my own."

"You don't go to Paris with a man, and walk around it on your own," Grace said. "That's missing the fucking point of Paris."

Anna walked back into the main room. When Grace caught up with her, Anna was staring out of the window. "He wants me to marry him," she said.

Grace bit her tongue. *Say nothing,* she told herself. *Just pray.*

"I turned him down," Anna added. She turned and looked at her mother. Up from the street below drifted the sound of traffic. "You've never liked him, have you?" she asked.

Grace kept her mouth firmly shut.

"You were right," Anna said.

Grace promptly sat down with the relief of it.

"Say something," Anna prompted.

"I daren't," Grace told her.

Anna gave a ghost of a smile.

"Is there a specific reason?" Grace finally asked.

Anna sat down on the floor and looked at her. "Good question," she murmured. "Is there a specific reason for refusing a man who's supported and financed you and your child for five years, and been nothing but gentle and kind?"

Again, Grace said nothing. She was practicing her old trick of pressing her fingernails into the palm of her hand, so that her mouth wouldn't run away with her.

"Gentle and kind," Anna repeated, in a low voice. She ran her hand along the grain of the wood floor. "Did I tell you about a woman called Sophia Cruz?"

"No," Grace said. "Who is she?"

"A client of James's," Anna replied, in a smooth, soft tone. "A millionairess. A divorcée. He sleeps with her." She didn't look up.

"She came into the gallery one day just before we went to Paris," Anna said. "She had on her usual uniform. Little black dress. Little black jacket. She stayed for an hour. She went into the office. I saw her take off the jacket. She had bruises on her arms."

Grace frowned.

Anna sighed, and leaned back against the wall. "I saw James . . . it's hard to describe. He put his hands on her arms. He put his fingertips over the bruises. And he looked at her. They looked at each other."

"Did you ask him about it?" Grace said.

"No," Anna replied. "I thought, *That's just paranoid,* you know? But . . ."

"But what?"

"I've seen him take someone's hand sometimes. Clients. Women. He takes their hand. But it's not their hand. It's their wrist. He closes his fingers over their wrist."

Grace got up, walked over to Anna, and sat down on the floor next to her. "He tried this with you?" she said, trying to keep her voice calm. "He hurt you?"

Anna met her mother's eyes. "No," she said. "That's the weird thing. That's the horrible thing."

Grace shook her head. "What?" she asked, confused.

"He apologizes," Anna said. She blushed furiously, and bit her lip. "It's over in a minute. When it happens at all. And then he apologizes."

"For what?"

"Touching me."

Grace put her head in her hands. "Anna," she murmured.

"I know, I know." Anna shook her head slowly. "I asked him later about Sophia. He admitted it. He said it was of no matter at all. No consequence. When I asked him about the bruises . . ."

"You asked him?" Grace repeated. "What the hell did he say?"

"Nothing," Anna answered. "He smiled."

Grace looked at her daughter with fury, and then horror. "Anna," she said, "you have to get out of this. You have to get out of it now."

"I know," Anna said. "But he told me I could never get out of the contracts. I would never be out of his life."

"Ridiculous," Grace countered. "See a lawyer."

Anna smiled wanly. "That's exactly what I intend to do," she said.

Twenty-four

ANNA HAD NEVER SEEN rain like the torrential rain that streamed past her now. A vertical drop, like a waterfall. It was dark, and there were no lights but the reflection of the rain in the pools that stretched out in front of her. Tiered pools; those in front of her curved as they followed the edge of a hill. Those beyond in rows.

It was like looking at the seating of an open-air stadium, an auditorium. The curves played back the echoing drumming of the water. The country—a country with no lights, no roads—was rippling away from her; and then she solved the conundrum of the shapes around her. These were some kind of fields. Fields built into slopes, over one another like green shelves. Green shelves filled with the pouring rain. So much rain that the crops were almost flooded, and only the merest tip of the rice shoots showed in the water, so that the shelved ranks of rain-filled pools had a faint green fluorescence.

Behind her, in the darkness, she heard noises.

A group of men—twenty or more—were coming along the track at the edge of the field. They walked with dogged purpose, their heads down, each man carrying a pole across his shoulders from which woven baskets hung. The baskets were drenched, the men were drenched, their feet bare in the mud and rain except for the slip of leather sole fastened around the ankle, with a narrow strip passing between the toes. They wore caps of dark cloth pulled tight across the forehead.

In the center of the group was, incongruous in this storm, an empty sedan chair, with a curved roof. Inside it was some sort of luggage, a banded box, and a gun case. The men who carried the poles of the chair slithered in the rain, and the chair rocked from side to side.

"Anna," said a voice. "Can you see . . ."

She turned her head, trying to find who had spoken to her. Threads of vanishing sound, the merest breath. Echo within echo.

She looked back to the fields.

The men might have been starving, their bodies were so narrow, their wrists and hands so thin. Long tunics stuck to the flesh like second skins, revealing small shoulders, and the ridges of vertebrae. They did not speak; they walked with a concentrated rhythm, without comment, without raising their eyes.

At the back of the group came a taller man. He wore what might have been European clothes, although it was hard to tell in the shadows and the rain. A broad-brimmed hat was pulled down over his face. He had a long dark coat, and breeches, and boots. Anna stared at the boots as he walked within ten feet of her, and realized that she had nothing at all on her own feet. She was naked, except for a cotton gown that reached to her knees.

But she was not cold, and the rain had not touched her.

"Anna," the voice repeated. "Listen to me. Follow this road."

And this time it was inside her body, reverberating in her hand, the very tips of her fingers, as if the syllables were solid, as if she could touch them. She frowned. There was no road; only the rain.

And then, out of the darkness came the shape of a village.

Its small street, a tunnel under the overhanging and almost touching eaves of the houses, was a river of flowing mud. To the left-hand side was a limestone wall, and, below it, the roughest kind of footpath, raised up from the street with uncut and unfinished slabs crossing piles of stones. One by one, the men climbed onto the lower wall, and negotiated the slabs. Only then did Anna notice the two dogs, two large liver-and-white spaniels, saturated and silent, threading their way between the feet of the men.

Somewhere in this greater gloom of touching roofs, a door was opened. The men stopped on the slab walkway; as Anna reached them she put her hand to her mouth. Mixed with the mud of the street was human sewage. The Chinese porters were leaning against the wall, philosophical about the stench, or immune to it. In any case, the rain was fast and acting as a sluice; she saw one man rest his head on the limestone and look upward, so that the rain streamed down his face and neck.

Voices were raised along the street. She edged past the men and looked down into the house. It was full of smoke from a fire in the center of the floor, and it was also crammed with people. Children crowded to the front. The European had taken off his coat and hat and flung them over the arms of the Chinese boy who had come in the house with him, and who was speaking to the owner. Calmly, the taller man looked around him. His bearded face was broad, his eyes small and deep-set, and his skin was sallow, with almost a jaundiced tinge.

An argument began to break out. The porters came through the door, bowed under their burdens, pushing and shoving to gain entry. A wail of protest went up; another set of doors, in the rear of the room, was opened, and those who had already been in the house were forced backward, into the animal quarters. His expression unperturbed, the white man sat down closest to the fire.

She inhaled the smoke; it began to choke her.

With every breath, the room receded.

It seemed to her that she slept, although she had no grasp of time. In her sleep, she heard the mechanical pumping of a machine. A heart that was not a heart. An intake of breath without life. There was a liquid in her veins that was not blood. It was too icy. She tried to see herself, and saw only a tissue shell, like the discarded carcass of a larva, or the dead body of a crane fly, caught in a web.

Morning came, and the ice flowed out of her and into the air, turning it raw and cold. The same men set out along a steep track that rose quickly away from the houses, and she followed them, seeing them from extraordinary angles. From above, a dark line among the rooftops; then, so close that she could feel the moisture of their breath on her face. Closer still, so that she saw the straps cutting into the flesh of one man's shoulders.

The roofs rapidly disappeared with every step, swallowed into the cloud through which they were ascending.

The dense forest of silver fir that had once covered the mountain of Wa Shan mostly lay rotting where it had been felled for charcoal. She counted the paces alongside one tree as they passed it; fifty meters from root to tip. There was no oak, or beech, or hornbeam on these slopes. They trudged on upward, the dew clinging to the still-damp clothes of the men around her.

The track began to be crowded on each side with rhododendrons; then it gave way to bamboo, thick enough to slow their progress. She saw how high they were—eight, nine thousand feet—when they reached a plateau, half a mile wide and full of bamboo scrub. Long tracts of grasses and weeds scratched at her; with amazement she saw her own bare feet placed in the bearers' footprints. The ground was cool under her rather than cold; and occasionally, as she glanced up, she saw the sky begin to appear above them, an eggshell blue threading between the bands of fog.

They passed a clematis that was still in bloom: the pale pinkish blossom of *montana*. The soil of the plateau thinned, and then gave way completely to rock. They began to climb in earnest now, hand over hand. She smelled the fragrance of the green tea they had brewed. For a second, she thought she tasted it in her own mouth.

And then the clouds cleared.

"Look," the voice murmured.

At ten thousand feet, the mountain was covered with rhododendron, mass upon mass of them, everywhere she looked. Too fantastic to be a dream. On some thirty-foot-tall bushes, the flowers were so huge and so profuse that they almost hid the leaves. Their

twisted stems, distorted by the extremes of weather, and by gain-
ing purchase on the thin ground, were covered in mosses and
lichen. Anna's gaze trailed over the panorama of color that fell below them: darkest crimson, brightest red, silver pink, yellow, white.
An ocean, a borderless steppe of moving color. *Rhododendron fargesii*, with its massive pink bloom, freckled with a darker pink inside
the petals, was here in its hundreds and thousands.

"It flowers here," the voice murmured. "And below your window, right here. And all across the country, all across the state, all
across the city. He brought it home."

Which city? she wondered, confused. *Which state?*

It was midday, and very warm. In front of them, the mountain
ledge that they were standing on was only ten or twelve feet wide.
The leader of the party was looking back along the line of men.
He filled a clay pipe with tobacco, and took two or three long
pulls, exhaling the smoke. He took his tea, standing while the
bearers were crouching or sitting; his dogs came to lie at his feet.
When he had finished the pipe, he tapped it out on the sole of his
boot; and then, almost casually, he walked to the edge of the rock,
and looked down.

She saw it with his eyes suddenly: an abyss three thousand feet
deep, and the roar of a river somewhere far below. She realized
that the man was merely assessing the further climb, and searching
the rocks below and to the side for specimens. He seemed almost
bored at the sterility of the sheer walls of the mountain; calling his
dogs, he set off again, striding forward without glancing to see
how quickly his party followed.

They came almost to the summit.

It was lit in strong sunshine; the top seemed flat and square,
approached by a series of rectangular fortress walls that formed
precipices. They were completely sheer. It looked as if God had
been playing with building blocks, and left them evenly placed one
on the other. At some unimaginable point in the past, ladders had
been made and secured to these sheer flat faces of rock, and each
ladder was forty feet long, and at the end of each ladder was a small
ledge on which to stand.

Anna clung to the granite behind her. She didn't want to go forward; she didn't want to put her hand on the ladder, even if this journey were a dream, or she merely a ghost haunting the journey that these men were making. Then, to her amazement, she saw the man pick up the larger of the dogs, hold the spaniel firmly to his side, and begin to climb the first ladder.

There was no balustrade; no handrail. Just the edges of the ladder itself. They were at ten thousand eight hundred feet, and the narrow ledge that the ladder reached was no more than eight feet wide. Anna felt her arms and hands tingle painfully with vertigo; she began to gasp. Her heart was beating strangely, with an almost mechanical, rasping knock in her chest. As the man got to the top of the ladder he saw the remaining path, narrow and steep and inexpressibly dangerous, winding upward with scree slopes falling away on both sides into nothingness. The world swirled far below him. Anna could only vaguely make out the thin wisps of gray that represented the clouds they had come through.

He put his foot on the next ladder.

After only half a dozen rungs, the dog suddenly began to whine. The man's arm shifted to hold it tighter; but the dog only struggled more. Anna could see its body begin to slither down his side; the bearers below him stopped, looking up. The dog's back feet were scrabbling, their claws digging in. Soon, the dog had slipped so far that, as the man climbed, his own body swaying from side to side with the dog's movements, his right hand was gripping the dog by only the scruff of its neck and its collar. On the very last rung, the dog dropped; the bearers below cried out a warning. The man himself lurched to one side, hanging on to it now by its collar alone. A bearer below, suddenly coming to his senses, climbed rapidly and pushed both dog and master, and the trio fell onto the ridge above.

The moments passed in silence, and Anna had a sense of them all, clinging to the side of this vast wilderness of rock, suspended in their brief and insignificant seconds in time.

★   ★   ★

They were on the summit.

It was a plateau, undulating and grassy, like a meadow. The first thing that Anna saw was another clematis, and a spinney of silver fir, and then, stretching away from her, the most amazing sight—a woodland, just like any North American or English woodland in spring, the ground covered in white anemones and primula. More astonishing still was the temple, built of timber.

The European walked forward through the grass, took off his hat, and went through the doorway, to where the image of Pu'-hsien Pu'ssa was seated on a plaster elephant. He sat down and regarded it wordlessly and expressionlessly, as if to climb ten thousand feet, and cross the abyss, and find a natural parkland, looking like his own home, looking like Kew on a fine morning, and, at the center of the park, a plaster elephant in a wooden temple, were the most natural, and least surprising, thing in the world.

She began to feel the thin air of the mountains.

She wanted to lie down; the ground at her feet rotated slowly.

She heard her name called again, the same indistinguishable voice.

The short, flower-strewn grass of Wa Shan faded; she stood on a bridge, a wooden cantilever bridge.

"This is the Pi-tao Ho," the voice told her. And she saw how, as the road rose, the river became deeper. She saw, with giddy certainty, how the journeys would all rise and fall, interminably; they passed juniper, black pine, poplar, black birch, yew, larch. The ravine dripped with moisture, woods thick with actinidia and viburnum.

The road became worse; where it failed, and holes were left in the cliff sides, planks had been laid to form a kind of crossing; where the direction took them over a river, the bridges were nothing more than half-rotten logs. Under them, the icy torrent swirled.

They were at Hsiang-yang-ping, at eleven thousand and six hundred feet, and before them the alpine passes soared. The trees lay three thousand feet below, and snow lay in patches on the path. As they descended from the last mountain pass, they saw countless numbers of yellow poppy, the supposedly unattainable and mythical *Meconopsis integrifolia,* rolling away over the sandstone and the snow.

"Anna," the voice repeated. "Can you see these paths? Can you see these bridges?"

"Yes," she murmured.

She looked down at her hands, thinking that something had touched her. The heavily weighted head of the poppy drooped just out of her reach, hanging on its thick stem as cherry blossom hung down, with the same heavy fist of flower.

She wondered if it was this strange, delicate petal that was caressing her skin.

"Anna," the voice whispered to her. "Follow me."

Twenty-five

JEN WAS COMING BACK from school in the afternoon, a child on either hand, when she saw the van in the street. It was parked outside Anna's: the back was down, and she saw crates and boxes inside. She puzzled over it for a second or two, her youngest pulling on her arm while trailing her coat along the ground. She glanced down to pick up the coat, and, in that moment, she realized what was happening.

She started to run.

"Mommy!" her little girl complained.

She found the door propped open; inside, there were men's voices. "Hello?" she called. "Hello?"

They were somewhere far up in the house. She walked down the hallway, looked in the kitchen.

"Grace," her boy said.

"I don't think that Grace is home, honey," she told him. "Here ... here." She fumbled around with the seats, and looked hastily in the cupboards. "You sit here, sweetheart, and take care of Sadie."

"I want to go home," he told her.

"In a second," she said. "Here's the lemonade. Pour your sister something to drink. And don't go out in the yard. Don't move, OK? Just for two minutes."

She raced up the stairs.

On the landing, she found James Garrett.

"What's happening?" she asked him. "What are you doing?"

"Hello, Jen," he said. He looked gray, she noticed; exhausted.

"Is Grace here?" she asked.

"No," he told her. "Grace is at the hospital."

She looked at the portfolio that he was holding. He had it balanced over one arm, and had evidently been turning the sheets of paper.

"Who's upstairs?" she asked.

"I'm just arranging something for Anna," he said. "A collection she wanted."

Her gaze kept drifting to the portfolio. It contained Anna's botanical drawings.

"I always liked these," he mused. "They're really well done." He turned one of the pictures for her to see. "What is this called?" he asked.

"I don't know. James, who is upstairs? What are they doing?"

"And this?" He was holding up another drawing.

"It's the *Meconopsis*," she said, only half paying attention, her eyes fixed on the stairwell.

He smiled sadly at her. "The what?"

"I believe it's some kind of poppy." She looked back at him, feeling herself blush. Upstairs, she could hear something heavy being maneuvered across the floor.

James was looking steadily at her. "You didn't say a poppy," he said. "You gave it half of its Latin name." He glanced down at the sheet. *"Meconopsis integrifolia."* He nodded to himself. "And what would *Meconopsis punicea* be?"

"I don't know," Jen said.

He closed the portfolio carefully, and tied the cloth string to fasten it. "It's red, Jennifer," he said quietly. "It's another poppy, and very rare."

"Is it?" she said.

"I wonder," he mused, putting the portfolio by his feet, "if we might stop playing games?"

"Games?" she echoed. "What games?"

"Well," he said, "for instance, the game where I show you something that has been under lock and key—along with a number of other items—and you at first seem to have some sort of understanding and recognition of what I show you, and then, in the next moment, you pretend that you don't."

Jen's heart did a slow somersault. "You've broken into Anna's desk," she said.

"Broken into it?" he repeated. "Do you know, until this afternoon, I had no idea that there *was* anything locked in that room?" He shook his head, almost sorrowfully. "No, I didn't break in," he said. "But I found a key sitting on top of the table, and I found that the key opened the desk."

"Those are Anna's private things," Jen said.

"Not private to you, apparently," James answered.

"If Anna's shown them to me, that's no business of yours, either," Jen retorted.

There was another noise from Anna's studio above them. "What the hell is going on up there?" Jen muttered. She put her hand on the banister to start up the steps.

Immediately, James put his hand on her wrist. "They're bringing something down," he said. "Don't get in their way."

She tried to pull her arm away. "Bringing what down?" she demanded.

He didn't answer her. But he looked down at his own hand rather bemusedly, as if he were surprised to see it on hers. His gaze fixed on their two sets of fingers on the stair rail. "You know," he mused, "I've really been rather slow in putting two and two together. I never thought that '*cinnamonifolium*' had any significance."

It was her turn not to reply.

"And let me see," he said, making a show of recalling. "Other names of her abstract work. The one I sold on Long Island, 'Koyamai.' I thought it was Japanese—I said as much to Anna. She let me believe she had a Japanese influence. And 'Corydalis.' Do you know that I looked up the word *corydalis* in an opera guide? I thought it was the name of a character. That gray-green and yellow. It reminded me of a heraldic symbol. She laughed about it," he said. "She implied it was simply manufactured."

Jen had moved no further than the first step of the stairs. The tone of his voice had frozen her. She couldn't remember ever having seen James Garrett angry—or, if he had been, he had never shown it to her. He had always been formally polite to her.

"Mommy!" Sadie yelled from below.

James had still not released his hold on her wrist. She glanced warily at him. His hand was almost cold. She looked over the banister. "What is it?"

"Want to go!"

"OK," she replied. "Wait . . . wait."

Above them, two men started down the stairs. One was carrying a large four-by-six portfolio, the other a box. She stood in the way, and looked back at James.

"You're stealing her work," she said.

"I can't steal something I already own," he said.

"But you don't own it," she said. "How can you own everything in her studio? How can you own unfinished paintings?"

"Jennifer," James said. "Would you let these men get down the stairs."

"I won't stand by and see Anna's possessions taken from her home," she said. She tried to pull her hand from under his, but he was pressing down on the rail.

"I'm taking work for framing," he said. "Look in the portfolios. They're not unfinished. They're finished pieces that we're preparing for sale."

"And Anna wants you to do this?"

"I have a contract with Anna for all her work," he said. "Did you forget that?"

There was a protesting scream, the sound of an argument, from downstairs. Jen hesitated, torn between her children and Anna's defense. In the second that she looked back, James took her wrist and disengaged her hand from the banister, nodding to the men to walk past her. She watched them go in utter frustration.

"All her ceramics?" she asked. "Notebooks, everything?"

He waited until the last man was on the second stairway. The face he turned back to her had changed from the affability of the last few moments.

"I have a contract," he repeated.

"Not for everything in that room."

"For everything Anna does."

"And you—" Suddenly, she stopped. "If you're taking *every-thing*," she repeated, aghast. Her eyes widened. "What's happened to Anna?" she said.

He didn't reply at first. For a moment, his eyes strayed upward. When he resumed, his tone was almost conversational. "I never connected the names at all," he said. "Until I saw the tray."

The tray, the drawer, she thought. *Oh, no.*

"Do you know what *cinnamonifolium* is?" he asked. She heard a hitch in his voice now; a little twist of grief. "It's an extraordinary name, isn't it? Botanical names are rather rhythmical, aren't they? *Cinnamonifolium* is a blue-black version of a plant called viburnum. And *koyamai* is a species of spruce." He shook his head, and gave a short, exasperated laugh. "It's all perfectly easy, once you have the key, once you know what it is you're dealing with," he told her. "And *corydalis* ... *corydalis* is a common weed, a climbing weed with a yellow flower." He gave a great sigh. "Extraordinary," he murmured to himself, "that I never realized. But why would I? I had no idea."

"Mommy!" Sadie called. "Mommy!"

"Realized what?" Jen asked. She didn't like the way he was looking: haunted almost. Sick.

James took a step toward her. "All these years, and I never knew that everything she painted, everything she drew, everything I sold for her, every single name of every painting, every abstract, had a botanical name. Or a shortening of a botanical name, or was an anagram of a botanical name. Isn't that amazing?"

Jen heard Sadie start up the flight of stairs below. "Michael is outside," her daughter called. "Michael went in the yard."

"You don't find that amazing?" James repeated.

"All right, Sadie," she called. "You call him back. You tell him to come here to me."

"I suppose," James said, getting close to her, "that you knew all this?"

"No," Jen said.

"No?" he repeated. "She must have thought I was very stupid."

"I don't think Anna would call you stupid," she said.

"But I even thought she had made the names up. It must have given her hours of amusement!" He had gripped her wrist again.

"Let go," she said, frightened. She backed away across the narrow stairwell. He stepped up alongside her, and began pulling her up the stairs.

"Let me go," she repeated. "My kids ... Let go ..."

They reached the top floor. He yanked her in through the door. James let Jen's hand drop, and walked to the other side of the studio, where he picked up the tray.

"You've seen this," he said. "You know what's in here?"

"Things from college," she breathed. "James, look—"

"From college," he said. "Ten years ago. More than ten years. That's right." He snatched up a cardboard box, and tipped the contents out onto the tabletop.

She saw the smaller white envelope of the oak leaves fall out. He snatched it up.

"What's this?" he demanded.

"I don't know," she lied.

He took out the leaves and held them out to her on the palm of his hand. "What significance are these?" he said.

"I really don't know."

"Leaves," he said angrily, bitterly, almost to himself. He threw down the envelope. "And this?" He was holding the Oxford map.

She said nothing.

"And this? And these?" He threw the postcards and essays down on the table.

"Everyone keeps things from college," she murmured.

He glared at her. He opened the watercolor pad, and turned the pages, staring at her as the images echoed each other. The *lonicera,* the lilies. He picked up another pad, and almost tore the front sheet as he opened it. On each page, Anna had written an explanation of the watercolors, noting the location.

Here were images of strange and beautiful landscapes: the Great Wall at Shanhaiguan, snaking down the mountains and across the coastal plain to the sea, and at Jiankou, scaling the bladelike summits; Po Lin monastery on Lan Tau Island. The red sandstone peak of Longhua Shan, near Tingtan, looking like a complete fairy tale citadel, the river snaking at its feet, and yet more promontories behind it, one after the other, each as breathtaking as the last, rising from fields whose shade of green was almost too emerald to be real. Heaven Lake in Jilin province; and, lastly, the village of Meirendao in the Three Gorges, the Yangtze storming at its side, its tiny fields of maize looking like sculptured lawns.

"China," James said. "China … China … China …"

"I've got to go," Jen told him. She could now hear Sadie and Michael in the hall. She was also acutely aware that, downstairs in her bag, she had left her cell phone. *I must call Grace,* she thought. *I must tell Grace.*

James stepped in front of her. "This is him," he said. "Isn't it?"

"Who?" she asked.

"David Mortimer. This is all him. This is what he does. He's a scientist. He told me." James cast about himself, his gaze moving from one image to another and from the maps and cards back to the drawings, as if simply by looking at them he could make sense of them. "Is he interested in China?" he asked. "Did he go there? Had he lived there?"

"I don't think so," Jen said.

"He must have," James replied. "Look at all this. He must have been there, or they were going to go there, or he had some sort of connection with the place …"

He was taking more items out of the tray. For a second, he seemed to have forgotten that Jen was there. "And for five years," he muttered, "she never mentioned his name. I knew of course that Rachel had a father somewhere. But I thought that he was less than nothing to Anna. And yet she'd kept these things, she named every painting for him. What that meant to her, to dedicate her work to him ... And she never told me," he said. "She never told me a word about him."

Quite suddenly, Jen felt sorry for this man in front of her. *You're just not equipped for life,* she thought. *You have no idea.*

"James ..." she murmured.

"I gave her a necklace, and she wouldn't wear it," he said.

She didn't know what he was talking about.

"It's here," he told her. "It's here, in this box, in this drawer."

He fumbled about in the tray, and brought out a long blue jewelry box. He held it tightly for a second. "Lilies," he said. And pointed to the drawings. "Lilies, like these. That's why she wouldn't touch it, isn't it? Because that's what *they* were about. She and David Mortimer. Something to do with them ... something ..."

He looked at Jen, but she purposely did not look up at him to return his gaze, even though she could feel his stare boring into her.

"Do you know how many drawings of lilies there are in here?" he asked her. He threw the jewelry box down in frustration. "But she never drew them to sell," he said. "They weren't for sale."

She looked behind her, to the door.

When she looked back, he had David's letters in his hand. He saw her expression, and gave a faint smile. "I've read them," he told her. "Have you?"

"No," she said.

"Never read them?" he asked. "Never had them read to you?"

"No."

"How extraordinary," he said, opening one. "Let me enlighten you."

"I don't want to hear," she said. "It's not right."

"*Anna,*" he read, holding the letter at arm's length, as if he were giving a speech. "*Anna, please write to me. Call me. If you can't get through at Magdalen, here's Sara's number ...*" He glanced at Jen. "Who is Sara?"

"I ..."

"It doesn't matter," he said. "Don't bother." He went back to the letter. *"You didn't give me a chance. I just want to talk to you. I'll come to Boston if you want me to."*

Jen put her hand to her face.

"Pitiful, isn't it?" James asked. "Almost tacky. Embarrassing, don't you think?"

"No," Jen retorted. "I don't, actually."

"Here's another," he continued, in the same tone of fastidious revulsion. "Dated three weeks later. *'Why didn't you tell me you were leaving? That's all I want to know. I want you to come back, or I'll come to you . . .'*"

James dropped the letter, with the rest of the things, on the table.

"And why was that?" he asked her. "Why did she leave him?"

"Look, James," she said, "if Anna has never told you about this, then I can't."

"Had they argued?" he asked. "What had they argued about?"

"I can't say."

"You can't say because you don't know, or because you won't?" he demanded. "She came back to Boston, suddenly. That much is obvious. She left him during the university year." He pointed at the last letter, where it had fallen. "That is dated March," he said. "She left in March. Before the end of the term. Why?"

She couldn't meet his face.

There was a silence.

"Rachel," he said. He was staring down again at the date of the letter. "Rachel was born that year." He suddenly walked around the end of the table, and grabbed Jen by the shoulders. "She never told him about Rachel," he said. "Why not?"

"My kids are downstairs," Jen said, stepping backward, trying to fend off his hands. "I've got to go. I'm going now."

"Grace knows," he said. "Doesn't she? She knows how Anna felt about this man. That's why she called him, isn't it? But Anna never asked him to come here. Why not?"

"If you don't take your hands off me, I'm going to start screaming," Jen told him. "Try explaining that to your hired help down there."

It had no effect on him. "Why did she leave him?" he insisted. "Why?"

His tone frightened her. "Because she was afraid that he was somewhere else," she relented, at last. "Somewhere she couldn't find him."

"But he loved her," he said. "Look at those letters."

"She was afraid that he was like his father."

"His father?" he repeated. "What about his father?"

She frowned, passing a hand over her forehead. "I don't really know," she said. "Anna only met him once."

He thought for a moment. "If she only met him once, it must have been something striking."

She shook her head. "She didn't go into it in detail."

He was staring at her. A look something like triumph flickered in his expression. "I thought so," he said. "I asked him about it. He deflected the question. I was right. David Mortimer inherited something that Anna was afraid of."

"He wasn't sick," Jen said. "If you think that."

"No," James murmured. "Not sick, exactly." And he shocked her by laughing. At last, he dropped his hands from her. For a moment, she saw a thwarted, isolated child in his face. He looked away, across the studio, fixed his gaze on the leaves for a second. "How very ordinary," he whispered. "Just like any other woman."

On the stairs, Jen heard the footsteps of the moving men.

Garrett looked back at the table. Then, he walked back to it, and slowly picked up the two drawing pads. He smoothed down the pages.

The men came in the door; he inclined his head to indicate the plan chest on one wall. "There are about twenty more pen-and-ink studies," he told them. "Pack between cartridge, like the others."

And he smiled a coarse smile; shocking, not because of the greed, but because of the disgust in it.

Twenty-six

IT WAS MID-AFTERNOON WHEN Grace saw the neurosurgeon again.

She was walking back from the rest room when she saw Daniel Coram standing in the corridor.

"Have you got a moment?" she asked him.

"I was just coming to find you," he told her.

As she entered his office, she found herself wondering how old Coram was, and how many years he had been watching the lives and deaths of people like her daughter. She noticed a waterproof jacket hanging on the peg behind his door; a pair of worn driving gloves on the desk. Next to them, in between the files and folders, were two cardboard models of rainbows: colors drawn onto cardboard and looped over, and stuck down with tape.

"My grandchildren," he said, when he saw her looking.

"How many do you have?" she asked.

"Five," he told her. "And you?"

"Just Rachel," she said.

She gazed for a second more at the colors scribbled on the card, and then turned away. She found it hard to think of Rachel now. She was frightened for her; frightened to know what she would do without a mother. A constriction of grief in her throat silencing her temporarily, she looked in her bag for cigarettes, and shook out an empty pack.

"My dad had a coat just like that," she said absentmindedly, nodding toward the Barbour. "He wore it for fishing."

"So do I," Coram told her. "I go sea-fishing." He smiled at her. "Rarely catch a thing besides a cold."

She smiled back. Looking again at the pack, she crumpled it in her hand, and threw it in the wastebasket. "My father fished near Deerfield," she told him. She sat down in the chair he indicated. "He would go out early," she murmured. "Dawn. There's a dam just upstream from where we lived. Sometimes they would let water from the dam, and if you hadn't listened to the radio, you had to watch the river level. You would see it drift over one stone, then another, rising . . ."

And this thought of her father, fishing but rarely getting lucky, but being happy to be on the river with her in the first light, and the sweet bright expectation of those days, and the cracked plastic seats of the truck cab, and the sight of the house at the bottom of the hill as they bounced down the rutted drive while the sun burned away the last of the night . . .

It was too much. She longed for her father now, for his good guiding sense. She wanted to be back in the truck, seeing the house emerge between the trees, and feeling summer heat on her arm at the open window, and her naked toes making patterns in the dust of the truck floor.

She plunged her head in her hands.

Daniel Coram came around the desk, and put a handkerchief in her grasp. Without opening her eyes, she pressed it to her face, and sat soundlessly without sobbing, pressing the material hard against her eyes to blank out the past and the present.

After a minute or so, she sat back, breathing heavily. She opened her eyes and looked at him. He was sitting in a chair by her side.

"Is it bad?" she asked.

"Pretty bad," he said.

She put the handkerchief in her lap.

"Mr. Garrett was here this morning," he said. "I spoke to him."

She didn't look up. "I phoned him," she murmured.

"What did he tell you?"

"Nothing," she said.

"I don't know that he understood me," Coram told her. "He seemed to have made up his mind."

"To what?" she asked.

"To Anna's death."

She gasped, and pressed her back to the chair, as if this would help her move away from him.

He raised his hand. "That's not what's happening," he said.

"Her *death* ..."

"It's not what's happening," he repeated. "Grace, do you hear me?"

Stripes of light and shade confused her; the room was rippling. She blinked. He emerged as before, solid and still, looking hard at her. "Yes, I hear you," she said.

"Let me get you a drink," he said. He got up, and poured her a glass of water. She took it and drank in sips; he took it back, and put it within her reach on his desk.

"Anna had a seizure this morning," he said.

"The nurses said so ..."

"I know that this sounds strange," he said. "But it's a good sign."

"It is?" she asked.

Coram put his fingers to his lips for a second, apparently deciding how to phrase the next sentence. "When a patient's in a coma," he told her eventually, "one of the questions we ask ourselves is if the brain is functioning, if there is brain stem activity. A patient can be on a ventilator, apparently breathing, but there is actually no activity in the brain stem, and without the ventilator, they would cease to breathe."

"Anna is on a ventilator," Grace whispered.

"But we have some motor response to stimuli," he said. "And a seizure rules out the diagnosis of brain death."

"Then why did James think the opposite?" she asked.

"There was no response following the seizure," Coram said.

"You mean, what? What kind of response?"

"Eye opening, verbal responses, reaction to pain."

"She didn't react to pain?" Grace echoed.

Coram leaned forward, elbows on knees, hands clasped. "Anna is responding now," he said. "She was vocal this morning, before you came. After Mr. Garrett had left. And she flexed when we tested."

"Vocal?" Grace said.

"She gasped a little."

"Did she move?"

"No."

"But this . . . all this is good?"

"It's not good," he said. "But it's not bad. It's not the end. I wanted you to be clear on that."

"OK," she said. And it sounded childish to her, the thin and expressionless way she had said OK like that. "I'm clear," she added, forcing her voice up.

He sat back, looking at her kindly. "You have Mr. Mortimer with you now," he said. "I notice he's talking to Anna."

"Yes," she said. "He knew her in college. They once talked about writing and illustrating a book about China. So he had this idea . . ."

"That he would talk to her about the book?"

"About China, yes. About certain journeys . . ."

"It's a good idea," Coram said.

"You think so?"

"I know so," Coram replied. "Coma may look like an unresponsive state, but coma patients often report having been able to hear what was going on around them." He smiled. "I see Rachel is helping him."

"He thought they would do it together," Grace murmured. "Draw a map, make the journey . . ."

She stopped. Rachel was so intent on the drawing. They had bought a long scroll of paper, and a roll of masking tape, and they had been allowed to tape it to the wall opposite the bed. Rachel was creating her rivers, just as she had done when she was five and six, across the wall in the apartment.

David had sat down next to Anna, and begun to speak in a low, soft tone. Occasionally, he would glance at Rachel and watch her as she leaned against the wall, head at an angle, eyes fixed on the pencil point. Grace had sat silently between them, seeing, in the depths of her concentration, how Rachel's speed dipped at times. There was no obvious indication that Rachel was listening to David, other than this fleeting slowness at certain points. When David reached the Wa Shan summit, Rachel actually paused. She redrew the curve of the coastline several times, like a failing printer copying over a line it had already typed.

"Is Mr. Mortimer related to Rachel?" Coram asked.

"He's her father," Grace told him. "They had never met before this happened. He never knew about her until now."

Coram took this information in with a bemused expression. "That is quite some news for them both," he said, eventually.

"Yes," Grace agreed. "It's been a newsy kind of week."

He stopped, trying to figure her out. Then laughed softly, sympathetically. "Newsy," he repeated. "OK. That's one way to put it, I guess."

Grace shrugged helplessly.

"And you are alone yourself?" Coram asked.

"Yes."

"Anna is your only child."

"Yes." She looked hard at Coram. "Do you think Anna will recover?" she asked.

"Do you want my opinion, or the statistics?" Coram asked.

"Both."

Coram nodded. "OK," he said. "Let's see what the odds are here. At any one moment in this country, there are ten thousand people in a coma ..."

"Ten thousand?" Grace echoed. "Ten *thousand* ...? My God. No."

"We used to think that in cases like Anna's, all the damage was done to the brain right at the point of impact," he told her. "In

Anna's case, that would be the moment that she hit the dashboard of the car. But now we think that probably isn't true. The damage is done afterward, when the brain can't get enough blood or oxygen."

He crossed his arms, looking at the floor momentarily. "There are two types of coma," he said. "One, from head or spinal trauma. Here, you'll see labored breathing, limbs extended. You might see a clenched jaw. When we do a lumbar puncture, we find blood in the spinal fluid. The blood pressure goes up, the pulse goes down."

Grace continued to stare at him, silent.

"Then there's the second kind of coma," Coram continued. "The breathing is bad, the pupils are always pinpoint . . . and that's caused by damage to the brain stem. When you see a case like that, the prognosis is grim."

"And Anna . . ."

"Anna doesn't have damage to the brain stem," Coram said. "But she's sustained a lot of injury. She has some primitive responses, a gag reflex, response to pain. She has opened her eyes a little once or twice. But she hasn't spoken, and she hasn't interacted with anyone . . . recognized your voice, turned toward it, squeezed a hand . . ."

"No," Grace agreed. She felt sick, drained. She noticed that the very tips of her fingers, clasped over the handkerchief, were blue. She curled them into a fist, and hid them.

"Do you want me to go on?" Coram asked.

"Yes," she murmured.

"Are you sure?"

"Yes," she said.

"OK," he answered. He watched her closely. "Between five and ten percent of coma patients aren't capable of conscious behavior," he said. "They end up like this for life. For what remains of their life."

"They never get any better?"

"No."

"But the others," Grace said. "The ones who start to react . . . they do get better. They improve, they get well . . ."

"Even those without brain stem damage," Coram said, "may never get further than the immobile state in which you see Anna now."

She raised her hand to her face. "Never get further?" she repeated. "What do you mean?"

"They might make facial grimaces sometimes," he said. "Or swallow, or open or close their eyes. But there's no evidence that they're aware of anyone or anything."

"And this goes on . . ."

"Maybe for weeks. Maybe for years."

Grace had leaned forward in her chair. "I've heard of this," she whispered. "It's when you turn the machines off. When you talk about the machines."

"We're not talking about switching off any machines right now," Coram replied.

She took this in, her own breath shallow. "But you will," she said. "If she doesn't improve. If she doesn't respond . . ."

"That's a long way down the line," Coram said.

There was a silence.

"You asked me for the truth," Coram reminded her.

She glanced at him; she had been staring, without knowing it, at the paper rainbows on his desk. "Yes, I did," she acknowledged.

"And I've told you the absolute worst," Coram added. "You understand, Grace? That's the worst. The worst that can possibly happen to Anna."

"All right," she said.

She closed her eyes, and saw Rachel's hand fisted around the pencil, and the relentless, concentrated scribbling. She saw Rachel and Anna, posed on a bridge, a bridge with a fathomless drop on either side. And Rachel sitting, the habitual preoccupied look on her face, sitting down at Anna's feet, and carefully unknotting the strands of the cables, unraveling the steel as if it were cotton, meticulously unthreading each line. And Anna, strand by strand, dropping away, little by little.

There was nothing practical that this child could do to hold her mother, Grace thought. She was making shapes at the edge of Anna's consciousness, unable to talk to her, unable to hold her. And with each silence, the silence of distracted, misplaced concentration, Anna fell further away from them.

"God," she breathed. "God."

Coram had gotten up. He stood uncertainly at her side for a second, then put his hand on her shoulder. "Let's be positive here," he said. "The odds are in Anna's favor. She's a young woman with no prior health problems. She has every motivation to get well. She has a daughter, a mother, a partner, and a friend in David." He paused. "What does she do?" he asked. "Does she have a job?"

"She's an artist," Grace said. "That's why we brought the map for Rachel to draw. We thought, even the atmosphere in the room, the sound . . ."

"Yes," he said. "I see."

"It's not much."

"But it would mean something to Anna," he said. "People say music and familiar sounds are useful. There are tapes of the ocean, or birdsong. Or people sometimes record the everyday noises of a house, or a city . . ."

"OK," she said, trying to remember. "Tapes . . ."

"The things that meant most to her," he suggested. "You could bring in paint for Rachel. The smell of paint or ink? Or whatever she worked with."

"OK," she repeated. She looked again in her handbag, this time for a pen and paper. She found her checkbook, and wrote on the back: *paint, ink, tapes, sounds.*

And she thought of the sounds of Anna's life: the landscape of sound she would make if asked to describe her by note and vibration alone. The changing conversation of the wind in the Appalachian trees; the murmur of the ocean; her grandparents' voices; the feel and sound of wrapping paper from parcels that she used to hoard as a child; the barking of the neighbors' dogs on the other side of the hill. Ogunquit in high season, with the sound of the trams slowing at their stops, the hum of crowds on the beaches; and everything that was Rachel—her cry as a baby, her TV tapes, over and over the same songs. Rachel on the piano. Somewhere in her house, Grace had the first recording she had made of Rachel trying piano scales. And she had others: a Chopin piece, a polka, and Debussy.

There was so much else. Anna's favorite old Motown on the radio; and the small, touchstone details of the house in Jamaica Plain: the doorbell, the screen door, the squeak of the kitchen door to the garden; the silence of the studio, the intimate proximity of brush on paper. The store on the corner with its wire mesh gate by the register, and WXKS always playing in the back; and the sound of kids playing tennis across the road in the municipal courts, and of Jen's children; the sound of a ball kicked against concrete; the gentle plash of leaves against leaves in a summer night, when all the windows were open.

And even less consequential things. The sound of coins in her pocket. The acceleration of traffic, the grinding sound of the old Chrysler engine; the click of light switches, the rattle of curtain-hooks as curtains were drawn; the ticking of clocks. The turning page of a book or newspaper. The hush of the Beacon Hill apartment, and the echo on its stairs, and the muted voices of the city below the hill. The splash of water, and the soft rustling settling of sheets, and the whisper of her own voice.

Anna had none of those with her. Not one of those things.

Her life was rolling back, like a tide ebbing the sounds of the world away. It was amazing how a life was made, and what was carried with us, Grace considered. And to bring the sounds to Anna's bedside would be like walking into her memories. Which memory would turn her head toward a sound? Which memory would turn her away?

She looked up at Coram. "Will she get back," she asked, "to where she was before?"

Coram gave her a smile. He held out his hand, and helped her to her feet. "If she wants to," he said.

Twenty-seven

ANNA OPENED HER EYES to a city.

It was morning, and summer; and the sound of the place swept down at her like a tide, one great relentless wave of color and sound.

The air was full of a peculiar, rhythmic noise: Anna recognized the beat as the heavy, speeding clatter of looms. Crowds pushed up the street where she stood. Sunk in shadow, the sun touched only the tops of the temples and the garrison walls; but the street and its shade were multicolored, with lacquered and gilded shop signs hanging from each building. She was carried by the busy stream of humanity, carried as effectively as the sedan chairs with their curved poles that lifted the chairs above the heads of the pedestrians, edging past pushcarts and wheelbarrows, down other streets, each devoted to a different trade: skins and furs, embroideries, goldsmiths, silversmiths, silks.

She looked up at the silks—indigo from P'eng Hsien, held in straw-braid baskets from Shuangliu Hsien and every shade from the palest ivory to the deepest blue-green, fluttering like flags on their stalls and in curtains from the doorways, and lying in rolls, color after color, delicate to the touch. She stretched her hand to the closest display, and felt the brush of it, strangely, pass along her arm to her face.

"This is Chengdu Fu in 1910, a city of three hundred thousand people," said her guide.

She turned her head, tried to find him. She looked in the faces that were passing her, reached out her hand to stop someone. Her grasp closed on nothingness. Yet she knew that voice, that familiar voice whispering beneath the clattering looms. . . .

"Surrounded by a nine-mile wall pierced by four fine stone gates. The wall was over sixty feet broad at the base, forty feet broad at the top, and thirty-five feet high. . . ."

Anna was suddenly completely aware of this construction, of its importance, of the shape and slope of the brick as it tapered upward. Her heart suddenly went out to it with a peculiar strong passion, and she thought of Rachel, and her drawings; and she suddenly understood entirely, in a flash, Rachel's fascination with the way that things were put together, and the vitality and ingenuousness of the imagination behind them. She found herself staring at the walkway that ran along the top of the wall; it boasted a fortress balustrade, squared and patterned. Her eye ran from the walkway to a gate, and she drifted through it, trailing her fingers along the inner facing, the forty feet of stone.

"The bridges," the voice said. "The bridges."

There were ditches, canals, and streams beyond the city walls.

Anna could hear these waters, the snowmelt of spring, the grudging race of a dry autumn, the bubble and trickle over weirs and dams; she could hear them like the blood moving in her own body, the pressing and receding beat of her own pulse.

"Every stream had its bridge. This one is Han Chou," whispered the voice. "This is the Bridge of the Golden Goose, this rests on six stone piers, this is ornate, it is carved—look . . ." And she thought immediately of the covered wooden bridges of home: of the red- or green- or blue-painted, slate-roofed bridges of Vermont, the trellis-sided bridge at Brattleboro, the English church lych-gate splendor of the span at Franconia Notch in the White Mountains of New Hampshire.

"This is Marco Polo's bridge . . ."

It was filled today with wagons, each with its curved bamboo roof; and at either end of the bridge were timber-framed houses, looking exactly like the black-and-white-framed Tudor houses in England; while down in the weedy shadows of the river they were emptying the fish baskets, and the river widened and slowed.

Anna looked ahead of her. Out on the road were thirty men. The morning had grown hot, and the mist that never quite left the plain was hanging low, ochre under a gray and humid sky. She walked with them, under memorial arches and gates—arches where even the road surface failed, and there was nothing but dust and the high bamboo on either side of the track—arches to gods and ancestors, capped by crouching tigers, embroidered with leaves. They passed fields of millet and sugar; pulse, indigo, and tobacco; rice and hemp and cotton.

They reached the river gorge. The road swept upward, upward, skirting the valley sides above the river. There were no more trees now, only the low shrubs with thick and felty leaves that illustrated the uniquely dry atmosphere of the gorge. At single rope bridges of plaited bamboo, they met the foot soldiers of trade, carrying huge packs on their backs of potash salts, charcoal, and oil cake.

At the desolate little hamlet of Peh-yang Ch'ang, they came to a breathtaking piece of heaven.

There was spread out before them mile upon mile of *Buddleia davidii,* the intensity of the violet color so striking that each man put down his load, and the whole party stood for minutes, staring out across it.

After a few moments, Anna saw the tall man walk forward. He crouched by the roadside, and put his hand to a smaller shrub. It was not more than four feet high, but it was a single albino form of its royally colored sisters. He took its flower heads and seeds, and those of the *Hydrangea villosa* that stood next to it.

Anna watched him wrap the seeds in paper, and then in cotton, and put them in his pocket. Then he walked away, brushing the dust from his jacket. It was a little gesture, an automatic gesture, as though the plant were of no consequence. Ten years later there would be white buddleia in America, edging the gardens in Boston with a neatly nodding white hem.

They reached Hsao-kou at six thousand feet. On all sides the mountain walls sheered upward, culminating in razor-sharp peaks; and yet at the door of the inn and around all the houses, magnolia grew, along with aconite.

It was the last they saw of any kind of cultivation. After less than a mile, the magnolia, buddleia, and hydrangea fell away, and the climb became dangerously steep. The pace slowed until the summit, and, on the other side, they saw the Lungan side of the pass, and a graveyard of trees: the relics of giants long cut down for their timber.

Suddenly it began to rain, as they came down from the summit. The light began to fail. And Anna saw, as the men around her slipped on the steep shale, and then gradually, as the height dropped, gained more and more purchase on soil and grass, that through the gloom all kinds of plants surrounded them, like ghosts in the low cloud.

They walked deeper into woodland, where maples hung with rain, and the floor was covered with anemone, and astilbe and spirea, meadow rue, and drifts of yellow and pink impatiens. She stopped and looked at them in amazement. She bought impatiens every year for her flower tubs; she bought them as seedlings, and repotted and nurtured them, and waited for weeks for the first buds and flowers. Last year, Grace had grown white and pink impatiens along her paths, and complained at how long they had taken to flower, and how thin and leggy they had become through the dry summer. Yet here they were, in huge drifts in the twilight; and the bearers trod on them as they passed.

She let the men go past her, and stood and watched them as they walked out of sight between the trees. She did not question the slow dream; she was grateful for it. It was the strangest of gifts. But when she looked at the last draining light between the trees, she felt suddenly sure that she was alive only in this curious other world, and that she was never going to wake. And she was never going to go home.

★ ★ ★

The night was spent at San-chai-tsze, at thirteen thousand feet.

They woke the following morning to a glorious day.

The path down was full of alpine flowers—larkspurs, gentians, and aconite providing stunning blues; saxifrage of all kinds, especially the purple *Saxifraga oppositifolia,* which was sometimes called snow purple.

It was as they reached the very top of the pass that Anna saw the senecio.

She paused at the word in her mind, *senecio,* a word she had never heard before. She could not understand where it had come from, why it had suddenly emerged in her thoughts. In the cool breeze blowing on the upland she looked to left and right, across the ruins of a fort where a prayer flag still fluttered. Below it, in the sunshine, she saw a raised mound of stones, a flat cairn, and something balanced on top of it. The bearers walked down to it, and stopped silently in front of it.

"Senecio," a man's voice whispered. "Remember."

She put her hand to her head, frustrated at this returning whisper, this familiar echo. It was so close and so intimate, and whenever she heard the voice she also heard the peculiar pulselike ticking that accompanied it, and, even further in the background, the muted rise and fall of other voices.

She walked down to the rubble of the ruin.

The coffin was balanced on top of the cairn; a man lay inside it, mummified by the dryness and cold; and, on top of the coffin, lay what he had been carrying when he had been attacked and robbed. There was not much. He had been a poor man. There was just the framework of bamboo poles out of which he would have made a carrying load on his return from Lungan. His two thin cedar-strip sandals lay on top of it, and a prayer flag had been attached to the stick that he had been using to walk. Anna looked down at the granite and sandstone underneath him, and the alpine flowers, a blinding carpet of yellow, around the rocks.

Anna couldn't look at the inhuman face in the coffin; she concentrated her gaze on the plants at her feet.

And then, abruptly, she knew.

She knew the word. She knew the voice. In this desperate place, it came back to her.

The plant beneath her was senecio. It was a sister to that other senecio, the *Senecio squalidus,* the plain yellow weed that had spread out of the Botanic Garden and along the railway lines from Oxford. And David came back to her, David sitting opposite her at a bar table.

"It's part of the daisy family, ragwort . . ."

"Am I going to get a botany lecture?"

His smile.

". . . Listen, this is interesting . . ."

She had begun to laugh.

"Oh, I'm transfixed . . ."

The afternoon that she had chased the names down in *Flora Britannica,* for no other reason than that they sounded exotic to her, even the names of the ragwort weeds and the incomprehensibly bland-looking lichens that had so amused her. And she remembered his talking of trees and her own thoughts, that this was possibly a very single-minded man, a man who hid behind what he knew, all his lists, all his names, all his theories. A man she wanted to find and keep close to her. The man who had walked with her through Godshill and up Godshill Ridge to Island Thorns, and who had looked at the perfect white rim of the water in the pool. The man who had touched her, and who clung to her, like a tune she would never get out of her mind.

Transfixed.

Senecio.

She turned around.

Transfixed . . .

David was standing behind her on the slope, below her, holding out his hands. Her heart jumped. She felt a terrible pressure in her chest, as if she were in the coffin that was weighted down with the stones, piled with all she had achieved. As if she were being compressed, the life squeezed out of her. She had a sudden crushing image of her paintings piled on top of her, and among them, the lilies, the *Davidia,* the trailing, peony-headed poppies, their faces turned to the ground.

She began to gasp. She tried to walk.

"Anna," he said, "can you hear me?"

His gaze was centered on her. Irrationally, she thought she could feel his hand in hers.

Somewhere beyond him, Rachel.

Somewhere beyond, on a thin, impossible bridge.

"Yes," she told him. "I can hear you. I can hear you."

But the words were taken away by the wind, swept away in the violent sunlight.

Twenty-eight

AS SOON AS DAVID turned into Newbury late that afternoon, he saw the gallery.

Sandwiched between the designer outlets on either side, it looked suitably modest and understated, with its dark wood door and plain window, and the sign denoting Anna's exhibition placed in the center of a single piece of silk.

He crossed the road, and tried to open the door. Finding it locked, he began to hammer on it. There was no reply. He leaned with his forehead on the frame, his weight resting on one shoulder, his head down, crashing his hand against the wood. People passing in the street glanced at him warily.

The day was warm; his clothes stuck to his skin. But the day, the street, the people passing close to him, the heat, did not register at all.

After a few seconds, he heard bolts go back, and the door opened. A young woman—a girl with smooth black hair—stood in the entrance.

"Yes?" she asked. "Can I help you?"

He stared at her, trying to think of an explanation. Then, he simply pushed past her.

Once in the gallery, he stopped.

James Garrett was standing on the lower floor, talking to a man in his sixties, who had a much younger wife on his arm. At the sound of his entrance, all three had turned, and now looked at him with both surprise and irritation. The client's wife was blond, painfully thin, and equipped with a vacant expression. David's glance strayed to the picture they had been looking at: the sepia study. For a second, he felt that they were looking at her, looking at Anna, spread naked, her flesh flayed to the desiccated skin of parchment.

He walked toward Garrett, and, without saying a word, hit him.

Taken utterly by surprise, Garrett lost his footing, staggered a few feet, and then fell to the floor.

"James!" exclaimed the girl. "Oh, God! James!"

The couple moved back, the man putting his arm across his wife.

"Get up," David told Garrett.

The girl ran over. "James, are you all right?" she asked. She crouched next to him, looking up at David. Their eyes connected: he noticed a bruise on her arm, just above the elbow. He looked away, back at Garrett.

"Get up," he repeated.

Garrett did so.

"What the hell are you doing?" asked the client. David only glanced at him, at his too-young leather jacket and clean, clean chinos. His wife took off her sunglasses and smiled.

"Why don't you two go away," David suggested.

"Go? What's going on here? Why—"

But David never heard why. Blood was pounding in his head. Anger had taken hold of him, like a cold passion. He stepped forward with what looked like a shrug, and slammed his fist into James Garrett's face.

"Oh, Lord," the wife murmured.

Garrett slumped backward, holding his mouth. David followed him. He caught him by his lapels, and shoved him against the wall. "What are you selling?" he demanded. "What is it you're selling?"

"James, James." Olivia was crying. She turned to the other man. "Help me," she said.

"To do what?" the man asked.

She stared at him in astonishment for a second, then, "I'm calling the police," she answered. She started to run along the gallery to the front desk and the phone.

"Don't," Garrett called.

David had Garrett's jacket bunched up against his throat, clenched in his free hand. He saw with satisfaction that Garrett's nose was bleeding. He put his face close to his. "Call them," he said to the girl, over his shoulder. "That'll be good."

"Leave the phone," Garrett instructed.

By this time, Olivia was standing with the receiver in her hand.

"Leave it," Garrett said. "Put it down."

David turned to look at the clients. "Are you still here?" he asked.

"It's all right, Brendon," Garrett said. "I'm sorry about this."

"We'll go," the man said.

David suddenly dropped his grip on Garrett. He walked up to the couple. The man stepped back; the woman, seemingly still amused, held her place, one hand on her hip. She looked David up and down. "You British?" she asked.

David ignored her. He looked at the man. "OK," he said to him, "he's selling, and you're buying." He looked at the painting behind them. "You're buying this?"

The man eyed him warily. "Maybe," he replied.

"Maybe?" David asked. "Fantastic. Wonderful. Brilliant artist, isn't she?"

"Yes," the man answered. He had rolled his copy of the exhibition brochure into a tube, as if that would protect him.

"That's right," David said. "She's very talented. But you should know that all this is stolen."

The man looked from David to Garrett.

Olivia had given Garrett a handkerchief, and tried dabbing ineffectually at his face. He had snatched it from her, and was wiping himself down. David noticed with deep satisfaction that the expensive Italian suit was stained.

Garrett caught the man's gaze. "It's the property of the artist," he said. "It's not stolen."

"It is *not* stolen," Olivia repeated, aghast.

"This is Anna Russell we're talking about?" David asked.

"David," Garrett said, shaking his head. He glanced at Olivia. "Get me some water," he told her. He walked forward.

"That's some shiner you'll have," the blonde observed.

Her husband caught her arm. "We're leaving," he said. He looked at Garrett. "You're going to let him do this to you?" he asked. "Just let him do it?"

"This is a very difficult time," Garrett said. "David is upset. I understand that."

David started to laugh. "Ever the diplomat," he retorted. "Ever the fucking politician."

"You're distressed," Garrett said.

"Oh?" David asked. "How sympathetic of you. How understanding. But why would I possibly be *distressed*?"

"David . . ."

"No, come on," David answered. "Why am I so fucking distressed, James?" He walked away, breathing heavily. He looked at the door with the dead bolts, the closed-circuit TV camera, the security pad. He stared at the TV for some seconds, and then waved at it contemptuously. "Getting all this?" he asked the screen. He turned back toward them. "Hell of a setup," he said. "Protecting the investment."

They all stared at him, silent.

"Got to protect your investment," David repeated. "Got a lot of potential money in here."

He looked from them to the other paintings on the wall.

"No," Garrett said.

"No what?" David asked.

"Don't touch them, please," Garrett answered.

David watched him, tapping his fingers against his leg, considering. "Why?" he asked.

Garrett shook his head, keeping his gaze.

"Can't replace them?" David asked.

There was utter silence.

Olivia started to cry.

"Jen rang Grace," David said.

"Who the hell is Grace?" the customer asked.

David smiled bitterly at him. "Grace is Anna Russell's mother," he said. "Jennifer is Anna's next-door neighbor. This afternoon, Mr. Garrett here went to Anna Russell's home, and took every single thing out of her studio."

The man frowned. "I don't get it," he said.

David looked at him with disgust. "Then let me explain it to you," he said. "This afternoon, this man cleared Anna Russell's house of everything she's worked on, everything he could sell, despite her neighbor's objections, and without asking her mother."

"Why should I ask Grace?" Garrett asked.

"Because you can't ask Anna, and Grace is her next of kin," David retorted.

"Rachel is her next of kin," Garrett said.

"What is this about?" the man interjected.

"Where are they?" David demanded. "Where did you put everything?"

"Oh," Garrett answered. "Why? Do you want them?"

David started forward.

"No!" Olivia cried.

"You're going to get yourself in trouble here," the man observed. He held up his hand, a placating gesture.

David looked at him, away from Garrett, away from the paintings.

"Do you know where she is?" he asked.

"Who?" the blonde said.

David stared scathingly at her for a second, then back to the man. "Do you know that Anna Russell is in hospital?" he asked.

"She had a car accident," the man said. "I know."

"That's right," David agreed. "Did he tell you how bad?"

"Bad?" the man echoed.

David took a deep breath; he looked at his feet for a second, his hands clenched at his sides. Then, he looked back at him. "I'm going to give you the benefit of the doubt," he said. "I'm going to assume you're not a couple of vultures picking over a carcass."

"That's uncalled-for," Garrett interrupted.

"Shut your mouth," David answered equably. His eyes were still fixed on the client. "She's in a coma," he said. "She's critically ill. In fact, Mr. Garrett here thinks she's as good as dead." At last, he looked back at Garrett. "Isn't that right, James?" he asked.

"When was all this?" the blonde asked. "This with the paintings?"

"This afternoon," David said.

"Oh, my God," Olivia whispered.

David looked at her. "Didn't you know?" he asked conversationally. "Doesn't surprise me. I don't expect he told anyone. Would seem a tad ghoulish, wouldn't it? Selling her stuff and making money out of her, on the day she's between life and death, or on the day she actually died?"

"She died?" the man asked.

David nodded. "As far as James here knows," he said. "So you'd better buy quick, because a dead artist is worth more than a living artist. Ask van Gogh. This exhibition was a great success last night. Said so in the papers this morning. And to die young, die tragically, that's terrible, isn't it? You can add on another hundred percent for that. This time next year," he said, waving his hand around the gallery, "she'll be worth twice what you're paying today, and all the stuff that James cleared out this afternoon will be worth a fortune. Of course," he added, "minor detail. But, if Anna Russell were dead, they're not his property. They're the property of Anna Russell's estate. They belong to her daughter and her mother."

All at once, he advanced on the man. "Get your checkbook out," he told him viciously. "Get out your checkbook, quick. Snap up a fucking bargain while you can."

The man stared at him.

Olivia was sobbing.

"I'm sorry," the man said. "I didn't know."

"To me," Garrett said.

They looked at him.

"What?" David asked.

"To me," Garrett repeated. "Anna left her paintings to me."

All at once, the truth of the situation dawned on the blonde. She started to laugh. "Oh, my," she said, gazing at Garrett. "What a shit."

"Honey," warned her husband.

"You see what he did?" she asked, waving her sunglasses in Garrett's direction. "That's pretty cool. He took the paintings from under their noses."

"You don't know what you're talking about," her husband retorted.

"Oh, don't I?" she asked. "I know tricks, and that's a pretty nice trick. If she's alive, he's got the paintings, and if she's dead, he's got the paintings. Heads you win and tails you win." And she shook her head in admiration.

David was staring at Garrett.

He took one, two breaths.

Then he turned for the door, and opened it.

Garrett ran through the gallery. "David," he called.

Garrett reached David just as he was on the doorstep, looking out into the street. Everything had left the younger man. His gaze was full of bewilderment, as if the world outside had surprised him with its clarity and life.

Garrett dropped his voice. "She gave them to me freely," he said. "I've taken nothing away from her. I've stolen nothing from her."

David blinked as he watched the people pass. Then, he looked back at the other man. "You've given up on her," he said.

"A ventilator is keeping her alive," Garrett answered. "I've got the courage to face that fact."

"Courage?" David repeated. Then he nodded, slowly. "OK," he murmured. "If that's what you think."

"People don't recover from injuries like that," Garrett told him. "Even if, technically, she lived, if her body lived, Anna is gone." An emotion—not grief, not pain, but some kind of desolate confusion, bemusement that she had slipped away from him—showed for just a moment in Garrett's face. Then he straightened his shoulders. "None of your histrionics will change that."

David looked at him.

"I don't care for your opinion," Garrett said. "I don't have any interest in what you think of me. You may think what you like."

"I will," David said. "There's been nothing but lies since I met you."

Garrett smiled. "You have a version of Anna's life from Grace," he said, in almost a whisper. "But I have had *her*. Anna herself. Not a version. Not a memory, like you."

David flinched.

"And whatever stories she told to herself about you," Garrett added, "I've been the one by Anna's side. I looked after her child. I housed her and paid for her."

"You *paid for her*?" David repeated, disgusted. "You *housed* her?"

"That's right."

"Like a dog," David said. "Like a pet. Or a possession."

Olivia walked up behind them, and stood at Garrett's back.

David looked from her face to Garrett, and then back again.

"You know what?" he asked. And he looked concentratedly at Olivia again before he continued. "You take those paintings. You have them all. Keep them. Because Anna isn't in them." He gestured toward the back of the gallery, where the couple were still standing. "You think that those paintings in there are Anna?" he asked. "That thing on the wall? That's not Anna. That's something you've manufactured. That's something you've twisted into shape. It's not Anna."

And he stepped into the sunlight of the street.

"She's gone," Garrett said. "Let go of her."

"Never," David said, without looking back. "Never again."

Twenty-nine

HE GOT AS FAR as Massachusetts Avenue before he hailed a cab.

He sat in the back, his hand over his eyes.

"Where to?" the driver asked.

"Jamaica Plain," David answered. He felt sick to his stomach.

"Where in Jamaica Plain?"

"I don't know," he said. He pressed down harder on his eyelids, wishing he could blank out the glare of the day completely. "Forest Hills . . ."

"Forest Hills station?"

"Yes," he said, not caring. "Anywhere."

It was five or ten minutes before he could take down his hand, and look out of the window. The traffic was heavy; it was coming up to five. He wound down the window, and took deep breaths of the fumy air.

The driver looked in his mirror. "You OK?" he said.

"Yes," David answered.

"Don't look OK," the driver said.

"I'm all right," he said.

He had never hit anyone before. At least, not since he was eight years old in the school playground. If you could count pretend punches that never connected. He looked down at his hands.

Stupid thing, he thought. Stupid bloody thing, to let himself get so out of control.

It had been half past three when Grace had taken her cell phone out of her bag. They had left the ward, and taken the elevator downstairs, and walked a way to the river. It felt better there: more air. He had found a place for Grace to sit, worried at the ashy color of her face. Rachel had stood looking at the water.

"I'm going home," Grace said, after a few moments' silence.

"You found the car?" he asked.

"It's impounded," she replied. "I called my neighbor at home. She's coming to pick me up." She had lit a cigarette, drawn in the smoke. "I ran out of the house without even locking the door," she said. "I need a change of clothes. Find my cat." She smiled wanly, raising her eyebrows at him.

"You've got a cat?" he asked.

"A tabby. Rachel loves him," Grace said. "He'll be sitting on the porch with an evil glint in his eye by now."

They smiled.

"Will you be OK with Rachel?" Grace asked. "Jen will help you."

"We'll be fine," he reassured her.

She looked in her bag for the phone. "I'll speak to her," she said.

The phone had been switched off in the hospital; now, Grace saw the text message waiting. "Oh, my God," she whispered. She showed it to him; then immediately dialed Jen's number. As she sat with the phone to her ear, he saw her face grow even paler. Then her eyes filled with tears.

When the call finished, and she told him what had happened, he got up. A kind of white fury filled his head. "I'm going to see him," he said.

"David, wait a minute—"

"I'm sorry," he said. "I can't. Where shall I meet you?"

They had looked at each other, then she waved her hand. "I'll bring Rachel to the house," she had said, finally. "Be careful."

"With him?" he'd asked. "Yeah, right."

★   ★   ★

It was some fifteen minutes later that, as the cab came through an intersection, he suddenly leaned forward and tapped the driver's seat.

"What is that?" he asked.

"What is what?"

"The trees over there?"

The driver gave him a look. "Guess it's a lot of trees," he said.

"Can you stop?"

"Sure." He pulled onto the side of the road, taking David's money without comment.

There was a fence around the parkland, and shrubs crowding close to it. David looked up and down the street, and then began to walk. After five minutes, he came to a gate. Inside, he saw a flight of steps, and a broad building that looked down on the acres below. He walked past the gate, up the steps, and stared at the frontage. He tried the front door, but it was locked. The note on the door showed the public opening hours: ten to three.

He walked down a few steps, and sat down on the stone flight, and looked out over the trees ahead of him: dawn redwoods, katsuras, tulip trees, magnolias, lindens.

He knew exactly where he was. He knew that there were mountain laurels here, and cedars of Lebanon; honey locusts, hemlocks, sweet gums, ginkgos, catalpas. Japanese zelkovas, probably still in flower; mountain ash, bamboos. There were over two hundred varieties of lilacs here, all still heavy with their blossom. And a dove tree. There was a dove tree near a place called Bussey Hill. If he walked down the asphalt lane opposite him, he could probably come to it.

He put his head in his hands.

Anna's house was probably less than twenty minutes' walk from here, he thought.

Maybe she had come here. Maybe she walked here often. Took Rachel to the greenhouses. If she remembered. If she . . .

He thought that she had responded this afternoon.

He had been sitting with one hand propping his head, and the other holding her hand. Rachel had been sitting on the floor; they had found a small coffee table for her, and she had a smaller piece of paper weighted down. She was totally concentrated on the China map, copying the route of the river. A nurse had switched on the lights of a neighboring bed, and that was when he thought he saw Anna's eyelids flicker.

"She moved," he had said, barely breathing it.

The nurse had turned around.

"I saw her move," he had repeated. "Just now . . . just now!"

The woman had come to the bedside, and checked the monitors and Anna's pulse.

"She moved her eyes when you switched on the lamp," he told her.

"Did she look toward it?"

He shook his head. "Yes . . . I don't know," he said helplessly.

"Move her head?" She was still solicitously looking into Anna's face. She brought out a pinpoint flashlight, and tested Anna's pupils.

"No."

"She's reacting," the nurse commented. She gave him a small smile. "But then she's already been doing that."

"What does it mean?" he asked.

"Maybe reflex," she said.

But he was convinced Anna had heard him.

He had been talking about the sunlight.

She had actually heard him.

He put his hands to his eyes.

"Can I help you?" asked a voice.

He looked up. A woman was standing on the step next to him. She carried a small briefcase, and had her car keys in her hand.

He wiped his eyes with the heel of his hand, and stood up embarrassedly. "This is the arboretum?" he asked.

"The Arnold Arboretum, yes," she replied.

He felt a great wave of emotion slam into him: unexpected, uncontrolled, it had all the force of a blow. It was as if the air had been knocked out of him. He turned away from the woman, overcome.

She put a hand on his shoulder. She was much shorter than he, and he abruptly felt the absurdity of it, a six-foot man being comforted by a total stranger, a woman eight or nine inches shorter than he, who had to reach up to put her hand on his shoulder. He took a gulp of air. "Christ," he said. "I'm so sorry."

"What's the matter?" she asked kindly. "Here ..." She looked in her briefcase, and brought out a tissue.

"No," he said, "I'm OK. Look, I ..." He tried to explain what couldn't be explained. The whole unwieldy mass of the last few days had suddenly rolled away from him, out of his grasp, as if it were a load he had been trying to carry, and he had finally lost control of it. He looked across at the trees. "I have a picture of this place," he said, his voice wavering. He cursed himself inwardly, tried to even it out. "I've got a picture—a photo, in a book—of a man called Ernest Wilson, standing on these steps."

She was looking steadily at him. "Wilson used to work here," she said.

He surreptitiously tried to wipe his face. "I know," he murmured. He balled up the tissue and put it in his pocket.

The woman turned and gestured toward the building. "He had an office right there, on the second floor," she said. "We have his records," she added. "In the archives."

"I know," he repeated. He glanced at her and grimaced an apology. "You must think I'm some sort of idiot," he said. "I knew this was near here. I saw the sign ..."

"Are you English?" she asked.

"Yes."

"And you came here to see the arboretum?" she asked.

"No," he replied. "I've always wanted to. But I came to Boston for another reason." He looked down the steps. "I ought to go," he said. "I'm really sorry. I don't usually sit on steps and cry." And he gave her a painful smile.

She started to grin. "I do," she said. "I cried like a baby at my son's Thanksgiving play. I had to go out and have a drink of water."

He nodded.

"Why don't you come back and have a look through the

records?" she asked. "You can make an appointment, and we'll show you what we have." They began to walk down the steps. "Did you study Wilson at some time?" she asked.

"Yes," he said.

"You know about his journeys?"

"Yes," he said, still struggling to get the words out. He paused with her as she reached her car.

"Do you work here?" he asked.

She smiled. "I guess," she told him. She held out her hand, and he took it. "Come back and see us," she said. She gave his hand a lingering, comforting press. "He's here," she said. "He'll be waiting for you."

David got to Anna's house like a dying man. He actually had to drag himself up the steps. "Jesus," he muttered to himself. "Pull your bloody self together."

Jen was coming down the hallway, with a basket of laundry in her hands. She opened the screen door.

"What the hell happened to you?" she asked.

"Nothing," he said. "Everything."

She smiled, took his arm, and led him down the hall and into the kitchen. Grace was sitting at the table, looking at the sandwich on her plate.

"Look who I found crawling up the path," Jen said. "Sit," she ordered David. "Drink?"

"Yes. Please."

"Coffee?"

"Have you got anything else?" he asked.

"Scotch," Grace said. "Second cabinet, top shelf." She put her hand on David's, withdrew it, and looked at his knuckles.

"He didn't feel a thing," David said. "Dead before he hit the floor."

Jen put the drinks down and stared at him. "You're kidding, right?"

He picked up his drink. "Here's to James Garrett," he said. "Lover, partner, and first-class shit."

Grace didn't move. "Is he resting in peace?" she asked.

He smiled. "No," he said. "He's walking and talking." He looked at his right hand. "I think I hurt myself more than I hurt him," he observed. "Feels like I broke my hand."

Grace took a deep breath, and drank her whisky. Then she lifted David's hand and flexed it gently. "Bruised, is all," she said.

They looked at each other. Garrett and Anna seemed to fill the room. They sat in silence, the weight of the days pressing on them. There was nothing to say. David looked at the evidence of Anna's life all around him: the flea market kitchen chairs against an old pine table; the magnets and memos pinned to the fridge. A shopping list, still tacked to the wall, in her handwriting. It seemed impossible that she should not be here.

There was a ring at the doorbell.

"I'll get it," Jen said.

Grace stood up, and rinsed her glass. "Want another?" she asked.

"No," he said. "Thanks."

She dried the glass, and then stood with her back to the window, resting against the worktop. "Tell me something," she said.

He looked up. "What is it?"

"Why didn't you reply to the letter?"

He frowned. "What letter?"

Grace folded her arms. "The letter she sent to you when Rachel was born."

He stared at her. "I never got a letter," he said.

"But she sent it to your college. And to your father's house."

He sat back in the chair. "I left Oxford," he said. "I didn't finish my Ph.D."

"She wrote in February . . ."

"I left at Christmas," he told her.

"And they didn't forward to you?"

"They would have sent it to Dad's, I suppose."

"So there would have been two letters at your father's house," she said.

He rubbed a hand across his forehead. "I didn't go home."

"But he must have told you there was mail waiting for you."

David shook his head. "I didn't speak to Dad much," he said. "I went abroad. I went to Gambia. Teaching. VSO."

"Even so . . ."

"I never saw them," David said.

"When you didn't reply, she thought it was as much as she deserved," Grace said.

"Oh, God," he murmured. "I would have come."

Grace sat back down again at his side. "Garrett asked her to marry him," she said.

"He did? When?"

"Just recently. In Paris."

"She didn't accept?"

"No."

"Why not?" David asked. "He had everything, didn't he? Money. Influence. Looks." He laughed shortly. "The full picture book. The house on the hill."

Grace gripped his hand. "It wasn't the same thing," she said. "She left you because she was panicked, not because she didn't love you. She refused him for exactly that reason. She didn't love him."

"Yet she stayed with him," David said.

Grace shook her head sadly. "She had decided to get out of the contract." She sighed. "I'm sure he guessed it."

"But she left him her pictures, her work," he said.

Grace straightened up with the shock of it. "She did what?" she asked.

"Left him her paintings, in her will," he said.

For a second, Grace sat with her mouth open. Then, she suddenly began to laugh. "She *what*?" she demanded. "David, Anna hasn't got a will."

"But—"

"I told her over and over again to make one," she said. "It was always one of those things she was going to do."

"But he told me just now," David said. "He told me that's why he took them."

Grace's look hardened. The laugh died down as quickly as it had come. "Because he thinks she's dying," she said.

"Because he thinks that, yes."

She simply shook her head. "Oh," she whispered. "That man, that man ..."

"Does he ever do anything else but lie?" David asked.

"I don't think he even knows the distinction anymore," she murmured.

The hall door opened. Jen came back in the room. She was carrying a little package.

David looked up at her. "Who was at the door?" he asked.

Jen smiled at them bemusedly. "The police," she said. "They brought this."

And she opened the brown paper wrapping, and put the little toy on the table. It was a battered blue plastic bridge.

"They said they found it in Anna's car," she told them.

Long after Grace had gone, David sat in the same kitchen chair, staring at the bridge.

Then, he took the toy and walked upstairs, and knocked at Rachel's door.

When there was no reply, he pushed it open gently. His daughter was sitting on the floor, surrounded by her model buildings and cars, all arranged on a wide plastic floor rug: one where a city map was laid out, in garish yellow blocks, with red traffic carriageways. It was the kind of toy made for preschool kids, sized up to take big plastic cars. But on each block, Rachel had put her stores and garages. At each street corner was a bridge.

"Hello, Rachel," he said.

She glanced up, then away.

"Look what I've got," he prompted her. He held out his hand with Mofty in it. There was a pause, while she looked at his hand; then she got up, took the toy, and walked to the very end of the room, the closest she could get to the corner, holding it to her chest.

"A policeman brought it," he said. "They found it for you."

"You had it," she said.

"No," he replied quietly.

"You brought it in," she said.

He saw the brutal logic of it. "Yes," he said. "I brought it upstairs. From the front door. A policeman brought it to your house, and I brought it upstairs."

She nodded, satisfied. He didn't know what else to say. He looked at the shelves along the wall, for inspiration. They were full of McDonald's figures.

"Rachel," he said. "Who are these?"

She didn't answer. He picked up the nearest.

Immediately, she took two or three steps, and then stood still, looking at the floor. "That's a Disney merchandising figure," she said. "It's a cartoon character from a film."

"The Lion King," he said.

"His name is Scar," she said. "He's the bad brother."

"You have a lot," he said, replacing it carefully.

"I have the series," she said. "There are different series."

He looked at the floor map. "You want to play a game?" he asked.

"I'm constructing the block," she told him. She held out Mofty, and he saw that she was considering where to place it.

"There's a gap by the petrol station," he pointed out.

"The gas station."

"That's right, the gas station."

She calculated a moment. "The dimensions don't fit," she said.

He looked across at the bed. The covers were very plain, and dark blue.

"Rachel," he said. "Want to play a board game?"

Her eyes flickered once to him, then away.

"Chess?" he asked.

"I play Othello," she said.

"OK," he replied.

She stood next to him, hesitating, looking at the map and back to the cupboard where the game was stored.

"You can sit on the window chair," she said, abruptly. "You put that white chair in the window. That's where it goes. You can sit on it."

He walked across the room, and did as he was told, watching her bring out the game, arrange the table, pick up and put down the last bridge she had been making.

"Does your mother play with you?" he asked. "This game?"

"You can play white," she said. "Until she comes back."

He looked at her face, and his father in her face. Behind him, in the garden, the light reflected blue, the color of the dusty clapboards of Jen's house, a blue that was almost gray, even in the sunlight.

Time slowed down to almost nothing. To the click of the counters on the board. He thought of Anna, and the click of the ventilator, the breathing of the machine. He wondered how long they would all wait. Whether it would be weeks, or months. Whether it would be years.

"OK," he said, to Rachel's downcast face. "Just until she comes back."

Thirty

IT WAS DARK; ALMOST dawn.

The village street was sandy, and strewn with leaves, as if a wind had been blowing hard, and scattered them. There were only half a dozen houses, with deep porches raised off the ground. An oil light burned under one of them, pasting the faintest pool of yellow light. Under it, a dog was asleep, his scrawny body twitching as he pursued phantoms in the fields of sleep.

Anna was standing on one of the porches now. Something had been put close to her hands. She touched the smooth, lacquered surface in the darkness, her fingers feeling around the square packs that were stacked one on top of the other. On each corner, she could feel metal fastenings, and, between each thick wooden frame, the edges of paper. Each frame, in turn, was packed in a wooden box. She ran her hands down the boxes, counting them. Nine.

Nine plant presses, to take the herbarium specimens for the arboretum. Nine plant presses, and a thousand driers. Every night, the driers and the specimens were changed. She saw the European now, in this dark, rain-soaked place, carefully unfolding the paper from its rubberized wrapping, lifting the leaves with the edge of a penknife, replacing them again on dry blotting paper; each leaf, each seed, each flower, while the rain dripped incessantly from the roof above him, into the unpaved mire of the street.

She walked down the porch, and saw the rest of the baggage piled in the doorway, ready for an early departure. Compass, barometer, pedometer, and altimeter; the journal, the camera; the quinine sulphate to treat malarial fevers; permanganate of potash, salts, insect powder, and opium. Close to the man's bed would be his gun, and the money supply. String cash, strung on cords around his neck, little coins no bigger than a dime, with a square hole cut in the center, a thousand on each string.

Next to Anna, the dog stirred. She looked down at it, and at the first gray details as the light strengthened. Then, she walked into the hut.

The man was lying on a bench by the door. He was awake, and lying motionless with his palms crossed on his chest, staring up at the beams of the roof. Flattened by his hands and held to his chest was a piece of paper. Then, he turned on his side, and swung his legs over the edge of the makeshift bed. He pulled on his jacket, picked up his boots, took them to the door, where he slowly inspected them, shaking them out. He put them on, and laced the puttees over the top. Then he turned back, picked up the piece of paper, and took it back to the door, turning it so that it caught the light from the oil lamp.

She saw then what it was that he had been holding.

It was a map, drawn on a notebook page. There was no scale. Two parallel lines along the top indicated the route of the Yangtze; two dropping vertically down showed its tributary, the Kuan Ho River. To the north, someone had written in capital letters, Patung District. To the west, Wushan; to the east, Chienshih. A small rectangle to the very right of the page was named Tai Ho Shan, a mountain that did not even appear on any map yet drawn. Neither did Mo Chang Kou, a settlement indicated by a little pencil circle. Yet it was vitally important that he find these places. It was why he was here. It was why he had traveled thirteen thousand miles. It was the reason he had gone to Yunnan to see Augustine Henry.

Because, in the center of the page that Henry had drawn for him weeks before, was a tiny scrawled message. Sandwiched between the words *Wushan* and *Chienshih* was the word *Davidia*.

The area where Augustine Henry had said it could be found, represented on the piece of paper now in the dawn light, was not too accurate. In fact, a lesser man might have given up entirely as he had watched Henry draw it. Because it was the equivalent of a needle in a haystack; perhaps one very small, almost microscopic needle in the largest haystack imaginable. The map represented an area of twenty thousand square miles. And the *Davidia* was in the center of it. One flowering *Davidia,* a solitary specimen that Augustine Henry had witnessed only once, ten years before.

The village was above five thousand feet, and the only inn was set on a steep slope.

After two days' march, and having stayed in what could only have been described as a hovel the night before, where the lice kept the men awake, and the stink was overpowering, they had tramped through what seemed to them a numberless amount of ascents and descents. Standing on any summit, there was no level ground to be seen in any direction. The razorlike ridges cut north to south, their sides and valleys covered in thick woodland.

In the valleys, the musk rose was everywhere—Anna could smell it now—and flowering cherries; and honeysuckle and philadelphus, mock orange. As they came down through one of the descents into woodland, Anna saw the man ahead of her stop, not to collect seed, but simply to close his eyes and inhale the perfume of the place. It hung so heavy in the air that to walk through it was like parting invisible veils. The aroma clung to her. She walked all around him, and thought she saw David in his face.

They began descending an almost vertical slope, slipping on the leaf mold underfoot. She looked up and saw the beeches over her head, some almost upright with a single trunk and a vastly spreading head of branches; others, much taller, but springing from the ground in eight or ten evenly-sized trunks slanting away from each other, as if someone had arranged a great bouquet of light gray stems.

"We're almost there," David said. "Hold on to me. Walk forward."

She did as she was told, though her feet were numb with cold. Her hands, too. Her lips, and mouth. She felt the faint resin grain of her tongue against her teeth. She felt her index and second and third fingers, but not her fourth, and not her thumb. She felt her chest, heavy as though pressed by a weight, barely moving to breathe. To walk with this body was both difficult and easy. She was carrying an assemblage of parts. Sometimes her progress was swift, faster than a thought. Sometimes she hesitated, at breathless drops into nothingness. At the shadow of a fern leaf across her path.

The inn was a rambling, two-storied place, with outhouses and a large courtyard. Because the ground sloped so steeply away, the front of the structure was supported on posts. As they came closer to it, the fragrance of the mountain behind them was rapidly lost; she realized that there were piggeries among the outhouses, and the stench from the inn itself, mixed with burning incense and candle wax, almost choked her.

The man passed in through the low doorway. The owner of the inn appeared out of the half-darkness. There were minutes of po- lite introduction; of the brewing of green tea, and the taking of it in the gloomy stink of the only room. Finally, the man asked the question he had traveled so far to answer. Was there a tree nearby that the Chinese called the k'ung-tung?

The owner furrowed his brow until the tree was described. Then, he smiled broadly.

Yes, there was such a tree.

And was the tree close by?

It was down the mountain further.

Only a mile.

Just a mile, Anna thought. Beyond exaltation or hope. Only a mile.

They got up, to the accompaniment of more polite bowing. The man walked out, back into the sunlight. With the houseboy trotting ahead of them along the path, with a sheer drop at one side, and the low outhouses on the other, they followed him until the inn was swallowed up behind them by thick groves of willow.

They saw two or three houses along the path, tiny places with bamboo roofs. Then, at last, they came to a clearing, where a larger house stood.

"Is the tree here?" the man asked.

Yes, the boy nodded.

This is the tree.

And he ran and put his hand on the house, and on the low roof beam that almost skirted the ground. He was smiling broadly and with pride. It was his father's house. His father, he said, was a good builder, and he had cleared the ground. He had taken down the house that had been here, and built another.

The man didn't understand. Utter confusion filled Anna's head. "Where is the tree?" he asked again.

The boy walked forward, and touched the overhanging eave of the house.

"Sir," he said. "I am very sorry. But they have cut down the tree for the roof." He turned back, spreading his hands in a helpless gesture. "It was a very old tree," he said. "And it was an excellent wood for building."

Thirty-one

GRACE GOT HOME AT eight.

Walking down the path toward the clapboard house, seeing its porch with the Lloyd loom chair, and her newspaper still wedged behind its cushion, she felt as if she had been away for weeks, and not days.

The same neighbor who had brought her back had locked the door for her, and given her the key on the return journey just now; she put it to the lock with the same sense of distance, strangeness. Even the sound of the lock turning and door opening were peculiar, as though she had never heard that particular click of the latch before. She threw down her bag inside the door, and took off her shoes, and stared at her hallway, and the pictures. The *Daisy and Mike* cartoon by the stairs looked odd, misplaced; the work of a stranger, a remnant from another life.

She went upstairs slowly, opened the windows, and stared out at the sea. It was a milky blue today, with a fine mist on the horizon. She stared for some time at that wide blue arc.

Stripping off her clothes, she got into the shower. The water was blissfully cool; she stood with her hands on the tile, leaning her weight against it and letting the water run down her back.

When she came out, her cat was standing in the room. He

stood in a patch of sunlight on the stripped wood floor, feet placed just so, looking like a statue, an Art Deco representation of a cat, his shoulders hunched to an angle with the surprise of seeing her, his tail lifted.

She lay on the bed for a while, exhausted. The yellow quilt felt as peculiar and otherworldly as the hallway had seemed; her fingers explored it curiously. The color seemed not to be right. The window looked wrong.

She got up and dressed herself in a cotton shirt and skirt. In her mirror, she noticed the weight that she had lost. She looked like a bony old woman, she thought. Bone and skin, a jaundiced face, and shock in her expression. It would have been impossible to believe, a few days ago, that shock could actually be drawn in someone's features, but it was there, as obvious as scrawled letters on her forehead. She had taken a blow. There was surprise and dislocation—almost a strange kind of disapproval—in that look.

In the kitchen, she took deep breaths while she waited for the coffee to brew. She looked in the fridge, and found fresh milk had been put there. Milk and fruit and the brioche that she liked. She gave a faint smile of gratitude, tearing the brioche into pieces, and eating them as she stood by the window.

She had come to Ogunquit as a woman of thirty. She had made a life, used a talent, brought up a child. Such a child, a little changeling, with wiry reddish hair that was difficult to comb. Green eyes, so green. All the precious memories. The hand in hers standing by the school gate; the sugar cookie dough at the kitchen table. Interminably long stories because she wouldn't sleep. Birthdays; a warm hand clasping hers under the bedclothes before it got light, and a small voice asking if she were awake. Anna at four, naked in the sea. Anna at ten, shy for the camera. Slamming doors at fifteen. The tears over her father.

He had been dead for twenty-four years now. Dead of a heart attack on a Miami street. The funeral had made the papers. No one had invited her, but they had sent a newspaper clipping. An anonymous clipping put into an envelope, followed by the summons to her lawyer's office. The annuity was cut off, and then they who had had so little of him had nothing at all.

She put her hand to her eyes. The cat had come in, viewing her warily. She picked him up and put her face into his fur. "Thinking stupid thoughts," she told him. "Stupid thoughts."

She took him out into the garden, laid across the crook of one arm like a pillow, her coffee in her other hand. She walked down the lawn and looked at her flowers, thinking of David's voice, with its flat, smoothed-out accent and its little Dorset lilt. It was a musical voice, she had decided. A good voice. He ought to sing. But when she had mentioned it to him, he had raised his eyebrows in mock despair. "Can't hold a note," he'd told her. And she had looked at him keenly, as he sat half-turned back to talk to her, his hand still holding Anna's, and the things spread out on the bed next to her daughter: the serrated-edge leaves from the shrubs in the street below, and a piece of silk he had bought. He had asked the nurses to buy a whole list, and they had brought it in that afternoon: a brown lacquer trinket box, an ornament from a souvenir shop, the kind that trickled water over stones. And he had a stone he had picked up from the street, an ordinary piece of stone, and a small shard of concrete, the broken edge from a windowsill or wall. She had watched as he ran Anna's fingers over them. He had been talking about a plant called *senecio*. He had stumbled in telling the story; pressed his face into the bedcover, rested on his arm, before he went on.

It was a pretty name for a wildflower, *senecio*. Anna would like that. Grace repeated it now to herself: a prayer, a psalm, a talisman. *Senecio,* the ragged wanderer.

David had asked her if she could bring something from the garden when she came back to the hospital. He had asked her for honeysuckle, but she knew that she didn't possess any. She thought that she could walk down to the beach later; there was a house down the road, close to the shore, that she had noticed had a great yellow blanket of honeysuckle in their garden. She would go down, and ask them if she might take a cutting.

Meanwhile, she looked at the border that she had planted in the spring.

She had no roses—she was never successful with them—and David had talked of roses a lot. She had cinquefoil, though, the five-petaled flowering shrub that looked a little like a rose, and was part of the rose family. It was a blinding yellow. She could take that. And its petals certainly felt like roses—satiny and soft.

She kneeled down by the cinquefoil, and suddenly felt a thump in her chest, as if someone had knocked her hard over the sternum. She sat back on her heels, and gasped. There was a pressure there for a second. Her throat ached fiercely. She waited for the familiar crush of angina, but nothing came. Frowning, she bent over the cinquefoil, and snapped off three flowers between thumb and forefinger.

When she stood up, her head reeled.

She waited for it to pass, looking at the blue rim of ocean beyond the fence and trees.

When this with Anna was over, she would take a drive into the mountains with her daughter, she thought. Just the two of them. They would go into Vermont. Down into New Hampshire then, and Massachusetts. They would go back to the village and see her father's house. Anna would like that. To walk down the long drive again, and see the green roof and shutters. And perhaps whoever lived there would let them look at the drawings in the outhouse.

Grace saw them again quite clearly, as clearly as she had done in her childhood. The pencil-drawn horses, the lion; all almost hidden behind her father's winter stack of apples. He would come in the room occasionally and turn the fruit gently in its tissue paper. The smell of apples in winter, the sweet secrecy of them. And, as he closed the door as he left and bolted it, he would stand on the step and look out over the trees, his roughened hand in hers; his fingers closing comfortingly over hers.

A crushing pain centered in her chest, and radiated down her back and arms. Despite herself, Grace dropped the precious cinquefoil on the ground.

The mist came up from the ocean. She saw it rolling toward

her, up the coastline, and slowly and steadily covering the sand. It passed up the slope from the beach, obliterating the road, and the houses below her.

It swept over the grass softly, gathering the garden in its embrace.

Thirty-two

DESPITE HIS EXHAUSTION, DAVID barely slept that night.

He kept thinking that he could hear Rachel moving about in her room, but when he got up to look in on her, she was sound asleep. When he did sleep himself, it was to dream in lurid color. He saw Sara walking through Lewesdon, the beech trees a surreal, blazing green, and Hannah dragging at her heels; and Grace somewhere behind them, standing silently on the path, her face turned away from him. He pursued them down the ancient track, coming to the field and then suddenly losing sight of them altogether. He woke up in confusion, without a clue where he was. He had to stand up and look around the room, and go out into the hallway before the house actually registered with him.

After the second time of looking in on Rachel, he fell into a deeper dream, this one of complete terror. He dreamed that Anna was lying in a pool of water, her body submerged just below the surface, and only her face showing, framed by the reddish hair floating in tangled weed. It was exactly like the Millais painting.

He tried to reach out to her—her eyes were open, and she was looking at him, apparently aware of her predicament, the fact that she was sinking, that the water was rising around her face; but as quickly as he walked, his feet sank deeper and deeper into mud. He couldn't get hold of her; when he thought his hands were on her, she dissolved. Only her face was left, a grotesque oval disc, the water creeping close to her eyes and mouth. He woke with a shock, his heart racing, and stared at the darkness of the room. For a second she stayed imprinted on the shadows; then, she vanished. He sat forward on the couch, heart pumping, fear racing through him. Only with an effort could he lie down again; but he couldn't close his eyes. He was afraid to see her again, drifting from him, drowning as he watched.

At six, he gave up the uneven battle to sleep.

He went into the bathroom and washed, went downstairs and made tea, and then walked up to Anna's studio, pacing the floor, looking at the open and empty drawers.

Rachel got up soon after that. He endured the breakfast routine with her, which drove them both to frustration. She liked the bread cut in just one way. She wanted the hot chocolate in a different mug, one that he couldn't find. He turned and saw her sitting rigidly at the table, with an expression of misery on her face.

"I'm sorry," he told her. "I'll write it down. Everything you like. To try not to forget."

She seemed genuinely uneasy. He didn't know what to do to comfort her. "Shall we go to the hospital?" he asked her, eventually.

"We're waiting for Grace," she said.

"We have to meet her at the hospital today," he reminded her. Her face puckered with fury.

"Rachel," he said quietly.

"You're a wrong person," she told him.

He put his face in his hands and laughed softly, with a sad black humor.

They rode the T with hundreds of other commuters into Boston. It was a mistake. He hadn't realized that the cars would be so crowded, and eventually he had to maneuver Rachel into one corner, where he stood a couple of paces back from her, his arms on the wall and the door, shielding her from the other bodies. She literally squirmed. She hated the proximity of others. People behind him, noticing, murmured to each other. As the T came into Back Bay, she began hitting the door.

"Rachel," he said. "Stop it."

It was no use. When the door opened, she got out, and began running along the platform. He ran after her and caught her as she started up the stairs. "Stay with me," he said.

She pulled to get away from him.

"What's going on?" a man asked him.

They struggled on the crowded steps for a moment; David glanced at him. "It's all right," he said.

"It don't look all right to me," the man said.

"She's my daughter," David told him.

"Don't make it right," the man retorted.

"Look," David said. "You don't know what you're talking about, OK? Just leave this to me."

Rachel began to make a keening noise, totally overloaded by the press of faces, the noise.

"What's the matter here?" a woman asked.

"This guy," the man told her.

"It's really all right," David said. "She's ... it's a medical problem ... she hates crowds ..." He looked at the woman, pleading. "I need to get her out into the air," he said. "Outside." The woman frowned at him. "It's all right," he repeated, desperate. "We just need ..."

They followed him up the stairs. Rachel fought off his hands. At last they got out into Dartmouth Street.

"Where are you going?" the woman asked.

"Mass Gen," he replied. "Her mother is very ill."

"You needed to change at Downtown, and get the other line," she pointed out. "You should have stayed on the train."

"I know that," he told her grimly. "I know."

"It's a long walk ..."

"We'll be OK," he said. "Thank you. Thanks."

He picked up Rachel's backpack. She had put it on the floor. She took it from him only with repeated persuasion, and then walked a little ahead of him as they crossed the road.

All the time, he felt the gaze of the other passengers on him as he fought the long battle up Dartmouth, to turn right at James Avenue.

When they eventually reached the hospital, he was devastated to find that Grace wasn't there.

He stood at the nurses' station, utterly perplexed.

"Did she ring?" he asked.

"No," the head nurse told him. "Did you try her home number?"

"I haven't got a mobile," he said.

"A what?"

"Cell phone," he corrected himself. "I haven't got a cell phone."

She gave him the ward phone with a smile.

He dialed Grace's house; but there was no answer. He looked at his watch. Nine-ten. Maybe she was already traveling. He dialed her cell phone number. It asked him to leave a message. Surprised, he gave his name. "Are you on the way in?" he asked. "Rachel is . . ." He paused. "It doesn't matter," he said. "Forget it. See you soon."

Pausing a second, trying to think, he rang Jen's house.

"Grace isn't here," he said. "I tried her house. There's no reply."

"But I thought she said she would be there early," Jen murmured. "She even said she might try to get to Anna's before the hospital."

"I know," he said.

"Maybe she slept in," Jen offered.

He didn't reply. He thought that impossible.

"I'll phone her neighbor," Jen said.

"You've got her number?"

"I think it's on Anna's list in the kitchen."

"Thanks," he said.

"You're welcome," she told him. There was a slight pause. "David?"

"Yes?"

"Are you OK?" she asked.

"Yes," he lied. "I'm OK. I'm fine."

He put down the phone, and walked into the ward. Rachel was not working at her map or her drawings of the bridges. She sat on the chair next to Anna's bed, her arms crossed tightly over her chest, her chin lowered. She was watching Anna's face, looking at the ventilator tube taped in place.

David pulled up a chair next to her.

"You can talk to your mom if you like," he said.

She was silent.

"Tell her ..." But he didn't know what to suggest. Impossible for Rachel to pick up her mother's hand and talk to her. Impossible for her to unravel the perplexity of her mother's silence. Impossible to get all the shaken shapes back into line and make life look as it had been before. It was agony for Rachel, that much he could see; but not the agony of grief. It was the agony of frustration, knowing that the logic of life had been overridden. And that was not actually so far from the grief that anyone could feel, he thought. He looked at his daughter's profile, and imagined her reaching the same point as he, by a different route. What was his fear, except a fear that his life and Anna's life would never run straight again, would never follow the ordained lines they had made for themselves? What was anyone's grief but a selfish desperation to get back to a point in the past?

He opened his own backpack, and brought out the piece of chipped stone, and the leaves from Island Thorns. He went around the opposite side of the bed, glancing at the monitors.

Carefully, he opened the envelope, turned Anna's palm, and placed the oak leaves in them, and curled up her fingers around them.

Thirty-three

SILENCE.

Never silence this profound.

The man was sitting in the woodland far above the inn, and listening. There was not even the murmur of wind in the trees, because the afternoon was warm, and the whole mountain was still.

He had ceased to look around him. For a moment—just for a few moments—he no longer cared what was growing on these slopes. Defeat, and the extraordinary absurdity of the search, consumed him. Anna felt his desolation: a blankness, his energy drained. He closed his eyes, and wished himself a world away. She saw that, too, the picture of the lilac in the arboretum coming into flower. Two hundred trees, their flowers passing through every possible shade from white to the blackish purple.

One day, his own lilac would be there, *Syringa wilsonii*, found on the Ta-p'ao Shan Pass near Tibet, on the Tibet border, on the road to Tatsienlu. He would remember coming down from that pass, with the lilac carefully stowed in the packs, and passing the mule ponies, passing in the opposite direction on the road to Tibet, loaded down with brick tea and raw hides.

He blinked, and sighed. Staring out across the mountains with misgiving in every fiber, she felt that keening emptiness. He had come thirteen thousand miles, and failed. And, at that moment, he doubted what he was doing. A single man, chasing a single tree in a wild and uncharted country; it was almost comedy. Sheer foolishness. Away from the bearers, alone on the mountainside, Ernest Wilson put his head in his hands.

Anna sat down alongside him. She had traveled so far with him, and understood him and known him, without the name ever resonating in her thoughts. But now it came: Wilson. Wilson.

She wanted to touch him, but her hands passed through him. Frustration raised her breathing, pumped her heart. Her body was shaking with effort to speak to him. She heard the rattle in her throat, the pinching of pressure. She turned around, looked at the panorama of razor peaks and the gorges, the sage-dark lines between them.

She had to show him his future, and she reached out her fingers and drew on the empty spaces of the sky, and the valleys rose up to meet her hands.

She drew the rose *omiensis* that he had brought from the sacred mountain Emei Shan. Ten thousand feet of flowers. She drew the white flowers with their four plain petals, brought down from the summit, in sight of the borders of Tibet. She drew the color in front of him now, lifting his face to it, and showing him all his eighteen glorious gifts to the world, his eighteen unknown roses, now living over and over again, summer after summer, in countless gardens.

She showed him the dark, still woodland under Emei Shan, filled with his silver fir, *recurvata,* and the thick undergrowth full of butterflies. She drew the violet line through his buddleia, and then changed it to rose-purple through the *villosa* hydrangea. She painted the delicate vein of pink on the *regale* and the dense, glamorous petals on the *fargesii,* and the blood-red fruit of the *sambucus,* the five-foot elder he found in Northwest Sichuan clinging to a coarse fringe of herbs.

She drew his magnolia, its generous, wide, hand-sized leaves and the color of the flowers so perfectly white as to seem unreal; the *sargenti* that he would think was the finest of them; the *soulangiana* that he sent to Wakehurst Palace as seed, where it grew double-flowered, bright red stamens showing against the white, and each flower full of scent. His own *wilsonii,* that flowers after the leaves come, and the flowers turn down to the soil so that they look like white bells in the late spring.

She showed him his honeysuckles, the racing *tragophylla,* that climbs through shade carrying clusters of ten or twenty flowers; the evergreen *nitida,* with their glossy leaves, the darkest of which was finally named for him. *Pileata* that, unknown to Anna, grew in gardens through Maine, New Hampshire, Cape Cod, and Connecticut, green through the winters, green under snow.

She walked down with him through the painted days.

She showed him the weeks to come.

Only three weeks later, in May, near the village of Ta-wan, the world would change again for him. Five days southwest of Yichang, he would find a *davidia,* in full flower, fifty feet tall, drowned in blossom. In the subdued light on the mountain slope, the tree would be a mass of luminous white, and he would stop dead, astounded at the unexpectedness of the find, and the flowers moving in the breath of breeze, as if hundreds of white moths were trapped between the leaves.

And from the seeds of this one tree would rise thirteen thousand others. Almost every *davidia* that grew in the western world would be descended from them.

Ernest Wilson would see *davidia* again in the next ten years. He would see it in the northwest of Hupeh and in the forests of Wen-tsao. He would find it because he walked over passes where few men had ever been, and on native paths that were little more than pale depressions in rock; and in places where there were no paths at all.

Anna opened her eyes, and looked down at her fingers.

In her right hand were the oak leaves from Island Thorns.

They were faded, but she saw the colors in them. The green of *recurvata* and *pileata.* The whiteness of her hand curled around them.

Magnolia wilsonii, Davidia involucrata, white against green.

She looked up, and saw David.

He was standing by a window, with his back to her.

She looked at the sunlight pouring through the open blind, at the prism it cast on the floor.

With a slow curiosity, her daughter extended her hand to Anna's; and, at the same moment, David looked back at them.

Postscript

MOST OF THE HOUSES at Ogunquit were shuttered against the blinding day, silent in their gardens above the beach.

Sara and Matt came up the hill from the beach, looking over their shoulders at Hannah and Rachel. The two girls walked some way behind them, barefooted, brown from the sun, Hannah with her hands slightly outstretched, balancing shells carefully in her cupped palms. Occasionally, she would look up at Rachel, who walked steadfastly beside her, so much taller, so much more silent, head bowed, carrying their towels.

From where she sat on the porch, Anna could see them coming. She smiled. This had been her viewpoint for the last few months, every morning watching the sea from exactly the same point where her mother had sat each day, coffee cup in her hands. Thinking of her now, Anna could almost see Grace superimposed on the picture ahead of her, almost see her turning at the gate, where David now stood, to glance back at her daughter.

Anna bit her lip. She rested her hands on the paper in front of her. She looked down across the porch, at the cat lying in the deep shade on his side; at the newspaper lying on the chair, and at the tubs of flowers. She tried to remember what they were called, these beautiful pink blooms that almost swamped their container, and were echoed along the path to the gate. Sometimes when the light was strong, like today, she had to wait to let herself understand the world in front of her, to put a name to shapes. It had been two years, but she still had a problem naming. It was only colors that she could remember easily.

Colors, and her mother among the same shades; her mother bending over the flowers, watering them carefully, brushing back the almost-white hair from her face. And her mother's eyes, her own eyes, and Rachel's—that color—green of such depth. Green, David's color. The color of life.

She looked at David, imagining Grace next to him. Her mother would have stood with her arm casually linked in his. They would have been talking together. She could visualize them, even though she had never seen them together in life. They were cut from the same cloth, David and Grace: single-minded, unshakable. Tears came to her eyes, and she smiled at herself. It was always like this now. Everything flowed close to the surface. Some kind of defensive circuitry in her head, the system that had kept her feelings in check for so many years, had been defused. She cried often. In frustration at her incapacity to do the most seemingly simple tasks. In grief, at remembering. In joy, in David's arms. Most often, this last. He had never left her. He had never gone home, or even considered it.

Anna looked down now at the palette beside her.

The oak leaves were long dead, and their shade was dull to any ordinary glance. But, in one sense, in the sense of color, in the sense of Grace's tender and ghostly presence, they lived. In them she could see the palest cadmium red and lemon yellow, the raw sienna, and phyllo blue. She looked at them with an almost idle speculation on their possibilities.

A mixing of pigment to their color would produce a minor miracle. She could add permanent rose to them, and they would become mid-blue, or violet. Ultramarine would turn them pink. Cadmium yellow would make the shade green again.

Even the dead leaves. Deepest green.

David was opening the gate now. He was talking to his sister, taking the beach mats from her hands; laughing at something that Matt had said. Then he glanced back at Anna, and smiled.

She closed her eyes for a moment, and saw the flooding images.

The woods and the water, the long reaches of open fields. Wilson's world of miracles. Ravines in shadow, the falling of rain, the mile upon mile of scent and shade; the passes of light and isolation. The lilies that grew, that flourished, in the driest places; the trees that clung on to life, established from the merest thread of soil, out of nothing, and climbed out of the dark; drenched woodlands full of overpowering sweetness. The snow, the sunlight.

All the paths that she had walked with David in the past.

The sure road that ran between them, unfolding ahead of them, a way through the mountains.

About the Author

English author Elizabeth McGregor has held jobs as a patent attorney manager, teacher, and antiques dealer. But it was winning a national short story competition that brought her finally to her passion for writing.

Her last book, *The Ice Child,* turned her life around and established an international reputation, selling in seventeen countries, and *A Road Through the Mountains* was written soon afterward.

Elizabeth lives with her daughter Kate on the south coast of England, in Dorset, where she is completing her new novel.